Bourbon Creams and Tattered Dreams

MARY GIBSON was born and brought up in Bermondsey, where both her grandmother and mother were factory girls. She is the author of the bestselling *Custard Tarts and Broken Hearts*, which was selected for World Book Night in 2015, and two other novels, *Jam and Roses* and *Gunner Girls and Fighter Boys*. She lives in Kent.

Also by Mary Gibson

Custard Tarts and Broken Hearts
Jam and Roses
Gunner Girls and Fighter Boys

Bourbon Creams and Tattered Dreams

MARY GIBSON

HEAD
of ZEUS

A catalogue record for this book is available from
the British Library.

ISBN (PB) 9781784973353
ISBN (eBook) 9781784973322

Typeset by Ben Cracknell Studios

Printed and bound by CPI Group (UK) Ltd,
Croydon, CR0 4YY

MIX
Paper from
responsible sources
FSC® C020471
www.fsc.org

Head of Zeus Ltd
First Floor East
5–8 Hardwick Street
London EC1R 4RG

WWW.HEADOFZEUS.COM>

Dedicated to the memory of my aunt, Ellen Halstead,
who once sang on stage at the Star in Bermondsey
and who was a real trouper to the end.

Prologue

New York

May 1930

She waited for midnight – her flight must be cloaked in darkness, and it must take him completely by surprise. When the phone call came she had to move quickly. She snatched up the receiver at the first ring.

'Matty, go now!' a woman's voice whispered urgently in her ear. It was Maria, Frank Rossi's sister, signalling that the first part of their plan was under way and that the New York police were at that very moment raiding Frank's club for illegal booze. Frank would be occupied for the rest of the evening, handing out bribes or answering questions, depending on which sergeant was on duty that night.

She hung up and hurried to her bedroom. Too scared to keep a packed bag in the apartment in case Frank discovered it, now she stuffed into a suitcase whatever clothes and belongings came to hand.

She'd had so little time to plan. After his trip to Los Angeles spent trying to drum up backing for her next talkie Frank had returned to New York an unhappy man. So, very soon, Matty Gilbie had become an unhappy woman. There was no reason he should blame her for the studio's cold feet, but he did. In the new film Matty was to play an Amy Johnson type heroine, a singing aviatrix who flies half way round the world to find love: Frank had pitched it to the studio bosses with the byline *The Cockney Canary Flies!*

She would be flying all right, but not in a film. Her flight was as real as her terror of Frank and if she didn't go tonight, she knew she would never escape him. She quickly checked the cash in her purse, it would have to do. She'd squirrelled away as much of her money as she could, but Frank was as intimate with her bank account as he was with her, and he had been emptying it at an alarming rate trying to get the new film made.

Maria was a good woman; she'd come up with the plan and booked Matty's passage. After a lifetime with Frank, Maria understood just how necessary it was for Matty to get as far away from him as possible. Matty only wished she'd taken notice of Maria's veiled warnings about her brother earlier. At first she had thought him as loving as the rest of his warm-hearted, Italian clan – they'd reminded her of a Bermondsey family and it made her feel at home. But she'd discovered Frank's love flowed only as long as his every whim was pandered to. He expected to get his way and when he didn't there were always consequences.

She shoved the suitcase lid shut and winced as pain shot through her – just one of the 'consequences' of Frank's displeasure. She put a hand to her side, probing the sore places around her ribs and stomach. She bit her lip and, fumbling with the suitcase catch, she forced herself to breathe deeply in spite of the discomfort. In and out, each breath like the slice of a knife, once, twice... Her singing training had taught her the importance of the breath. For her voice it had always produced strength, power, grace – but now she would use it to steady her nerves and gain her freedom. She breathed deeply a third time, and felt the pain ease a little. She took one last look round the bedroom, grabbed her passport, tickets, money, and flew.

The apartment was in a canyon of buildings she'd always hated. Now, in the darkness, they were like towering fortress walls, hemming her in. Rain sheeted down as she scanned the canyon for a yellow cab, traffic swished along, sending up sprays of rainwater, soaking her feet. She looked desperately from right to left, willing a cab to appear. Her heart hammered out the

2

seconds as car after car passed; in desperation she hoisted up the heavy suitcase and began walking. A man turned the corner and came towards her, a black fedora pulled low over his face, rainwater dripping from the brim. She froze, sure it was Frank's bodyguard, and almost turned to run. But she forced herself to think. Why would he be here? Frank would need him at the club tonight. The man lifted his head and gave her a cursory look as he passed, then hurried on. Just then a cab came into view and she waved frantically at it. The gutters were streaming and she slid on the slick, inky sidewalk as the cab drew up. Stumbling forward, she reached out to the cab roof to steady herself.

'Careful, lady! Where to?' the cab driver asked.

'Harbour, quick as you can.'

'Sure, hop in.'

She fell gratefully into the dry interior, ignoring the pain stabbing her ribs, she heaved her case inside, slammed the door and the cab moved off. She stared out of melting windows and with the windscreen wipers racing she saw her old life being washed away. Leaning her head against the dark streaming glass, she was shocked at her own reflection – it was the face of a stranger, rigid with fear. In the deluge it felt she might already be on board ship, sailing on a torrential stream down towards the harbour, across the Atlantic Ocean and home. She gripped her suitcase, ready to leap from the cab as soon as it stopped, and prayed silently for a way to open up whenever cars or traffic lights halted their progress. She willed herself not to look back. If he was following, then it was better she didn't know.

Matty woke to an unsettling watery world. The rocking waves had not lulled her to sleep during her first night at sea; instead they had intensified the nausea she'd been suffering during the past few weeks in New York. Her cabin was cramped and deep in the bowels of the ship, but at least she had it to herself. She'd tossed and turned for what remained of the night, imagining Frank's reaction to her desertion. She only hoped poor Maria could remain strong enough to play the innocent, for if Frank ever suspected she'd helped, he'd soon beat the truth out of her. Frank was not a man you walked out on, but if he simply assumed she was fleeing another beating, perhaps there was the slim hope he might write her off as a failed business venture, lose interest and let her go. Maybe she was fooling herself, but she had to believe Maria hadn't put herself in danger for no good reason.

As the ship came to life around her next morning, she stretched out her long limbs in the narrow bunk and allowed herself the stirrings of relief that she'd never have to see Frank again. She heard laughter coming from the corridor and recognized the voice of a cockney steward who'd directed her to the cabin in the early hours. He'd recognized her and asked for an autograph. Cabin doors banged and she heard passengers on their way to the dining room in search of breakfast. There would be no more sleep this morning. She propped herself up and let out a groan as her stomach heaved once more. Flinging aside the blanket, she was about to swing her legs out of the bunk when her attention was caught by two bright red spots on the sheet. Her heart paused between beats as she registered what they might mean. Pulling the blanket off the bed, she began frantically searching for other telltale stains. There were none and the cold fear which gripped her receded a little. Should she go to the ship's doctor? But she wasn't ready to face the inevitable frosty disapproval when he failed to see a wedding ring on her finger. Perhaps bleeding was normal at this stage. She wasn't sure.

But when she stood up and felt a gush of warm water flood her thighs, she knew this was anything but normal. At only just over four months into her pregnancy, it was far too early for her waters to break. She stared at the pool of water at her feet and lowered herself slowly on to the bed. Bending forward, she cradled her stomach in a bid to keep her baby safe, just where it was. But as she felt the first sinister pull at her womb, hope drained from her and she let out a whimper. 'No, no, no! Stay there, don't come yet! It's too soon,' she pleaded with her unborn child.

4

The pains came on quickly, like waves of menstrual cramps, but deeper, stronger and more vicious. One after another they came, till she thought her body was being torn apart from the inside. Pain forced her to cry out, but she bit down hard on her own knuckles. She didn't want to attract the attention of any passing steward or passenger. Matty gripped the bedsheet and yanked it taut, twisting it with every tearing spasm of her body, till it formed a rope she could stuff in her mouth to stifle her screams as the pain ripped through her again and again. There was no mistaking what was happening to her, and it filled her with a sickening dread. The contractions were crippling and close together. Another long scream escaped her gag, ending in a deep sob, for she knew that the baby, if it came now, could not possibly survive.

The sheet became sticky with her blood as she fought her own treacherous body's instinct to push. She screamed against it and tore the bloody sheet, as life and death had their relentless way, finally forcing Matty to thrust the tiny baby from her body. She fell back on the bed in exhaustion, letting tears wash her cheeks. Instinctively she reached down and drew the baby up between her legs, to lie on her chest, wiping its fragile body with the sheet. Feeling its warmth against her, a surge of irrational hope forced Matty to sit up and look at her child. It was a girl.

She was flooded with love and grief. The tiny baby lay enfolded in the palm of her hand. She was a person, however small. The legs were drawn up and minute feet crossed each other at Matty's wrist. Perfectly formed, the miniature hand rested on Matty's fingernail. Five diminutive fingers, with delicate nails of their own, barely spanned the width of Matty's finger and she felt them curl around it in a feather's grip. She watched the little heart beating, caught in a miniscule ribcage, like a struggling bird. Translucent skin, un-resistant as air, gleamed as Matty traced the red filigree of veins, still pumping life into the small being. She cupped the tiny child with two hands now and raised her up, so that she could examine eyes, fast shut, and a mouth set in a serene smile.

Caressing the smooth head and cheek with her thumb, Matty watched as the heart slowed and finally ceased to beat.

A wave of sadness overwhelmed her. Her daughter's eyes had never looked upon the world, nor on her mother's face. She held the baby close to her breast, and whispered into the barely formed ear. 'Goodnight, my angel. I love you.' And as kind darkness closed over Matty, she clung to the hope that somehow her daughter had known how deeply she was loved.

The cockney steward had discovered her swaddled with her dead child in the bloody sheet. She didn't remember how she'd got to the sick bay, but when she woke her baby had gone. The ship's doctor came to attend to her physical healing, but there were no ministrations to her grief. She asked for her baby over and over again, and the doctor had to repeat several times that 'the remains of her pregnancy' had been removed. At first her grief-numbed mind would not allow her to understand that he was referring to her baby, but when she did, she wished she could scour the phrase from her memory. After he left she lay on the bed, burning with anger that her baby's life seemed to have been so coldly dismissed simply because it had been so short. All she knew was that those few precious minutes with her tiny daughter had awoken a love stronger than she'd ever felt, and she was filled with gratitude for that brief life.

1

The Cockney Canary

May–June 1930

The minute the ship docked in Southampton she realized she couldn't go home. Her Bermondsey family would have too many questions and she had no strength to keep her secrets. Her body was still bleeding and so was her heart. She had no plan. She had only thought to escape Frank and then figure out her next step on the voyage home. But the voyage home had been a fog of desolation. Of all the dreams she'd had when embarking for America, this last, unexpected one of having a child of her own, had captured her most fiercely. And now it had been ripped away.

When the train drew into Charing Cross, pure instinct led her to Mrs Melior's, a small lodging house a short walk from the station, down by the Thames. They were the old digs she'd always used if she was playing in the West End for more than one night at a time. The place had the advantage of familiarity and obscurity. Besides, Mrs Melior was one of the few landladies in the business who could be relied upon to be discreet. Now she returned to the haven of the small room on the top floor of Mrs Melior's, where the sash window always stuck and the river constantly slapped against the Embankment, filling the room with a sharp, musky smell.

Mrs Melior's expression of delighted surprise turned quickly to one of concern as Matty arrived, asking if her old room was free.

'Goodness, Miss Gilbie, you look exhausted! Come in! I've only got one gentleman staying at the moment, second back, but even if I was full I'd turn them all out for you!'

The woman insisted on taking her heavy suitcase and lugging it up the narrow staircase. Matty followed meekly, having no energy to protest. She simply wanted to lie in the familiar narrow bed and hide away forever.

When later Mrs Melior brought her tea and toast on a tray, Matty explained that she didn't want her arrival in the country to be known just yet. It was a private visit, she said, some personal troubles that had required her to come home suddenly, nothing to do with work. The woman grasped her hand, taking in the single suitcase and Matty's appearance. Her hair, which normally shone like spun copper, was dull as rust, unwaved and combed straight back off her forehead. Her perfect oval face, pale at the best of times, was stark and bare of make-up. She'd barely eaten during the week-long voyage home and her mismatch of clothes hung loosely on her tall figure. She felt all angles and planes, sharp enough to cut through all her normal veneer of effortless elegance and grace.

'Whatever troubles have come, Miss Gilbie, I hope you know you can stay here as long as you like. It goes no further than me.'

Matty noticed the woman's eyes stray to her lap and, horrified, she saw that blood had seeped through the front of her skirt. She began to cry.

'Now, now, there's no need to get yourself upset. It happens to us all,' Mrs Melior said. 'I'll get you something for that.' But by the time the woman returned, Matty had already fallen fast asleep in the chair by the window, soothed by the regular sough and slap of the river below.

When she woke, there were pads, hot water and soap on the washstand and she noticed Mrs Melior had placed a vase of pansies on the window sill. She went to push up the sash further and was rewarded with a warm breeze and a view of the Thames, spanned by Waterloo Bridge. The old bridge had begun to crumble while she was away and was now shored up against collapse by beams at crazy angles. The musky river smell rose up as the day's heat waned and she leaned her elbows on the rotting sill, resting her chin in her hands.

Was she right to have come here? From the moment she'd stepped off the ship she'd felt exposed, jumping at every American accent she heard on the London train. Whatever optimism she'd had when she set out on her voyage had been lost along with her baby, and she'd begun to fear that the Atlantic Ocean wasn't wide enough to protect her from Frank's reach. But for now she needed a place to heal, somewhere safe she could draw together all the pieces of herself that Frank seemed to have stolen from her.

That night she dreamed she was back at the New York Hippodrome, where she had taken a dozen curtain calls. But as the heavy plush curtains closed in front of her face, she heard a fluttering, and looking up, saw a real canary caught in its folds, battering itself against the plush, plum fabric, breaking its wings. Frantically she called to the small bird, but it seemed blinded by the footlights, caught in their upward-slanting beams. The bird fell senseless to the stage at her feet and when she stooped to pick it up, limp wings fell across her palm. She cradled it until she felt its heartbeat weaken and warmth and life drain from its tiny body. She woke in a cold sweat, feeling tears trickle down her cheeks till the pillow was wet with them.

She kept to her room, sleeping for hours, resenting the sunlight when it woke her. Mrs Melior, asking no questions and breaking all house rules, brought up her meals, which largely remained untouched. On the third morning when Matty didn't come down again, Mrs Melior brought her breakfast. The woman placed the tray by her bedside and seemed to be waiting for Matty to start eating. But the thought of food made her feel sick; the idea of eating to stay alive filled her with guilt. Why should she be living when her child was dead? If people knew, they would tell her not to blame herself, but Matty *was* to blame. If she'd left Frank earlier, then there never would have been that final beating.

'Eat a bit of it, Miss Gilbie,' Mrs Melior said. 'You're wasting away!'

And she waited until Matty had cracked the boiled egg and eaten a spoonful. At the door she stopped. 'I've run you a bath, nice and hot. I've told the gentleman second back, it's for you, so don't let it get cold!'

Mrs Melior had never been subtle. Matty knew she needed a bath, yet it had seemed far too arduous a task. But after eating the egg, she forced herself to get up and go to the bathroom. In the mirror she saw the gaunt face of a stranger; she could barely meet her own dark eyes, red-rimmed and haunted as they stared back at her. 'All right, all right,' she urged herself, gripping the basin. 'A bit of slap, Matty.' But she would have to dig very deep into her store of stage make-up tricks, if she were to erase the signs of her grief and pass for a woman who cared whether she lived or died.

But if she was going to carry on staying here, then she would have to work, for Frank had bled her dry. Which meant there was one other person who must know that she'd returned from America – her agent, Esme Golding. Going there was a risk she would have to take, for it was the one place in the world where Frank might know to come looking for her.

Esme's office was not far from Mrs Melior's, in a side court off Charing Cross Road. As she left the lodging house, the uneasy feeling she'd had on the journey home returned and she glanced up and down the street. She had no idea what she was looking for, someone who looked out of place, a flashy American suit or a bronzed face. But she couldn't hide in Mrs Melior's forever and so she began walking away from the riverfront towards Charing Cross Road.

Matty had washed and waved her hair, borrowing some vicious-toothed wave clips of Mrs Melior's. She'd dressed in her white suit, bought last year in California. She'd been surprised to arrive home during a London summer rivalling that heat, and was grateful for the cool lightness of the soft skirt and loose, long jacket. But by the time she was crossing Trafalgar Square, smuts from the sooty old town had begun to speckle the white suit.

She passed the Hippodrome, remembering how she'd brought the house down at the Hippo the year before going to America. Back then her music hall triumphs had seemed mere stepping stones to Broadway and a screen career, but hindsight had turned the Hippo, the South London Palace of Varieties, the Star – and all the others – into safe havens she fervently wished she'd lingered in.

Esme's office adjoined her flat on the first floor of a narrow old house squashed between a coffee shop and a sheet-music sellers. The front door had been wedged open in hopes of letting in a breeze and Matty walked straight up the stairs. Esme's waiting room was empty, which Matty found slightly worrying. She knocked on the office door and pasted on her brightest smile.

The woman's head was bent over the desk, her grizzled hair cut into a futile bob, ruined by wayward frizzy curls. She was peering at a contract through a fug of smoke.

'Got any work for a cockney canary?' Matty said and Esme's head shot up.

'Matty Gilbie! What in God's name are you doing here?' Esme hastily stubbed out her habitual black Turkish cigarette and got up.

'My dear, why didn't you tell me you were coming?' she asked, giving Matty a warm hug.

'I didn't know myself until a fortnight ago. Thought I'd surprise you.'

Esme paused, studying Matty. 'A fortnight! You were in a hurry. I should think the family were surprised to see you.'

'Yes... yes, they were surprised.'

'You look tired, Matty. Have you just got off the boat? But weren't you supposed to be in LA making the next talkie?'

While Esme was firing questions at her Matty had taken a seat; she didn't only look tired.

'Oh, Frank's still getting the money together for it... and to be honest I thought I'd come home and raise a bit myself. Every little helps!' she replied, trying to sound casual. But not even her acting skills could hide the tremor in her voice as she said his name.

'What's happened? Don't tell me your American, Frank whatsisname, has been stupid enough to lose everything in the Crash!' She paused to light another black cigarette and narrowed her eyes as she inhaled. 'I told you he was bad news.' Steel-grey eyes assessed Matty, who tried not to flinch, for the woman had felt understandably betrayed when Matty chose Frank to manage her American career.

Matty flicked a tarry speck from her white skirt and took a deep breath.

'Esme, the truth is, the new talkie has been a bit of a drain on me. I really *do* need to make some money.'

Esme looked hurt, as though Matty's shortness of funds was a slight on her.

'I'll do my best, sweetheart, but you've been away three years, and things have changed. It'll have to be gradual...'

Matty flushed. 'You were the one who told me America would be good for my career!' Knowing even as she said it that she was blaming the wrong person.

The woman raised a placating pair of palms. 'I know, I know, but none of us foresaw the Crash, did we, darling?'

But Esme was too fond of her to be angry for long. 'All right, darling, I'll see what I can do, just have a bit of patience. I won't say I told you so, but if you'd taken a percentage on *London Affair* as I advised – you'd at least have some money coming in now.'

'Frank said an upfront fee was better—'

'Better for him,' Esme muttered, pursing her full lips, so that they curled back on themselves. But Matty couldn't face any more 'I told you so's' today and got abruptly to her feet.

'I'll need something soon, Esme,' she said, trying not to let the desperation she felt show in her voice.

'I'll let you know, Matty darling.'

And Matty allowed herself to be enfolded in the woman's cigarette-smoked embrace.

Every day for a week she went back to Esme's office in Charing Cross Road and by the end of it she still had no bookings. Her agent was apologetic.

'I told you I needed to get back to work, Esme. Is there really nothing about?'

Esme turned to some files on her desk, which she began flicking through. Matty could tell she wasn't really reading them.

'Truth is, Matty, there's nothing worth your attention *just* at the moment. Only a few little piddling jobs over in South London. There's always the "good ole Saahf",' she said in exaggerated cockney. Matty had heard that the once illustrious South London Palace had entered a sad decline, like so many of the old music halls that had made her name. 'It's only a couple of nights. Wouldn't want to waste your time with those. Let me see, the Star does a few shows between films these days...' Esme shrugged. 'It's the economy, darling, and I can't do much about that. It's cheaper to go to a talkie than a West End show...'

Matty slumped back in her chair; she knew Esme was right. 'I know it's not your fault, Esme. But if all you can get is the South London or the Star, then just book them.'

'You really don't mind going back to the South London halls?' Esme asked.

Matty didn't mind, but she felt a current of panic. It was a strange feeling and reminded her of the time Frank had driven the wrong way down Broadway in his swanky Cadillac. Instead of turning round, he'd reversed all the way back to Time Square. Her heart had been in her mouth the whole way, a sick waiting for the inevitable crunch to come. She'd found that reversing when she'd been cruising so heedlessly forward was disorienting. But whatever her feelings about returning a failure, she couldn't delay her homecoming forever and the fact that very soon she'd have no money to pay Mrs Melior the rent forced her hand. She left

Esme's and went to the nearby post office to send the telegram. *Surprise! Arrived Southampton, home tomorrow.*

*

Sunlight glanced off grimy bus windows, blinding Matty alternately with its brilliance and its absence. The rhythmic flickering obscured Bermondsey's streets and with the heat of this scorching summer sun beating on the window, she was transported back to Los Angeles. She closed her eyes. The silver and the black penetrated her closed lids and she saw again the flickering silver screen, alive with her own image, larger than a human being had a right to be, her face a pale oval, her eyes wide as moonlit lakes and just as bright. She shuddered at the memory. She could hardly believe it had been over a year since she'd sat in that darkened screening room, watching the rushes of her first film with Frank. He'd sat so close that his body heat had been uncomfortable, and his cologne had hung heavy as the scent of California Poppy now drifting in the air from Atkinson's cosmetics factory as the bus passed through Southwark Park Road. The smoke from Frank's cigar had stung her eyes as it curled up into the light from the projector, just as now, smoke from Woodbines writhed in the fuggy heat of the bus's top deck, almost as if last winter's fog had been captured and preserved there.

How excited she'd once been watching those rushes. Frank had insisted the film would make her a star. Yet she'd been more interested in hearing the sound of her own voice than seeing herself on screen. But to her ears the voice hadn't quite the sweet, pure quality she'd always aimed for on the stage and she'd been determined to improve it.

'Everyone's voice sounds tinny on the talkies, honey,' he'd assured her. 'And besides, we got no time for fine-tuning! We gotta finish this thing, before the other backers get cold feet. You're hot property, Matty! A British accent, a voice like an angel, just when the talkies are taking over. I'm telling you, they won't be able to get enough of you!'

So she'd let it go and the film, *London Affair* – a romance set in a Victorian London, full of fogs and gas lamps, with herself playing the role of a kind-hearted consumptive flower seller, had been a success, *Hear the Cockney Canary Sing!* the film poster proclaimed, for that was the name she was known by on Broadway.

She tried to recall that feeling of excitement – a bubbling, expansive feeling that anything was possible. But that had been before the Crash, and before everything had gone so wrong with Frank. She had imagined a very different homecoming to Bermondsey. As it was, she'd prepared herself to face her brother Sam's disappointment and she'd been prepared to challenge Eliza, the sister who herself had brought up an illegitimate son. But she hadn't been prepared for this emptiness, this dullness at her core. She had expected to return to Bermondsey with her arms full – the child would be the only explanation she'd need. But all she had to show for three years in America was a film people were fast forgetting, a few hidden scars and an empty heart.

She could have wished for a longer walk from the bus stop, but if she'd failed to rehearse her story well enough during her weeks at Mrs Melior's, she doubted a few hundred yards of Bermondsey pavement could help her. Reverdy Road was a respectable street of terraced brick houses, with round arched windows and front doors. Lined with newly planted trees, it still felt small and warren-like compared to the soaring canyons of New York or those wide streets of Los Angeles she'd once cruised along in Frank's gleaming tan and cream Cadillac. The soot-blackened brick and grey slate closed in around her, bringing her back with a jolt to the Matty she'd been before ever the Cockney Canary had graced the stage of the Star music hall in Abbey Street. The feeling was an uncomfortable one, a claustrophobic mix of shame and failure – she was meant to have escaped all this.

Matty lifted her head, straightened her back and strode towards her sister Eliza's house. She would need all her stage presence for this performance.

The street had a midweek afternoon dullness about it, with its residents still at their factories or schools. The small terraced houses burned quietly in the afternoon heat. A black cat, sunning itself on the wall in front of her sister's house, was her only audience. She slowed her steps. The cat's unsmiling eyes fixed her, staring insolently at this stranger in its territory.

'Who are you looking at?' Matty challenged the cat, staring back at it. But for some reason, under its unblinking scrutiny all her resolve melted away. The old Matty Gilbie never ran away from anything, but life with Frank had taught her that however brave it felt to stand your ground, sometimes it was wiser to run. But this was home, and if she didn't stop running now, then she never would.

The woman who answered the door could have been Matty's mother. With the same faded auburn hair and pale, translucent skin, Eliza's resemblance to their mother, Lizzie Gilbie, was striking. But Eliza's embrace was full of a delighted vigour and the tall figure, though perhaps a little more stooped than when Matty had last seen her, was nothing like the enfeebled woman their mother had been at forty-nine. It struck Matty now that Lizzie Gilbie had died too young, not much older than her sister was now. As she allowed herself to be held, Matty was caught by a deep, unexpected wave of sadness at that old grief – the loss of her mother. For a moment she imagined that Eliza's embrace was her mother's. It was a fruitless, bittersweet comparison and Matty was ashamed of it.

'Matty, why didn't you let us know you were coming home?'

'I did, I sent a telegram.'

'But we've only just had it. You could have sent it before you set sail!'

Eliza was holding her at arm's-length and gazing with undisguised pleasure. 'Look at you – you're even more beautiful than you were three years ago!'

Eliza cupped her cheek with a hand, and Matty armed herself against the intensity of her sister's dark-eyed gaze. She had never

16

quite understood the late blossoming of Eliza's interest in her, but she knew that after a lifetime of union activism those intelligent eyes could prise the secrets from the toughest factory boss, and so now she made sure to veil her own. With a graceful sweep, she removed her oyster-shaped hat and presented it to Eliza.

'Ain't you going to ask me in for a cuppa then?' Matty beamed.

She had been on the stage since she was twelve, and she told herself that this was just another part for her to play.

Eliza led her into the parlour. The room was simply but tastefully furnished. Two glass-fronted bookcases were crammed with political pamphlets, some of which Eliza had written, along with other heavy-looking economic tomes. There were a few pieces of good oak furniture. A drop-leaf table stood in front of the window and two upholstered armchairs were placed either side of the fire. On the mantelpiece were photos of Eliza's son, Will, when he was a schoolboy at Dulwich College, wearing a cap and striped blazer; a wedding photo of their brother, Sam, and his bride, Nellie, standing on St James's Church steps; a studio portrait of herself when she was twenty-three and at the height of her career. Eliza's past was intertwined inextricably with her own.

Taking Matty's summer coat from her, Eliza fixed her with a knowing look.

'Let me make us some tea – then you can tell me the real reason you didn't let us know you were coming home.'

Eliza gave a wry smile and was gone before Matty could protest. She turned back to the photos on the mantelpiece, picking up a faded sepia photograph of a young man on a penny-farthing bicycle, wearing a cycling cap and hooped jersey. Standing beside him was a rather careworn young woman in the dress of an earlier generation.

She smiled at her parents as they were when they'd first made the journey from Hull to London, her father riding all the way on the penny-farthing and her mother following reluctantly on behind.

'Oh, Mum, if only you were still here,' Matty whispered to her mother's younger image.

She heard the teacups rattle and turned to see Eliza placing the tray carefully on the table. As she handed Matty the teacup, Eliza fixed her with that intelligent, probing gaze.

'So, what's brought you home?'

Matty felt a spasm of pain shoot through her stomach, as if the muscles had been twisted and tightened into steel ropes. She lifted her chin and, taking a deep breath, raked the tiredness up from her chest. She gave Eliza her brightest smile.

'Oh, there was a lull between shows and Frank's still getting up the backing for the new talkie. I thought I'd make the most of it. Booked my ticket on the spur of the moment... it all happened so quickly, and anyway, I wanted to surprise you all, make a grand entrance!' Matty said with a laugh.

'Well, you've certainly done that. And all on your own – no Mr Rossi with you?' Eliza asked lightly.

'Oh no, it's really more of a holiday for me. Frank's too busy setting up everything for the next film.' Matty waved her hand, as though the thousands of dollars needed for the project were a minor matter.

Matty's acting skills had obviously deserted her, for it seemed Eliza was not convinced. Her sister glanced at the photograph of their parents, back in its place on the mantlepiece and said, 'I can't promise to be as wise as Mum, but you can always talk to me, Matty, you know that, don't you?'

Matty knew now would be the time to confide in her sister. If anyone could understand about the baby, it was her sister. But as the seconds ticked away, she found herself choking back the words. Then the sound of a key in the front door interrupted her thoughts and the moment was gone. Matty shot Eliza an enquiring look.

'Anyone home? Ma?'

Matty recognized the voice and was about to rush out to greet him, when Eliza caught her hand.

'In here, Will.' Eliza put her finger to her lips and Matty went to hide behind the door.

He stuck his head round the door and Matty leaped out, throwing her arms round him, spinning them both across the room till they tumbled in a heap on to one of the armchairs.

'Matty!' He recovered first and then, grabbing her round the waist, he tossed her up into the air with a whoop.

'Be careful, Will!' Eliza warned, but he'd already caught Matty.

'Blimey, you've turned into Tarzan!' Matty laughed.

'He doesn't know his own strength.' Eliza apologized for her son, but Matty was already getting her own back by pretending to strangle him with the white cotton scarf he had tied around his neck. His hands on her waist and his effortless tossing her about told her that he was no longer a schoolboy. He wasn't going to be a tall man, but he'd inherited all the contained, hard-muscled strength of his father. Now she stood back, breathless.

'Let's have a look at you then.'

She loosened the white scarf from his neck and he removed his flat cap. He stood in front of her, smoothing down his dark curls, and it was obvious to Matty which of his two worlds he'd chosen to inhabit.

Matty's nephew, Will James, had been an awkward fifteen-year-old when Matty left for America. She remembered how embarrassed he'd been by the tears of his Bermondsey family when they'd all waved her off from Waterloo. Will had always felt more like a younger brother to Matty, in spite of the difference in their upbringing. His had been as privileged as hers had been deprived. Will's education at Dulwich College had been funded by his father, Ernest James, a wealthy politician Eliza had lived and worked with for many years. He'd attended as a day boy and Matty often felt he'd grown up feeling neither a Bermondsey boy nor a public-school boy. At fifteen she'd seen him begin to flounder in both worlds.

After looking him up and down she declared, 'You look like a bloody stevedore. I thought you was going to Cambridge!'

'And I thought you were in America!'

Matty noticed that his exaggerated Bermondsey vowels were fighting with his correct public-school accent. She felt suddenly sorry for him; her years in America had taught her how painful it was to never feel at home.

'He is, and she was.' Eliza answered both their questions. 'Here, give me those ridiculous items. You don't have to dress like a docker to be of use to the working classes,' she said tartly and took her son's cap and scarf. But Matty saw her look of indulgence as she left the room.

'I'll make us some dinner while you two catch up,' her sister added, leaving them alone together.

'Guess where I've been? At the docks, helping organize a mass rally to Hyde Park,' he said proudly. 'They ain't going to listen to someone dressed like a banker, are they?'

Matty could remember a time when Will had been ashamed of his Bermondsey background, refusing to have friends home. Now he took the trouble to deliberately drop his aitches and affected a cockney accent he'd never had – she thought it must be hard work.

'Working men can't afford to listen to anyone but their bosses – who generally dress like bankers,' she retorted.

'Rubbish! You're a theatre type, you don't know you're born.'

Matty had to smile – here it came. She was almost grateful for the familiarity of this banter with Will, whose contrary nature would turn any conversation into an argument.

'Do I need to remind you that at twelve I was making matchboxes at home so we could pay the rent!'

'Sweated labour, it's a disgrace, still going on!' He shook his head earnestly.

Looking towards the door, he said loudly so that Eliza could hear, 'I'm not going to Cambridge.'

'Don't be a soppy 'apporth, of course you are. And then you're going to be a great politician and improve the lot of the working man,' Matty told him.

'I don't need a Cambridge education to do that. Look at Ben Tillet!'

'I would if I knew who he was,' she replied, and Will raised his eyes in disgust at her ignorance.

'I haven't got time for university, Matty. I can't sit in a bloody ivory tower while thousands of people are getting their dole cut.'

'Last I heard, it's your socialist prime minister that wants to cut it—'

'And that's my point – he's no socialist and it's all going to hell in a handcart!' Will's face had hardened. He stood up, and Matty thought he might even start banging the table, when Eliza walked in with a tablecloth. She shoved it into Will's hands.

'Lay the table, Will. You're eighteen and you're too young to be a politician. You're going up to Cambridge and that's that.' Eliza went back to the kitchen and Matty broke into the chorus of 'He's Only a Working Man!' She began strolling up and down the parlour, ringing out in her broadest cockney.

I wake 'im every morning when the clock strikes eight
I'm always punctual, never, never late
With a nice cup of tea and a little round of toast
The Sportin' Life and the Winning Post
I make 'im nice and cosy, then I toddle off to work
I do the best I can
For I'm only doing what a woman should do
Cos he's only a working man!

It made Will laugh and she was glad to have diffused his simmering anger. Sometimes she teased him that he'd been born on a soapbox. He'd been a whirlwind of a child, barrelling everywhere at speed, and it seemed that same energy was following him into adulthood.

Over dinner he directed a barrage of questions at Matty. What did she think of the Wall Street Crash and how many unemployed did America have? Did they have the dole? And sometimes his boyish fascinations interrupted his social concerns. Had she ever met Tallulah Bankhead? Did she know any gangsters? Had she been to a speakeasy?

Matty felt the weight of a million more questions bearing down on her and, closing her eyes, let her head fall back against the chair.

'Oh, Will, of course Matty doesn't know any gangsters and look, now you've worn her out.'

'No, I'm fine.' Matty jerked her head up. 'It's the journey...' she lied, tired only of keeping up the act. 'I'll be right as rain in the morning.' Matty gave Eliza a small smile, weak enough to indicate that an early end to dinner would be welcome.

'You poor thing, you must be exhausted.' Eliza got up from the table. 'Come with me, the spare bed's made up.'

''Night, Will.' Matty yawned, kissing the top of his dark curly head. 'I did meet her, Tallulah, at one of Frank's parties, told me she liked my accent, pissed as a puddin' she was.'

Eliza was already halfway up the stairs and Matty followed wearily behind. The bedclothes were turned back and a jug of water was on the stand by the time Matty reached the room.

'Thanks, Eliza.' She kissed her sister gratefully. There was no one quite like Eliza in a crisis, even if she didn't yet know quite what that crisis was.

2

No Place Like Home

June–July 1930

Matty was nervous. She dreaded her brother Sam's disappointment more than anything. She suspected he would see through the charade of her success where Eliza had not. She'd never worried about disappointing her sister.

'Are you coming with me to Sam's?' Matty asked her the following day, hoping she would say yes. Eliza's presence might at least deflect some of Sam's questions.

'I wouldn't miss the look on his face when he sees you!' Eliza replied.

'He shouldn't be surprised – I sent a telegram saying I'd be there this afternoon.'

'Not surprised. I meant he'll be so *pleased*. He's missed you, Matty.'

But Matty didn't have to be told that. He'd never wanted her to go to America, but her brother's letters had been regular and affectionate. Now she was regretting that her replies had been so infrequent. She told herself there'd been good reasons: first she'd been taken up with work, and later she simply couldn't bear to fill her letters with lies about her life with Frank. But Sam had deserved better from her.

They walked to Sam's and on the way Matty was assaulted by her past, the myriad smells of Bermondsey conjuring up her life with Sam and Nellie in Vauban Street and her stint as a factory girl. How could she have forgotten the overpowering scent of strawberries wafting from Lipton's jam factory or the sickly vanilla of Pearce Duff's custard? Matty glanced up at a row of tall windows.

'God, look at that custard powder still on the sills, Eliza! I swear it's four inches deeper than when I was last here... I don't know how Nellie stands it.'

'Oh, Nellie's not on the factory floor any more, didn't you know? She's cleaning the offices now – part-time. It's easier with the boys.'

Matty felt guilty that she didn't know this small but important detail about Nellie's work. Once their lives had been as intertwined as mother and daughter. She *should* have known. But achieving her own heart's desire had resulted in casualties. Going to America had meant walking away from her friends, her family, and abandoning Tom, the man who'd wanted to marry her. Not for the first time, she rued the day she'd ever persuaded herself to leave. Yet she knew she could have done nothing else.

'Ah, home sweet home! Can't beat that old boneyard smell, can you!' Matty took an exaggerated breath of the smells from Young's glue factory. Its two tall brick chimneys loomed up at the end of Vauban Street. They belched smoke that billowed between the rows of crumbling terraced houses. She was only partly joking, for in spite of the smells and dirt from the surrounding factories it had been a sweet home that Nellie Clark had made for her and her brother Charlie after their mother died.

Eliza pointed up to a huge hoarding on the side wall of a grocer's shop on the corner. A man on a ladder was in the process of removing the old poster in readiness to put up a new one. Although half of it had already been scraped away, Matty recognized it immediately.

'Oh dear God, I don't believe it!' Matty tipped back her head. There was her own face, looking back at her, sad and haunted, haloed in the glow from a gas lamp, against a backdrop of a foggy London scene. In the other corner a villainous-looking man with a long chin and slicked-back hair looked at her lasciviously. *Hear the Cockney Canary Sing!* was emblazoned over the top of the film title *London Affair*.

'Well, I'm glad you got to see it,' Eliza said. 'It's been up there for months. The boys have been so proud. When they showed the film here the queue went all the way round the Star and back up almost to Dockhead!'

Matty clapped her hands in involuntary delight. 'Oh, I wish I could have seen that, Eliza! It would have meant more to me than any New York showing.'

And suddenly she was surrounded by a crowd of excited children.

'That's my aunt! She's famous, she's American!' She heard her nine-year-old nephew, Billy, before she saw him, running towards her, followed by his two younger brothers. She was glad she'd defied the smutty air of Bermondsey and worn her pale pink, shawl-collared coat, with matching kid gloves and shoes. The outfit might be more fitting to the sun-washed streets of Los Angeles, but she drew herself up, ready to be Matty on the stage, just for Billy.

A woman poked her head out of the nearest window to see what all the commotion was about and soon neighbours were standing at their doors.

'Giss a song, Matty!' a young fellow trundling a handcart full of vegetables from the greengrocer on the corner called out to her. She laughed and caught up a cabbage, holding it in front of her, like a bouquet, then did a twirl to show off her costume and sang a snatch of '*Why am I always the bridesmaid, never the blushing bride?*' which elicited a cheer from the little crowd. Billy dragged her to the nearest open front door and into the beloved old house.

'I've a good mind to tan your hide, Matty Gilbie, how was I meant to put on a spread with one day's notice!' Nellie pulled her into a strong embrace. Her boys, Billy, Sammy and Albie, were ranged for inspection, neat in grey shorts and white shirts. Poor Nellie must have had a morning of it trying to keep them clean and off the street. They broke ranks and gathered round as Matty dug into her bag, drawing out her gifts, model cars that brought cries of joyful recognition. 'A Cadillac, a Bugatti, a Chrysler!'

'Come on now, boys, give Auntie Matty a bit of room.'

Albie, the youngest, threatened to be swallowed up in the depths of her bag, looking for more, and Nellie pulled him out.

'Sorry, Matty, they're just over-excited. We all are.' Nellie showed her to the kitchen table, which in spite of the short notice, she'd managed to load with sandwiches and cake and trifle – no doubt courtesy of Pearce Duff's jelly and custard departments.

'Where's Sam?' Matty asked, puzzled that her brother hadn't rushed to greet her with the rest of the family.

'Oh, I think he's just having a smoke in the backyard, I'll go and get him.'

She saw a look pass between Nellie and Eliza and immediately felt excluded from an inner circle that she'd once taken for granted.

'No, I'll go,' she said, and slipped past Nellie into the backyard.

Her brother was standing with his back to her, a cigarette held between finger and thumb. She doubted that he hadn't heard the commotion of her arrival.

'Sam?'

He took a long drag on the cigarette and for a moment she thought he wasn't going to turn round. Then he faced her. His weather-bronzed face looked older and there was more grey in his dark hair, but it was his dark eyes that she searched for the signs of forgiveness.

'Hello, stranger,' he said, flicking the cigarette to the ground.

How could Eliza have pretended he would be pleased to see her? He didn't seem pleased at all. Then she ran to him and flung her arms around his neck. 'I'm sorry I didn't write much!' she blurted out, refusing to let go as he tried to unpeel her arms.

'Well, it's like Mum used to say, I suppose, "out of sight, out of mind".'

Now she was sure she'd hurt him. 'Never out of mind, Sam.'

He shrugged. 'Nellie's had to rush round getting a tea together.'

She couldn't bear this coolness from her once adoring brother.

26

If he knew, she told herself, why there had been no notice, why there had been so few letters, he wouldn't be so hard. But they were the last excuses she would use to defend herself.

'I've not had an easy time of it lately. I just needed to get home.'

At the sight of her tears, Sam's eyes softened and she felt strong arms enfold her.

'Well, I'm happy our little canary's come back to us,' he whispered into her hair. And when he used the phrase, it had nothing to do with the six-foot poster at the end of the street. It was just her old family nickname, earned when she'd sung from morning till night just because it was as natural to her as breathing.

After tea the boys were allowed out into the streets with their cars and as Nellie cleared the tea things, Matty offered to help wash up.

'No, you won't, you're the guest of honour. Eliza will help me.' Both Matty and Eliza knew when not to argue with Nellie and her sister followed meekly into the scullery, leaving Matty alone with Sam, who silently rolled another cigarette.

She stood at the kitchen window, looking along the row of houses where roofs dipped at drunken angles and fences were rotting. She was still feeling a little awkward, even though she knew she'd been forgiven. Sam followed her gaze.

'The council are talking about pulling the whole lot down and building flats here.' He plucked strands of tobacco from the roll-up. 'Not a moment too soon, it's driving poor Nellie up the wall. The place is crumbling with damp and the rats are coming in from the boneyard. We're up half the night making sure they don't go on the boys' beds.'

'Oh, Sam, I didn't know it had got that bad. But where will you go?'

'We're down for a council flat, in The Grange – you know, by the leather factories. Just hope they finish building them soon.'

Matty felt a familiar guilt. She had planned to come back a rich woman, able to buy Sam and his family a semi in a nice suburb rather than a council flat opposite some of the smelliest factories in Bermondsey.

'I wish I could do more,' she said lamely and saw Sam bristle.

'My family's not your responsibility, Matty. Besides, the new job at the Bricklayer's Arms pays better money than I've had all me life.'

Sam drove a horse and cart, working out of the huge railway depot up by Old Kent Road; it had been a step up from working for Wicks, the local carter, and the extra wages would at least mean he could afford the rent on the new council flat.

'You've done enough for me, Sam, over the years.' She went and sat on the arm of his chair, draping her arm round his shoulders as he smoked silently for a while.

'I've only ever been glad for your success, duck. I'm sorry about before. You mustn't feel you owe us anything.'

It was going to be now or never; she just had to be brave.

'Sam, I've got something to tell you.'

'What's that?' He put out his cigarette between his finger and thumb, saving some for later, and looked at her expectantly.

'I'm thinking of making it a longer stay, perhaps try to get a run in the West End, what do you think?'

Eliza and Nellie came back just in time to overhear her question.

'Ah, I knew there was something!' Eliza declared, smiling triumphantly first at Sam then at Nellie. 'She's been homesick. I feared as much. But, Matty – a London show? What would happen to your screen career – aren't these things all a matter of timing?'

Matty would rather have explained things to Sam first, but now she went on.

'I can't pretend I haven't been homesick. I've missed you all, and I've missed the London stage, my home crowd… you know.' Matty could normally hold a smile for hours, but unaccountably she felt her lower lip tremble. Suddenly Eliza leaned forward and took her hand.

28

'Rubbish, of course you've been homesick, Matty. And God knows I wouldn't blame you. When I was in Melbourne with Ernest I used to walk by the river and pretend it was the Thames! There's no shame in that.'

Had Eliza seen shame on her face then? There seemed little point in trying to deflect her. 'Well, yes... but it's not only homesickness,' she said.

'If you're not happy in America, you don't have to stay there, duck,' Sam said matter-of-factly. 'God knows, we'd be happy enough if you come home. Besides, don't they make talkies in England too? But I suppose Mr Rossi would have something to say about it.'

'Oh, I don't take orders from Frank!' Matty declared, perhaps a little too strongly.

'No, of course not – nor from anyone else!' Sam raised his eyes and they all laughed.

'But it's not been so easy financing the new film, since the Crash that is. There's been a bit of a hiccup... I thought I'd make the most of it, see my family, you know.' Matty felt she was stumbling.

'Talking of Mr Rossi,' Eliza interrupted with a knowing smile. 'He's been a great friend to your career – but is it a little more than a business partnership between you two?'

Matty felt a flush rising and was glad of the pale face powder she'd dusted herself with so liberally. She dipped her head to her handbag, feeling around for her cigarettes.

'Leave her alone, Eliza, you're making our Matty blush.' Nellie tried to come to her rescue and Matty shot her a grateful look, but Eliza would not be put off.

'I saw the photograph you sent Sam and Nellie of you two in his beautiful car, where was it? Los Angeles? He's very handsome, Matty.'

Matty smiled as if Eliza had caught her out. Yes, Frank was handsome. She hadn't been able to take her eyes off him that first day they'd met, when he came backstage at the New York

Hippodrome. Hair black as a raven's wing, swept back from his forehead, brown eyes fringed with dark lashes, long as a girl's, and teeth like sharp pearls, flashing a smile as warm as the Italian sun he'd been born under. Oh, he was handsome all right, and Matty, to her intense annoyance, had felt the power of his charm pierce her normal defences with ease.

'All right, if you must know, it is more... or rather, it was for a while.' She shrugged her shoulders and flicked a tube of white ash into the fire grate. 'It just... didn't work out.'

Eliza, never one to ignore an awkward silence, plunged on. 'Are you very upset about it?'

'Upset? No! Not at all.' And that part at least was true.

That evening Matty called in at the Star to see the manager, Bernie, for old time's sake. These days it was primarily a cinema, but they still staged variety shows and a weekly talent contest when young hopefuls such as she'd once been could try their luck. She stood before the front steps, looking up at the old building which was dominated by huge film billboards. She was sad to see the old 'Lardy', as it had been known in her day, was no longer looking so 'la-di-dah'. Bernie had let the place go and she thought it looked a bit of a fleapit. She pushed through one of the front doors.

'Is Bernie in?' she asked a young woman who was clearing up after the afternoon's tupenny rush. The girl looked up and blushed, recognition dawning on her face.

'I'll get him for you, Miss Gilbie.' She hurried away and while she was waiting Matty poked her head into the cinema. If she needed any convincing that the glory days of the old music hall were numbered, this was it. The carpet was still littered with the detritus of the tupenny rush, and a young boy was going along the rows collecting empty bottles of pop and sweeping up peanut shells. The ironwork was rusting on the ornate horseshoe-shaped balconies and great chunks of ornamental plaster were missing from the ceiling. That much hadn't changed – the plaster had been crumbling for years – and she searched out above the stage the very patch which had fallen during one of her performances and nearly killed her. She seemed to hear the echo of her former self ringing around the place. All those rousing patriotic songs, God forgive her, she'd sung on that stage during the war. How many young men had been inspired by those to take themselves off to the battlefields of France? She shuddered, then turned at the sound of Bernie's voice.

'Matty, you're a sight for sore eyes! Come here, beautiful.'

Bernie gave her a loud kiss and laughed. 'What you slumming it down the old Lardy for? You should be in Hollywood making yer next talkie!'

He beckoned her out and she followed him to his tiny office. The walls were plastered with old programmes and posters proclaiming the luminaries who'd graced the Star's stage over the years: Marie Lloyd and Vesta Tilley, Dan Leno and Charlie Chaplin – she doubted *he'd* ever be popping in to see Bernie again. And of course, she was up there too – the Cockney Canary. Bernie poured her a gin and fixed her with his professional eye. It was Bernie she had to thank for her first singing job – last on the bill a couple of nights a week during the war, and although the Star was now past its prime Bernie still knew the business inside out.

'Between you and me, Matty, and it won't go no further, I heard about yer bit of trouble.'

Matty froze. How much did he know? Nobody knew all of it, not even Esme. She took a gulp of gin and leaned back against the torn leather chair. Keeping her face expressionless, she waited for Bernie to carry on.

'I heard Mr Rossi's been finding it hard – getting you a backer for that new talkie. Not surprising the way things are over there. Is that why you've come back? Drumming up a bit of home-grown support?'

Matty let out a silent breath. If this was all Bernie knew, then she had nothing to fear. She'd brought home with her secrets far more dangerous than a failing career.

'Times *are* hard, Bernie. To be honest I'm looking forward to having a break from the acting, getting back to singing while Frank's doing all the financial stuff.'

Bernie nodded his head. 'Esme's been on the blower. I told her these days we only have a show once a month... the Lardy's not what it used to be.' He flung his arm wide, taking in all the past stars in its firmament. 'But we'd love to have the Cockney Canary back... if you're sure it's worth your while?'

He fixed her with an appraising eye. Where was her star? He seemed to be asking himself. Was she still in the ascendant, or was she even now dipping low in the night sky, soon to disappear forever? Perhaps she might have to disappear one day. If Frank came looking, he'd only have to scan the show bills to find her. But for now she needed money and the down-at-heel old Star, tucked away in the maze of Bermondsey's streets, was the least risky place she could earn it. Besides, the possibility of singing again had been the first thing to lift her heart since she arrived back in England. If she had to give up singing, then she might as well give up breathing.

'For old time's sake!' She smiled and lifted her glass.

'To the good old days!' Bernie lifted his own and she noticed his shirt cuff was frayed. Times were hard for all of them it seemed.

As she left Bernie, with a firm booking for top billing at the next variety show, she reflected on the 'little bit of trouble' Bernie had referred to. She was relieved he only knew the half of it, but she'd been surprised that particular piece of showbiz news had made its way across the Atlantic already. Her first talkie had given her minor fame, but she'd known for a long time that a second would never be made. The Cockney Canary's flight had in some ways been cut short by the flights of others.

They'd called them 'the flyers', the ruined men who couldn't face life after the Wall Street Crash last year. She'd seen one with her own eyes, casting himself from the skyscraper on to the merciless wind. Matty had looked up, following Frank's excited, pointing finger. She wasn't worried for the man, caught like a disjointed puppet on a whirling eddy. That ridiculous optimistic streak of hers had made her certain that he could fall hundreds of feet and at the last minute be jolted back from death by the invisible wire. Her years in the theatre had taught her that a flyer always had a harness and a wire; she'd flown with one herself, that year she'd played Peter Pan at the Alhambra. But instead the poor man had exploded on to the sidewalk like a ripe watermelon and Frank had to hustle her away into the nearest speakeasy, plying her with bourbon till the trembling gave way to a shocked numbness. She couldn't know how in that moment her own fortunes had already turned, diving with the flyers whose ruined fortunes would leech money from backers of Broadway shows and talkies alike.

*

Matty's show at the Star sold out in days. Her Bermondsey fans filled the balconies and she gave them her trademark selection of music hall favourites and new jazz songs. Her versatility had been part of her success; she could sing anything. She was pure and bright with 'Silver Lining', smoky and sultry with 'Am I Blue?' Then she made sure to make them laugh with her native cockney version of 'Don't Have Any More Missus More'. It felt good to be back here, in the place where she'd started. It reminded her of an earlier, simpler self, when all she needed to do was follow her desire to sing. She felt all the scattered parts of herself returning and as she sang, she felt the weight of her grief begin to lighten.

She was aware of Sam and Nellie and the rest of the family sitting in the front row, but in her imagination she placed another two in the audience: her mother, Lizzie, and her father, Michael Gilbie, who had died when she was only eight. They would stand her in their little kitchen when she was small, teaching her to sing from the stomach, indulging her fanciful 'shows' and praising her efforts so that she knew she could only ever be a success. Whatever stage she was on, in New York or London, it was always to them that she sang, and tonight was no different. The applause was so thunderous she thought the balconies might collapse along with a bit more of the ceiling plaster. After the show well-wishers called backstage, where Bernie had put on a party for her.

'They gave you a good old Bermondsey welcome, didn't they?' Will James plucked two drinks from a side table and offered her one. Tonight he was dressed in a sharp evening suit and looked nothing like a docker. Matty felt the collar. 'Nice whistle, you wearing that for the next rally to Hyde Park?'

'Very funny, I'm just making an effort for you! But I bet all this must seem small beer after those glamorous Hollywood parties?'

Matty shook her head. 'This is the best audience in the world!'

Eliza had overheard them. 'She's in no hurry to rush back to America, are you, Matty?'

And Matty smiled, perhaps a little too fixedly, for Eliza drew her to one side. 'Is everything all right, Matty? If you're tired we can leave. Sam and Nellie need to get back for the boys anyway.'

Matty nodded. 'I'm ready to go.' She was tired, but she was also worried. Esme had been unable to get her any more bookings. The Star once a month and the occasional appearance at the South London Palace wouldn't keep the wolf from the door. Esme had promised to try the provinces for her. But Matty knew her tiredness was mostly the result of keeping up the charade. She had never been good at keeping secrets, and now she felt weighed down by layers of them.

Will walked them as far as Reverdy Road, but the night was still young for him and he stopped on the doorstep.

'Actually the "whistle" wasn't just for you.' He smoothed down the well-cut jacket. 'I'm off to a little club in Soho and you'd be surprised how many well-heeled young men will cough up for International Red Aid, especially if the person asking is wearing a decent suit!'

He winked at Matty, who found herself relieved he wasn't coming home with them. Grateful for time alone with Eliza, she'd learned that her sister could be a wise confidante. Perhaps it was time to be more truthful. Who knew, she might be able to help?

They sat in the parlour with sherries, which Eliza had insisted they end the evening with.

'It's a triumphant return – you can't go to bed on a cup of tea, Matty!'

Matty gave a tired smile and heaved a deep sigh. 'Eliza, the truth is, it's not a triumphant return at all. I've not been straight with you,' she said in a rush. 'And my career's not going well, it's going badly – has been since the Crash.'

She let out a breath. It was a relief to finally tell even that much of the truth, but she felt a blush rise to her cheeks as Eliza stared at her doubtfully.

'Not going well? How can that be, Matty? Didn't you see that poster in Vauban Street they were taking down? And look at tonight! They love you here, they loved you on Broadway, and what about Mr Rossi – he's getting you into another talkie, isn't he?'

'Well, he did have plenty of ideas about my fabulous screen career. But, Eliza, he never counted on the Crash. The money ran out.'

'But your Broadway show was a big hit. Surely they'd want you for another one.'

Matty raised her eyes and cocked her head to one side, in what she hoped was a plucky-looking gesture.

'Truth is the show closed a few weeks after the Crash and there's no backer for a new one.'

'Oh, Matty, I'm so sorry, my dear. You've had all this worry and you never said a word to us.'

'You couldn't have helped me, Eliza. Not unless you've got any advice on how to revive a failing music hall career. If you have I'd be all ears!' And she pulled at her lobes in a stage gesture which didn't have her sister fooled for an instant.

'Matty, dear.' She put her arm round her. 'If they don't want you over there, you must just come back home, everyone loves you here.' And she looked down with eyes full of an unaccountable love, which had always surprised Matty and sometimes puzzled her, since she'd done nothing at all to deserve it. For an instant she let herself lean against her sister, pretending that this was the extent of her problems, that all she had to do was pick up where she'd left off three years ago. As if the world was still bounded only by the West End and the Old Kent Road and she'd never heard of Frank Rossi, nor any of his plans for her great screen career.

'It's not as simple as that, Eliza.'

'Actually, it is, Matty. The simplest thing is always to go where you are loved, and leave where you are not.'

It made Matty cry to hear this, after her months of feeling so alone with her secret loss, and she wished she could tell Eliza the whole truth. But instead with her finger she traced an old scar on the inside of her wrist. It looked like a wild strawberry, but was nothing so sweet; it was the trace of a cigarette burn earned for questioning one of Frank's business choices.

'My agent's having trouble getting me bookings. I'm a bit worried about funds.'

Eliza looked shocked.

'I put my own money into the new film...' Matty explained.

'Ohh, I see. And has that taken up all your savings?'

Matty nodded.

'But things will get better, Matty, and until then you'll always have a home here and you're not to worry about money, do you hear me?'

Matty grasped Eliza's hand. 'You've always been so good to me, Eliza, not that I've deserved it. I know I used to be such an ungrateful little cow, but you've been the best of sisters.'

Eliza held on to her hand and Matty saw her eyes pool.

'That means the world to me, Matty.' Eliza closed her eyes and a spasm passed briefly across her face as she was caught by a coughing fit that left her breathless and unable to speak. She put a hand to her side, trying to cushion the effect of the coughing.

'Liza?' Matty asked, alarmed to see her in pain.

But then her sister opened her eyes and smiled. 'Those old seats at the Star have wreaked havoc with my back muscles. Let's go to bed, and remember what I said, this is your home now and it always will be.'

She got up and put her arm round Eliza. 'I don't deserve you,' she said, and together they walked slowly upstairs, Matty's heart feeling lighter for having shed at least one of her secrets.

3

Am I Blue?

August–September 1930

Esme had drummed up a few bookings after Matty's successful return to the Star and now she was on her way to her agent's office to discuss them. The sense of being followed, which she'd had since arriving back in the country had abated in Bermondsey. The place was little visited by outsiders. Peopled by dockers and factory workers, it was a village in the middle of London where strangers stood out a mile. But now, back in the West End, where the world came and went, she had lost that feeling of safety.

As she turned into the side court from Charing Cross Road something made her look back. She didn't know who he was, other than that he'd been the one haunting her dreams. The side court was a cul-de-sac, and he stood blocking her only way out. She could tell he wasn't English. He lacked the London pallor and the way he stood was expansive, as if he owned the ground he stood on. His bulky wide-shouldered figure was draped in an extravagantly striped suit and a fedora was pulled low over his olive-skinned face. She knew he had come for her. Her heart pounded in her chest as he began walking slowly towards her. Perhaps she could call out to Esme, but it was unlikely the woman would hear her, way up in her top-floor office. If Matty was quick enough she might dodge round him before he could grab her. She knew her long legs would carry her at a speed, if she could only slip past.

But she did nothing, paralysed by the crooked smile on the man's face as he approached. He reached into his inside pocket and Matty flinched, waiting to see the flash of metal as he withdrew a gun or knife. She'd expected to feel terror when the moment came, but instead she experienced an odd calm. It would be all right, she told herself, remembering her child, how still, how peaceful she'd looked. It would be like that for an instant, and then Matty would be with her again. She felt almost eager as she closed her eyes and sensed his bulk block the sun.

'Matty Gilbie?' The accent was American. 'Mr Rossi asked me to look you up. Open your eyes, honey. He wants you to see this.'

Feeling cool air brush her cheeks, she forced her eyes open. The man was fanning her face with a heavy cream envelope. 'It's a message from Frank, and he says it won't be the last.' Then he pulled open his jacket to reveal the gun.

She could have fled to anywhere in the world – Canada, Australia, Timbuktoo... what on earth had made her risk coming back here? However vague Frank's geography might be, even he would expect the Cockney Canary to come home to London.

The man grabbed her hand and pulled her close. The lop-sided smile never leaving his face, he slapped the envelope into her hand.

'Oh, and Frank says he'll be seeing ya – soon.' He flicked his hat and turned on his heel, calling back over his shoulder. 'I think he really misses you!' And he disappeared into Charing Cross Road, laughing.

Esme Golding was unable to speak. Smoke from her black cigarette caught in her throat and escaped slowly through her nose. She choked, waving her hands, while Matty banged her on the back.

'Are you completely mad, darling?' Esme eventually coughed out. 'You're not actually thinking of paying?' Esme threw the letter that she'd been reading back across the desk in disgust.

Matty went to the sideboard and poured Esme a glass of water.

'I need something stronger than that,' Esme said, indicating the tray of drinks on the sideboard. Matty poured whisky for them both. 'And I'll need more than a finger full.' She gave a sour look at the single Matty had poured.

'Come to think of it, so do I.' Matty topped up their whiskies and took a gulp of her own. It didn't calm her. In fact her heart beat faster and her hand trembled as she handed Esme her drink.

'I knew he'd come after me.' She sat down, a wave of nausea catching her. She took a deep breath. 'But I'd started to hope... Still, it's just like him to let me think I'd got away. I should've known better.'

'Why would he need to come after you?' Esme looked at her suspiciously. 'I thought you were here raising money for the new talkie. What's really been going on, Matty?'

Matty lit a cigarette and took a long draw before she answered. 'I saw a man throw himself off a skyscraper once,' she said, recalling the flyer who'd smashed on to the sidewalk on the same day as the Wall Street Crash. 'It was horrible, Esme, seeing that, but do you know, Frank thought it was funny. He said I just needed a stiff drink and took me to a speakeasy. Turned out he owned it and I never knew.' She paused, blowing out a long plume of smoke. 'There was a lot I didn't know about Frank. After the Crash I found out he wasn't much of a film producer, you were right about that, Esme. Seems he'd made most of his money providing bodyguards for film stars. Once our backers started pulling out he went back to doing that... and other things... which he didn't bother hiding from me any more.' Matty gave a bitter laugh. 'There's me, thinking he was my Rudolph Valentino and he turned out to be a bloody croo. Might as well have stayed home and got myself tied up with a good old Bermondsey villain!'

She fingered the scar on her wrist. It felt as if he'd reached out to burn her all over again.

'Oh, Matty, I'm so sorry. I should have known it was something more serious, when you went to Mrs Melior's and not straight home. Have you even told your family?'

'I told Eliza some of it. She knows I'm not just here for a short visit. She's offered to help me out.'

Esme nodded. 'That's good, but look, Matty, you can't give in to him. Besides, how do you propose raising that amount when I can't even get you the provinces?'

The letter detailing how much Matty owed Frank for their failed film enterprise had been drawn up by a lawyer, but its civilized legalese meant nothing. He was just playing with her. Matty knew Frank always collected debts personally, and though he hadn't come himself, it was obviously the messenger and not the letter he wanted her to worry about.

'I need to pay it, Esme, otherwise I'll never be free of him.'

'Oh, you've got such a stubborn streak, Matty Gilbie.' Esme scrubbed at her untamed salt-and-pepper frizz. 'I'm just worried about you, sweetheart. You owe him nothing!'

'In his eyes, I do. I walked out on him. And if paying him off keeps him out of my life it'll be money well spent.'

Matty screwed up the letter and, stuffing it into her bag, hesitated briefly. 'I'm sorry to ask, but could you deal with the lawyer? I don't want Frank to know where I'm living.'

'Of course I will, darling. But if he's sending thugs to watch this place, you'd better not come back here for a while.'

She was moved by Esme's protectiveness; the older woman had taken her on as a fifteen-year-old and could never quite accept she was now grown up. And though Matty had told her about the messenger, she'd said nothing about the gun. It seemed pointless to terrify her.

'Don't worry, I'll wire him the money and you can repay me when you're back on your feet,' Esme went on. 'I just hope Mr Rossi never takes it into his head to come a'hunting you himself. He seems the type who doesn't like to waste an investment!'

And, with Esme's words ringing in her ears, Matty decided to walk through the back streets, just in case Frank's associate was following her. Something made her doubt he would. He'd simply been Frank's opening gambit. She hurried on towards the river, intending to cross Waterloo Bridge on foot. The bold summer was continuing unabated but, today, as she turned down to the Embankment, huge white clouds rolled up the Thames. She needed to think and stopped at the river parapet. Looking westward, she was forced to hold on to her hat as a welcome breeze lifted it and, staring into the river's choppy waters, she shivered in spite of the heat. The letter had brought back memories of her terrified flight home. What did Frank want? She'd known that there would be consequences for walking out on him, but if it was only money he was interested in, then she'd got off lightly. Standing now in the shadow of Hungerford Bridge, the thunder of steam trains above her, purple smoke snaking down to where she stood, her attention was caught by a playbill on the side of the Playhouse theatre advertising a production of *The Dishonoured Lady*. It seemed that even the billboards were accusing her, but not as much as she had accused herself.

*

'Rent? I wouldn't hear of it! In fact I should be paying you! I'd be so lonely rattling around here on my own when Will goes to Cambridge – I'll need your company!'

Eliza had suggested to Matty that their temporary arrangement should be permanent and that she should make her home at Reverdy Road. 'I promise you, Matty,' Eliza insisted, 'you'll be nothing but an unpaid companion and I'll be exploiting you worse than a pickle girl at Crosse & Blackwell's!'

'But you're never home long enough to be lonely! What with Labour Institute meetings every other night and all the trade union work... I know you're only trying to spare my pride, Liza...'

They were sitting either side of the fire, enjoying the novelty of silence that had fallen over the house while Will was out. His presence dominated the household; his conversations and his opinions were always paramount. Matty was surprised at how much Eliza still pandered to him, but he was, after all, her only child, and she'd had to battle hard with Ernest James to keep him and then to bring him up as a single mother. Matty was comfortable in her sister's company, surprised at how companionable a silence could feel. Now Eliza leaned forward, hands clasped as earnestly as though she were explaining the finer points of employment law to a factory girl. Flickering flames lit her face from below and Matty saw a flash of the firebrand she'd been in her youth.

'You're my sister, Matty. And if I can't help my family, then what use is all my campaigning against dole cuts or unemployment?'

Matty knew this hadn't always been Eliza's line; there had been desert years when she'd never come near her family. Their father had blamed Ernest James's influence, and it certainly seemed that Eliza had remade herself after leaving him and taking their child with her. She'd been trying to remake herself ever since.

'Eliza, you're going beyond what most sisters would do... you're supporting me. Is it because of what happened to you?'

'What happened to me?'

'Well, when you left Ernest – supporting yourself and a baby. It must have been hard – doing it all on your own.'

Eliza nodded. 'It's just because I had to do it alone, Matty, that I'd never want the same for you.' Her sister searched her face, and seemed about to say more, but Matty turned her gaze back to the fire, her silence about her lost child weighing on her heart heavy as lead.

'But at least I had savings for a house and I had regular work...' Eliza said finally.

And Matty gave a wry smile. 'When you put it that way, things don't look too bright for me, do they?'

Matty knew there was no point in pretending she could afford much more than a room anywhere else.

'Let me help?' Eliza grasped her hand. 'It would really make me very happy.'

And when Matty agreed, her sister squeezed all the tighter and nodded her head. 'Good! It's settled,' she said.

In the end Will had given in gracelessly to his dead father's wishes, saying he could help organize the struggle just as effectively from

Cambridge as he could from Bermondsey, and he'd already begun to act the part. One morning later that week he came down to breakfast wearing what she thought of as his student costume: a dark button-down collared shirt with a knitted tie and pale baggy trousers.

'So, Matty, still swelling the numbers of the unemployed?' he asked provocatively, taking a large bite of the toast she'd made him for breakfast. 'What do you say to joining me at the NUWM tomorrow?' he jibed. Will had informed Eliza that he'd be spending the time before going up to Cambridge working with the National Unemployed Workers' Movement.

'Only if you promise to come dressed as a docker,' Matty said, passing him his tea.

She had always known the best way to deflect Will's acerbic humour was to sprinkle a little vinegar on his own wounds. Sometimes it worked, but this time he was obviously in a critical mood. Matty had discovered he had a vein of resentful anger, which she sometimes found wearing, suspecting his political opinions were merely the posturing of a young show-off.

'So, have you signed on?' he probed.

'No.'

'Ah well, you don't need to. You've got Ma, haven't you?'

Eliza paused, a slice of toast halfway to her mouth. 'Will!' she said in a shocked voice, and Matty felt her sister's foot seeking out Will's so she could no doubt kick him under the table. Instead she only succeeded in cracking Matty's ankle.

'What?' the boy said in mock innocence. 'I'm not saying anything against it. I'm a communist – I believe in the redistribution of wealth. Besides, you've always had your lame ducks, Ma, haven't you.'

Matty wasn't quite sure which of them Will was attacking, but she was gripping the teacup handle so tightly she was endangering Eliza's bone china.

Her sister stood up, her face red and her fists clenched so that the knuckles were white. Matty had never seen her look quite so angry, not even when decrying the latest unemployment figures.

'I won't have you speaking to your Aunt Matty like that. You're a spoiled brat and I blame your father for it. Now get out!' she shouted at Will. 'And don't come back until you can apologize to your aunt. She doesn't deserve such rudeness from you of all people.'

Will's normally florid complexion deepened to a livid plum and he slammed away from the table. 'This house never could take too much truth... could it?'

Matty had never felt so awkward with her own family. Will had made her feel like a stranger in the house, but she would not reveal her hurt to Eliza. Her sister couldn't be held responsible for the outbursts of her volatile son, who was old enough now to know the power of his own words to hurt.

*

Will had apologized before leaving for Cambridge in late summer. But the incident had soured her new easiness with Eliza and burdened Matty with even more guilt at relying on her sister's generosity. She was relieved to get a phone call from Esme one evening but it left her with a dilemma, which she spent all night puzzling over until Eliza returned from giving a talk to the local TUC Women's Committee.

'What are you looking so worried for?' Eliza asked as she dumped her briefcase on the floor and hung up her coat.

'Esme's got me some bookings,' she said. 'Do you want some tea to warm you up?'

When Matty came back with tea, Eliza was seated by the fire, holding her side as a coughing fit took hold of her. Seeing Matty's worried look, she banged her chest. 'It's chilly out, the cold always makes it worse.'

'Your hands are white, here,' Matty kneeled by the fire and took hold of Eliza's long tapering fingers, rubbing some warmth back into them.

45

'Ouch, they sting, bad circulation... But bookings, Matty! Tell me all about it. Surely that's a good thing?'

'Well, they're only one-nighters at the Regent and the Lyceum in East Anglia, but I could have a week in Hull afterwards.'

The shows were being staged at the new hybrid cine-variety theatres – half cinemas, half show theatres – and she desperately needed an extra injection of cash to pay Esme back the money she'd wired to Frank. It would mean leaving the relative sanctuary of Bermondsey, but she judged that these provincial theatres were every bit as low-profile as the Star.

'So why aren't you happy about it?' Eliza asked. 'It's not what you've been used to, but...'

Matty shook her head. 'No, no, it's not that.' She blushed, and went on quickly. 'To be honest, I haven't got the train fare.'

Eliza looked shocked. 'Matty, have you no savings left at all?'

Matty gave a dry smile. 'Would I be living off you if I did?'

'What went wrong out there, Matty? And don't tell me it's all down to the Crash. You've not really been yourself since you got back. You're jumpy and nervy and sometimes it feels to me like you're not here at all... even Sam's noticed it.'

Matty groaned and, resting her head in Eliza's lap, she stared into the fire. She didn't want Eliza to see her face, which was already burning with shame.

'It's Frank... I suppose he realized I'm not such a good business prospect after all. And now his lawyer's sent a letter to Esme, says I owe him money!'

'Matty, look at me.' Eliza drew her round to face her. 'You're not to blame yourself. He should have been protecting your interests, blame him!' Her eyes flashed and her expression sharpened. Matty thought she looked as she must have done in the days when she sat opposite factory owners, assessing their offers. Eliza picked up her tea, drained it and put the cup and saucer down with finality. 'We'll see about Frank Rossi. I can get you a lawyer from the TUC – we'll give him a dose of his own medicine.'

46

Matty knew her sister would want a fight.

'You don't know him, Eliza. When I say his lawyer, I don't mean some cosy old cove in a wig. Believe me, the best thing I can do is pay Frank off and pray to God he never crosses my path again.'

'You're frightened of him. Is he a criminal, Matty?'

'Oh yes, Liza.' Matty gave the answer to both questions without hesitation. How many stage-door Johnnies had fallen in love with her over the years, and she had let them come and go like the tide? But Frank had been different. His impossibly handsome face; the confidence he exuded, an innate power which enabled him to bend others to his will... and then there was his passion for her, which had been as dangerously addictive as the cocaine which dusted his parties so liberally.

Only gradually had she discovered that all his silvered words were worthless. And like the soft pads of a big cat's paws, they could be withdrawn in a moment, ready for sharp claws to strike. When those claws had come out, she'd seen him then for what he was, a sleek, stealthy predator and she, little more than prey to him, a cockney canary in a panther's grip.

'It took me a while before I realized he'd just been feeding off me, Liza. I really thought he loved me. Perhaps he did for a while. But I think he loved the money I brought in more. Let's just say that when I saw his true colours – I didn't like them.'

'All right, Matty, if you think paying him off is the safest thing to do. I can't bear the thought of you frightened of anything.' Eliza took her hands and Matty was surprised to feel her trembling.

'Oh, you know me, I'm tougher than I look! I'm not proud. I'll work till I drop to pay him what he *says* I owe him, just so long as it keeps him away from me... and the people I love. But I think I'll need to get a day job. They say Peek's are hiring!' Matty grinned.

'No, you can't go there!' Eliza said quickly, alarm on her face.

'Why not? Too good for factory work? If I hadn't had the voice, it's what I would have done anyway.'

'I'm not saying you're too good. I just mean… you can't go back, Matty, not once you've seen a different life. I should know. You at Peek's? It would be like letting a caged bird loose in the woods, my dear. No. You're going on tour and I'm paying the train fare!'

*

She played to a full house at the Ipswich Regent, which wasn't many people, she had to admit, but what had once been a joy was now almost an agony. Her singing had always been an abundant source of comfort, but now she was singing to keep the wolf Frank from her door that comfort had turned into a torment. She didn't know how she would get through the following week in Hull. The last time Matty had been in Hull was to attend her old Auntie Annie's funeral with Eliza and Sam. But the Hull she saw now was a very different place. Eliza had told her that unemployment was higher up here, but she was shocked to see the boarded-up shops, and even the old seed mill where her father had worked was closed, its gates padlocked.

It had been a mistake to come on tour on her own. Secret grief for her child still clung to her and though she'd not confided in them, being back among her family had somehow helped ease that loss. But the loneliness of nights in digs and solitary train journeys had left her too much time to think and she'd arrived at Hull drained and ready to go home. That night Matty tried to turn her despair into fuel for her performance. It was a matter of professional pride that she didn't bring her own sadness into the hall. Though the tune playing in her own head was 'Am I Blue?' still she gave her audience a programme of old music hall favourites, which lifted the crowd's spirits if not her own. She deliberately avoided all songs of missing and loss, choosing the brightest and silliest of her repertoire, ending with 'The Old Apple Tree' and a comical drunken dance from imaginary pub to pub, which brought the house down.

She was so effective that the manager came up to her after the performance. Sucking on a large cigar, he blocked her way to the shared dressing room, which was little more than a cupboard in the basement.

'Well, love, they don't call you the Cockney Canary for now't! You couldn't a' bin more chirpy 'n that if I'd taken you up there in a gilded cage! You've got 'em laughin' and the poor buggers certainly need cheering up! Half on 'em won't have jobs this time next week, so we got to make the most of it while they're still earnin'. Come 'an have a drink wi' me.'

'No thanks.' Matty leaned heavily on the basement wall and dabbed her face with a lace handkerchief. The greasepaint was melting and she wanted nothing more than to get the heavy sequinned dress off and return to her digs. She felt no obligation to keep up the act with the manager.

'I'm bone tired.' She sidestepped round him but he grabbed her arm.

'Come on, Matty, aren't you lonely on tour, you could do wi' a bit of company.' He pushed his face closer to hers. She sighed, this was the last thing she needed. She'd played Hull a few times in the early days of her career and knew Nat had earned his reputation in the business as one of the more persistent stage managers when it came to his female acts; in fact he treated his theatre as though it was his personal fiefdom.

'Yes, Nat, I am lonely...' For a moment his face brightened. 'I miss my family and if you want to thank me, you can let me use your telephone. I want to ring home.' Matty glared at him. Knowing Nat was a married man, she hoped that the mention of home would sober him. And she saw his face change.

'Oh, sorry, Matty, 'course you can use the phone, love.'

It was late, but Eliza kept late hours and in all her years of touring Matty couldn't ever remember needing to hear a familiar voice so much. Though she hadn't told Eliza the full extent of Frank's mistreatment, it was as though she'd let off the emotional stopper of some pungent poison, which only now was making its way through her system. She wasn't one for self-pity. But tonight the only antidote she needed was her sister's voice.

After the fifth ring she realized no one was going to answer, but she let it ring twice more, just in case Eliza was upstairs.

The voice when it came didn't sound like Eliza's. 'Hello? Is that you, Matty, why aren't you on stage?' Her sister's breathing was laboured and Mattie could hear a soft rattle on each intake of breath.

'I've just finished. I'm still at the theatre. I've been ringing for ages – where have you been? Have you just come in from a meeting?'

'Ah, you're checking up on me!' There came a pause and another harsh breath. 'No, it just took me a while to get to the phone. How's the Hull audience been?'

'OK, but I'm looking forward to coming home.'

Matty heard a muffled wheezing which turned to a phlegmy cough, rattling down the telephone line.

'Eliza, that cough's terrible. Have you seen the doctor?'

'Don't fuss, Matty, dear. I'm fine. I spent all yesterday in Trafalgar Square with the hunger marchers. It was freezing but marvellous...' Her enthusiasm disappeared in another wheeze. 'But I shouted myself hoarse on the platform.'

'Will it make a difference, do you think?' Sometimes Matty wondered where this dedication of her sister's came from, the passion to right everyone else's wrongs. But she'd certainly been grateful for it in her own case. So Eliza's answer was a surprise.

'I'm not that optimistic, Matty, it's like raising the dead. Even our Labour government can't conjure up work when the factories are dying.'

Matty wanted to hear more cheering news.

'How're Sam and Nellie, have you seen them?'

'Nellie brought the boys round. They're all bright as buttons, but I think Billy's got the family talent for music. He sang us "Mother of Mine" all the way through without a mistake.'

'Not another one destined for the stage, I hope.'

There was a moment's silence and Matty thought they had been cut off.

'Hold on, Matty.' Matty heard the phone clatter on to the table and then what sounded like a coughing fit.

'Eliza?' Matty gripped the telephone, suddenly wracked by an unaccountably strong certainty that something was really wrong with her sister. 'Eliza!' she shouted down the phone. 'Are you there?' And seized by a strong wave of panic, Matty called to her again. 'Where have you gone?' But there was only silence. 'Eliza!' Matty screamed, now really afraid.

'Yes, yes, I'm all right, Matty. Just a coughing fit, teach me to stand on a freezing cold podium in the middle of winter.'

Immediately anger replaced concern. 'Well, you should be taking better care of yourself! You frightened the bloody life out of me. I'll come home.' Matty was already reaching for her bag and coat.

'Don't be so melodramatic. You're not on the stage now, Matty. Really, it's just a cold. I'll be fine, trust me.'

4

Pal o' My Cradle Days

September–October 1930

At first she thought the house was empty. She dropped her bag in the passage and threw off her coat. She hoped Eliza had a fire going; she was stiff with cold from the journey.

'Eliza? I'm home... it's perishing out!'

Then she heard it. A crackling, hacking cough, unbroken by any breath. It sounded as if it were coming from the chest of an eighty-year-old man, but when finally it ended with an attempt to call her name she knew it was coming from her sister. She leaped the stairs two at a time to find Eliza propped up in bed, her hair falling down in untidy strands, face white with tiredness.

Matty ran to her. 'Why didn't you let me know you were so ill?' she said accusingly. 'I would have come straight home.'

'I thought I just had a cold—'

'A cold! Eliza, you can barely breathe...' Matty's voice rose in panic. 'I should never have listened to you.'

'Matty, it's just I've been awake all night, it's worn me out. I only need something to clear the pipes.' Her sister patted her chest weakly and let her hand fall back on the sheet.

Matty shook her head. 'I think it's more than a cough. I'm getting the doctor.'

At that moment there was a loud knocking on the front door.

'I already sent the boy next door to fetch Nellie,' Eliza explained.

And soon Nellie, who didn't stop to take off her coat, was at Matty's side. She placed the back of her hand on Eliza's cheek. 'She's burning up and I don't like the sound of her.'

'I'm here!' protested Eliza, who still had enough strength in her to resent being treated like a patient.

'Shall I ring for the doctor?' Matty asked Nellie, who nodded in spite of Eliza's protests.

The doctor was with them quickly as his surgery was on the corner of Reverdy Road. A kindly man with an unhurried manner, he took his time examining Eliza while Matty hovered anxiously by the bed. Finally he pronounced it pneumonia. Eliza, he said, needed to be in hospital.

'Come on, Matty. I'll wrap her up, you get your coat on,' Nellie ordered.

And Matty sprang into action, glad she could finally do something. She swaddled Eliza in a papoose of blankets so thick that Eliza appeared to shrink in size.

She attempted a weak laugh 'Stop, Matty, you're like a mother hen… you'll suffocate me before the pneumonia does!' she said, trying to push off the covers. But Matty ignored her and was glad she had, for it was cold as death outside and even the short distance to the ambulance had Eliza shivering.

'Try not to worry, Matty,' Nellie said, laying a hand on Matty's before they stepped up into the ambulance.

Guy's Hospital was a scene of calm professional activity. Nurses in starched hats wearing white and purple striped dresses attended Eliza, surrounding her in an unhurried, synchronized dance that Matty at first found reassuring. The ward held the forced hush of those saving all their energies simply to get well. But Eliza's cough tore through the quiet like a ferocious beast, and it was obvious to Matty that her once vigorous body was wearing itself out in these repeated paroxysms of explosive force.

A nurse hurried up to them. 'Are you the next of kin?'

Matty nodded.

The nurse walked briskly to a side room. She fired questions at Matty, but Nellie answered, as Matty had no idea how long Eliza had been coughing, nor what her temperature had been. She felt the poorest of sisters, ashamed even to open her mouth.

Eventually the nurse finished making her notes and looked up at Matty; in spite of her reassuring veneer, there was something in her eyes that made Matty afraid.

'Can't you do anything to help her breathe?'

'Try not to worry!' the nurse said pointlessly.

Eliza was gasping for air now, clutching at the bedclothes. Matty had never seen her brave sister scared – but now the fear in her eyes spurred Matty to action.

'Look at her! For God's sake, get some help!'

The nurse didn't argue, but dashed out of the room.

Matty gripped her sister's hand. 'Oh, I feel so bad, Eliza. I should have come home when I knew you were ill!'

But Eliza had no breath left for words and simply gripped Matty's hand.

'Shhh, Matty, that's silly talk. Besides, when have you ever known Eliza take anyone else's advice?' Nellie reassured her.

They heard the nurse before they saw her; she was trundling an oxygen canister on wheels. She quickly spun dials and adjusted a small mask over Eliza's face. She'd brought the doctor with her.

'This will help for now,' the doctor explained, 'but I'm afraid you'll have to leave her with us, she needs to rest.'

As Eliza calmed and began to breathe more easily, Matty's pounding heart began to still itself too. Her eyes locked with Eliza's, and Eliza gave her a small, nod, almost of permission.

'We'll be back tomorrow!' she said, but Eliza held up her long tapering fingers in a beckoning gesture and Matty went to her side. The voice was muffled behind the mask, so Matty leaned in close to hear her laboured words. 'I always loved you, Matty, right from the day you were born...' She was silenced by a long shuddering breath and closed her eyes. Matty turned to leave, but Eliza grabbed her hand with surprising strength.

'You were always here...' and she rested her other hand on her heart. Matty thought she heard the words. 'Goodnight, my angel,' as Eliza's eyes closed again and her hand dropped to the bedclothes.

Matty was rooted to the spot. Perhaps she'd been mistaken, for it was an endearment Eliza never used. But their mother had. Always, before tucking them into bed at night. Perhaps that's why they were also the last words she'd spoken to her own tiny daughter, and as she bent to kiss Eliza goodbye, tears flooded her cheeks at that unbearable memory.

That night when she finally got home, she glanced in the hall mirror as she took off her hat and was shocked by the toll the anxious night had taken on her. She looked almost as exhausted as Eliza. She traipsed upstairs and laid down to sleep, kept awake by the creaks and groans of the empty house and by guilt for the way she'd treated her sister in the past. She remembered how hard Eliza had tried to be friends when she'd returned, buying her presents, asking only to be given a chance to make up for the lost years when she'd been exiled with Ernest James in Mecklenberg Square and later Australia. Matty tossed and turned, eventually hearing the voice of her mother, always practical, never sentimental. Lizzie Gilbie would be getting so impatient with her now. 'You can't turn back the clock. It's what you do today that counts, not what you did gawd knows how long ago!' she'd have said, with a flash of fire in her eyes, reserved for those less practical than herself. And Matty smiled through her tears of regret, for even from the grave Lizzie Gilbie was right, and Matty would do everything in her power to prove to Eliza how much she'd grown to love her.

The following morning as she was preparing to go to the hospital, Matty was surprised to hear the clip clop of a dray and the creaking of a cart as it came to a halt outside the house. She ran out, grabbing her hat and pulling on her coat.

'Sam! What are you doing here?'

It seemed his delivery round out of the Bricklayer's Arms had brought him past Reverdy Road and he offered to take her to Guy's Hospital.

'That's if the Hollywood star don't mind being seen sitting up on a cart!' He laughed.

'Mind! Have I ever minded? Shove over.'

As she clambered up on to the seat beside Sam, the smell of horse and leather harness transported her back to the days when, as a child, Sam would hoist her up on to his cart and take her for a ride. Now she leaned against him, putting her hand on the arm of his worn work jacket.

'Drive on, James, and...' she said, pausing for Sam to complete their old chant.

'*Do* spare the horses...' He obliged, smiling.

He gave his familiar click and the horse lifted its head. They jolted forward, cartwheels hissing and hooves clipping sharply on the frosty cobbles as Sam urged the horse onward.

'Nellie told me they gave her oxygen. How do you think she is?' he asked, above the roar of a passing lorry.

'A little better, I think, Sam. I'm praying she'll be able to breathe on her own today.'

Her brother nodded, his jaw set, as he concentrated on the traffic. But when he glanced at her, she could see his own anxiety written there.

'We'll keep our hopes up, eh, Matty love? Nellie's put a sandwich for you in here.' He indicated a wrapped package. 'She says you won't think to eat.'

'As if she didn't have enough to do looking after all you lot! Say thanks for me, Sam.'

Sam shook his head. 'Our Eliza... if she'd spent less time putting the world to rights organizing hunger marches and more on looking after her own health...'

Her brother had always been hard on Eliza, and whereas once Matty would have agreed, now she defended her sister. 'It's what she's lived for, Sam. And besides, she might not have been looking after herself, but she's certainly been looking after me lately. Do you know she's not taken a penny rent?'

'And so she shouldn't…'

Matty gave up trying to convince him as Sam brought the cart to a halt outside the old Victorian hospital building. She hugged him and jumped down. It was impossible to imagine how she could have got through the last couple of months without him, or Nellie, or Eliza. They were all the world to her, and sometimes she felt almost grateful that she'd been blown back across the Atlantic and into the warmth of their arms again.

'Can you come in for a minute?'

He shook his head. 'I'll try to get time off tomorrow. But be sure to give her my love, won't you?' he said deliberately.

Eliza's eyes were closed. She looked thinner than yesterday, her eyes dark sunken circles above the oxygen mask. Matty sat at her bedside and took her sister's hand.

'Sam sends his love, Liza. And Will's on his way home, he'll be here soon…'

In fact Matty didn't know where Will was. She'd telephoned the porter at Trinity, but he'd said Will wasn't there, and when she'd explained how ill his mother was the man had relented. 'I think he's gone off with that other young Bolshie, son of Lord Fetherstone, though you wouldn't think it. Walks around in sandals, filthy feet. The family pile's up north.'

But when she asked for the telephone number he refused. Matty pretended to cry; she could do sad equally well as chirpy.

'Now, now, young lady, no need for tears. Best I can do is pass on a message, let the young gentleman know he's needed at home.'

So Matty could only hope the message had got through.

The nurse came to the bedside. 'Let's see if she'll make an effort for you today.'

Matty let go of Eliza's hand.

'We'll try without the oxygen,' she said, gently lifting the mask off Eliza's face.

'Come on, Liza,' Matty urged, 'prove I'm not the only trouper in the family.'

Matty's fingers dug deep into her palms as she clenched her fists, willing her sister to take just one calm, unhindered breath, one effortless intake and one smooth sigh out.

'One breath for me, Liza,' she begged, reaching again for her sister's hand, and seeing, she thought, a flicker of effort crossing her face. Eliza's lips moved as though struggling to speak.

Matty held her own breath for what seemed like minutes, but must have been only seconds, when, with a shudder and a half smile, Eliza breathed in, one deep, life-promising gulp of air and then one long sigh out which ended, not in a paroxysm of choking but, instead, in a palpable calm, a stillness that filled the seconds. Matty had felt that stillness before, she had held it in the palm of her hand, and with a cold recognition she stared at her sister's chest, waiting for it to rise of its own accord. She lifted her eyes to the nurse, but the woman's expression had turned from one of expectancy to alarm.

'I don't think this one's ready to breathe unaided, just yet,' she said, hastily replacing the mask.

'What's the matter?' Coming nearer, Matty saw instantly that the stillness hadn't left her sister. 'She's not breathing!' Matty's voice rose in alarm and the nurse ran to the door of the ward, calling for a doctor.

The next minutes passed in a red blur of searing focus, with the image of her unmoving sister burning itself into Matty's vision. When the doctor arrived, he was almost rough, pushing Matty aside so that he could get to Eliza. Hands flat on her chest, he began to pump the frail ribcage, and with each plunge of his hands Matty cried, 'Breathe, Liza, breathe!'

Finally the doctor stood up, defeat in his eyes. 'I'm so sorry, my dear, the disease had weakened her lungs too badly...'

Matty, with a voice trained to project to the back of an auditorium, screamed at him 'No!' so that the walls seemed to reverberate and the loose old windows rattle in their sashes at her denial. Refusing to believe that the sister she'd come to love had been snatched away, so suddenly, she protested again – '*No!*' – wanting to be the breath that could fill her sister's lungs, wanting to be the pulse that could set her heart in motion once more and finally. 'No,' as defeated and hoarse, she realized she could not.

At one point someone must have brought her tea, for she was seated, with a cup in her hands and curtains drawn round her. The nurse crouched by her side. Taking the cup from Matty, she asked, 'Is there anything I can do, telephone anyone for you?'

Matty shook her head. 'How can she be dead? I don't understand, what did the doctor mean about the disease weakening her? She's had nothing wrong with her but a cough and a back ache... It was a cold, that's all.' She looked at the nurse in numb disbelief.

'The back pain would explain a lot. It really must have been quite bad.'

'She didn't complain... she was always concerned more about other people than herself.'

'Well, the doctor says she's been suffering from pleurisy for some time and sadly it turned to pneumonia... Would you like to sit with her before you leave?'

Matty nodded mutely; for some reason her voice had deserted her.

'I'll leave you alone for a bit. I'm just outside.'

She heard the swish of the curtain and finally let her eyes rest on Eliza's face. Now that the illness had finally, so capriciously and cruelly, decided to abandon her, all her sister's fire and energy had stilled. Calm and restful as she'd never been in life, her eyes were closed, a half smile on her face as though there were things she knew that Matty did not. Matty took up the long, thin hand, skin translucent as the finest bone china, and let her lips rest there for a moment. As she reached to wipe a strand of faded auburn hair from her sister's untroubled brow she saw, more than ever, the resemblance to their own mother. She remembered her twelve-year-old self, seated, very much as now, watching as Lizzie Gilbie slipped out of the world. And she thought back to yesterday and Eliza's final goodbye. There had been too many goodbyes, too many losses. She let go of Eliza's hand, which felt lighter in death, as if the weight of everything substantial had already flown.

*

'Have you found the will yet?' Sam had come to Reverdy Road to discuss Eliza's funeral.

'Will? No, I don't know where he is. He's meant to be with a friend,' Matty said distractedly.

'No, love, not Will. I meant *the* will, Eliza's last will and testament! She told me ages ago she'd made me executor, so I know she's got one.'

'Oh no. I haven't even thought...' Matty looked around vaguely as though the document might magically appear on the table.

Since Eliza's death an uncharacteristic daze had punctuated the perpetual state of heightened alertness she'd felt since Frank's henchman had shown up at Esme's.

'But, Sam, I really am getting worried about Will. I persuaded that porter at Trinity to give me the Fetherstones' telephone number and according to the butler the boys haven't been there at all. So God knows what he's been up to.'

'And Eliza never said he was going away?'

Matty shook her head. 'But then again, they weren't getting along very well.'

'Why not?'

'He resented Eliza helping me – accused me of being a sponger and said she was a hypocrite!'

'He's going to regret speaking to his mother like that. But he's always been so bloody headstrong, he wouldn't admit it.'

'I just wish he'd come home. I feel so bad for him, Sam, we're all he's got now. His father's family certainly don't want anything to do with him, and that's been half his trouble. He's never felt good enough for them...'

'And always felt too good for us...' Sam said.

'No, that's not true.' She leaped to Will's defence, remembering the forward, confident child he'd been, charging into their lives and capturing her heart.

Sam put an arm round her shoulder. 'I'm a bit hard on him, I know, Matty. But it just gets under my skin, the way he thinks his upbringing's been a burden, and you've had none of his advantages, but look what you've done with your life!'

She laid her head on his shoulder. Ever her champion, she felt a cold fear that one day he might think she had done less well with her life than he now imagined.

'Will's got a lot of growing up to do, Sam. Think of me when I ignored you all and went to be a munitionette at the Arsenal. You all begged me not to and did I listen? You do some bloody stupid things when you're young...' She sighed.

'And sometimes when you're not so young too... I've not always been the sensible one. But come on, this is not getting that will found.'

They searched Eliza's bureau, but apart from some notes for a speech to the Labour Institute and a few bills, there was little there. Then Matty had a thought. 'She did say once that she had a very good solicitor, someone the TUC uses. Perhaps she left the will with him?'

Sam agreed to try the Labour Institute in Fort Road to see what he could find out about the solicitor and after he left Matty went up to Eliza's bedroom. It hadn't been touched since the night she was taken ill. Matty began folding and putting away clothes. It filled her with sadness to see how few belongings her sister had. She'd lived her principles, and what little she'd earned had mostly gone to worthy causes. Sam might worry about the will, but Matty guessed there would be little enough for Eliza to leave, apart of course from the house, which Will would have. Though it occurred to Matty he might not keep it as he was forever telling them that all property was theft. She smiled to herself at how Eliza would raise her eyes at her son's extreme views. As she patted the clothes into the bottom drawer of the tallboy, Matty spotted an old Peek Frean's biscuit tin that looked pre-war. She took the tin out and prised off the lid. Inside she found a prayer book, of the sort they were all given as leaving presents from school, a number of folded, yellowing documents and a few photographs. She recognized the dark curly-headed toddler in one photograph as Will, and another of Eliza, looking awkward and gawky in her hideous scullery maid's uniform. *God, you must have loathed it*, Matty thought, imagining her bright and powerful sister scrubbing other people's floors. Matty sat on the bed, sorting through the rest of the photos.

She smiled fondly at Sam in his army uniform. She picked up another of a young girl, her long wavy hair tied back with a bow, wearing a pinafore frock from another era – reaching halfway down her legs. Was that Eliza as a child? The lines of washing in the courtyard looked faintly alien, not like a Bermondsey street. On the back was written in old-fashioned copperplate: *Our little ray of sunshine, Eliza aged five.* Matty knew it was her father's hand, for her mother's skills never lay in that direction.

It must have been taken when they lived in Hull. How sad, that his little ray of sunshine should have so disappointed him. At the bottom of the pile was a picture of another little girl, about the same age, and it made Matty gasp. It was undoubtedly her younger self. In spite of her sister's declaration in the hospital, Matty had never imagined Eliza taking an interest in her childhood, let alone having a photograph of her. She turned it over, and recognized the much poorer handwriting of her mother. She'd written in pencil: *Another little ray of sunshine, our Matty.*

Matty held the two photographs side by side, herself and Eliza. Why had she never seen the resemblance before? It was almost the same face.

'Oh, Liza, I wish I'd known you back then,' Matty whispered, feeling keenly for the first time how robbed she'd been of her sister for so many years. She put the photos back in the tin. At least she'd had dear Nellie, a sister and a mother all rolled into one, and even now, when she was feeling particularly low, Nellie was the person she invariably turned to. Not wanting to be in the house alone, she decided that she would go to Vauban Street and went to make herself look presentable. She had no intention of walking out of the house looking grief-ravaged. She powdered her face, applied her lipstick and changed her dress. But as she passed Eliza's bedroom she went to the Peek Frean's tin in the tallboy and took out the matching pair of photographs. She must show Nellie and Sam the resemblance between the two little rays of sunshine.

On the day before the funeral, Matty was in her bedroom, trying on her new black dress and coat. Black was a colour she rarely wore. The stage had taught her not to be frightened of strong colours and she now felt strangely conspicuous in this unrelieved black, as if she was outlined in bold, instead of obscured, which was what she wanted to be tomorrow.

She heard a noise behind her and whirled round.

'Did someone die?' Will grinned and then stopped short at the door, his smile fading. 'Oh fuck, somebody did. I'm sorry, Matty,' he said.

He looked dishevelled, as though he'd been sleeping rough. There was mud on the turn-ups of his trousers and his shoes were scuffed and caked with dirt. His dark curls were plastered greasily to his head.

'Will, where have you been? I've been trying to get in touch for days!' She ran to him and held him in a tight embrace, not wanting to let him go because it would mean having to tell him.

Finally he extricated himself. 'Me and Feathers have been tramping. We're writing a piece about doss houses for *The Daily Worker*. What's happened, Matty?' His face was alarmed now, perhaps reflecting her own.

'Will, love, I've got bad news. It's your mother... she caught pneumonia. It all happened so quickly... I'm sorry.'

'Ma?'

'She's gone, Will.'

His young man's face turned into a boy's, crumpled and creased as he slumped to his knees. Matty dropped down beside him and he laid his head on her lap and wept unashamedly.

When he lifted his wet face to hers she wiped it with her handkerchief, trying to answer all his questions that now tumbled out.

'I was away in Hull and she caught a chill at the rally and it turned to pneumonia... she was only in Guy's a couple of nights. They told us she'd had pleurisy a while, but we never knew... There was nothing they could do...'

'Why didn't she wait for me?' Will asked, almost angrily. 'I was so bloody horrible to her last time I saw her! Why didn't she wait, Matty?' His face screwed up in an agony of regret.

Matty put her hand on his greasy curls and drew his head on to her shoulder.

'She didn't need to wait to know you loved her, Will. She was your mother. She knew you didn't mean what you said.' And the boy was overcome with a new burst of grief so violent that Matty had to hold him tightly for a long time, until the front of her new black coat was stained with the darker black of his tears.

Matty had thought that she was the celebrity in the family. But as she turned to look back from the front pew at the hundreds of people pouring into St James's Church, she began to realize how wrong she'd been. She'd taken little interest in Eliza's political work, and only now did she understand how popular it had made her sister. Labour party dignitaries sat in the front pews with herself, Sam, Nellie and Will. Their MP Dr Salter was at the front too and would be giving the eulogy. But as she took another discreet look around she saw the back pews filling up with groups of factory women, no doubt coming to show their gratitude for all those pay rises Eliza had gained for them over the years. A few of their remaining Hull family had made the trek down and even their father's cousins, George Gilbie and Betty Bosher, were there. But the crowd became a blur to Matty, her focus of attention now finely tuned to Will. In public he had been a model of strength and restraint, but she had shared the house with him last night and his sobs had been audible through the bedroom wall. She sat next to him and when Dr Salter praised Eliza's selfless work she felt him stiffen, for Will's opinion of Eliza's politics had often been dismissive. Matty sometimes thought he hated her politics because they'd taken her away from him too often as a child. She squeezed his hand. She knew he was in turmoil and although she could never replace his mother, she had held the boy as a baby and sung him to sleep at night, and she would give him what comfort she could now.

The official reception was a rather proper affair at the Fort Road Labour Institute, with tables laden with sandwiches and cakes, and cups of tea served by an army of willing volunteers. Matty was standing by the tea urn, and had attracted a few admirers who wanted to engage her in conversation about her next talkie. But she was anxious to evade them and looked round for someone to provide an escape. She saw a short, buxom woman heading her way. It was Katie Gilbie, cousin George's wife and landlady of The Land of Green Ginger. As a young girl she'd been known as Bermondsey's own Marie Lloyd, though Matty thought her singing career had mainly been confined to Bermondsey pubs. The woman had grown rounder as she'd grown older, retaining the piled-up hairstyle of thirty years ago, so that she now resembled a cottage loaf. Matty sighed. Katie Gilbie had a determined look in her eye, but anything was better than the crowd of doe-eyed young men who'd surrounded her.

'Matty, darlin'! You poor thing, come and give us a kiss,' Katie cried out, though her bulk and short arms prevented a full embrace. Matty told herself to be patient. It was a family funeral, old sores were to be forgotten, but Matty had inherited her mother's long memory. Cousin George, a stiff-mannered man who prided himself on being a respectable publican, had always looked down on her father and during the war he'd even accused

Sam of letting down the family name for not joining up in the first week. Matty could not forgive George that. Yet Katie wasn't a mean person; she'd just had the misfortune to marry George Gilbie. It was well known he wouldn't have had such a successful business if he hadn't married Katie, with her outgoing ways and knack for bringing in the customers. Since Matty's success in the halls, Katie had developed an unwanted interest in her.

'Now, me darlin', you and the family are coming back to the Green Ginger after this. I know it's a wake but gawd, you'd be gaspin' for a decent drink here, wouldn't you, love? All signed the pledge by the looks of 'em!'

Matty tried to protest, knowing that it was the last thing Sam would want to do.

'Sam and Nellie's coming back, and you make sure you bring her boy.' Katie nodded towards Will, who was locked in earnest discussion with one of the Labour councillors.

Katie patted her arm. 'Me and you'll do a duet, eh?'

Matty smiled weakly and Katie leaned in confidentially.

'I heard you're having trouble getting the bookings. Well, people ain't got the money, have they, darlin'? I know what it's like meself, when I was trying to make a living in the halls... Don't take it wrong, but if you need a bit of extra cash, there's always a spot for you at the Green Ginger.' Katie smiled encouragingly, the thick coating of face powder cracking in all the wrong places. Matty's heart sank momentarily, but then who was she to be fussy? She had Frank breathing down her neck, and no doubt Will would be selling the house soon so she'd have to find rent for a new place.

'Thanks, Katie,' Matty said. 'I might just take you up on that if I don't get some work soon!'

Just then Matty spotted a well-built, fair-haired young man coming her way.

'Freddie!' she called. 'I haven't had a chance to talk to you.' Grateful to escape the subject, she veered off from Katie into his path.

Nellie's brother, Freddie Clark, was part of Matty's second family, acquired when Nellie had taken her and Charlie in during the war years. Married now and with his own family, Freddie owned a thriving haulage firm. Although in his younger days his business dealings hadn't always been legal, Nellie had assured Matty his new wife, Kitty, had straightened him out.

He was carrying a plate of sandwiches, but with his large, free hand caught her round the waist, kissing her on the cheek.

'Hello, Matt! Sorry about your Eliza, bit of a shocker, eh?'

'It was sudden, Freddie. But how's your family? I hear you've got a new baby?'

'She's beautiful, Matt. And Kitty's here.' He lifted the plate of sandwiches, as if to convince Matty that they were all for his wife, which she doubted, remembering Kitty's small frame. 'Left the baby with her mother. How's life treating you? Not doing no more talkies?'

It was a question she was coming to dread. 'I didn't really like America, Freddie.'

'Nah, not all it's cracked up to be. Eh? You're better off at home. You got any new shows on? I promised Kitty I'd take her to see you.'

Matty smiled, not wanting to explain her dwindling bookings to Freddie.

'Well, I'll make sure you get some comps next show I do!'

In the end Katie hadn't found it too difficult to persuade the family back to the Green Ginger for free drinks, but Matty had trouble with Will when she broached the subject.

'No! I'm not setting foot in that place. They had no time for my mother when she was alive. The only reason they've asked us back is because they think you're famous!'

'Shhh, Will. They're your family and your mother wouldn't want you to be rude.'

'My mother cared too much about appearances. It was all compromise with her!'

Matty put a hand on his arm, which he shrugged off.

'Will, please, just let's get through the day.' She couldn't understand where this anger towards Eliza had come from. Perhaps he really did blame her for not waiting for him to come home before she'd died. 'We'll stop for a quick drink and then go,' Matty said soothingly.

'Oh, all right, just one, but then I'm off.'

But at the Green Ginger, Will found that he wanted more than just one drink and when he rolled off his chair halfway through her duet with Katie Gilbie, Matty began to regret persuading him to come. For Matty, drinks were never free. She always had to pay with a song and now she was trying to accompany Katie's cigarette-smoked gravelly voice with her own sweeter tones in a version of 'Pal o' My Cradle Days' – a choice Matty had tried to dissuade Katie from, given the occasion. They had reached the final lines and the whole pub was singing along in a heartfelt harmonious crescendo:

I took the gold from your hair, I put the silver thread there,
I don't know any way, I could ever repay you,
pal o' my craaaaadle days!

It was the drink, Matty thought, rather than sentimentality, which caused Will's locked-up grief to burst, for now he began sobbing audibly, and as he got up to push out through the crowd he stumbled and fell. George tried to help him up but Will turned on him, snarling like a terrier and upending a table.

'Take your hands off me, you bloody hypocrite. You hated my mother, though God knows her politics were nearer yours than you ever thought. Bloody moral cowards...' He now seemed to be in conversation with himself. 'Both of them, father and mother, moral cowards... pal of my cradle days? Inconvenience me, ashamed of me, both of them... and that's the truth...'

He would only have got louder if Sam hadn't intervened, casting a look of mute appeal to Matty. She left Katie to carry on singing, with a hissed instruction to the pianist as she passed.

'Play "Silver Lining", for gawd's sake – anything but this!'

Taking Will's other elbow, she and Sam hoisted him out on to the street and Nellie followed with the boy's coat and scarf.

'Come on, son,' Sam urged him. 'You're disgracing yourself.'

'Disgrace? My parents were the disgrace.' He turned unfocused eyes on Sam. 'Him, bloody snob, and her, wishy-washy turncoat, betrayed her own class...'

Suddenly Nellie was in front of him. She was not a tall woman, but years of hard work had made her strong, and now she looped Will's scarf over his neck and pulled him closer. Fixing him with bright blue eyes that had witnessed Eliza's greatest triumph in the famous Bermondsey women's strike twenty years earlier, she said in a low, fierce voice, 'Betrayed her own class? Your mother did no such thing! She helped more working women than you've had hot dinners at that expensive school of yours. So you keep your opinions about Eliza to yourself till you know what you're talking about!'

Something of Nellie's ire must have penetrated Will's alcoholic fug, for he nodded, obedient as one of her own well-behaved boys, and submitted as she helped him on with his coat. It made Matty laugh out loud to see Nellie rout the young communist and she felt that, of all the eulogies she'd heard that day, Nellie's was the most heartfelt.

5

Tattered Dreams

November–December 1930

Eliza's will still hadn't been found. There had been no response from the TUC solicitor to Sam's enquiry and he had come to Reverdy Road to search for the missing document. Will was sitting on the parlour floor, surrounded by a pile of his mother's papers, huge bundles of yellowing correspondence and dusty documents all relating to past union causes and strikes, as well as notes for speeches and pamphlets. He was flicking through some letters from his father to Eliza.

'Crikey, the old man was head over heels! Never knew he had it in him,' Will said, waving the almost transparent remnant of his parents' affair.

'Will, you don't have to go through their old love letters! Give them their dignity,' Matty said, snatching it from him and returning it to the ribbon-tied bundle. She was actually thinking of the letters she'd written Frank while she was in California and he was in New York. Even as she'd written them she feared that one day all that passion would turn to bitter regret. There were only so many slaps, burns and losses that a love could survive, but she'd stayed with him for longer than most would have done. Typically, Frank had rarely replied to her letters, preferring the telephone. But she understood why Eliza, usually so unsentimental, had kept those old letters even when the thing had ended badly. She had often thought she would love to burn every word she'd written to Frank. But, perversely, she'd kept his few replies, perhaps as evidence that she'd had good reason, at one stage, to believe in his love.

'I'll have to leave you two to get on with it,' she said and went to get dressed for a stint at the Green Ginger. She'd felt obliged to start paying Will rent and Katie's offer had at least given her the chance to earn some instant cash. When she returned in a sapphire-blue cocktail dress with a fur-trimmed bolero, Will was tipping his mother's papers upside down, growling with increasing frustration. Matty could smell the dust of her sister's past rising as the boy rifled through the pile. He looked up distractedly.

'I must get it sorted out before I go off with Feathers.' Will had informed Matty that he would be staying with his friend at Fonstone, the Fetherstones' large country house. 'I've promised Victims of German Fascism they'll have the money this year and I've decided the proceeds from the house are going to International Red Aid. Ma won't have left me a lot, but it's probably enough to keep a revolutionary cell going for ten years!'

He held Matty's gaze, seeking her approval. 'I'm obligated, Matty. It's no good preaching solidarity, is it, if I don't follow it through?'

Matty was silent for a moment, as she looked in the mirror above the mantlepiece. She pressed her auburn waves into position, but her hair and make-up were immaculate and didn't really need checking. She was looking instead at the reflection of Will's earnest face and realizing how much he was his mother's son. His physical resemblance to Ernest James meant Matty had always thought Will took after his father, but in his extreme desire for justice, he was just like Eliza.

'Of course you've got to stick to your principles, Will. It's your money and your property – you do what you like with it.'

She perched a shell-shaped blue hat with a cockade on the side of her head. Just because it was the Green Ginger didn't mean she needed to abandon all vestige of her West End style. Satisfied, she turned away from the mirror and picked up her bag. Inside were a lipstick and powder compact, and a purse containing three shillings and twopence ha'penny. The earnings from her provincial tour had gone to pay off some of Frank's demands. She was officially broke.

This wasn't the first time Will had spoken of his intention to give away the inheritance from his mother. His father's money was in trust and would only come to Will once he'd completed his reviled Cambridge degree. Matty thought this was a wise proviso on the part of Ernest James. Perhaps he'd taken a keener interest and known his son better than Will ever gave him credit for.

A loud thud from above was followed by the sound of slow footsteps on the stairs. Sam pushed through the door, holding a cardboard box – it looked like an old Worth dress box.

'This is the last one from the attic,' Sam said, letting it fall beside Will, coughing as a thick layer of dust was dislodged from its top. 'You'll have to go through it, Will. I promised to be back home before the boys go to bed.'

Will drew the box towards him with a groan. 'The perils of having literate parents,' he muttered.

'I'll walk down with you,' Sam said to Matty and, though unreadable to most people, Matty could see that he was irritated.

Once out in the crisp night air, she put her arm through her brother's. 'Has he been getting on your nerves?' she asked immediately.

'Oh, I know he's young… and he's got his principles,' he said, 'but doesn't he know charity begins at home? There's people in the family might need it just as much as a Russian revolutionary!' He gave her a pointed look which she didn't like.

'Sam, it's not up to us to judge. We can only guide him and we'll do it for Eliza's sake, won't we?'

He shrugged. 'I suppose you're right, my little canary!' He gave her hand a squeeze. 'But it's as if he can't wait to get rid of Eliza's money and her house and her things… and her family! Besides, he *knows* she didn't approve of bloody Stalin… I don't think we'll see much of him now she's gone.'

'And you know you're turning into our dad, don't you? He was always complaining about Eliza having time for everyone else but her family!'

She felt Sam sigh. 'That was different.'

'But you might be right about not seeing him much... he's going to stay at his friend's for a while.'

'See what I mean! Not a thought that we might need him to be here. We've lost her too.'

For all her brother's censure of Eliza in the past, Matty knew that for him, family ties were everything. He shook his head. 'Well, I won't go on about him, he's an orphan and we're all he's got. I suppose when he needs us he'll be back.' He bent to kiss her before turning down Spa Road. 'Good luck tonight, Matty, knock 'em dead!'

She treated him to a stage smile and a pirouette, then watched him walk away shaking his head and smiling.

'Always knew you'd be famous!' he called back to her.

Her dear brother had, with a tact born of love, never mentioned her dramatic fall in popularity or her lack of bookings. To him she had always been a star, whether it was as a seven-year-old mimicking Vesta Tilley or as a young woman in the music halls or in a Hollywood talkie, it simply didn't matter, because Sam was always her greatest fan, and, apart from Nellie, Matty was his.

*

Will's face looked like it had been turned to stone and his normal high complexion paled in an instant to alabaster. With his curls and his youthful clean-lined profile, he reminded Matty of a Greek statue she'd once seen on a trip to the British Museum. But only for a moment, for in the next instant it was transformed by fury, animated from within by a fire that reddened his face so intensely Matty thought she felt heat radiating from it.

'But that's not possible!' he finally spluttered. 'She can't have!' He looked to her and Sam for confirmation that the solicitor had interpreted it wrongly. But the lawyer looked back impassively, no doubt having seen such incredulity before in the face of an unexpected last will and testament.

He read out the same passage again. '*Half my estate to go to my son William Michael James and the remaining half to Mathilda Gilbie, including sole ownership of my house...* It's perfectly in order, Mr James. It's regrettable you didn't know that the will was lodged with us, but your mother made her wishes quite clear when she came to see me. This is the change she wanted, along with the added small bequests to her brothers Samuel and Charles Gilbie.'

Will looked at Matty with such venom that she felt it as a blow, her heart drumming in her chest.

'I didn't know!' she said in reply to his unvoiced accusation. 'It's not what I would have wanted, Will. I don't understand it.' She felt as shocked as Will looked.

'Here is a letter she left for you, Mr James.'

Will snatched it from him. The silence was filled with Will's audible, short breaths and the maddening ticking of the solicitor's clock. Matty stared at the pendulum, wishing it would hypnotize her into a state less approaching a heart attack than she felt at the moment. She looked at Sam, who was shifting uncomfortably in his seat, pulling at his tie.

'What could have possessed her, Sam?' she whispered as Will read the letter.

'I know what possessed her,' Will spat out. 'You came home with your sob story and she favoured you over me. Here, read it.' He flung the letter at Matty.

Her mind in a turmoil, she had to read it twice before she could accept that it was true. Eliza explained her decision, saying that Will's needs at Cambridge had been fully covered by his father's trust and that afterwards, when he graduated, he would indeed be a wealthy man, free to do whatever he wished with Ernest James's money, but that meanwhile their dear Matty was in great financial straits and needed a home. As a young man of principle, Eliza said, she knew he would not begrudge his beloved aunt this gift. And she had signed the letter with the endearment that made tears prick Matty's eyes. *God bless, my angel, my darling boy.*

'I'm so sorry,' Matty said, not referring to money or houses, but to the loss of his mother. But the eyes burning back at her were not those of an angel, and any grief was obscured by a stubborn determination that his own wishes shouldn't be thwarted.

'I'll contest it,' he said, and slammed out of the office, leaving Sam to apologize. But the solicitor was unperturbed and assured him that the will would hold up in court. Once outside the office, which was in the City, Sam suggested they walk back to Bermondsey across London Bridge.

'I think I need to clear my head a bit before I go home and try to explain this to Nellie,' he said.

It was lunchtime and office workers crammed the pavements, darting down the marble steps of offices in search of cafés and pubs for a rushed sandwich or pint. The place had its own particular smell, with roasted coffee aromas wafting from side alleys as they wove through back courts, and the smell of beer and spirits seeping through open doors of ancient lop-sided inns. As they walked towards the river and London Bridge, the crowds began to clear; it was only during the morning and evening that the bridge became unpassable, but at this time of day the commuters were firmly shut inside the square mile. Finally, Matty asked, 'What do you make of it all, Sam?' There was a tremor in her usually well-controlled voice. She'd been gripping her handbag so tightly her fingers were stiff.

'I'm shocked, of course I am, but she did think a lot of you, Matty,' he said in his understated way, looking at her as though gauging her reaction.

'But no fonder of me than of you or Charlie, and not enough to leave me the house!' She was remembering Eliza's surprising last words to her, how she'd always loved her. Was Will right – was it simple favouritism? 'Why me? I don't feel entitled. Can I refuse it?'

He shrugged. 'I don't think you can, and perhaps you shouldn't if that's what Eliza wanted. You could give it back to him, I suppose, once you've inherited it. But he's so pig-headed he probably wouldn't take it from you. Besides, he's in a hurry.' Sam jammed his hands into his pockets and as they reached the end of the bridge he took her elbow.

'He's always been in a hurry,' Matty mused, remembering the whirlwind presence Will had been as a child.

The square-turreted tower of Southwark Cathedral rose before them as they reached the end of the bridge.

'I'm not ready to go home, Sam. Feel me, I'm shaking.' She held out her hand for him to take.

'Let's have a sit down then, duck.' And he led her down some stairs to a little garden outside the cathedral. As they sat on a bench beneath its ancient chequered flint walls, the hiss of traffic from the bridge and clatter of carts from Borough Market faded to a cloistered quiet.

'I'm not so sure it's about the house and the money anyway, Matty,' Sam said, leaning his elbows on his knees. He had worn his Sunday suit for the meeting, and he felt about in his pockets.

'Left my tobacco in my work jacket.'

She took out her own cigarettes and they lit up.

'What do you mean?' she asked, blowing out a long stream of smoke. She hugged her jacket more tightly around her.

'She idolized him, and he knew it. Suddenly she's favouring you. I think it's plain jealousy.'

'I wish she'd told him what she was planning. It's too much of a shock for him.'

'Perhaps she meant to let him know, probably thought she had all the time in the world. Like all of us.' He coughed a little and banged his chest, and seeing her anxious look, patted her hand. 'Don't worry, you won't lose me too. I'm fit as a fiddle. It's just the roll-ups.' He paused. 'Matty, is there something you're not telling me?' he asked suddenly.

'I should think so, what do I want to tell you all me secrets for!' She laughed and was glad to see him smiling.

'I just mean, Eliza obviously knew more about your money worries than I did. I don't want to pry, but are you really on your uppers, love?'

She nodded briefly. 'I made some bad choices in America, Sam, and the work's drying up. In fact I've been thinking I'll have to get a proper job soon, Peek's or Duff's. Can you see me in the hat?' she tried to make light of it.

Sam looked shocked. 'What? Factory work? Why didn't you tell me?'

'I didn't want to worry you with my problems. You've got your own, what with those three boys eating you and Nellie out of house and home!'

He waved the suggestion away. 'No, it's a good job at the Brick.'

But Matty knew that money was tight for Sam as well, and was pretty sure the 'good' suit he was wearing today was the same he'd been married in.

'But, if you really are brassic,' Sam went on, 'I reckon you should just accept Eliza's gift gracefully and if the boy wants to waste a load of money contesting the will, then let him. But he's only got one family. That James lot don't want to know him. Sooner or later he'll realize.'

Matty stood up. 'I hope so. Come on, Sam.' She was shivering, partly from cold and partly from shock. 'But I tell you what, it's going to be bloody awkward at tea tonight!' she said.

But Will never returned to Reverdy Road that evening. When Matty went up to his room, she found a note on the bed.

Enjoy your house was all it said.

Matty raised her eyes to heaven. 'Thanks, Eliza,' she muttered, crumpling the note.

She sat heavily on the bed and smoothed the ridged candlewick cover. How could her sister have thought this wouldn't cause trouble? But Eliza always had a way of ignoring the finer points of people's feelings, either for a principle or to get her own way. She heaved a deep sigh. Who did that remind her of?

Matty held on to Billy's hand as they inched forward along the double-fronted elegance of the brand-new Trocadero cine-theatre. The queue snaked behind them back round the corner of the cinema and Matty was unable to see the head of it due to the dense pea-souper that shrouded them. Billy was constantly craning his head round the people in front of them.

'Do you think we'll get to the front before it starts?' he asked.

'Stop worrying! They'll make sure we're all inside first,' Matty said.

She pulled the fox-fur stole up around her neck. She could understand why Billy was excited; they were to be among the first to enter the vast dream palace. True, Matty would have preferred to be seeing the opening of the cinema from the stage. She'd hoped to be offered a spot in the variety show that would accompany the two new talkies. But Esme hadn't been able to get her a booking – instead she'd sent two complimentary tickets for the opening. Matty might be disappointed, but she certainly wasn't going to waste the tickets and had brought Billy along. Always singing, he seemed to have inherited the Gilbie love of music, and she'd even managed to teach him a few tunes on the upright piano Eliza had bought for Will. It turned out that of the two cousins it was Billy who'd inherited the family's musical talent, and Will had cheerfully admitted defeat after only a few attempts.

Over three thousand of them were waiting. The excitement rippled along the queue, all the more intense for being conveyed through a thick cloak of invisibility formed by the fog. Chatter and muffled laughter and the crunching of thousands of feet on peanut shells was the soundtrack to an irresistible shuffling force which moved them forward whether they wanted to or not. When at last they reached the front entrance, and the crowd rolled into the cinema, so did the fog. Swirling in a dense grey mist, it gave the ornate gilded foyer an even more fairy-tale feel. Once in the auditorium Billy's mouth opened wide as he tilted back his head to gaze upwards. Billowing fog rose to a circular turquoise ceiling recessed and lit from within, golden eagles guarded it as though it were some heavenly home of the gods, and the clouds of sulphurous-smelling mist added to the illusion. Lozenges of light hung from the ceiling, but the visibility was so low that when Billy let go of Matty's hand she lost him.

'Billy? Billy?' she called, feeling around her, trying to catch his blazer. Her hand landed on his cap and she pulled him close. It felt unsettling to be marooned in the fog inside this brand-new palace of light.

'Good job we're up the front!' Billy said cheerfully, grabbing her hand and pulling her along unceremoniously through the crowd.

And he was right, rank upon rank of seats stretched in front of her, but the fog that had entered with them was so dense it obscured the stage. As they settled themselves into their third-row seat, she looked behind her and doubted that any of those up in the immense curving balcony would be able to see a thing on the screen, let alone the tiny figures on the stage when they appeared for the variety show. It struck her as ironic that she'd been mourning her place in the show on this opening night. To walk on to that vast stage and sing to over three thousand people, to garner the reviews which inevitably the opening night of such an impressive picture palace would attract, had given her a vestige of hope. But it looked like it would be no loss. Few would have seen her, and her clear voice would have been muted, filtered through this blanket of thick fog.

A startling boom from the great Wurlitzer organ rumbled through her chest, and she found herself actually feeling sorry for the opening live acts, who trooped on to the stage, carrying on gamely through their turns. Fortunately, the huge crowd didn't blame them. Matty knew too well the ferocity of an unhappy audience, but this crowd was still so buoyed up by the excitement of the evening they barely seemed to notice that they couldn't see a thing.

It was an odd experience, to sit in the audience for a change. The screen, set in such golden-curlicued brilliance, now felt to her more like a barrier than a portal to her dreams. It was almost a relief when the fog rolled in front of it and veiled the moving images. But then she felt Billy, squirming at her side, half out of his seat as he strained to glimpse the opening shots of *The Storm*, a western that he'd been so looking forward to, and she was glad when the intrusive mist began to dissipate. In Billy's eyes she was still a star, and as each new character appeared he hissed in her ear, 'Do you know him? Have you met her?' Finally, when the beautiful Mexican leading lady made her entrance, she could actually say yes. Lupe Velez was her stage name and Matty had spent a couple of afternoons hanging about the lot, talking to the young woman during breaks from making *London Affair*.

In fact Lupe had tried to warn her off Frank. 'That man's bad for women,' she'd said in a whisper, as if he might have spies on the lot. 'I should know. I went out with him a while back, and he was mean, Matty. Roughed me up when I said no to carrying a little cocaine for him... nearly broke my jaw! Dump him!' But in those early days Frank was still all charm and Matty was in love. Besides, Lupe wasn't the most reliable of people. She'd struck Matty as strangely flighty. On one occasion she had pulled out a pair of roller skates and given Matty an impromptu show, scooting up and down the lot, narrowly missing cameras and crew transporting bits of set. She'd insisted Matty try, which had only resulted in her tumbling and grazing her chin, much to the annoyance of her director, who'd told them both off as if they were schoolgirls, before sending Matty off to make-up to be made presentable. It was easy to spin out of control in such a world – the extremes of who you were seemed to poke out and catch you, sharp and unexpected. Like Matty, Lupe had been poor as a child. And though her star had still been shining, Matty had wondered for how long. Now, a world away from those days with Lupe, she looked up into the face of the dark-eyed beauty on the screen and finally accepted that her own short-lived screen career was over for good.

That night, fitful between wakefulness and sleep, as moonlight flickered through the swaying branches of one of Mrs Salter's newly planted trees, she was transported back to the days of promise, the screen in front of her flickering with her own image and reflecting back to her all the stillborn dreams which she had once so cherished.

6

Broken Biscuits

December 1930–January 1931

Frank's warning shot of sending his henchman had been designed to keep her on edge and it had worked. She still jumped at every ring of the telephone or knock on the door. So when the phone rang she snatched up the receiver.

'Hello, darling!' It was the husky voice of Esme Golding, an infrequent caller in the last few weeks.

'Esme! Have you got me some work?' Matty crossed her fingers.

'Sorry, Matty, the reason I'm ringing is that something rather unpleasant has happened. I don't want to alarm you but I've had another demand from that bastard across the pond – it came wrapped round a brick that smashed through my window this morning. Glass all over the bloody place.'

'Oh, Esme, I'm sorry, were you hurt? Did you see who did it?' Matty gripped the telephone so tightly that it shook in her hand. She'd felt suddenly cornered as if Frank were already stalking the streets of Bermondsey.

'I'm fine. When I got to the window whoever did it had gone... perhaps it was the same thug Frank sent before? Why he can't use the postal service like everyone else I don't know!'

'Because the postie wouldn't scare the living daylights out of us. But what does he want this time?'

'Well, I think you're going to need every penny of that inherit- ance when it comes through, sweetheart.'

Matty heard the sound of Esme inhaling on one of her Turkish cigarettes and she could picture her narrowing eyes. 'Look, try not to worry, darling. I'll stall him, but he's a mean badger, isn't he? Bloody man just won't let go!'

Matty put the phone down. Esme's reassurances hadn't helped. She needed to make some money to get Frank off her back and she couldn't rely on Eliza's bequest. She came to a decision. If her voice was no longer her fortune, then elbow grease must have its day.

*

Matty felt as if she had been catapulted back to the very place she'd started out, but instead of making custard powder at Pearce Duff's it would be custard creams. She threw back her shoulders, held her head high, and walked through the gates into Peek Frean's biscuit factory in Drummond Road as though she were making her entrance at the South London Palace.

I've played worse places than this! She bolstered herself, scanning the yard.

It wasn't so much a single factory as a conglomeration of huge, many-storeyed buildings and long sheds, sprawled across such a vast area that it had earned the name of 'biscuit town'. Hard by the railway viaduct that bisected Bermondsey, its tall, white clock tower wouldn't have looked out of place on top of a church. Matty had glanced at its white face as she'd approached the factory on this, her first day of hard manual labour in many years. The fluttering feeling in her stomach was only a kind of stage fright, she told herself, and that was something she knew how to deal with.

She walked with her confident, long-legged stride across the courtyard, looking straight ahead, though aware of a gathering audience on the periphery. She'd waved her auburn hair, had on only a touch of make-up, and dressed down in one of her simplest pleated dresses with a long edge-to-edge jacket, but still she'd almost immediately attracted wolf whistles from some men standing on a loading bay high in the nearest building. So much for keeping a low profile. She looked up with a smile and a wave, but carried on walking as a few girls, who'd obviously been waiting at the gates, fell in with her. Word had obviously got round that the famous Cockney Canary would be joining them.

'What you doing working here, Matty? Why ain't you made another talkie yet?' one of the braver ones asked.

'Fancied a rest cure!' Matty said, and the girls laughed.

'We loved that *London Affair*, didn't we, girls?' A young woman with round glasses, looked up at her almost adoringly. 'Are you making a film about a factory girl, Matty?'

'Why else would she be at Peek's? Certainly ain't for the money, is it, love?' another one answered for her.

'How did you guess?' Matty shot back.

But she was beginning to feel awkward. How long would it be before these women realized that she was as hard up as they were and as grateful for a job on the production line as any one of them?

She was rescued by a round-faced woman, about her own age, who smiled at Matty as if she should know her. But then many people did that, assuming a familiarity because they'd seen her on the stage or the screen.

'Let the poor girl through!' the woman said. 'She's on the clock, same as us!' And she elbowed her way between Matty and the others.

'Come with me, Matty. It's your first day, ain't it? I'll show you where to go.'

How did they all know she was coming? She'd hoped to slip in this morning like any other worker, but there was obviously an efficient Peek's grapevine at work. The young woman grasped her elbow, steering her out of the crowd, but Matty heard a bold-faced woman say in a deliberately loud whisper, 'She's come down in the world, ain't she? Research for a factory film my arse.'

'Ignore Edna, you'll get a few jealous ones like her.' The young woman gave her a shy smile and a sidelong look. 'But don't you recognize me, Matty?'

Matty smiled back. She thought she recognized the voice and was desperately trying to put a name to the face, when the girl said, 'It's Winnie! Winnie Roberts.'

'Oh, of course, Winnie! How've you been?'

Matty was mortified. How could she not have recognized Tom's sister? If she'd made a different choice four years earlier the woman could have been her sister-in-law by now.

'Well, I've put on a bit of weight, eating too many of them bleedin' biscuits!' Winnie said, seemingly unoffended that Matty didn't immediately remember her. Her round face dimpled and her chin doubled as she laughed, so that Matty forgave herself for not recognizing the young woman. The last time she'd seen her Winnie had been as slim and lithe as Kitty Godfree.

'Tom says I should never have given up the cycling!' Winnie said apologetically. 'But standing on your feet ten hours a day, you don't feel like doing much afterwards, do you? And I'm a terrible gannet for the biscuits...'

Matty hoped she never developed a taste for pat-a-cakes and garibaldis.

'Of course I recognized you! You haven't changed a bit.'

She gave Winnie a hug, feeling a surge of warmth for at least one friendly face in this bewildering maze of a place, where everyone seemed to have a fixed purpose but herself.

'You're a bloody good actress, Matty, I'll give you that. I'm like half the side of a 'ouse, look at me. I can see why you wouldn't know me.' Winnie opened her wrap-around coat, to reveal her generous form, widening her eyes in mock horror.

Once at the offices Winnie stopped.

'Go up to the first floor, they'll sort you out. Wait till you see the hats we have to wear – it ain't a pretty sight!' She put a reassuring hand on Matty's shoulder. 'Don't worry about what people say in this place, you can't escape the tittle-tattle, but most of 'em will love havin' you here. Little bit of glamour around – can't do no harm!'

'Thanks, Winnie...' Matty hesitated before leaving her. 'How's Tom?'

'Oh, he's fine, love. Got over you eventually!'

Matty searched her face. It was the 'eventually' that bothered her. Had it taken months or years, and did Winnie blame her for breaking her brother's heart? But she seemed genuinely pleased to see Matty, and she had gone out of her way to be helpful.

'I'll tell him you're back when I see him... got to go, Matty. Chin up, it ain't that bad here. Want to meet me in the canteen dinner time?'

Matty nodded gratefully, and mounted the stairs, her thoughts returning to Tom. She'd been thrown by the mention of his name. She hadn't expected that their paths would ever cross again. He'd wanted to marry her once, but she'd closed that door when she chose to get on the boat to America, telling herself it was the price she'd have to pay for fulfilling her dreams. Still, the memory of him had recurred over the years, like the refrain of some old song that evokes a time and a place long gone. In fact there was a song that she'd always thought of as theirs and 'I'll See You in My Dreams' started to play now in her head as she walked up the echoing staircase. She'd always avoided including that song in her sets. It had been the one that meant most to them, and she remembered now how Tom would sing it to her softly, in his not very good voice, with his eyes locked on to hers as they danced. No, it had never seemed right for her to sing it on the stage, almost as if she were shining a twin spotlight on to his heartbreak and her guilt at shattering those dreams of his. Now she almost wished she hadn't bumped into Winnie.

She reached the top of the stairs and turned her mind to the day ahead, wondering if the hat would really be as hideous as Winnie had promised. Matty's parents always said she was pretty and men had praised her beauty, but her parents were biased and Matty no longer had any faith in what men said. There was, however, an old dresser at the Gaiety who'd once told her she could look good wearing a sack and she believed him. But when the foreman held up the mob cap and shapeless white overall that all the women wore, Matty thought she'd finally met her match.

They were as far from the chic couture of her Hollywood days as she could imagine. Wearing the hideous garments, she was escorted back downstairs by the foreman, and she drew no wolf whistles as they crossed the courtyard where sweet vanilla breezes swirled in warm eddies from the bakehouse. He led her into a long, many-storeyed brick building, where they passed endless rows of women standing at benches, hands moving in a blur so that the biscuits they packed became almost invisible. Following him at a half trot, she came to the production line where she was to work. She spotted Winnie, who paused for just long enough to give her an encouraging nod, without breaking her rhythm, and it seemed to Matty that in their ceaseless activity all the women were like mechanical marionettes, following the will of some invisible puppet master. But the foreman had stopped and was attempting to get the attention of someone who had her back turned to him.

'This is your supervisor, Matty,' he said as the woman turned round. 'Edna here will show you the ropes. Nothing she doesn't know about Bourbon creams, eh, Edna?'

Matty's heart sank. It was the bold-faced, middle-aged woman who had been unconvinced by Matty's brave show at the factory gates earlier on. Matty smiled at her, but when the foreman had gone Edna raised her eyes to heaven. 'Trust me to get the film star. Come on, cock linnet, or whatever yer name is, follow me.'

Edna indicated a space at the line between two other women. 'I'm only showing you once,' she said, picking up the bottom half of a cooked Bourbon biscuit from a moving conveyer belt. She held it steady beneath a delivery nozzle, which squirted a blob of chocolate butter-cream on to the biscuit base. Edna plucked another half of biscuit from the belt and deftly placed it on to the chocolate cream, squashing it down to form a sandwich. She passed it to the woman standing next to her, who was sorting and packing the biscuits. It looked simple enough and Edna stood back, leaving her to get on with it.

She set to with confidence, surprised that her first attempt was not very pretty. She had obviously been too heavy-handed and the chocolate cream oozed from between the biscuit sandwich, covering the bench with gooey brown sludge.

'No! Not like that, you'll have no cream left in the biscuit!' Edna said, snatching away the offending Bourbon and flicking it into a bin. She swiped a cloth over the bench.

'Do another one, quick. She's waiting on you.' Edna pointed to the woman on Matty's left, who stood holding a half-filled packet of Bourbons.

But this time Matty didn't press down hard enough and the top biscuit wobbled unsteadily on the cream. The next attempt had the right amount of cream but the bottom biscuit pointed one way and the top pointed another. Edna tossed it away and sighed, looking up at the clock.

'They're on piecework and you're costing 'em money!' Edna scolded.

'Sorry,' Matty said, each time she ruined a biscuit, feeling humiliated and ridiculous in the stupid hat and the ugly apron. It took all her determination not to squash Edna's disapproving face on to the next squirt of chocolate cream and walk out. But after half a dozen attempts the forelady was satisfied and Matty began working as a team with the woman next to her doing the packing. Her name was Sophie, a slight, worried-looking woman, whose eyes were continually glancing up at the clock. Once Edna was gone she whispered, 'You'll get the hang of it, I'll slow down me packing till you catch up.'

That was obviously a great sacrifice for Sophie and Matty smiled gratefully. But even so, she simply couldn't make her Bourbon creams quickly enough, so that by dinner time she was in a state of breathless anxiety, conscious only that Sophie's pay packet was going to be a lot lighter this week than last.

If only she hadn't been put on Bourbon creams. She could have taken Vita Wheat, or even shortcakes, but the sludgy brown filling made Matty feel nauseous. It didn't help that Len, a gangly ginger-haired young man in charge of the filling machine, refused to use the scoop provided. Instead, he dug two splayed hairy hands into the solid brown mass of chocolate cream and dumped handfuls of it into the filling machine. Matty tried not to look, but the machine needed constant replenishment and every time she saw his chocolate-clogged hands relieving themselves of their gooey burden Matty's stomach heaved.

'Shouldn't he be using the scoop?' Matty eventually whispered to Sophie, who stopped long enough to break into a smile.

'Vile, ain't it? He'd pick up the scoop bloody quick if the bosses come round. But hands is quicker. By the end of the week when you're up to speed you'll be grateful. Quicker he is, more we earn,' she said.

Matty doubted she would last a week. She didn't think it would be her stamina that let her down – it would be her stomach.

The following day Matty's fumbling attempts to create the perfect Bourbon cream were beginning to improve and though she told herself this was only a temporary job, she couldn't bear to be bad at anything and was determined to get up to speed. By the dinner-time hooter Sophie was congratulating her. 'Look at her, Win!' she said, calling Winnie's attention to Matty's increasing deftness. 'She's quicker 'an a blue-arsed fly, I won't be able to keep up soon!'

Matty grinned and pushed up the mob cap, which she'd contrived to flatten into a beret shape. Edna was patrolling and had witnessed the exchange. As she passed Matty, she grabbed the cap and tugged it down low over Matty's forehead. 'Keep it regulation. This ain't a fashion show, cock linnet!'

Matty's face burned like a schoolgirl's. But she bit her tongue and stifled a laugh as Winnie waved two fingers at Edna's retreating back. Edna seemed to circle her perpetually, like some carrion bird waiting for a creature to die. Why she was so eager to see her fail, Matty didn't know. But her heart sank when she saw the woman walking determinedly towards her holding a single biscuit in her hand.

'What d'ye call this?' She shoved the biscuit under Matty's nose.

'A Bourbon cream?' Matty ventured and heard a few giggles from the girls around her.

'All right, clever dick! I'm talking about this. Edna pointed to a ginger hair curling out of the chocolate-cream filling of the biscuit. 'I told you to keep your hat on proper and now one of yours has got in the biscuit!'

'I'm auburn!' Matty said.

'I call that ginger,' Edna said, and though Matty knew she should keep silent, her instinct for putting down hecklers kicked in and she shot back: 'There's only one ginger nut around here and he never come out of the bake ovens!'

The girls around her burst into laughter and even Len, who had picked up the scoop as soon as Edna came into view, gave her a wink.

'Have your laugh, but you'll be smiling the other side of your face when your pay's docked one and six for bad hygiene!' Edna threw the biscuit into the bin and walked off with a small smile of triumph on her face.

But Matty wasn't to be cowed. She persisted and was proud of herself when she was handed her pay packet at the end of the week. With the docked money it didn't even amount to two pounds, but she'd earned it herself and, supplemented by her pub singing, she'd have enough to live on, putting any spare towards paying Frank off. Before leaving the factory that Saturday lunchtime, she went along with Winnie to the staff outlet to buy one of the cheap packets of broken biscuits the workers were allowed to purchase. They were the assorted rejects from all the lines, and though her nephews might not be enjoying the reflected glory of their film-star aunt any longer, that night when she went to Vauban Street Sam's boys seemed even more impressed by the packet of broken biscuits she presented them with.

Matty found the only way to make her new life bearable was to sing as she worked. Soon the girls around her on the Bourbon-cream line were encouraging her.

'Give us a song, Matt!' Sophie would ask, and Matty knew that the woman had an ulterior motive, for the more Matty sang the quicker she worked. Then Winnie would call out for a particular song and the requests would flow faster than she could meet them. She buoyed the production line up with cheery songs – 'When You're Smiling' or 'Sunny Side of the Street'. Then the older women would shout out for the music hall favourites, raucously singing along to 'A Little of What Yer Fancy Does Yer Good'. The saucier the song the more they liked it and the more rumbustious they got. Sometimes the choruses reverberated so loudly in the high-ceilinged building that they were hard put to hear the foreman when he came in with the day's orders.

Then one morning as they were in full flow during a particularly boisterous version of 'Oh, Oh, Antonio', they heard Edna's voice shouting above the din.

'No singing! No singing!'

There were a few stragglers who carried on regardless, but soon these realized they were on their own and gradually fell silent. Edna's strident voice broke through.

'Oi, you lot, look at this! What does it say?' She was pointing at a painted sign by the door, which Matty hadn't seen before and she assumed must have been put up overnight.

'No singing!' Edna repeated, only to be drowned out by boos from some of the girls.

'Management say it's a distraction and the subject matter is lewd! There's to be no more singing.'

'Miserable bastards!' Winnie shouted.

'Oi, that's enough of that, Winnie Roberts, or you can go up to the office and get your cards for swearing!' Edna called back.

Matty had been astonished to learn that the firm's Quaker founders had set a high moral tone for the company and operated a strict no-swearing policy, which she thought would be nigh on impossible to enforce. But Edna was obviously going to try. Winnie pursed her lips defiantly, but there were no more protests and the muttering soon died away. Matty was left dumbly facing a line of Bourbon creams with no cream in them, wondering how on earth she was going to get through the day without music. The production line had become a surrogate stage for her, and singing had helped her to ignore the sickly sweet smell of vanilla and chocolate that greeted her each morning along with the blocks of fat, sacks of flour and sugar that went into the vats of cloying biscuit mix. At least there'd been the consolation of entertaining a floor full of women while they worked. But now it seemed even that would be taken away from her. It was ironic; the Cockney Canary had landed herself in the one place where she was expressly forbidden from singing.

As she turned her face to avoid the sympathetic gaze of Winnie and Sophie and all the other silenced workers, for some reason her mind went back to her time as a munitionette at the Arsenal. It had been a braver time, when she was fearless and confident about her future – now she'd meekly allowed herself to be silenced by a martinet. *Give me the stink of cordite and the terrors of TNT*, she thought. *I'd rather be back there with my skin turning yellow as a canary, than spending my days up to my eyes in Bourbon creams.*

That evening as she walked home black, bare branches of cherry trees fractured a leaden sky. Planted a decade earlier by the Bermondsey Beautification Committee, she tried to imagine a time when their fat pink blossoms, hanging against a deep blue sky, would dance and splash their shadows on the pavements. She blessed the lady mayoress, Ada Salter, with her vision of a Bermondsey in which there was 'no house without a window box, no street without trees'. But today Matty's own imagination, which had always been able to supplement harsh reality, failed her. And she couldn't imagine that spring, that better time. Grief for her child, for Eliza and for her own lost future seemed to have fractured her, and the weight of it was as heavy on her chest as the leaden sky above her.

Perhaps she was just weary after a ten-hour day in the hothouse of Peek Frean's, but she thought it was more the 'no singing' that had made her feel so defeated tonight.

She walked through the back kitchen and out into the yard, which, even though she'd tended it better than Eliza had, still accused her with bare patches of earth. She found it as oppressive as a prison yard, for it was surely Will's house and Will's garden, not hers.

Matty was booked to sing at the Concorde pub that night, but as the house with its ticking mantle clock, its hissing Ascot and its sun-striped parlour seemed to be rejecting her, she decided she might as well go there early. She shrugged off her coat and went to change.

Winnie had told her she'd come along to boost the audience at the Concorde, which was the pub favoured by the Peek's workers. They had taken up an easy friendship where they'd left it three years earlier. Though Matty had reservations about her being Tom's sister, she'd got the impression from Winnie that he was long over her. So, if they bumped into each other, at least Matty wouldn't have to agonize over ruining his life, nor torment herself with regrets about what could have been. When she arrived at the pub she was surprised to find Winnie already there, with Sophie and a few other girls from the Bourbon-cream line. She barely recognized them without their caps and aprons. For now, seated in a row, with their perfect marcel waves, painted eyebrows and bright lipstick, she thought they wouldn't have looked out of place on a chorus line. Matty broke into her trouper smile, the one that could ignore the state of her heart.

'Hello! It's Peek's very own Tiller Girls!' she exclaimed, giving them a minstrel wave.

They held up their hands, gave her a wave back and shouted in unison: 'No singing!'

7

Inheritance

February–March 1931

Matty was nervous. But then, the courts were designed to make anyone dressed in normal clothes nervous. Barristers sailed through the high-ceilinged entrance hall like white-headed, black-winged birds, their robes billowing, chins thrust out in determined flight. They knew where they were going; this was their realm and she and Sam were mere interlopers. She recognized the feeling of a closed world. What else was Bermondsey after all? They stood in front of a solid oak door that led to the courtrooms. They were waiting for their barrister.

'He's late,' Sam whispered, glancing nervously towards the glass-panelled entrance doors at the far end of the vestibule.

'He'll be here, don't worry,' Matty replied, refusing to whisper.

And then she spotted him pushing through the entrance doors, a bundle of documents under one arm, small glasses glinting in the shaft of light streaming from a high window. He crossed the black and white tiled floor with a speed that belied his bulk, which was accentuated by a voluminous black robe. He bore down upon them like a well-fed bird of prey that had spotted two unsuspecting mice.

'Mr Gilbie, Miss Gilbie.' He gave Matty a firm handshake. 'Are we ready?' Not waiting for an answer, he swivelled on his patent-leather shoe, pushing through the oak door into a narrow corridor, expecting them to follow. More doors led off the corridor into various courtrooms. He stopped at the last.

'Now, I must warn you, Mr James *does* have a case.' He tilted his head to one side, judging the effect of his words.

'But that's not what Eliza's solicitor told us!' Sam said. 'Matty is entitled to benefit.'

He said it with such finality it almost seemed a truth. Yet Matty hoped it was not, for her life would be simpler, if harder, without the burden of this inheritance.

'I am not saying he will *win* the case, just that he *has* it.' The barrister attempted a smile, but Matty had seen bad actors do better. 'His "reasonable expectations" as the only child of Miss Gilbie are the basis of his claim. As a dependent with no other income… you understand?'

'But that's a lie, he's got an allowance for Cambridge and later on he'll have his father's money…' Sam attempted to explain what the barrister must already know. But her brother had taken his role as executor so seriously, and had been so intent on getting justice for her, that now she could see the suggestion they might lose had really shaken him.

'Sam,' Matty laid a hand on his arm, 'let's not start accusing Will. Perhaps he really is struggling.'

'Struggling my eye.'

But their barrister ignored Sam's flash of anger and looked down at his watch. 'I don't want you to worry, I have every confidence. The will is undeniably valid and we'll have our judgment well before lunch!'

As he turned away to open the courtroom door, Matty puffed out her cheeks and patted an imaginary belly, mouthing 'he's hungry already!'

She was rewarded with a suppressed smile from Sam at her larking around and she took hold of his hand, to steady herself as much as him as they entered the courtroom. But once inside Matty was surprised. It was much smaller than she'd imagined, little more than a windowless, wood-panelled box with another smaller raised box at the front and a few wooden benches, which she doubted would hold more than fifteen people. When she thought of the thousand-seater theatres she'd played in in New York and the West End suddenly this didn't seem so frightening after all.

She heard the door squeak open and looked round. Her eyes met Will's, but his gaze slid away and he gave no sign that he'd seen her. He inclined his head, listening to his barrister, before sitting down on one of the benches alongside hers. He looked paler, thinner, and though he was the one responsible for putting them all in this position, she found her heart going out to him. What did he think he could gain? Matty had known riches and she had known poverty, and her happiest days had certainly been her poorest, living in Beatson Street, with her parents still alive, making ends meet in their tiny terraced house down by the river. Even now, when she was struggling to earn a few pounds a week, she knew she'd rather be at Peek's than living a life of luxury with Frank in New York. She tried to study Will's face without making it too obvious. His dark eyes had a bruised look about them and she wished he had not made himself such an exile in his grieving for Eliza.

But then the judge came in and interrupted her musings. They all obediently followed the clerk's instructions to stand. The judge, wearing a more ornate wig and robe than the barristers, mounted stairs to his bench and picked up his gavel. He reminded her of Bernie at the Star, in the days when it had been a full-time music hall and he had been master of ceremonies, banging his gavel with abandon at each new wonder, announcing each act in a more convoluted fashion than the last. 'And here for your delectation,' he would declare, 'that charming chanteuse, contrapuntal crooner and cantatrice of captivating coloratura, Bermondsey's very own Cockney Canary, Matty Gilbie!' Then Bernie would go mad with the gavel, getting up a sweat and rousing the audience, so that by the time she stepped on to the stage they were roaring for her and she already had them in the palm of her hand. Those days were beginning to seem very far away, and she, a very different Matty Gilbie. When the judge's gavel cracked down hard, she was jolted back to the present, yet something of her youthful confidence returned with the sound and she looked full into the judge's hooded eyes, knowing that his stage was no finer than hers had once been.

The barristers took it in turn to put their cases. Their own was matter-of-fact, almost off-handed in his performance, as he gave a mumbling summary of the facts. He sat down, checking his watch, and Matty saw him yawn as he began shuffling documents into order. Will's barrister seemed much more impressive. He was vehement and convincingly certain of his client's 'reasonable expectations', as Miss Gilbie's only child, laughing sometimes that the thing had even come to court.

He appeared to have finished and was about to sit down when he sprang up again, waving another document in his hand. 'Furthermore…' he continued, 'there can be no doubt that Eliza Gilbie changed her will because of the *undue influence* of her sister, Matty Gilbie, an *actress* and *variety artiste*—' he wrinkled his nose with distaste – 'who associated with American mobsters and after hitting upon hard times fled her debts in America to graze upon pastures new!'

Matty felt a flush rising to her cheeks. 'Now that's a bloody lie!' she shouted out and was silenced by the judge. She didn't give a jot about losing her inheritance, but being branded a manipulative money-grubber was an accusation she'd fight. She turned to their own barrister. 'Did you know about this?'

He pushed his wig back and scratched his head, which she took to be a no.

Matty saw Will hand his barrister a couple of documents, which he presented to the judge. She had no idea what they were, but it became clear they were proof of Frank's demands. She felt a rising panic, though she had done nothing wrong. But how had Will got hold of them? The only one who knew was Esme. Matty could see no reason why she would give evidence to Will. But she must have. Matty's heart lurched as she felt another of her anchors slipping away. It seemed there was no one she could trust to be what she believed them to be and she reached instinctively for Sam's hand. At least she could be sure of him.

Their own barrister asked to see the documents and, after scanning them, threw them on the desk in front of him and picked up one of his own folders, dipping his head deep into it, lifting his glasses, peering closer, mumbling. She felt Sam fidgeting nervously, and at one point she heard him say under his breath, 'Why don't he get a move on? Answer him, man!' And if he'd had his carter's whip with him she thought he might have given a little snap to the back of the laborious lawyer's head.

She was surprised to see their barrister darting forward with a little jump, like a bird for a worm, up to the front bench, where he whispered to the judge, head cocked listening to the reply. Then, nodding his head, he came back to where they sat. Matty was bursting with frustration. They were talking about her, talking about her difficult, complicated relationship with Eliza, boiling her motives down to greed. She wanted to shout into their insouciant, bewigged faces, 'It wasn't like that!' But without warning the judge banged his gavel, mumbled something about an adjournment to consider the new evidence, and in minutes they were back in the entrance hall.

'You should have told me about the debts...' Their barrister looked down at the floor. 'Bit of a surprise, not keen on surprises.' He hummed a little tune. 'The demands for money are unlike the work of a lawyer... more "demanding money with threats" – was it?'

And Matty nodded miserably. The barrister laid a heavy hand on her shoulder. In a surprisingly sympathetic voice, he said, 'I'm sorry. They have no proof of debt and no proof of undue influence, but the wheels of justice turn slowly and the judge must consider the evidence.'

The result was that they were given a new court date for a week's time, which was a problem in itself as Matty would need to take another day off work. As they walked towards

Waterloo Bridge, Sam kept his arm firmly round her and they were almost there when he stopped. 'I think you need a drink, love, and so do I.'

They were outside an old inn called The Punch and Judy. The public bar was a smoke-filled fug of journalists and lawyers and office workers, but Sam found a table in the quieter snug. When he came back with a gin for her and a pint of bitter for himself, she was screening her face with her hand, swallowing her tears.

'What you getting yourself so upset about, Matty? It's not your doing, love. Here, drink this.'

Her gin and tonic tasted of salt tears, but she swallowed them along with the alcohol and managed to answer. 'I loved him, Sam, from a baby. It just hurts that he's turned on me, for no reason. He looked at me as if he hated me in that courtroom.'

Her brother squeezed her hand. 'You've done nothing wrong. That boy's always had a chip on his shoulder, never felt good enough for his father's family and too good for ours. Eliza did her best but...' He shook his head. 'I know I've said it before, but...' He lifted her chin. 'Believe me, Matty, you're entitled. If only...' But he paused, as if thinking better of it.

'If only what?'

'Nothing. Drink up, Matty love. Let's get home and tell poor Nellie she'll have a few more sleepless nights to look forward to. She hasn't been able to sleep a wink over all this.'

'Sam, would you mind if I didn't come home with you?'

'No, 'course not, not if you don't want to.' But Sam looked surprised and Matty felt the need to explain.

'I thought I'd go and see my agent, while I'm over this side.'

'Right oh, love. Fingers crossed you'll be able to get out of Peek's and back on the stage, eh?'

And Matty nodded, but she was going in search not of a job but an answer. Why had Esme Golding betrayed her?

Esme was seeing a young hopeful. So Matty sat in the waiting room, an airless square of quiet desperation, filled by other clients of Esme's looking for work. The man sitting next to her suddenly extended his hand.

'It's the Cockney Canary, ain't it?' he asked, smiling.

He was a red-faced, middle-aged man who looked vaguely familiar.

'Tommy Turner. Terpsichorean? Sand dancing? I used to be a double act, with my brother Timmy?'

'Oh yes!' Matty remembered Tommy, but he looked different without the black tights, short checked jacket and elongated patent dance shoes he'd worn on the stage, and he had aged badly.

'Remember now? The "Lardy" and the good old "Saahf"? Happy days, eh, Matty?'

'Yes, Tommy, they were. So you're on your own now, what's Timmy doing?'

'Poor old Tim. When the act went downhill, so did he. Topped 'imself.'

'Oh, I'm sorry.' She hadn't known the Turners well, but they'd always been the sort who would give a word of encouragement if your act went down badly. Now she didn't know what to say.

'No, he didn't know nothing else but the halls and when we had to go on the relief, that did it for Timmy.'

'But you're still working?'

'I come every day, gives me something to do, but she can't find nothing for me. What about you?' His eyes filled and Matty was worried he might cry; she was almost glad she had no success story to rub his nose in.

'Not much about for me either, Tommy. Bernie at the Star's been very good to me and I've had a few spots at the cine-variety shows.'

'They don't want sand dancers these days, though.'

Matty nodded sympathetically; it was limiting to have only one talent. At least she had learned to tap dance and play the piano, and she could tell a joke reasonably well. She was about to suggest he branch out into tap when Esme's door opened and the row of waiting clients looked up hopefully.

A young woman of about sixteen, with platinum-blonde hair and bright red lipstick, was kissing Esme on the cheek. She walked out of the office with a bouncy stride, beaming. Matty resisted an impulse to run after her and warn her that her big break might very well lead to breaks of a different kind – broken hearts not the least among them. As Esme called her in, she noticed that Tommy's face had fallen.

'I'll have a word with Bernie at the Star,' she whispered and he grasped her hand, muttering his thanks.

'Matty, I'm sorry to have kept you waiting, darling. But what are you doing here? I thought you were in court today?'

She offered Matty one of her black cigarettes, but Matty took out one of her own, lighting up without answering.

'Well? How did it go?' Esme asked.

'I'd have thought you'd know that already. Didn't your friend Will James telephone you with the news?'

'News? Oh no, you lost? I can't believe it. But what do you mean, my friend Will? That young rascal who's put you through all this is no friend of mine. What would make you think that?'

Matty leaned across to flick her cigarette in the ashtray on Esme's desk.

'We're adjourned. I haven't lost yet, but that's no thanks to you! I trusted you with all that Frank business. How could you have betrayed me to Will?'

Esme's face drained of colour and she pushed her hands through her tightly curled hair. 'I don't know what you're talking about,' she said in a stony voice. She got up and poured two whiskies. Placing one on the desk for Matty, she went on, 'But if someone's betrayed you, Matty, it wasn't me. Now tell me what's happened.'

Esme sat at her desk, gulped down her whisky and listened intently as Matty related the accusations about her debts and how they'd been used by Will's barrister to suggest she was nothing more than a gold-digger.

'But why would I give Will any documents?' she asked finally.

Matty stared out of the small, grimy sash window, from which she could just see the top of the Empire Leicester Square, until pigeons fluttered down on to the sill, obscuring her view. 'That's what I've come to ask you,' she said dully, bringing her attention back into the room. She realized that a numbness had taken hold of her and that her own glass was empty.

'Matty, listen carefully, you're not seeing properly. I want you to get out of Frank's clutches more than anything, so why would I scupper your chance of inheriting a bit of cash?' She waited for Matty's answer.

'There's no reason.'

Esme leaned over the desk. 'No reason. And who's always looked after you and put your interests first, since you were the same age as that little blonde I just had in here?'

'You have.'

'I have,' the woman repeated, grinding the black stub of her cigarette into the ashtray. 'Just because two people you loved have let you down, doesn't mean you need to distrust us all!'

Matty began to feel foolish. 'I'm sorry, Esme. You don't deserve it. But where did Will get the information?'

Esme took a deep breath, tapping well-manicured fingernails against her glass.

'I didn't keep the demands from Frank's lawyer, mostly because they weren't worth the paper they were written on. I'm sure I gave them back to you. Did you keep them?'

Matty looked at Esme guiltily and nodded. 'I did... can't think why.'

'To remind yourself what a bastard he is, should you ever forget?' Esme raised an eyebrow before asking abruptly, 'But listen, Matty, does Will still have a key to your house?'

When she got back to Reverdy Road Matty went straight to her bedroom. She had left America in such a hurry, stuffing any papers she thought she might need into a small leather document case. But filing had never been her strong point and the papers had stayed in their disorderly home, along with some photographs and reviews she'd wanted to save from her happier early days in New York. She remembered shoving Frank's demands into the case. Perhaps Esme was right about her reasons for keeping them, but Matty doubted it. She had enough physical and emotional scars as reminders. She pulled the case down from its home at the top of her wardrobe and tipped the contents on to her bed. Quickly sorting out the photos and cuttings, she sifted hurriedly through the other papers. Heart thumping, she spread out bills, old letters from Sam and Eliza, her passport and travel documents. The demand letters were gone.

That devious little tea leaf! Now she was certain he had been through her things. She would have given him anything and yet he'd crept in and stolen from her. White-hot fury coursed through her as she swept the papers back into the case and slammed it back on top of the wardrobe. She went to Will's room. When he'd stormed out last year he'd taken very little with him. Now she tugged open his wardrobe and chest of drawers – they were empty. Then something occurred to her and she rushed across the landing to Eliza's room. The clothes that she'd folded away so carefully in the tallboy after Eliza's death were now a jumbled mess. She felt around the bottom drawer, but the old Peek Frean's tin full of Eliza's memorabilia was no longer there.

Will could have rifled the house at any time over the past few weeks. She had no idea when he'd been back. Her ten-hour days at Peek's, along with whatever pub bookings she could get in the evenings, meant she'd seen little of the house in Reverdy Road. But the idea of Will sneaking around her home made Matty feel sick with disappointment and betrayal. The tumbled remnants of Eliza's things felt like a desecration. She kneeled on the floor and began slowly to refold Eliza's clothes. She picked up an old-fashioned shawl her sister had kept. It had belonged to their mother, who'd used it to wrap all the Gilbie babies in. She'd given it to Eliza for Will. Now Matty remembered herself as a very small child, being gathered in her mother's arms, enfolded in this same shawl and she realized with a painful jolt that it would have come to her, if she'd had a child. Eliza must have been keeping it for that day. Suddenly her losses seemed too bitter to bear and she buried her face in the shawl, but instead of its soft wool, she felt only the bloody sheet that was all she'd had to swaddle her tiny baby. She sobbed into the shawl and breathed in the scent of Eliza, and her mother and the child she had lost.

During the following week she barely thought about the coming court appearance. She had found since losing her child that grief was like a tide: it rolled in and it rolled out, and sometimes the waves crashed hard enough against her chest that the breath was knocked from her. That shawl had been one of those waves and no inheritance in the world could take away the hurt; she would just have to wait for the tide to roll out again. She numbed herself with the monotony of Peek's and let her thoughts be drowned by the raucous singing during nights at the Concorde.

So the verdict, when it came, took her by surprise with its swiftness. They were in the courtroom for no longer than five minutes before the judge pronounced, 'This evidence is inadmissible. I find no undue influence and declare that the will of Miss Eliza Gilbie is valid. Mr James to pay costs.'

Bang went the gavel and their barrister looked at his watch, smiled at Will's barrister and mouthed, 'Lunch?'

'Is that it?' she asked Sam, but looked instead at Will. His face told her it was over. His pallor had been replaced by a purple flush and his lips were thin, tight white lines. He snatched up the trilby he'd worn for court and was about to walk out without acknowledging her, when she stepped into his path.

'Will, don't go like that—' But he brushed past her and out into the dim corridor.

She hurried after him, vaguely aware that Sam was following. Will was already in the cavernous, echoing entrance hall by the time she caught up with him.

'Stop! Will, you can have it – take the bloody house, take the money. I never wanted it,' she pleaded, catching hold of his arm.

His bruised eyes suddenly lit fire. 'I shouldn't have to be given what's already mine!' His voice was trembling. 'It's the injustice of it. You'll never understand, Matty, you've never had a serious thought in that canary brain of yours, have you? What do you think all the marches and protests are about? That's what the struggle's for – people should get what they're due! I should get what I'm due!' he spat out finally.

She felt Sam's arm round her shoulders and sudden, hot tears on her cheeks, as her brother stepped up and addressed Will. 'Your mother would be ashamed of you for treating your own family like this. At least she earned her principles, but you ain't had a day's struggle in your life. Come on, Matty.'

And Will, rage overriding any sense of dignity, bellowed after them. 'Don't you dare talk to me about my mother! I've got no mother, and no father and no family either!'

8

Mother Love

March–April 1931

She was thinking of Frank. Her few hundred pounds inheritance might appease him for a while, but Matty doubted simply extorting money from her would be enough to satisfy him. She'd once seen the sort of justice Frank meted out to those who betrayed him and it wasn't the eye-for-an-eye kind. She knew he was just biding his time and she would have to wait for his next move.

Today, after her ten hours at Peek's, she'd gone straight to an evening entertaining the clientele at the Land of Green Ginger and was now drinking a cup of tea, trying to find energy to get herself upstairs to bed. She'd just eased her feet out of her tight shoes when she jumped at a loud knocking on the door. Had Frank made his next move? Cold fear gripped her; should she run into the backyard? The neighbours might hear her if she screamed loudly enough, but she decided it was better to try ringing the police. She might just have time. There was another rap on the door and with a thumping heart Matty crept to the front parlour. She made her way across the darkened room to the phone table by the window. She held her breath, picked up the receiver and at the same time peered out of the window. She let the receiver fall. It wasn't Frank, but it was still a very unwelcome visitor.

His eyes were barely able to focus on her and he supported himself by leaning on the door jamb.

'I'm surprised you didn't use your key,' she said, not inviting him in. She had no energy for a fight with a drunken Will tonight.

He grinned stupidly at her and his hand slid off the door jamb so that he tipped forward into her arms.

'Shorry,' he mumbled, sliding down on to the passage floor, where he sat staring up at her as though waiting to be rescued.

'You're as pissed as a puddin', you silly sod.' Matty bent down and draped his arm over her shoulders, then heaved him up and led him into the kitchen. His legs began to buckle and she propped him on the nearest kitchen chair.

'I wondered when you'd notice I'd paid you a visit, not very obsh, obsh, obsh...'

'Oh shut yer cake 'ole, Will, I've had about enough of you. If you weren't so blind drunk I'd tell you what I really thought of you sneaking round my room, going through my things, but I'm not wasting my breath.'

'Deshppicable is the word you're looking for, Matty dear, deshppicable...'

'I know what word I'm looking for but I wouldn't lower myself to use it...'

'Barshdud,' he giggled. 'True, Matty dearest, in every sense.' Then, looking at her with a sly smile, attempting to stroke the side of his nose but missing, he said, 'But ishh not just me... I'm not the only one, am I?' And he giggled again.

She turned away, sighing, and went to put the kettle on. She left him still giggling to himself while she set about making him strong coffee. Her first instinct was simply to put him to bed to sleep it off. It was what she'd normally do. But she couldn't bear the sight of him at the moment and certainly didn't want him spending the night here. The only way he'd be able to walk out of the house tonight was if he sobered up, and she forced him to drink two cups of strong coffee. She didn't intend to talk any more than she needed to, so she switched on the wireless and sat leaning her head back on the chair, listening to Jack Payne and his orchestra on the BBC, while Will slurped uncertainly at the hot brew to the strains of 'Sunny Days'.

Eventually she became aware of him staring at her. She stared back, as Jack Payne sang on – 'Sunny Days, never let the darkness fool ya, Sunny Days you've got something comin' to ya, smile with those bright Sunny Days!'

'You're just like her,' he said eventually, 'got your little secrets all tucked away in a box.'

'I don't know what you're talking about, Will,' she said wearily.

'That Yank – so-called manager of yours – you kept quiet about what he really is, didn't you? His little cocaine canary, is that what he called you? Let you entertain his gangster friends, did he? Singing the old songs, and what else did he expect you to do?'

Matty was still holding her own coffee, which she launched at Will's head. He was too drunk to duck and the contents dripped down his face like black blood, staining his shirtfront and trousers, as Eliza's bone-china cup bounced on to the hearth and shattered.

'All right, I will say it, you are a bastard! Now you can get out.' She stood before him, trembling, and he slowly got up, wiping his face with a handkerchief. 'I don't know what I've ever done but love you, but now I don't even care.'

'Of course you don't care. You've got what you wanted, stolen my inheritance.' He shrugged, holding out his hand, rubbing finger and thumb together.

'Do you really think that? I had nothing to do with it. I don't know why your mother wanted to give this place to me... she was a good woman.' She was tired of defending herself and, full of disgust at Will's behaviour, she blurted out, 'You really are an ungrateful, spoiled little git. Eliza didn't deserve a son like you!'

His face twisted with rage and he roared back at her. 'And she didn't deserve a daughter like you either!'

At first she thought she'd misheard him, a drunken slip of the tongue. But his expression had changed to one that she recognized from his boyhood: when he'd been found out in a childish crime, his lips would twitch in a nervous smile. It used to drive Eliza mad and Matty had often spoken up for the boy – he wasn't being deliberately insolent, she would explain, it was an involuntary thing. She knew that, because she'd done it herself whenever her cheeky ways had got her into trouble with her mother. Now Will's nervous smile told her that he hadn't made a mistake, and that he knew he had got himself into deep water. She sat down heavily, holding tightly to the arms of the chair, fearing she might faint. She opened her mouth to speak, but nothing came out. The wireless was still playing, and she tried to focus on the song, Ambrose was playing now, what was it? She hated it when she couldn't remember a song. It seemed vital that she identify it, then the vocalist broke in with '*Wrap your troubles in Dreams and dream your troubles away*' and she saw Will walk over to switch the wireless off. The silence roared in her ears as her world crashed around her. For some reason she saw again the flyer, the poor man who had flung himself off the skyscraper and landed at her feet. She understood now, how when there was no solid place left to stand, a person might have no choice but to fly, launch themselves into an abyss that seemed less painful than the remnants of their shattered world.

'How long have you known?' she finally asked. It never occurred to her to protest that it couldn't be true. She knew it was true. A light had been shone into the darkest, deepest part of her and illuminated what was buried there.

He reached into his inside pocket and handed her a folded birth certificate.

'She kept you in a Peek Frean's tin, Matty. Do you still want to defend her?'

Matty wasn't aware of Will stumbling out of the house. She sat with the birth certificate in her hands, reading it over and over. *Mother: Eliza Gilbie; Father: Ernest James; Residence: Mecklenburg Square.* The words were a meaningless jumble and she forced herself to concentrate on them, to make them have something to do with her. If the Wall Street Crash had stolen her glittering future, tonight had robbed Matty of her past as well.

Now there was nothing left of Matty Gilbie. No future, no past. She'd thought she could rebuild her life, here in her Bermondsey home, and she had stayed hopeful – the days of Peek's and pubs would pass, she'd told herself, better days would come. What had Jack Payne been singing earlier tonight? '*Sunny Days, never let the darkness fool ya, Sunny Days you've got something comin' to ya, smile with those bright Sunny Days!*'

But she had been a fool to trust her own optimism; the darkness had won. She dropped her head to her lap and wailed, as she hadn't done since the day her beloved mother had died. 'Oh, Mum, why did you leave me?' Like that bereft twelve-year-old, she rocked back and forth as grief tore through her, merciless and magnified by the knowledge that her mother had been stolen from her twice. Once by death and now by Eliza – her sister, her mother.

And Will was her brother? The thought made her sit up. Sam. Did Sam know? Did Nellie know? Did everyone know who she was but herself? Everything in her life had been a lie. She had loved her mother with a passion, tending the sick woman when only a child herself, praying all the prayers of innocence that God would spare Lizzie Gilbie's life. Her prayers hadn't been answered and now she felt the intense cruelty of fate that could rob her a second time of her mother. Had she been loving the wrong woman all these years? Yet how could she ever un-love Lizzie Gilbie?

She couldn't remember taking herself upstairs to bed, but it was in the early hours of the morning that she woke, and like a ravenous beast the memory of Will's revelation tore into her heart. In an attempt to shake it off, she got out of bed, but staggered as she stood, almost as if she were back on board the boat coming home and there was only the ever shifting ocean beneath her feet. But she knew that no matter how wide she spread her arms to balance herself, her world would never right itself again.

She felt like a caged animal with no place in herself to find peace and she went downstairs with the vague idea of making some tea. She took down a cup from the dresser, and found she'd forgotten what she was meant to be doing with it. She let it fall to the ground and, in an agonized attempt to wipe away all her memories, she lunged at the dresser. Piece by piece, she hurled Eliza's pretty rose-patterned cups, saucers, plates and tureens on to the kitchen floor. With each crash she felt a part of her old existence disintegrate and when there was nothing left, she walked across the shards, crunching her stockinged feet over their sharpness. She welcomed the stinging cuts, distractions from a pain in her heart which she knew would never go away.

It was Nellie who found her, curled like a baby on the bed, her sheets stained with blood and her pillow stained with tears. When she opened her eyes she watched silently as Nellie examined her stockinged feet. Whey were her stockings dark brown? That wasn't her usual colour at all, she wore lighter shades, and why was Nellie pulling at her feet? Matty yelped with pain and found herself staring into Nellie's blue eyes. Those brave eyes, which Matty had seen endure so much, were now clouded with fear.

'Matty darlin', what have you done to yourself?' she asked, coming to the head of the bed and taking her hand.

For a moment Matty had no idea what she'd done, only that the pain in her feet had been welcome at the time. But that wasn't last night, surely? Her kind memory failed her for as long as it could and then in a wave of sickness she remembered.

'I walked on the crockery.' Her voice sounded hoarse, for her tears had ripped through her throat.

'But how did it happen?'

Matty shook her head. 'I'm not sure... I think I smashed Eliza's place up, Nellie.'

'You? But why would you do that, love?' Nellie's bemused expression made Matty weary. She didn't want to explain; she wanted to sleep. She groaned and turned over, wincing with pain as her feet brushed against the sheets.

'All right, Matty love, you can tell me later, but I've got to clean them feet up or else they'll go septic.'

111

She disappeared downstairs and Matty heard her clearing a path through the ruined kitchen. Soon she was back by her side, with a bowl of hot water.

'Here, take these first.' She handed Matty a couple of Aspro, then set about peeling off Matty's stockings. Sometimes she pulled away china shards which had been embedded in her feet, making Matty flinch, but eventually the stockings came off and Nellie gently cleaned every wound, finally covering them with lint and brown sticky Lion ointment to draw out the hidden slivers.

'We don't want none left in, darlin', do we?' She spoke to Matty just as she had when a child. Matty knew she hadn't always been an easy charge for Nellie. Her mother had spoiled Matty and she'd taken a while to be won over by Nellie. But eventually she'd come to see her as a second mother. And now there was a third, the real one. Did Nellie know?

When Nellie went downstairs to make a pot of tea, Matty tried to recall what it had been like when Eliza had first come back into their lives. She had a vague memory of a visit from a tall lady with a wide hat, an imposing figure in her mother's tiny kitchen, and someone had told her it was her sister Eliza. And during the war she'd returned, wanting to befriend Matty. But like a door slamming shut, Matty refused to follow her thoughts into that past, for none of it was as it had seemed.

She eased herself up in bed as Nellie came in with the tea.

'I've swept up,' Nellie told her. 'You've not got a plate left to eat your dinner off, but I found a couple of mugs. Thank gawd the teapot's enamel.'

'Thanks, Nellie. I'll get up in a minute.'

'No, you won't, you're stopping there. I think that court case has been playing on your mind, it's been a shock to your system—'

'It's not that. I had a visit from Will.'

'What's he come round upsetting you for? Hasn't he done enough? I'll get Sam to talk to him, it's got to stop.' Matty could see that Nellie had gone into her protective mode.

Matty's eye was caught by a piece of yellowing, screwed-up paper sitting on her bedside table. She reached over for it and began smoothing it out.

'He brought this with him. He found it in Eliza's things,' she said, passing the birth certificate to Nellie. She watched her intently while she read.

Nellie closed her eyes briefly, then folded the paper and let out a long sigh. 'My poor little canary, you didn't deserve to be hurt like this. That boy wants shooting.'

'Have you always known? Does everyone know except me?'

'No, love, I didn't always know.'

'Will you tell me, Nellie?'

Nellie took Matty's hand and sat on the bed. 'All right, love. I will, but I want you to remember, that whatever was done was out of love. You was such a happy little thing before your mum died, and afterwards, well, me and Sam and Eliza, we wanted you to stay happy... But it's true, Eliza fell pregnant with you when she was in Ernest James's service. He wouldn't let her keep you, so she did what she thought was best and give you to your grandparents to bring up as their own. They thought it'd be better for you not to know and I suppose it was hard for Eliza, so she stayed away...' Nellie paused, waiting to see the effect of her words. But Matty felt almost frightened to breathe; the bed was a precipice and the next word from Nellie could propel her into an abyss.

'I only found out Eliza was your mother during the war. At first she wanted you back, but she could see it was too late. And your mum – Lizzie – she'd made me promise to look after you once she was gone. She didn't ask Eliza. She asked *me* to take you on, and Sam wanted that too. So in the end we decided it would be best not to tell you. You were such a fragile little thing in lots of ways, missing your mum, and Sam in France. But in other ways you'd got a will of iron.' Nellie smiled wistfully. 'I remember the day you told me you wasn't working at Duff's like the rest of us, you wanted to be a singer. I thought you'd have no chance, but you did it, Matty, you did it...'

'Who was it decided not to tell me?' Matty asked, aware that her face was a rigid mask, but needing Nellie to finish her story.

'We all agreed, Eliza, Sam and me. We wanted to protect you. There was a war on, we didn't know if Sam would come back... and there was the promise I made your mother.'

'My grandmother.'

'No, Matty, your *mother*, Lizzie Gilbie. Eliza gave birth to you, but you know who your mum was. I've never seen a child so devoted to their mother as you. God, you used to fuss round her like a clucking hen. And you couldn't even reach the stove, but you'd be making soup for her—'

'No! Nellie, don't. Don't talk about it. She lied to me half my life! And you and Sam and Eliza, well you've lied to me for the other half. So don't talk to me about how much I loved my mother!'

She saw alarm on Nellie's face, but she went on. 'You know what, I can understand our Will now. It's just like he said to me at court – I've got no mother and I've got no father, and I've got no family either. I want you to go now, Nellie, and tell Sam not to come round. I don't want to see him.'

It was only later that day, when Winnie turned up on her doorstep, that Matty found out how Nellie had come to discover her. After making sure that the caller was not Sam, Matty let Winnie in. Her friend explained that when Matty hadn't turned up for her shift at Peek's that morning she'd grown worried.

'Well, you hadn't mentioned nothing about taking a day off and I knew you wouldn't risk going off Tom and Dick if you wasn't. So I nipped round at dinner time to see if you was all right, the door was ajar and the state of the place! I thought you was dead in your bed and burgled. I lost me bottle and run round Nellie's. Mind you, it nearly killed me. I've got to get this weight off, Matt, I thought I was having a heart attack.'

Just at that moment Winnie was dipping a broken Nice biscuit into her tea, so Matty took her resolution with a pinch of salt.

'So I said to her I said, I think something bad's happened at Matty's, and she's done no more than left Albie with the neighbour and runs back round here with me. She's got no fear that woman – up the stairs she goes, you stay down here she says, they might still be in the house. But she come down and her face was white as a sheet. She just said you was all right but not feeling well... I never asked no questions, love, but you wasn't burgled, was you?'

Matty shook her head, choking back tears that she didn't want her friend to see.

Winnie dipped her hand into the white paper bag full of broken biscuits, then shook the bag at Matty, offering what comfort she could. 'Go on, love, you look like you need cheering up.'

'Oh, all right,' Matty said, with a weak smile, and pulled out a Bourbon cream.

And in spite of her tears Matty joined in Winnie's laughter at the sight of the reviled biscuit.

About a week after Will's revelation Matty was in her garden. She loved the way the roses defied Bermondsey's sooty air and she tended them like children. She'd never had a garden before moving to Reverdy Road, but she'd felt sorry for Eliza's untended patch and had made it her own. Now it was one of the few places where she could escape the turmoil of her own thoughts and she was examining an early blooming red rose. There had been an unseasonal snow shower, and its barely opened petals were outlined in frosty white. She doubted it would survive. She stroked the deep red velvety bloom and a song came to mind, 'My Love is Like a Red, Red Rose'. Her father's favourite, the song Lizzie Gilbie had asked Matty to sing to her as she lay dying. Tears stung her eyes at the memory and she opened her mouth to sing, but no sound emerged. What was the matter with her? She put a hand to her throat and coughed. She tried again to force a note from her mouth, but produced little more than a stuttering breath. It was as if a hand were tightening round her windpipe. Now panic gripped her. She realized she hadn't sung at all since hearing the truth about her parentage. *Sing, just sing it!* she urged herself. Still holding on to the rose, she took in a deep breath, but on exhaling let out only silence. Her hand closed around the rose stem and a thorn dug deep into her palm. She yelped with pain. It was obvious she hadn't lost her voice; she just could no longer sing.

No Singing. That sign over the packing line at Peek's now came as a blessed relief. For it felt to Matty that all her songs had been silenced. They simply didn't bubble up from inside as they had her whole life and to force them out was impossible. She had never been one of those singers who tried to 'save their voice' – she'd earned her family name of 'little canary' because she simply never stopped singing. Sometimes she thought it had driven Sam and Charlie mad, but her parents had always encouraged her. And perhaps that was why she could no longer sing. Now, every time she attempted to breathe deeply and let out a note, she would remember her mother saying *sing from your stomach, Matty,* and scenes flashed into her mind's eye of the little concerts she'd given for her parents in their kitchen. Who had she been singing for? Who had she been trying to please? There was no peace in those memories; there was only peace in staying silent. So she blessed the strict governors at Peek's who'd deemed singing an unnecessary distraction, for now she agreed with them.

Over the following weeks she tried again and again to sing. She wasn't going to let go of her voice without a struggle, however tempting it was to give in to the silence. But each time the result was the same: her throat closed up tight and the more she strained the more she was seized by fear that she'd never sing again. Without the company of Eliza or Will, and with no visits from Sam or Nellie, the quiet of the house began to close in. Sometimes she felt it would stifle her. Tonight, thinking it might help to sing along with the wireless, she tuned in to Jack Hylton's band. She'd always liked his upbeat arrangements. But the song they were playing seemed to mock her, and her attempt to join in with 'Happy Days are Here Again' ended in tears of frustration. She slammed her fist on the top of the radio so that Jack Hylton was momentarily drowned by static, but his irrepressibly optimistic singers soldiered on. 'Oh, shut yer row up!' Matty shouted at the wireless and switched them off, finding that she preferred the silence after all.

Sam respected her request; he never came to explain or justify himself – perhaps he thought he didn't need to. But if he was waiting for her to go to him, he would wait a long time. For she didn't know which brother she was angrier with, the one who had told her the truth or the one who had lied. It was easier to forget both.

Sam may not have come himself but he did send someone else. It was on a Saturday afternoon and Matty had not long been home from work. She was in the middle of shortening one of her simpler show gowns in an attempt to turn it into a day frock. Most of her wardrobe had been bought in America and was unsuitable as everyday wear for a Bermondsey factory girl. But she simply didn't have ten bob to spare for a day dress, for with no pub spots or variety earnings, her two pounds a week from Peek's was having to be stretched very thin. No one except Esme knew that all Eliza's money had gone to keep Frank at bay. Matty had thought it money well spent, even though it meant now she couldn't afford to clothe herself decently. Still, she refused to look shabby and, with no variety work, she doubted she'd need the long, pink crêpe gown again.

She was no seamstress and the result, which she'd spread out on the parlour floor, was not encouraging. So when the knock came, she was grateful for a reason to leave her sewing.

'What damn use is a telephone if you never answer it!' Esme Golding stood on the doorstep, immaculately tailored in her expensive belted check suit and beret. With her matching shoes and handbag, she was an immediate reminder of another world, which Matty would have liked to close the door on. But Esme did not wait to be asked in. She slid past her into the narrow passage, brushing Matty's cheek with a red-lipsticked kiss, trailing a perfume that smelled of money in her wake.

'You'd better come in then!' Matty addressed Esme's back.

'In here?' Esme walked into the parlour, circling the small room in seconds and finding the most comfortable chair to sit on. Matty followed, hastily shoving the pink crêpe dress into the sideboard cupboard.

'Spot of sewing? Is that your new hobby now you aren't interested in working?' Esme was lighting up and looked round for an ashtray.

'I *am* working,' Matty said, standing awkwardly in front of Esme, feeling as if she was up before the headmistress.

'I mean proper work, not making bloody Bourbon creams, darling.'

Matty gave a dismissive laugh, 'You ought to try ten hours a day at it, Esme, you might change your mind about what's proper work.' Matty wasn't going to be cowed. 'Besides, I've been begging you for so-called "proper work" in whatever fleapits will have me for over a year! I'm sorry but I can't keep living on hope alone.'

'Rubbish, darling. The Cockney Canary I know would never give up singing – she would sing in a sewer! So what I want to know, dear Matty, is where has she gone? What's happened to the Cockney Canary and why doesn't she ever pick up the fucking phone when I've got a booking for her?'

'You'd get your cards using language like that at Peek Frean's'.

'Aren't you at all interested in why I've come to this unlovely corner of London you insist on calling home?'

Matty knew the woman was trying to rouse a reaction, but she simply didn't have it in her to hit back. 'Tell me then, but don't pretend Sam didn't ask you to come.'

Esme widened her eyes in mock innocence. 'Would I lie to you, Matty? He *did* telephone, but only because he's terribly worried about you. But before I tell you the real reason I've come I'll need some refreshment. It's never too early for me, darling.'

She mimed a drinking action and Matty sighed, going to the sideboard to pour drinks.

'I've only got gin and nothing to mix with it, is that all right?'

'As it comes, Matty. I'm not fussy, so long as I'm not depleting your supply.'

Matty saw her raise an eyebrow at the nearly empty bottle of gin.

'Don't worry, this pub's in no danger of running dry,' Matty said, pulling out a full bottle from the back of the cupboard. She had been finding that sometimes a glass or two before bed was all that could halt the endless round of 'what ifs' and recriminations that had begun to invade her night-time thoughts.

As Matty slumped down in the chair opposite, Esme went on. 'Well, I'm only here to let you know that if you can bear to drag yourself away from your pat-a-cakes, then the Astoria, Old Kent Road, want you to appear twice nightly for a fortnight. And by the looks of that abomination of a dress you just butchered, you're in need of a bit more cash at the moment than Peek Frean's can supply!'

'I'm grateful you've come slumming to let me know about the Astoria, but you can tell them I'm not interested. You may as well know, Esme, I've decided to give up the business.'

Esme could not hide her shock or her disappointment. But her perennially mocking expression turned fierce.

'All right then, Sam *did* tell me what happened and of course it's a terrible shock for you. Clearly you can't forgive any of them, least of all your sister, Eliza. But tell me this, Matty, have you never done something you were ashamed of? Have you never had a secret that you'd do anything to keep from those you loved?'

Matty, fidgeting nervously with her glass, spilled spots of gin on to her skirt and rubbed at them ineffectually as Esme pressed on. 'And did you tell Eliza the real reason you came home? Have you told Sam? Really, Matty, I'm not such a fool as to believe you've told even me the whole story. So while you're in your biscuit factory next week counting shortcakes and all the sins of your sister, just remember what secrets you're hiding yourself!'

Silence hung heavy between them as Matty felt her words sink in. Esme had come perilously near the truth and as the woman waited for a response Matty felt the temptation to reveal she'd fled America to save not just herself, but also her unborn child, from a life with Frank. It would be a release, the uncoiling of a spring that had been wound tight inside her. She fingered the strawberry burn mark on the inside of her wrist and instead blurted out another truth.

'I can't sing any more! It's not that I don't want to... I've lost my voice.'

Esme let out a short bark of a laugh. 'Balls! Do you really expect me to believe that? You could have come up with a better excuse, Matty. Lost your voice? Impossible!'

'It's true! Ever since Will told me about Eliza. And I've tried... really tried.'

'Well, try bloody harder!' Esme's tone was fierce but Matty could see doubt beginning to unsettle her.

And as she went on to describe to her all the times she'd tried – in the kitchen, in the garden, at night lying on her bed – Esme's disbelieving expression melted away and Matty saw pity replace it.

'There'll be a tune running through my head, I open my mouth, and nothing comes out. Nothing at all. I don't know what to do, Esme.' Matty's face crumpled and she buried her face in her hands. How could Matty explain to her that it was as if she was being unmade. Day by day the strands of her past were unravelling, along with her inborn talent, the one she'd always believed she'd inherited from her father, who it seemed wasn't her father. She had no idea and no interest in whether Ernest James could sing.

'Oh my God, it's true,' Esme said finally, her voice dull with shock. 'My poor, dear girl.' For a minute Matty thought she might burst into tears, but instead she pulled a silk handkerchief from her bag and handed it to Matty. 'Here, dry your eyes and don't expect me to cry with you, because I know you'll sing again, my little canary. I know you will.'

9

Peek's

April–May 1931

Working at Peek's was almost a relief. There was little there to remind her of her old existence. It felt as if her life had fragmented, her past shattered into a thousand pieces. All her memories of a time before Will's revelation felt suspect and untrustworthy. She felt like an amnesiac who might piece together their past from other people's recollections but who never truly felt connected to the life they'd lived before. She almost wished she'd lost all her memories rather than have every remembrance tainted. She never thought she could be grateful for factory work, but she welcomed the mind-numbing monotony. She became a model Peek's worker. In the past Matty had invariably turned the weekly cleanliness inspection into a lark for the girls by adding the odd flounce and frill to the hideous mob cap and shapeless apron. Edna would doggedly pull them off, but it gave the girls a laugh and added a more festive air to the regimented inspections. But these days Matty appeared with unadorned cap and overall, which she laundered and meticulously starched herself. Now there were no quips about soldiers on parade as she thrust out her scrubbed hands and clipped, unvarnished nails for Edna to inspect. The girls had grown fond of the weekly show and the change in Matty had not gone unnoticed.

One dinner time in the canteen Winnie broached the subject. 'You don't seem yourself these days, Matty,' she said. 'You've lost your sparkle, love. Why don't you come on the beano with us? We're all going, all the Tiller Girls.'

Matty smiled at the name for the regulars who'd come to listen to her at the Concorde, which seemed to have stuck.

'Ramsgate ain't Hollywood, but we have a bloody good time! It's a laugh, we wear our work caps, stick feathers in 'em, pom poms – all sorts – and Edna can't complain! It's right up your street, you can lead the sing-song on the chara! Go on, Matt, say you will.'

Matty had never turned down an invitation to entertain anyone, yet she feared there was no point in agreeing. After all her failed attempts to sing, Matty didn't think she'd do any better leading the girls in 'I Do Like to be Beside the Seaside'

'No, I won't come, thanks, Win. It's kind of you to offer, but you're right, I'm not feeling myself at the moment – I wouldn't be very good company.'

'Perhaps you need a tonic,' Winnie suggested.

But somehow Matty didn't think the cure for what ailed her was to be found in a bottle of Wincarnis.

Though Esme's prophecy that Matty would sing again hadn't come true, her words about forgiving Eliza had stirred the beginnings of an uncomfortable understanding in Matty. For there were indeed secrets that she had lied about to keep hidden, so who was she to judge?

One day as she was approaching the factory gates, sniffing to see what the day's bake would be, she recognized the scent of shortcakes, and Esme's words returned to her. Would she spend the day counting shortcakes and her sister's sins or reflecting on her own? Neither would help Matty to get on with her life, which she reminded herself was not over yet, however much it might have changed. So when Winnie repeated her invitation to go on the works beano she finally agreed.

She met Winnie outside the Concorde along with the Tiller Girls and thirty other Peek's women. They were milling around, comparing decorated work caps, pinning carnations on to coats, waiting to board the long cream and brown charabanc. Word about the beano had got round to the local children and a crowd of them jostled for a place closest to the charabanc. The driver loaded crates of beer on to the back, then, just as they were boarding, a horde descended on them. Children of all ages, some raggedy-arsed and barefoot, others smart in shirts and grey shorts, but all shouting with one voice: 'Chuck out yer mouldies!'

The chorus got louder and louder and didn't stop until the women dug into their purses and flung coppers high into the air. Pennies, halfpennies and farthings cascaded on to the cobbles, signalling a ferocious scrum, with the biggest boys scooping the lion's share. In amongst them Matty spotted two dark heads that made her heart stop. She pushed her way off the charabanc. "It's Billy and Sammy!' she explained to Winnie and ran to them. They looked round as she called their names, and then she realized her mistake. They were about the same age, but Nellie wouldn't send her boys out with frayed shirts and dirty faces. Matty smiled at them and gave them a penny each. Realizing with a pang how much she had missed Sam's boys, she found herself wondering if they had missed her too.

On the way to Ramsgate the girls pleaded with her to sing, but she didn't dare risk trying and failing in front of them all. Winnie, seeing how uncomfortable she was, came to her rescue. 'Let's have our fashion parade first, girls! I've brought me bag of tricks!' She flounced along the central aisle of the chara, distributing fancy hats and feather boas from a large bag, and adorning herself with the most outrageous garments. She kept up a running commentary, as she pretended to model the latest Paris fashions to roars of laughter from the girls. Matty sat back, and let the show go on around her, laughing when Winnie got risqué. But her thoughts kept returning to Billy, Sammy and Albie, and how her anger at Sam had only served to increase her feeling of loss.

By the time the chara rolled into the little seaside town the beer crates were half empty, and it was a rowdy, cheerful crew that descended to the sands, still wearing their decorated Peek's caps and carnation buttonholes. Edna handed each of them their dinner money, for on this one day of the year, the firm was paying them to enjoy themselves.

'Where shall we go for dinner?' Winnie asked, already knowing the answer. 'Fish and chips?'

The coach had dropped them some way from the sea front and they made their way along a row of respectable two-tone brick villas. Their ornate wooden porches and balconies, freshly painted in green and cream, hinted at a sea view that none of them possessed. Most of them were B&Bs, and above window boxes packed with bright petunias were invariably *No Vacancy* signs. Ramsgate at the height of the season was overflowing with those fortunate ones who could find the money for a week's holiday by the seaside, the train disgorging crowds of pasty-faced Londoners and their excited children during the season.

'Smell that air?' Winnie asked and Matty inhaled obediently, confirming that the air was indeed much better than London's. Matty's parents had never been able to afford a holiday for them, but she'd since sampled Coney Island and had seen Blackpool often enough when she'd performed at the Grand. The crowds in Blackpool looked very like the Ramsgate holidaymakers walking alongside them in excited little flocks. Families passed them, trekking to the sea, like so many Bedouin tribesmen to an oasis, carrying brightly coloured windbreaks, red tin buckets and spades and rolled towels. Beyond the neat villas Matty caught the glint of sunlight bouncing off the sea and soon they reached the prom.

There was not an inch to spare. The pace of the milling crowd had slowed and now they were surrounded by couples and families, walking at that peculiarly slow stroll reserved for the prom. So intent was she on avoiding tripping over a pram that she collided with a family in front of her who'd stopped to have their photo taken at the Sunbeam Studio. The children were perched on a giant dog, desperately trying to keep their balance long enough for the photo to be taken.

'Shall we get ours taken later, Matty?' Winnie asked. 'Let's all get the showgirl costumes and we can pretend we're on the stage with you!' The other Tiller Girls agreed, but Matty hoped that by the time they'd had fish and chips and gone in search of an afternoon drink they would have forgotten.

She stopped to take a breath.

'Hang on, Win, let's at least have a look at the sea now we're here!' She hauled Winnie back and they leaned on the railing, looking down to the long stretch of golden sands below. Barely an inch of sand could be seen between the encampments of sunbathers and sandcastle-makers. Deckchairs demarcated each family's territory, and as she scanned the laughing groups of children her eye was caught by a game of beach cricket. Three young boys, one batting, one bowling, and the smallest, whose job it seemed to Matty was the hardest of all, chasing after the stray balls and retrieving them. The match was going on some way from where she stood, but something about the jaunty tilt of the batter's cap caught her attention.

This time she was not mistaken. If she'd been in touch with Sam she would have known this was the week he planned to take the family to Ramsgate. Sam had sent her photos of this place with his letters: he always tried to give the boys a holiday, paying into the holiday club all year and never dipping into it, no matter how tight money was. Suddenly Matty felt like a bird in a trap – she could not let herself be seen. Grabbing Winnie's arm, she urged her on.

'I thought you wanted to look at the sea!' she protested.

'Well, now I've seen it. Come on, let's get to the fish and chip shop.'

She turned and half ran, her arm through Winnie's, catching up with the other girls, who linked arms with them so they formed a phalanx bowling along against the tide of promenaders. Four young men coming in the opposite direction wouldn't break ranks and, as the Tiller Girls' little chain broke apart, Matty collided with a man concentrating on not dropping a handful of ice-cream cornets.

'Oh, I'm so sorry!' she apologized.

'Oh, not to wor—' He froze as ice cream trickled down his fingers.

'Your ice cream's melting, Sam,' she said, giving up any notion of flight, but dimly wishing she were Amy Johnson, so that, like the heroine of the day, she could have the means to stay aloft, flying high, never having to come down to earth again.

'Matty!' Sam's face flushed.

'I'm on the Peek's beano,' she explained, sadness washing over her at the awkwardness between them.

Winnie and the others were waiting patiently. 'You remember Winnie, Tom's sister.' Sam nodded a hello and smiled.

'Nellie and the boys are on the sands – do you want to come and say hello?' he asked finally.

'You go on,' she said to Winnie. 'I'll catch up with you at the pub.'

When the girls had left, Matty eyed the melting ice creams. 'For gawd's sake, Sam, go and give the kids their bloody ice creams before they melt,' she said, reaching for their old uncomplicated easiness.

'All right, wait here though, Matty, don't go away!'

She looked into his once dear eyes, seeing hurt and incomprehension, mixed with an unbearable hope, and gave a brief nod.

He turned down the stairs leading to the beach and she saw him trying to hurry in the deep soft sand, so smart in cap and blazer and white trousers. Sam, looking after his family first, just as he'd looked after her. It broke her heart to think how he'd deceived her and then she remembered Esme's words – the sins of her sister, the sins of her brother, what were they compared to her own? They had only been trying to protect her. Who had she been trying to protect when she kept from them the true nature of her life with Frank? How, knowing what he was, a common gangster when all was said and done, she had stayed with him. The love of an audience was a powerful narcotic; she had felt it.

126

Sometimes, after a show, she'd joined in Frank's cocaine parties, just to keep the euphoria going for a little longer and it had led her into situations she would be ashamed for her brother to know about. She was only protecting herself from the judgement of those she loved after all.

He found her where he'd left her.

'I've told Nellie I'm going for a walk round the harbour,' he said quietly.

As they walked side by side she glanced at Sam. She saw the slow clenching and unclenching of his jaw, which he always did when he was nervous, and then he said, not looking at her, 'Don't be angry with me.' Her brother dug his hands deeper into his pockets. 'I'm just asking you not to judge me and Nellie – nor Eliza – till you know what happened, Matty.'

'I'm not judging you. I'm just sadder than you can ever imagine, Sam. I've lost everything.'

He took his hands out of his pockets and they were balled into tight fists. 'No! That's not true, you've lost nothing, Matty, not if you don't want to. I loved you from the moment I saw you tucked up in Mum's old sideboard drawer. I was only a kid myself when you come to us and they told me you was me sister, and of course I believed them. Everything I ever felt for you I still feel. It didn't make no difference when Eliza came back and Mum had to tell me the truth. She was so scared, Matty, that Eliza would take you away, that she would upset your life. We didn't want to lose you and if it meant a tussle with Eliza, then I was bloody well going to fight her tooth and nail so Mum could keep you.'

Her brother was the mildest of men, she'd never been able to imagine him a soldier, but he'd enlisted in order to protect his family, or so he'd thought. It was that protective streak in him that had the power to overcome his gentle nature, and she saw a fire in his eyes now that she remembered from when she was small and he would fight her battles for her.

'Nellie told me Eliza came for me, during the war. I was horrible to her from the start. Is that why she agreed to keep quiet?'

'No, Matty, she agreed because she loved you. Don't you see? All the pain you're feeling now, that's what she wanted to save you from.'

They stopped and found a little shelter that looked seaward. The sound of children's laughter rose from the red-striped booth on the beach where Punch was battering Judy and her baby, and finally Matty asked the question that had been searing its way up from the deepest places of her hurt. 'Sam, why did she keep Will and not me?'

Children's laughter and the discordant squeals from Judy's baby filled the silence between them. Sam gave her a pitying look and said, 'Oh, Matty, she didn't have much choice. Ernest James gave her an ultimatum, he didn't want an illegitimate child sodding up his life – sorry, Matty, but it's the truth. If she didn't give you up she was out on her ear, and bringing up a kid on your own back then – it usually ended in the workhouse. So she did what she thought would be best for you, she gave you to Mum. James set aside an allowance for you and Eliza sent it to Mum every year, but he didn't want to know nothing about you or where you were.'

It was a common enough thing for an illegitimate child to be brought up by grandparents. But the thought of a woman being coerced into giving away her baby chilled her blood. She knew his blunt honesty was designed to show her that here, finally, was the unvarnished truth and she could trust him, but part of her perversely wished he'd had a different story to tell. It would have been easier to blame Eliza. But Matty had her own experience of being under the sway of a powerful man. It had taken all her courage to run away with Frank's child and she found herself understanding Eliza's plight.

'You've got to realize, she was only his housekeeper, well, that's what he told his family and friends. She didn't have no money of her own and she'd been at Mecklenburg Square since she was fourteen, I think.'

'So what changed when Will was born?'

'Eliza. Eliza had changed. They were out in Australia by then and Ernest was just the same when Will came along, said she had to give him up. But Eliza told me once that letting you go was the biggest mistake of her life and she wasn't going to do the same again.'

'She told you that?'

Sam nodded. 'And the other thing she said, Matty, was that what she was proudest of in all her life, was you and Will. You know I didn't always approve of her, but I'm sure of one thing, she always loved you, Matty.'

'So how did Ernest James come round? He met Will, paid for his schooling and left him the trust money.' Matty couldn't help the painful comparison with her own irrelevance to him.

'I reckon it's 'cause he was a boy. James was that sort of feller, didn't think much of women, didn't treat 'em very well either, if Eliza's anything to go by. But she got away from him, got her passage money together and brought the baby back to England before he could stop her. It took him a couple of years to track her down, but she'd got the better of him over Will by then. She told James he could pay for Will's schooling and see him, but she was going to keep the boy at home. Sometimes I wonder if she did the right thing.'

Matty was listening intently, rapt by the unfolding story of her own hidden past and struck by how closely her life had mirrored Eliza's. But now she interrupted Sam. 'How can you say that? At least Will's had his mother all these years!' Matty felt a flush of anger rise to her cheeks. 'Which is more than I have.'

But then she saw a matching flare in Sam. 'Oh no, I'm not having that. Mum – *our* mum – would have cut off her right arm for you. Don't tell me you missed out on mother love, 'cause you didn't!'

He was right, she knew he was right and yet the story he'd just told her made her feel he must be wrong.

'All I'm saying,' Sam went on, 'about Will, is that half his problem is he didn't know where he belonged, and he's spent all his life pulled from pillar to post. At least you were settled.'

Yes, she had been settled, so settled that when the chance first came up for America, she'd refused to leave her home, partly from fear, partly because Nellie needed her with Sam missing in action at the time. And when she'd finally pulled herself away from Bermondsey to Broadway, she'd been successful, but she hadn't thrived. Not one day had passed when she didn't wish she were home. And knowing what she now did about Eliza wouldn't have changed that. Eliza had sometimes called her a rose amongst thorns, as though Matty were somehow too good for Bermondsey, and she'd always assumed it was because of her growing fame, but now she understood. Eliza was simply feeling a mother's love, a mother's guilt.

She sat in silence next to Sam, staring at the restless motion of the distant incoming waves, rolling and rippling along the shore, dissolving into foam and disappearing into the golden sand; she thought they seemed to be seeking something to hold on to and yet never finding it.

'You're right, Sam,' she said finally. 'I *was* settled. But I'm not any more.'

Before they parted Matty asked Sam not to mention their meeting to Nellie: their former closeness had been one of the hardest things to lose and she couldn't face Nellie's hurt as well as Sam's. She went off in search of Winnie, finally tracking her down after trying three pubs on the front. The fish and chips had long been eaten and the Tiller Girls were lined up along a plush-covered bench in a dim corner of the pub, a table of half-empty glasses in front of them.

Her heart was in turmoil after her talk with Sam, but she was used to ignoring her own feelings in order for the show to go on. It was no good facing an audience with a face like a fiddle. She put on her brightest smile.

'What are you sitting in here for, when the sun's shining outside! Come on, let's go and get that photo taken, Win.'

She dragged them up one after another, forcing them out into the sunshine, linking arms with Winnie as they walked back to the Sunbeam Studio. Before long they were both dressed as matching cowgirls, not quite what Winnie had envisaged, but the showgirl outfit wouldn't fit her. Matty was quite happy to pull on a leather waistcoat and outsize leather chaps which flapped about like wings. She adjusted Winnie's cowgirl hat to match the angle of her own and they each picked up a whip.

'Now try and look fierce for the camera,' the photographer said. 'You're meant to be tough westerners!'

'That's easy, Win,' Matty said under her breath. 'Just imagine we're keeping Edna in line with one of these.' And she cracked the whip, just as she'd once seen a cowboy do in a wild-west show in California. The photographer jumped but seemed delighted with the pose.

'Perfect!' he said. 'This one's going on the front of the shop!'

Later, when they picked up the print, Matty could see why. Her expression, which she thought of as habitually mild, was in fact quite fierce. Perhaps just knowing that Eliza was her mother had begun a transformation, for she could see in her own face a reflection of Eliza as she once was, standing on the podium in front of the lions in Trafalgar Square, ready for a fight, taking no nonsense from barons of industry, politicians or hecklers. Matty in her cowgirl outfit might be a million miles from Trafalgar Square, but she knew she'd need every strain of inherited toughness if she was to find her way home.

On the charabanc going back to Bermondsey that night, she sat next to Winnie, pretending to listen to her friend's chatter. This time no one asked her to lead the singing. The girls started up themselves with 'I'm Forever Blowing Bubbles' and 'Four Leaf Clover'. When they moved on to 'Mammy', Matty turned her face to the window. She could see nothing, the night was so black, but as she listened to the refrain: *Mammy, Mammy, I'd walk a million miles, for one of your smiles, my Mammy!*', she thought she saw faces reflected in the glass: Lizzie, Nellie and Eliza, all

131

with smiles proclaiming that each one loved her as powerfully as any mother could. Yet Matty felt nothing but bereft, for there in the glass was another reflection, a tiny face with eyes fast shut and a serene smile. Wiping her hand across the glass, she erased their images from her mind's eye and closed her eyes to dam the brimming tears.

*

It became obvious that Peek's were laying more and more girls off. At first it was just in the fancy tin department, as demand for the more luxurious lines declined, but soon it became a regular thing for Matty to pass a bench of girls in the morning, only to find they were all gone by dinner time. Not that factory girls expected to get notice; when they were no longer needed they collected their cards and left the same day. The firm knew that when it was ready to begin hiring again, there'd be no shortage of women lining up for the jobs.

One day, as they were eating dinner in the canteen, Winnie, who had made short work of her own, cast a covetous eye on Matty's.

'Here.' Matty handed over half her sandwich. 'I'm not that hungry.'

'You sure?' Winnie asked, taking a bite. 'Thanks, Matt, Mum says I've got hollow legs.' They laughed, but then Winnie's expression turned sombre. 'Matt, I think I'm gonna have to leave home.'

'But why?' Matty knew that Winnie's father had been out of work for months. 'Don't your mum and dad rely on your wages?'

'Of course they do. But the relieving officer's been round and told 'em they've got to sell half their home, all the bits and pieces it's taken 'em twenty odd years to pay off! All because of my piddling eighteen shillings a week coming in. Don't matter about it being my wages, they say it goes to the household, so Dad's relief's been cut. They'd get more if I wasn't living there. Besides, Mum says I'm eating 'em out of house and home!'

When Winnie was anxious, she calmed herself with food, and the worry about her parents had sent her into a spiral. Not content with a packet of broken biscuits each week, she was now snacking on whatever she could filch from the lines each day. It was something everyone did occasionally, in fact they sometimes set up a competition to see who could pinch a favourite biscuit without getting caught. It was a dangerous game, though, earning a fine or even instant dismissal if they were discovered. But in the middle of a boring day, with five hours still to go, the risk of nicking a sugary Nice or a pink iced Playtime biscuit seemed a necessary distraction. But for Winnie it was more than that. Matty believed she genuinely mistook anxiety for hunger and, though she'd urged her friend to wait till their dinner break, the following morning Winnie found the temptation too much.

Winnie gave Matty the eye and mouthed, 'I'm having that one.' She nodded towards an approaching Bourbon cream. Quickly reaching round Matty to whip it off the line and into her overall pocket, she let out a little yelp as she touched it. The biscuit was still hot enough to burn her fingertips and as she dropped the Bourbon cream Matty's hand shot out to catch it. But it was like holding a hot coal and she batted it away, sending it spinning to the factory floor, where it landed at Edna's patrolling feet.

The forelady's face curled in disgust as she trod on the biscuit. Matty waited for the telling off. But instead Edna beckoned to Winnie, who blushed like a naughty schoolgirl as she left the bench to stand before her.

'I've seen you, Winnie Roberts, half-inching stuff off the line when you think I'm not looking, but this takes the cake, right under me nose!'

Winnie was squirming and Matty was mortified for her. The other girls dropped their heads, so as not to witness Winnie's shame – it could so easily have been one of them.

'You know the rules about 'alf-inching stuff! Well, you can just go and get your cards.'

Winnie's lower lip began to tremble.

'It won't happen again,' she said, then, lowering her voice, pleaded. 'Give us another chance, Edna. Me mum and dad rely on my wages.'

With any other forelady it might have worked, but Edna was a stickler. 'You should a' thought of that before, sticky fingers! Get yourself up the office.' Edna turned to walk further up the line, but Matty couldn't stay silent.

'Come on, you mean old cow,' she called after the forelady. 'It's one bloody Bourbon cream! And anyway, it looks like a broken one to me!' she said, eyeing the crushed biscuit, still on the factory floor.

This was a mistake, for the Tiller Girls giggled and Edna's face reddened. She walked towards Matty till her face was inches away. 'And you'd better watch yer cheek or I'll have you out an' all, for swearing.'

Matty saw that the woman wasn't going to back down, but the idea of Winnie going home to tell her parents there would be no wages this week was too hard to bear.

'Well, it wasn't Winnie – it was me. I just can't resist them Bourbon creams. It was me trying to nick the sodding biscuit, not Winnie!'

Edna broke into a smile. 'Well, you just made my day, they asked me to clear out the dead wood. Go and get your cards and you, gutsy...' she pointed at Winnie. 'I'm watching you.'

'But it's not true!' Winnie tried to explain and Matty gave her a warning shake of the head. 'It's all right, Win, I don't need this job. I'm only here doing research for the next talkie...' As she promenaded past the line of the Tiller Girls, whose hands hadn't ceased moving, she raised her voice to the level necessary to reach the back of the auditorium in the Star. 'I've found out everything I need to know about this place and when the film comes out there'll be an evil cow of a forelady in it you'll all recognize!'

Now the Tiller Girls paused, just for long enough to give her a round of applause, and she curtseyed low, before making her exit through the swing doors at the end of the factory floor.

In the office they were very quick to give Matty her cards, eager to take on a fourteen-year-old in her place at half the wages. No doubt the school leaver would be kitted out in mob cap and overall before Matty had exited the factory gates.

It was dinner time and she left the factory surrounded by a swarm of chatting, hurrying women. Still clutching her cards, she walked up Drummond Road towards the John Bull Arch, the reality of her situation slowly sinking in. Without her voice she had no other income and she had needed the money from this job simply to live. She realized she'd given Edna exactly what she wanted. But why had she done it? Perhaps a part of her had wanted the sack, and she'd simply given herself a far nobler motive than the true one, which was that at fourteen she'd never wanted to be a factory girl and she didn't want to be one now.

Bermondsey had always been a place of muted colour, with its dominant palette of soot-blackened brick and grey slate. Although the council's Beautification Committee had brightened it with flower beds and trees, Matty had always found the true colour of Bermondsey in its smells, and of these there was no lack. She could have made her way home blindfolded, just by following the smells. On the way up Drummond Road, leaving behind the buttery sweetness of Peek's, she was assaulted by the vinegary maltiness of the pickle factory. She spotted a group of women on their dinner break, standing outside the factory gate. Wearing long sacking aprons soaked in vinegar, they were literally pickled themselves. She smelled their reek of pickled onions as she passed them. Pungent brown liquor dripped from their aprons on to their clogs, staining the pavement around them. She realized that compared to these women's work her long hours on the Peek's production line had been a piece of cake, her revulsion at the Bourbon-cream filling a mere indulgence. At least it had been 'clean work', a bonus in a borough full of foul-smelling, dirty industries. No doubt any one of these pickle girls, with their swollen red hands, would have swapped with her in a heartbeat. But it was too late for regrets now.

She had to start thinking about how she would feed herself next week.

What could she do? She turned under the John Bull Arch beneath the railway and into the Blue. Mixed with the coke-tinged smoke from steam trains above came a sugary odour carried on the wind. Shuttleworth's chocolate factory was exuding its usual confection of aromas. Matty inhaled chocolate and raspberry, were they making raspberry fondant creams? She caught a hint of something more exotic, coconut? Perhaps it was coconut-ice day. She almost crossed the road to enquire about a job there. But something stopped her. Did she really want to be that factory girl she'd escaped becoming all those years ago? But the cold reality was that without singing, she had little option. If only there was a way to find her voice again.

She walked slowly along the Blue, trying to calculate her weekly outgoings as she weaved her way round market stalls. Arithmetic had never been her strong point and her early success had meant she never worried about budgeting. She cast her mind back to the days when she'd been one of five children living on Nellie's wage. How she'd managed Matty couldn't imagine, though she did remember they made matchboxes round the kitchen table for a while to help out. She found herself wishing she could walk round to Vauban Street now for a lesson in managing her money. But her days of turning to Nellie for help were over.

She supposed, if the worst came to the worst, she would have to bump on at the Labour Exchange. Her head was ringing with a litany of pounds, shillings and pence, when she became aware of a different music altogether. The sound of accordions and drums reverberated off shop fronts and she noticed pedestrians stopping to look in the direction of the music. She peered along the busy shopping street and glimpsed between market stalls a long line of men approaching. The banner held by the two foremost read *SAY NO TO DOLE CUTS!* Another banner proclaimed they were members of the National Unemployed Workers' Movement. There must have been a few hundred there, stony-faced marchers, orderly and as smart as their dole money would allow. Another banner further down the line caught her eye. Addressed to Ramsay MacDonald, it asked: *Prime Minister's Question Time: Could YOU live on 15/3d?* It gave her the answer to her budget questions. Fifteen bob would be her income if she was lucky, though she doubted she'd get the full dole. Even her poor maths revealed that she'd be hard pressed to live on less. At least she had no rent to find. Not for the first time she blessed the house in Reverdy Road. It was only as the line moved slowly past her that she noticed that one of the banners was being held aloft rather shakily by a lean-faced young man with dark curly hair. It was Will.

He seemed to have grown older, his youthful complexion dulled and his high colour turned to pallor. It seemed that all the fire of his character had retreated to his eyes, which burned with a bright fervour. Now they looked through Matty as she raised her hand to wave at him, in a foolish forgetting. He stared at her briefly, then deliberately looked away and the column passed on, leaving her with a stone in her heart.

10

And Troughs

May–June 1931

When what remained of her wages ran out and she still hadn't found another job, Matty's fears came true and she was forced to sign on at the Labour Exchange, or the bun house as it was known. She found out from the Public Assistance Committee that she would have to live on fourteen shillings a week, with vouchers for buying tea, sugar and margarine at certain grocers. When she queried the amount the relieving officer informed her that as she only needed five shillings and ninepence to stay alive, the Public Assistance Committee was being more than generous, bearing in mind she was a single woman, with no children and a house of her own.

Fourteen shillings was little enough to get by on, but after paring down to the minimum her expenditure on coal, gas, electric and food she thought she could just about manage on twelve shillings and threepence, leaving a couple of bob for emergencies. But the following week she was surprised to find the Relieving Officer on her doorstep. He was a protuberant-nosed man, who walked into the house snout first, as if ready to sniff out any deception. He waved in front of her an order to look round her home.

'But it's all settled, I'm getting fourteen shillings a week, for what good it'll do me.'

Matty had seen the cowed expressions on the face of other claimants at the bun house and she had hated the way they'd been treated, as if being out of work were a moral lapse.

'Now, Miss Gilbie, that attitude will do you no good whatsoever.' He sniffed the air, catching the scent of her perfume and wrinkling his nose as though it were pickling vinegar. To cheer herself up she'd dressed today in a flowing, silk dress, bought in California and totally unsuited for her days at Peek's. Perhaps she looked rich. But he eyed the dress with disapproval.

'I am here on a very serious matter,' he went on. 'It has come to our attention that you have another means of income.'

'No, I haven't,' she replied truthfully. 'I've not been able to get work since I was put off from Peek Frean's, and believe me I've tried.'

'You do realize it is fraud to mislead the Public Assistance Committee?'

'But I haven't got another form of income!' Matty protested.

The Relieving Officer's eye fell upon Eliza's piano, on top of which was a framed photograph of Matty on stage. He picked it up.

'Our informant has told us that you've recently inherited a substantial amount of money, which you haven't declared! What's more, you are a well-known singer and regular performer at variety halls all over London and you expect me to believe that you are in need of Public Assistance! You do realize you could go to jail if we find you've been lying about your circumstances?'

Matty had been standing during the interview, but now her legs turned to water and she reached for the back of a chair.

'The money's all gone,' she said, realizing how unlikely this sounded. 'And it's true, I was a singer, once, but I lost my voice.'

The man gave a dismissive bark and slammed the flat of his hand on the piano, so that the strings sent up a jangling resonance on the frame. 'That's a good one, very good. Well, if you can't sing any more, you won't be needing this. You can sell the piano and your dole is cut to twelve shillings a week. And we'll be watching you. If we find you on the bill at the Star, you'll be hearing from us. I'll see myself out.'

When he had gone Matty, still shaking from the encounter, poured herself a generous gin and sat down. There would be no money for another bottle, not unless she could ask Freddie Clark to get her some off the back of a lorry. As the clear liquid burned her throat she crossed to the piano. She lifted its lid and holding the glass against her cheek with one hand, she sounded a minor chord with the other, before leaning heavily on the keys and filling Eliza's sedate little parlour with echoes of her own discordant despair.

When Esme telephoned her and discovered Matty was on the dole, she'd insisted on taking her out for lunch. The restaurant in a hotel near Leicester Square was furnished with glamorous black and white angularity. Glittering with geometrical mirrors, it was a world away from the bun house. There was even a piano playing the latest tunes and it should have lifted her spirits. But it reminded Matty too much of the suite at the Ambassador, which Frank always took when they were in Los Angeles, and Matty was glad when lunch was over.

Esme insisted she come back to her office for a drink. As they went to mount the stairs, she bent to pick up a letter. Turning to Matty, her expression one of tight-lipped alarm, she said, 'For you, care of me. It's got an American stamp on it...'

Esme let Matty read in silence as she poured them drinks. Eventually Matty folded the letter and put it in her handbag. 'It's not from Frank,' she said in answer to Esme's enquiring look. 'It's from his sister.'

'Thank God for that!' Esme said. 'What does she say?'

'She wanted to let me know her mother had died.'

And Esme looked vaguely surprised. 'Well, I suppose even monsters have mothers,' was all she said before turning to her new radiogram and putting on a record. Perhaps Esme's motive was to remind Matty why she should fight to regain it, but when the voice of the Cockney Canary floated out Matty felt nothing but surprise at how beautiful that voice was, and yet it was the voice of a stranger, no longer hers.

But the letter had unsettled her. Matty had hoped never to hear from Maria Rossi again. She'd given her agent's as a forwarding address for emergencies, but they'd agreed it was best Maria knew nothing of where she was living, so that if Frank grew suspicious he wouldn't be able to scare or beat the truth out of her. When Matty told Esme the letter was about Mama Rossi's death, it was the truth, but not the whole truth.

That night, sitting in the parlour by the light of the standard lamp, she read the letter over again.

Dear Matty,

I hope you and my little nephew or niece are doing well – and being out of Frank's life, you got to be better off than you were! I know we said I should only write in emergencies, and honey, we got one. I did my best, Matty, but he was on at me from day one, saying he knew I was in on it. He roughed me up a little, but I never let on I helped – what's a black eye to me, cos you know I'm a tough old broad! Well, one of his guys was in London and told him you was there, and Frank said he was gonna take you for every penny.

But, Matty, Frank knows, he found out you were pregnant with his baby when you skipped. It's bad enough you walked out on him, but taking his kid, I've never seen him so mad.

I'm not blaming Mamma, it was my fault. She was dying, Matty, and I thought she should know she had a grandchild growing up somewhere. So the sonofabitch comes round crying, and after the way he treated her I says, don't water the flowers after they're dead! But Mamma, she wants to make him feel better so she tells him about the kid. And he promises Mamma on her deathbed he'll get you both back, treat you right. But after she dies he starts tearing the place up, all my room, all the letters, he tips them out, and then he's on at me again to tell him

*where you're living. I ended up in the hospital, with my
jaw wired up, but I told him I don't know where you live,
which I don't.*

*But I had to let you know, there ain't a chance he's not
coming for you, not now you got something of his. So if
you're living in London, honey, you lie low, or get outta
there if you can. I ain't seen you in no more films so I
reckon my brother put you off the business for life. Don't
write back here, Matty. If he found out I warned you I
reckon I'd be seeing Mamma a lot sooner than I'd like, if
you know what I mean!*

*Good luck, Matty, you was always too good for him,
and don't forget, give the kid a kiss from me.*

She had signed herself *Your sister, Maria.*

Matty's mouth had gone dry as she read the letter over again.
The idea that he wanted her back felt even more chilling than
if he simply wanted to harm her. As far as he was concerned
he'd owned her, and she was sure he'd feel the same way about
his child. Which was why she'd instinctively known to keep her
pregnancy secret and why she'd risked everything to get her child
away from him. Certain that now, with his skewed family pride,
he would never let her go, she ran to the front door and slammed
home the bolt, though she doubted any lock would keep Frank
out if he decided to come calling. It struck her then that losing her
voice had been a blessing; without it she had no need to go near a
stage or Esme's again. Instead she could sink into an anonymous
life as a Bermondsey factory girl.

*

So Matty dutifully accepted the green job tickets that the Labour
Exchange gave her and went along each morning to whichever
factory had issued them. Most times the jobs were already filled
and today, when she looked at the address on the ticket, she was

confident this one would be no different from any of the others she'd tried for in the past months. But when she presented the ticket in the factory office she was dismayed to find that it was accepted and she'd got herself a job at the pickle factory across the road from Peek Frean's. As the foreman led her down to the factory floor, she wished she'd been wise enough to lose the ticket on the way, which was what many people did if they didn't fancy the job on offer.

The foreman gave her an apron that was little more than a huge sack and took her down to the bottling room. Soon her sacking apron was soaked in malt vinegar and her fingers as pickled as the onions she was bottling. The onions stung her eyes, but the tears that pricked them had nothing to do with pickles and she dipped her head, focusing only on trying not to splash her feet with the slopping malt vinegar. When the dinner break finally came she tagged along with a group of women going out to smoke. She stood at the factory gates, alternately inhaling tobacco and taking in grateful gulps of air that didn't either sting her eyes or assault her nostrils. She realized she'd become one of those women dripping in vinegar she'd so pitied when she'd walked out of Peek Frean's. She hadn't been provided with any clogs, so the only decent shoes she owned were now squelching in vinegar. She looked down at her feet: her only other shoes were the high heels that she'd worn on stage and she doubted they'd last long on the pickling floor. Leaning her back against the brick wall outside the factory gates, she stared across at Peek Frean's clock tower, and found herself longing for the smell of a Bourbon cream.

The Peek Frean's dinner hooter announced a tide of hundreds of workers surging out through their gates. They flowed like a dark river along Drummond Road, hurrying with that particular head down, arm-swinging walk of the factory worker determined to make the most of their free time. Women were borne along in chattering groups and, without their aprons and caps, many of them emerged from the factory looking as glamorous as film stars with their dyed perms and freshly applied lipstick. Cloaked by the dense crowd, Matty hadn't seen who was coming until the bold face was almost level with her. The sharp eyes lit upon Matty and she saw in them a sort of cruel triumph as Edna lifted her head and raised her voice so that all her group of followers could hear.

'Oh look, if it ain't the cock linnet! Must be doin' *research* for a film about a pickle factory!' And the woman's laugh was echoed by her little coterie as Edna sailed past. Matty had no witty retort this time; the long queues at the Labour Exchange had driven out any lingering sense of defiance. Blood rushed to her cheeks, she clenched her fists and held her tongue. Only this morning when she'd picked up this job, there'd been a tussle over the green tickets. There simply weren't enough to go round. It had ended in a fist fight between men grasping at any chance to feed their families. The sense of desperation was catching and it had given Matty an uncharacteristic carefulness, which checked her normal defiance. Choking back tears of humiliation, hardly knowing who she was any more, she turned away in a sort of daze and came face to face with Winnie, whose look of fury told Matty she'd witnessed the whole thing.

'Come on, love. I'll take you for a cuppa down the Blue. Go and get that apron off ya.' Winnie spun her round and gave her a little shove. Matty didn't protest and soon the two were seated in the Blue Anchor café. Since Matty's sacking from Peek's, Winnie had become a regular visitor at Reverdy Road. Her friend had insisted on bringing the odd packet of tea or sugar, though Matty knew she was stretched near to breaking with supporting her parents.

'This is my treat!' Winnie insisted.

'Not on your life, you need your pennies more than me. How are things at home?' Matty asked.

'They've stopped Dad's relief altogether, he's been out of work too long and to be honest, Matty, if our Tom wasn't helping us out we'd be starving. Good for me figure though!' Winnie said, patting her stomach and trying to put a brave face on.

Poor Winnie, Matty could see that her girth had shrunk noticeably.

'So, is Tom living with your mum and dad now?' Matty asked. She'd avoided probing her about Tom's life, but being friends with Winnie again had brought him uncomfortably near. She was curious, but the less she knew the less chance she had of regret or guilt invading her life again. At least in America she'd been able to use the miles between them as a buffer.

'He's still got his own place, but he slips us a few quid, you know, on the quiet so the bun house don't know.'

Matty nodded. 'I hate it when the RO comes sniffing round. Since they cut my dole, they haven't left me alone.'

'I'm convinced it was Edna reported you!' Winnie said. 'Though what you ever did to her, the evil cow, I don't know.'

Matty shrugged. 'It could have been anyone, Win. People think we're all spongers, don't like the idea of their rates going into scroungers' pockets. Still, the way things are going, anybody could end up on relief.' And she told her friend about the fight over the green tickets at the dole office that morning.

'I'm sorry, Matty, I feel so bad. It should have been me got the sack.'

But Matty put her hand over Winnie's, 'If I had a dad and mum at home, you'd have done the same for me... but I haven't.'

One evening, after a particularly unpleasant day bottling pickled walnuts in a vile black liquor, she was trying to scrub black stains from her fingers without scraping the skin off as well when a knock came on the front door. A fist closed around her heart, and she tried to calculate if it was possible for Frank to already be in the country, but it wasn't, and immediately terror of Frank was replaced by a new fear, which had become as ingrained as the pickled walnut stains on her hand, and it was of the Relieving Officer. She'd been expecting him. He'd warned that he'd be paying another visit to make sure she'd sold the piano, though she'd hoped that being in work might forestall that necessity. She wiped her hands and steeled herself for the ordeal of having him sniffing round her home. She hadn't been able to bear getting rid of the old instrument, which both she and later Billy had learned to play on. Poor Billy, what must he think of her desertion? She shook her head to wipe away the image of his disappointed face and went to answer the knock.

In spite of herself her hand flew to her mouth. He'd obviously knocked, then taken a step back on to the red-tiled front path, perhaps so as not to startle her. But that couldn't have been avoided. He looked so different from the day she'd last seen him. Now he wore a dark, well-cut suit, with a grey trilby shadowing his lean, square-jawed face.

'Tom!'

'Hello, Matty,' he said, removing his hat. His light brown hair was now cut much shorter, brushed back from a neat side-parting to reveal his high forehead. 'Can I come in?'

Momentarily frozen to the spot, Matty stared into those distinctive, half-moon-shaped hazel eyes, which had once reflected back love, and which now revealed nothing. He waited a few seconds and when she didn't respond said, 'I'm sorry, I shouldn't have come.' And he turned to walk away.

'No, don't go! Of course you can come in, I'm just so surprised to see you!'

She felt herself flush and was glad to turn her back on him, as she led him to the parlour. She offered him tea, aware all the time that a surge of the old familiar excitement had instantly coursed through her at the sight of him. It was impossible to ignore or deny, but she realized at once it was merely an instinctive reaction. His face, like an old song, had called up the memory of a feeling – not necessarily the feeling itself.

Nevertheless, as she made tea in the kitchen she did glance in the mirror, making sure her waves were still in place. Since the cost of a hairdresser had soared beyond her reach, she'd started wearing her hair shorter, with softer waves that she'd achieved herself using just fingers and wave clips. Her dark eyes were red-rimmed and revealed too much of the anxiety she'd been feeling. She patted her cheeks to give them some colour and then smoothed the front of her dove-grey dress, wishing it wasn't quite so worn. She looked at her hands; the black stains said everything about how her star had fallen. She sighed and took the tray into the parlour.

'You're looking well, Tom. How've you been?' she asked, and for a moment she wondered if he was going to make this awkward.

He smiled politely. 'Fine, Matty, I've been fine. Got a new job, things are going well.'

Her heart sank. Politeness was almost more painful than outright hostility; it meant he felt nothing. His smile had never been anything other than infectious for her; it was what she had fallen in love with. A smile that began in his eyes, crinkled their corners and only then moved to his mouth. But of course he wasn't still 'her Tom' and it had been selfish of her to think that he might be.

'You look very smart,' she said, noticing the hat that he had taken off and was now twisting round in his hands. 'I love the titfer!' she said, taking it and planting it briefly on her own head, with a Burlington Bertie swagger. Again came the polite smile and she handed him back the hat awkwardly. She'd always been able to make him laugh, but that wasn't the only thing that had changed. He'd always been a flat-cap man. The new style suited him and if she hadn't known better, she would have taken him for an office worker. 'Are you going out for the evening?'

He shook his head. 'I've come straight from work. I'm in the Bermondsey Health Department these days – in the offices.'

She tried to veil her surprise.

'Don't look so shocked, Matty. You didn't expect my life to stay the same, did you?' There was an edge to his voice. 'I've moved on, the same as you.'

He even spoke differently, with no dropped aitches in evidence. She'd once known him so well, and yet she found herself looking at him with new eyes. The Tom she knew had never held down a job for very long; he'd flitted butterfly-like from one to another. She'd first met him when he was working as a mechanic for Freddie Clark in his haulage business – along with the other less legitimate activities Freddie had been involved in before he married. Tom had done a stint in the docks and when she'd left for America he was working at the borough cleansing station in a totally unglamorous but necessary job. As Bermondsey's old housing stock was riddled with bedbugs, cockroaches and lice, families regularly sent their mattresses and bedding to the cleansing station to have the vermin eradicated in huge steam boilers. At the time it seemed as far from Matty's increasingly glamorous world as could be imagined. But that wasn't the reason she'd decided not to marry him.

'Well, it's a bit of a leap from boiling out bedbugs to a clerk in the health department!' she laughed. 'But I'd love to hear how *that* happened!'

He looked at her for a long moment, his head cocked slightly to one side. 'Would you, Matty?'

And then she remembered how with Tom, a question was always a real question. He'd never had much time for small talk.

'Yes, I would,' she answered honestly.

'That's strange. I thought you'd lost interest in me and my life a long time ago.'

There was the sting she'd been waiting for, but he covered it well. 'But actually I've come to talk about you.'

'Me?' She realized she was flustered. How had that happened? Tom had never been able to fluster her. But she could only think of one reason he'd want to talk about her and she steeled herself to turn down his plea to take him back.

'Winnie told me she pinched a biscuit and you got the sack for taking the blame.'

Matty hid her surprise with a shrug, 'Oh, I hated it there anyway. Besides, it was wearing me out!'

'So it's true. I could barely credit it. They sacked you for a *biscuit*?'

'I did swear at the old cow of a forelady as well.'

Tom gave a sharp laugh. 'She came unstuck then. People always think you're softer than you really are.'

She realized with a jolt how well he knew her. 'Oh yeah, hard as nails me.'

But this time he didn't laugh. He gave her a cool stare until she blushed, remembering. It was a phrase he'd used about her the night she'd walked away from him. Tom may have moved on, but she didn't think he'd forgiven her, in which case why had he come?

'Well, our Win was grateful. She needs the money, not for herself but for the old folks. I help as much as I can, but as soon as the RO sniffs out extra money coming in they cut their dole.'

'Oh, I know all about the RO. They're making me sell Eliza's old joanna.' Her eyes rested on the piano for an instant. 'I wish I didn't have to.'

'But, Matty, what were you doing working at Peek's anyway? I can't believe you really need the money,' he said, with a puzzled expression. She remembered how his high forehead creased that way whenever he was searching out answers. She'd always found it particularly difficult to pull the wool over Tom's eyes and though he wasn't immune to her charms, he could usually spot if she was using them to hide something.

She wished she could feed him the lie that she was researching her next film, but he would never have been fooled and besides, her fingers had already betrayed her. She caught him looking at her hands.

'You in a pickle factory!' He shook his head. 'Matty, what happened?'

She let out a long breath. 'It's simple really, Tom – I'm broke. All my money went into the next film and it's not going to happen now, what with the Crash and everything.'

'Simple? I can't believe that. Nothing was ever simple with you, Matty.' He paused, as if waiting for the true story.

She shrugged again, not willing to enlighten him.

'I'm sorry you lost everything.' She could tell he meant it, but Tom was not one to take anything at face value and he persisted. 'But surely you could make better money from the stage than pickles?'

She blushed, and wished Winnie hadn't told him about her getting the sack, then he wouldn't have had to see her like this. But pickles were a fact of her life now and it was no good pretending she was something that she wasn't. Tom would always sniff out that sort of deceit.

'I know you've been on the bill at the Star since you came home.'

'Oh, did you see me?' she asked quickly.

'No, no... I didn't.'

She dropped her eyes, feeling unaccountably disappointed. 'Oh. Well, to be honest, Tom, I've had enough of the stage.'

And now he burst out laughing, his old laugh, the one she could elicit with a funny face or a witty remark. 'You? Fed up with singing?' he said in disbelief. 'Now I know you're telling pork pies. But you don't have to tell me your business, Matty,' he said, suddenly serious.

A part of her wanted to tell him the truth. There was a time when they'd shared everything, and perhaps that had been the problem. In the end, Tom had simply taken up too much space in her life and she'd had no room for anything else, least of all a career in America. She could see that he'd changed, but so had she, and life had taught Matty that an open heart was the most vulnerable. She folded imaginary wings around her pain, shielding all the hurt from his penetrating gaze.

'That part of my life's over, Tom,' was all she said and he nodded, seeming to accept it and surprising her, for the Tom she remembered would have probed until he'd got the truth.

'So you really do need that job at the pickle factory?'

'Oh, I need the job. I've tried Hartley's, Crosse & Blackwell's, Lipton's, not Pearce Duff's because of Nel— I mean, too many memories.'

He paused for a moment as if considering something. 'I know you're surprised I'm here, and to be honest it's only because Winnie asked me to come.'

'Why would she do that?' Matty felt a flash of anger; she would kill Winnie for putting her in this position. 'She told me herself you'd moved on—'

But he waved her aside. 'No, it's nothing like that. She told me you were on your uppers, not that I believed her, and she asked me to help you.'

Now she was even angrier. 'No, Tom, I don't want your money – thanks very much, but I'm managing.'

'In a pickle factory?'

'Have you come to gloat?' Matty snapped. 'I left you for a glittering career in a pickle factory? Is that what you really want to say?' She stood up, her face flushed, just wanting him to go.

'I knew this was a mistake.' He got up, jamming his hat on, but at the parlour door he paused. She saw his jaw clenching; it was something he used to do when he was being annoyingly patient with her and it had always made her blood boil.

'I don't care where you work, Matty. But you've done my family a good turn and Winnie asked me to help you. So, no, I didn't come to gloat. I came to offer you a job.'

*

'What's the matter with you, you silly cow? Fancy turning him down!' Winnie was furious with her. They were sitting in Matty's kitchen drinking tea and Winnie's expression was stoney. 'It wasn't his idea, you know, he didn't want to come. It was me. I kept on and on at him to do something for you, after the way you helped me, Matty. He said you'd take it the wrong way...'

Matty raked her pickle-stained fingers through her hair. 'I'm sorry, Win. I was a bit touchy with him and as soon as he went, I felt bad.'

'He was just trying to do you a favour.'

'I know that now,' she said miserably.

'I don't know what you said to him, but he had the right hump when he came round to us. He chucked this in the bin.'

Winnie fished a sheet of crumpled paper from her bag and pushed it across the kitchen table. 'I reckon it would've been right up your street.'

Matty flattened it out on the kitchen table. It was a list of duties for a part-time assistant in the borough health department. At first it seemed like a routine office job, which Matty couldn't say was at all up her street, but it certainly would be more pleasant than the pickle factory. Then something caught her attention. She read to the end and looked up at Winnie with a smile spreading slowly across her face.

Winnie's expression softened. 'Want me to have another go?'

Matty grinned. 'So long as he promises there won't be a Bourbon cream or pickled walnut in sight.'

She wasn't sure that working for Tom was such a good idea, but with her future perilous and her past ripped away, where did she have to go but the present? And a job with Tom was what was on offer, here and now. So, the following week she reported for work at the public health department. She found Tom's office tucked away at the back of the labyrinthine town hall building in Spa Road. He wasn't there, which gave her a chance to look round the place he'd migrated to from the borough cleansing station. It was little more than a cubby-hole, with a tall window looking out on to a brick wall. The room was crammed with filing cabinets, a plan chest, an easel and a pinboard, along with two desks with barely an inch between them. On the walls were health posters, featuring large molars and smiling babies. Two she recognized; they were the same posters as on the electric sign situated above the Underground public conveniences at the end of Grange Road. The electric signs were a marvel of modernity: illuminated by electric light at night, they flipped automatically to reveal different health messages. The one she was studying was in a series called 'The Tale of a Tooth'. It showed a bawling baby with the caption: *Once toothless, now four teeth have I, They're never cleaned,*

I don't know why. The next poster, in stark contrast, featured a healthy chubby infant with a kiss curl on its forehead and a Mr Punch toy in its lap. The accompanying caption read: *I came with none, but now have four, but Ma cleans mine, that's how I score!* The caption writer obviously had no qualms about making a mother feel inadequate so long as it resulted in healthy teeth for Bermondsey infants.

Matty had often seen kids hanging about the electric signs at dusk, waiting for the pictures to light up. They knew the captions off by heart and would sing them in lusty voices to whatever tune was popular at the time. But even without the captions, the pictures told the tale clearly enough.

She was smiling at the posters when Tom came in.

'They're good, aren't they? Our chief medical officer wrote the captions – he loves a bit of poetry!'

She turned on her heel. 'I was just remembering a group of kids I saw the other day – they were singing these captions to the tune of "Oh! My Sweet Hortense!" They did very well, actually.'

Tom smiled, then suddenly all business, he said, 'Let's get cracking. I'll show you the job for this morning. It'll be different from one day to the next – I'll warn you before we start!'

He led her to the plan chest in the corner and opened up a drawer of artwork.

'We're creating some more multi-posters for the electric signs and this artwork needs to go to the printers.' He pulled out the drawings and Matty could see the artwork dealt with TB, showing a child receiving sun-ray treatment from large lamps at the council's solarium in Grange Road.

Tom pulled out a filing cabinet and gave her a folder. 'Here's the printers' details, just give them a ring, then send off the artwork. It's all in there. I've got to go, Matty, the three musketeers want a meeting over at the skeleton room!'

And when she gave him an exaggerated look of puzzlement, he grabbed his hat from the stand and said, 'I'll explain later!'

'Hmm, busy!' she mused as he left her alone in the office.

He'd obviously got over his earlier pique at her ingratitude, at least enough to offer her the job. But she hadn't been able to guess what his tone would be once they started working together. He'd pitched it at cordial but businesslike, which she didn't mind at all.

She spread the artwork over the top of the plan chest and went to look for packing materials. As she rooted around in the store cupboard for cardboard and string she sniffed the air and smiled – only dust and paper and a hint of floor polish, with not a whiff of vanilla or vinegar anywhere.

When Tom returned at lunchtime, she'd already parcelled up the artwork, found the post room and sent off the material. She'd organized a stack of other artwork that seemed to have no home and presented him with a sheet of telephone messages that she'd answered. He looked impressed.

'You've made yourself at home,' he said, his eyes on his own desk, which looked considerably tidier than when he'd left.

'So, who the bloody hell are the three musketeers?' she asked as he threw himself into the chair behind his desk and fished out a packet of sandwiches.

'D.M., Birdy and Plum, the three musketeers we call them. Want one?'

'Did you make them?' She peered at the slices of limp bread, which had an inch thickness of cheese sandwiched between them.

He nodded and she declined.

'They're my bosses – and yours now. D.M. – he's Chief Medical Officer Dr D. M. Connan, Birdy – Mr Bush chief admin officer and Plum, that's Mr Lumley, a radiographer. I'm their assistant.'

'So what will I be doing?'

'Oh, all sorts, Matty – sending artwork, like today, arranging meetings and lectures, general office work and anything else that crops up. Sorry it's not very regular work, could be mornings or evenings. Can you do evenings? I forgot to ask.'

She ran her finger along the dust on the edge of his desk. 'Since I stopped singing in the pubs and halls I'm free most nights.'

'Well… that's good,' he said a little awkwardly.

But it seemed her tasks were over for the day and she left feeling that he hadn't really explained much about what she'd be doing. She would just have to take each day as it came and that suited her mood. If her hours didn't pick up she wouldn't be earning as much as at the pickle factory, but she'd rather starve than go back there.

It had been a strange reunion. She'd often wondered how Tom's life had turned out. She'd imagined him ruined by heartbreak and pitied him, or else she'd envisioned him married with children and then, perversely, had been angry with him, but after she met Frank she didn't think about him at all, not until things went bad, and then she began to remember everything she'd ever loved about him. But the reality was nothing like her imaginings. He'd been cool, professional and as far away from her as if the Atlantic Ocean still lay between them.

11

Silver Screens

June–July 1931

The next few days followed a similar pattern, with Tom largely out of the office and Matty left to get on with various jobs involving the health department's 'propaganda materials'. Then one morning she went into the office to find him in the middle of a telephone call, a harassed expression on his face. He hung up and put his finger to his mouth, his brow furrowing. He looked up, not really seeing her.

'What's the matter?' she said, tossing her hat on to the stand so that it landed neatly next to his.

'Ohh, I just lost another wife...' he said distractedly, and before she could question him he pointed straight at her. 'Trust you to make your entrance dead on time! Follow me!'

He picked up his hat and flung Matty hers before hurrying out of the office. She followed down the hushed, polished corridors of the town hall, out on to the steps and into Spa Road, not daring to ask him what he meant about losing his wife. Perhaps there was something Winnie hadn't told her?

He was the sort of man that was unhappy sitting around, which was one of the reasons she'd been surprised he'd gone into office work. Now, walking rapidly with an easy long stride, he explained as they went.

'Matty, you're going back into the film business – Bermondsey style!'

She smiled uncertainly. 'Are you pulling my leg?'

He stopped outside a large Victorian house in Grange Road that announced itself as the TB Dispensary. 'No! I'm dead serious, Matty. The health department propaganda doesn't stop at electric signs – we make films too!' He pushed open the front door and led her through a waiting room, out into a large back garden bordered with high trees.

'Welcome to the skeleton room,' he said proudly.

She was looking at something which looked very like a film set. Constructed of thick plywood and raised on a wooden dais, the three walls of the skeleton room were wallpapered, with painted-on windows and a real door to finish the effect. It was furnished like a typical overcrowded Bermondsey home, with two beds, a kitchen table and chairs all in the same room. The table looked set for tea and in the painted fireplace there was a notable absence of coal.

'So, I help Dr Connan make the health department's films – organize set-making, props, casting, lighting equipment, all that sort of thing.'

'Like a stage manager?' She immediately recognized the invaluable behind-the-scenes role without which any production would flounder.

'If you like.' He grinned. 'And today, you, Matty Gilbie, are the answer to my prayers.'

He looked her full in the eyes for a moment then quickly turned to the set, beckoning her over to meet a young man who stood beneath a tree, smoking.

'Reggie, meet Matty, your new wife.'

Reggie threw away his cigarette. 'Pleased to meet ya,' he said, shaking Matty's hand. 'I don't go much on bigamy meself, but you're the third trouble and strife I've had this week!' The young man's laugh turned into a cough.

'Don't look so worried, Matty, you're not really marrying him. I've been looking for someone to play Reggie's wife but they keep getting cold feet!'

'Sight of my ugly mug.' Reggie smiled good-naturedly.

'Don't worry, Reggie, she's not fussy about looks.' And for a minute she thought she saw a mischievous glint in his eye. But then, all business, he went on, 'Now before Birdy and Plum arrive I'll fill you in, Matty.'

Things were progressing a little faster than Matty could keep up with.

'Hang on, Tom, are you expecting me to act?' she said, feeling panicked. 'I'm not prepared!'

'Matty, you could do this with your eyes closed. It's a silent, no lines to learn. The storyline's simple. He's a consumptive.'

Tom nodded towards Reggie, who banged his chest and said, 'Good job I've already got a cough, eh? No need to put it on!'

'Reg's coming home to tell his wife – that's you – the diagnosis. You'll answer the door to him, but when he comes in you're waiting for your kiss and he walks right past you. So you get upset with him, but then he explains why,' Tom said.

'And I ain't got the 'ump, I've got the TB, and the doctor says I can't kiss no one, not even me wife, because that's how it gets spread,' Reggie explained.

'So now you just have to act upset and cry – a *lot*.' Tom went to the table and picked up an onion. 'And if you can't cry to order, then we'll cut the onion.'

'No, no onions!' Matty said in alarm. 'I've had enough of them lately. Don't worry about my tears, I can turn on the taps whenever I need to,' she said, thinking of the technique she'd always used when tears were required. She simply conjured up her own sadness, of which she had plenty at the moment.

Just then two men appeared, one middle-aged in a three-piece suit, the other younger with a jolly expression. They were laughing over something and didn't look at all like serious public health officials to Matty. Tom introduced the older man as Mr Bush and the other as Mr Lumley, a radiographer, who would be in charge of the camera. Matty gathered film-making wasn't their full-time job, which explained their high spirits – perhaps this was a welcome break for them both.

Mr Bush shook her hand warmly. 'Well I never, Matty Gilbie, the Cockney Canary! Bermondsey's own star of the silver screen! Thank you for gracing our set, my dear, we're honoured. I don't believe we've ever had a professional in one of our films before. Tom finds all our home-grown talent for us, but he has excelled himself this time.' Mr Bush stopped mid-flow, a look of concern clouding his good cheer. 'Tom, you did explain to Miss Gilbie about the, ah hem,' he gave a cough and lowered his voice, 'the remuneration?'

'Oh yes, Mr Bush, I know the borough can't pay me a Hollywood salary!' Matty answered for him, unembarrassed, though she appreciated his delicacy.

'Just so, my dear. Dr Connan – our Chief MO – is very keen to keep our costs down, we use only home-grown talent, our actors are usually council employees and our Bermondsey audiences are always willing extras!'

Matty could see this was film-making on a shoestring, but she was impressed by Mr Bush's enthusiasm.

'Plum, if you'll kindly set up the camera.'

It was a smaller version of the Hollywood studio cameras Matty was used to. Plum adjusted the tripod so that the camera pointed towards the door of the set.

'Actors in position!' Mr Bush settled into his director's chair. 'I believe the phrase is, lights, camera, action!'

Tom was right, she need not have worried. As soon as the camera started rolling Matty was in her element. Reggie had a little trouble opening the set door which stuck, but once he was through managed to snub her pointedly puckered lips in a very deliberate way, making a good job of looking weighed down by bad news. She pouted prettily and looked hurt; they were after all meant to be a young, married couple. Then he led her to the table, where after giving her the bad news, she sobbed effectively into a handkerchief, shedding real tears, without recourse to the onion.

'Cut!' Mr Bush called and sprang up out of the director's chair with a delighted smile. 'In one, my dear, in one!'

It seemed she'd passed her screen test.

They shot three more scenes, the last featuring Reggie setting up one of the garden sleeping shelters the borough provided for TB sufferers. Tom had shown her one already assembled in the dispensary garden and she was astonished that this was considered good for a sick person's health. Little more than a shed with a cot-bed and chair inside, it had louvre shutters on its front, which could be raised so that the consumptive slept virtually in the open air and away from his wife and family, all of whom would often be sleeping in the one room.

At the end of the morning's shooting Tom looked at his watch. 'It's about lunchtime. I'm off to the pub for a pint and a sandwich.' He hesitated, then asked, 'Fancy coming?'

This was the part of the job she was going to find difficult. Not that Tom had made her feel awkward. His focus had obviously been on getting the job done. She didn't think he'd hired her because they'd once been in love; she knew it was a practical decision and she'd seen how pleased he was by Mr Bush's praise for his ingenuity. But still she couldn't help wondering if he'd felt pressurized into asking her to lunch. He was her boss, after all, not her friend. But if he was her boss, she supposed she shouldn't upset him in her first week.

They went to the nearby Grange pub and over a drink he explained that this afternoon he'd be taking her to see one of the cinemotors that were used for screening the health films around Bermondsey's streets.

'You won't just be acting, Matty. You'll have to turn your hand to whatever needs doing. Setting up the captions or getting hold of equipment – we might need to pick your brains about a new camera soon.'

'But I was always on the other side of the camera!' she said quickly, hoping he hadn't overestimated her experience.

'Well, you'll know a lot more than we do! But remember I asked if you could do evenings? You'll be needed once the evening screenings start, probably just handing out leaflets, or helping

D.M. keep the crowd in order – you should be good at that, after dealing with the scrums at the Star for all those years.'

She was glad he wasn't being overly sympathetic about her changed circumstances. He obviously wasn't too interested or worried that the new Matty Gilbie had none of the fame or fortune of the old. Instead she found herself in the position of being the one intrigued by his new life.

'So – how on earth did you get into all this?' she asked.

'It wasn't such a leap really. I moved out of the cleansing station and started driving the disinfectant vans. The medical officer turned up at the depot one day, looking for a van he could convert into a mobile cinema. Our foreman got me to show D.M. the van. He asked loads of questions about converting it, how we could put a screen in the back, where we could mount a projector. Well you know me and motors. I came up with a drawing showing how to make the adaptations and took it to my foreman the next day, and that's how I got myself a new job in the film department!'

Matty was used to the idea of projecting on to a screen but she couldn't work out how that could be achieved with a van.

'You project it *through* a translucent screen. Anyway, you'll see this afternoon. But converting that van was the most fun I'd ever had – working! It made me feel as if I'd got something to live... work towards.'

He covered well, but Matty knew he had been about to say 'live for'. He must be talking about just after she'd left for America.

'So, I went to night school,' he went on quickly, 'got my qualifications and that's how I worked my way up.'

'I'm pleased for you, Tom. I always knew you could make more of yourself, not that I didn't love you just the way you were!' she joked, then seeing his face redden, wished the floor could swallow her up. She must remember, it had been her choice to go and, despite his detached air, his slip of the tongue suggested wounds that hadn't entirely healed.

'You never did have a very high opinion of me, did you? But there was a lot about me you were never interested enough to find out, Matty.'

It appeared she'd misjudged him again, for it didn't seem like a broken heart but wounded pride that had caused his outburst.

'Tom...' She wanted to explain that of course she'd been interested in him, she had loved him, but that would be no consolation, for she'd also left him.

He interrupted her. 'Sorry, Matty. It was a long time ago.' He spread his hands as though it were aeons, but Matty had discovered that in matters of the heart, time had a strange ability to coil back upon itself – past hurts could deliver a serpent's bite every bit as venomous as on the day they were first inflicted.

She was remembering even now the first time her impossibly handsome and always attentive lover, Frank Rossi, had narrowed his beautiful long-lashed eyes before slapping her across the face, shouting that she was a washed-up has-been he should never have wasted his time on.

'Where are you?' Tom asked, getting her attention.

'Oh, nowhere.' She smiled.

'Nowhere must be a nasty place then. You didn't look very happy.'

'Sometimes, when I remember America...'

Tom leaned back in his chair. His large hazel eyes were so transparent, like one of those screens in the cinemotors he was so proud of, with all his feelings projected through them. And as those eyes fixed on hers it was as if three years fell away in an instant. Tom had been the person she could tell everything to and now, before she could stop herself, she began to unburden her heart. Telling him, not everything, but enough, so that he understood how poor her choices had been in America. When she told him Frank's name and what his businesses involved, he nodded. 'I know the type, Matty.'

And she knew he wasn't just speaking generally. When they'd first left school, Tom and Freddie Clark had flirted with

162

membership in a gang based at the Elephant and Castle, who were every bit as tough as Frank and his boys. But it was a world Tom had always felt lucky to escape; he'd once told her that Freddie Clark had probably saved his life by insisting that they get out. Freddie, Tom said, with all his bent ways, was a pussycat compared to most of the Elephant Boys.

'So you picked up with a wrong 'un?' he said, his voice level and matter-of-fact.

'He didn't seem that way at first.'

'They never do,' he said dryly, and shifted uncomfortably in his seat.

She knew it wasn't fair, to expect him to still be the one she could tell anything to, especially when it concerned another man.

'Did you hear about Eliza?' she asked, quickly changing the subject, and he seemed to relax.

'Yes, I'm sorry. Winnie told me she left you the house in her will. You were always a favourite of hers.'

He waited for her to answer and when she couldn't, he leaned forward. 'Are you all right, Matty?'

Angry with her own weakness, she brushed away tears. But talking to Tom had unstopped them and she put up a hand to shield her face. He pulled out the handkerchief from his top pocket, handed it to her and waited till she was able to speak. 'Winnie told me that the boy took you to court over it. I know you idolized Will.'

'It was horrible, but that's not the worst of it. He told me something that's just turned my life upside down.' And ignoring all her resolves to keep her distance, she plunged on. 'It turns out Eliza wasn't my sister. She was my mother.'

Tom's face registered disbelief. 'Oh my God, Matty, you poor kid.'

She looked up sharply. She had only wanted to share the unbearable load of that knowledge with someone who would understand, but she'd always been 'his kid', his pet name for her, and for a minute she thought he might put his arms round her. But his expression revealed shocked concern, nothing more.

'I know what it means for you, Matty, you thought the world of your mum. It must have knocked you for six.'

'Thanks, Tom. I knew you'd understand. But the terrible thing is, ever since I found out, I haven't been able to sing and I can't work out why. I did everything I could to get it back – trying to sing around the house, doing voice exercises – and I even thought I'd go and see this hypnotist up the Old Kent Road!'

'You don't need hypnotism! You've had a big shock. It'll come back.'

'That's what Esme Golding said, but I've just about given up.'

It was a relief to have told him, yet she felt guilty to have traded on their past intimacy. But after they left the pub Tom seemed to slip back gratefully into work mode. So they were just colleagues again as they walked towards the borough disinfectant yard where the cinemotor van was garaged, and she found herself wistful for those long vanished days when they had been so easy with one another they could finish each other's sentences.

The cinemotor was about eleven foot long, with the slogan *Fresh air and fun* painted on the side. Back-door flaps opened up into a clever viewing box, shading the thin rubber screen from too much exterior light. Tom helped Matty through a side door into the back of the van, where a projector was clamped to a stand. He pointed to a stool. 'The projectionist sits there to run the film, which gets projected out through the back screen. The audience just crowds around outside. The screen's high enough up for them to get a pretty good view.'

'Seems a bit airless in here. Doesn't the poor projectionist get hot?' Matty ducked her head as she examined the bulb in the projector.

'Not really. It's a cold light, cos of the fire risk, and look...' He pointed to louvres in the van sides. 'You just open one of these for a bit of air! I designed them,' he said proudly.

'Well, I still wouldn't fancy being stuck in here for an hour!'

Tom looked a little sheepish and began fiddling with the lantern slides, which were also shown during the lectures.

'Tom! Don't tell me I've got to be projectionist as well!'

Ignoring her question, he demonstrated how the viewing screen slid along runners set into the floor of the van and out on to a lowered back board. 'This was my idea too. Means we can have a longer throw from the projector, gives a *really* sharp picture,' he said enthusiastically.

She crossed her arms, waiting for her answer.

'Well... you might have to work the projector... now and then. I did tell you the job was varied!'

That evening she was as tired as if she'd done a ten-hour shift at Peek's. It wasn't the day's work, which had been far more congenial than filling Bourbon creams or onion jars. It was, she thought, the unlooked-for nearness of Tom that had drained her. For so long he'd been thousands of miles away in body and a lifetime away in spirit, and she'd let him recede from the centre of her life. Now she felt as if she'd been swimming against a tide all day and she wasn't certain where that tide wanted to lead her, but at least she could take comfort in the knowledge that Matty Gilbie had a screen career to look forward to after all.

*

Her part in the consumption film only lasted a week. It was short, running to no more than half an hour, for as Mr Bush explained film was too expensive for anything longer. Besides, the attention span of the audience, many of whom would be children, had to be taken into account. But once she was no longer needed on set, Tom had plenty of other tasks lined up for her. She spent a couple of days in the office arranging the schedule of summer outdoor screening. The cinemotor would tour the borough in the summer evenings, showing the public health films in back streets and courtyards. Tom told her they could expect crowds of five hundred or more, so her job was to make sure the police were informed of each event. She had to arrange showings in factories and schools and decide

165

which films would be appropriate for which venue – she didn't think the tanners at Bevington's would take too kindly to a film about *Maternity and Child Welfare*.

It wasn't until early summer that the cinemotor began touring Bermondsey's streets. Though the children were still at school, Tom assured her that they would all be allowed to stay up for the evening screenings.

'You wait, Matty, you'll have a bigger crowd than the Old Kent Road Astoria!' he promised her.

It was a balmy evening in June when they set off for the first outdoor screening of the year. Tom drove the van and would be working the projector, while Dr Connan, the medical officer, would give a lantern-slide lecture before they showed the film. Matty wasn't entirely sure what her role would be, only that Tom said it would be 'varied', which she'd learned was a term they used quite a lot in the film department, especially when no one had a clue what would be happening.

Matty was a little in awe of D.M. The health films were the medical officer's brainchild and she sensed he was reserving judgement about his newly acquired Hollywood starlet. He was always smartly dressed and invariably wore a bowler hat and a three-piece suit, with a tiepin and a watch chain on his waistcoat. He was a brisk man, ever conscious of time as money. Tom had assured her he had a sense of humour, but she'd yet to see the evidence.

Matty seated herself in the cab, squeezed between Tom and D.M.

'Now, my dear Miss Gilbie, has Tom told you that you will be required for crowd control this evening and you are also to act as my plant?'

'Oh yes, Dr Connan.' She nodded, though in fact Tom had told her no such thing and she shot him a questioning look, which he avoided by pretending to look for a street sign.

'When we come to the Question and Answer section following the film the crowd are apt to become a little lively,

166

and if I should have mentioned in my lecture that the stomach holds two pints of liquid we can certainly expect some wag to declare that his stomach is able to hold far more – especially on a Saturday night!'

Matty let out an involuntary laugh, which D.M. met with placid seriousness so that she couldn't tell if he'd been joking or not.

'So it will be up to you, Miss Gilbie, to steer all questions back to the serious business of a man's – or indeed a woman's – cleanliness. Our subject tonight is the prevalence of germs in the average Bermondsey household!'

Matty said she was sure she could do that and out of the corner of her eye noticed a small smile playing on Tom's face.

They didn't have to go far to the first venue and soon Tom turned into Dunlop Place, a cul-de-sac that ran alongside the Salvation Army colony in Spa Road. It was parallel to Vauban Street and held a similar row of ancient houses, most of which were scheduled for demolition under the council's slum clearance programme. Tom had explained they preferred a cul-de-sac or courtyard as a venue, so that D.M. didn't have to compete with the noise of passing traffic during his lecture. As the cinemotor trundled over cobbles, Matty was astonished to see that a crowd of several hundred had already squeezed themselves into the narrow street. When they caught sight of the cinemotor a cheer went up that sent a shiver of excitement down Matty's spine, such as she hadn't felt since her first days at the Star. She turned to Tom and smiled.

'Hold on to your hat!' Tom warned, leaping out of the cab and helping Matty down. He slid open the side door and emerged with an electric cable, which he unrolled. He eyed the crowd as if they were Red Indians circling a wagon.

'Here's where we get our electricity,' he explained, producing a small key and unlocking the side panel of a lamp post. He plugged the cinemotor's cable into the lamp post.

'Come on, Matty, can't keep our public waiting! They start

to get mouthy if we take too long setting up. Here, hand these out, keep 'em quiet while I start the lantern slides.'

He shoved a bundle of leaflets into her hands and went to slide out the screen from the back of the van. The huge crowd, anticipating the start of the show, surged round him, organizing itself into a wedge shape and fanning out from the screen. Matty shoved her way into the crowd's solid core. Eager children jostled for a place at the front, hoisting smaller tots on to their shoulders. Women stood further back, while men hovered at the fringes of the wedge, hands in pockets, not looking at the screen, almost as if they were there by accident. But when Matty offered them leaflets, they were all eager to take them.

D.M. jumped on to a stool and asked for quiet, giving Matty the eye to shush the crowd as well. He pushed an electric bell, which alerted Tom inside the van to begin the lantern show. The first slide appeared and Matty was surprised as a hush fell over the crowd. They listened intently to the life cycle of the fly and its potential to spread disease. A slide showing flies' eggs – much enlarged – drew a comment from a scruffy, ripe-smelling boy standing next to Matty. 'They're not flies' eggs, they're Richmond sausages!'

Matty tapped the boy on the head and he gave her a yellow-toothed grin. He obviously hadn't seen the film about dental care yet. After ten minutes on dysentery, bedbugs and hair lice, the smaller children were becoming fractious, but Matty saw that D.M. was a pro. He ended his lecture with a carrot, the promise of the film, which would follow any questions. A large man, with a bulbous, red drinker's nose, piped up. 'I ain't been sick a day in me life! I puts it down to a pint o' Guinness for breakfast!' And the man patted his stomach.

D.M. looked down at him with a mild, unflustered expression. 'Sir, our concern would not be with your gut—' D.M. was interrupted by roars of laughter as the man had a belly the size of a beer barrel – 'but your liver, which is of course an entirely different part of the anatomy...'

'I know where me liver is!' the man declared and took off his cap to rub his head, at which point Matty saw a definite twinkle in D.M.'s eye.

He raised his voice and announced: 'We have a gentleman here who believes his liver is in his cranium, and in his case it very possibly is!'

Matty saw her chance. She burst into laughter and, joined by those who'd paid more attention to the lantern slides, soon shamed the heckler into silence. After a few more sensible questions Tom fired up the film projector. When the screen lit up and the film started rolling, a little gasp went round the crowd. Matty recognized the old magic of light and dark. The fading dusk had turned the street of crumbling houses into a shadowy, hushed auditorium and now the light of the silver screen, though only four feet wide, had made it into a cinema.

Tom had told her they must pack up quickly once the film was over, as they liked to fit in two showings a night and they were due in Thorburn Square in ten minutes. As she handed more leaflets to the departing audience she felt an insistent tugging on her skirt. She looked round to see an eager face staring up at her. She took a moment to recognize him until a familiar voice asked, 'Can I come round and play your piano?'

'Of course you can, Billy.' His expression was one of such sweet and innocent expectancy she couldn't refuse.

He was taller, thinner, outstripping his strength since she'd seen him last summer. She bent to kiss his cheek, but he grabbed her hand, dragging her towards the margins of the crowd. 'Mum and Sammy's here, Come and see 'em!'

Panic seized her. During the time she hadn't seen Sam and Nellie, she'd been able to surround her heart with a dull cladding, like the black cloth Tom hung in the van to keep out chinks of light. But facing Nellie again threatened to pierce that shroud and Matty wasn't ready to have all those painful places exposed again.

'Billy, I can't, I'm sorry...'

But now Nellie was in front of her, and Sammy, who'd acquired a pair of round spectacles, was demanding to be kissed. Nellie held tight to Albie's hand, and he looked shyly at Matty as if she were a stranger. Nellie had obviously known she was here, had no doubt seen her giving out leaflets, but Matty knew she would never have approached her if it hadn't been for Billy. Nellie was not the sort of woman to go where she was not wanted.

'Billy, leave Aunt Matty alone,' she said, putting her hand on his shoulder.

'Hello, Nellie.'

Nellie gave her a small smile. 'The kids have missed you.'

'Why didn't you come and visit us?' Billy asked.

'She was busy working,' Nellie answered for her.

So that's how they were explaining her absence. Ironic really, considering her weeks of unemployment. Just then Tom hooted the horn of the cinemotor and stuck his head out of the window.

'I'll have to go, we've got another showing.'

As Matty turned away Nellie laid a hand on her arm. 'It's not only the boys. Me and Sam's missed you too, Matty...'

Matty held her gaze, but Nellie was beckoning her across a chasm that Matty couldn't traverse. Try as she might, she could not find the bridge that would span it. She'd allowed an unbearable gulf to open up and it had only grown wider with time. She hesitated, struggling to ignore her own hurt. Part of her longed to throw her arms round Nellie, who perhaps seeing Matty falter, said quickly, 'You're welcome to come round and see the boys any time, stay for tea...'

'Oh, thanks.' But Tom tooted the horn again and the moment was gone. 'Sorry, got to go.' Matty kissed the boys and dashed to the van. Tom gave her a questioning look as she got into the cab, but she shook her head, feeling all her earlier exhilaration drain away.

12

The Value of Light

It seemed strange to see herself on the screen again, but the circumstances couldn't have been more different from those heady Hollywood days. They were watching the TB film for the first time and though her co-star Reggie was undeniably amateurish, she gave herself credit for a good performance under the circumstances. She wrung her hands with worry and hid her face in despair at the deadly diagnosis and then, when Reggie's character was sent off to Switzerland at the borough's expense for the sun cure, she let her face light up with hope, raising her eyes to God in silent prayer. In fact she thought her acting was far more convincing than anything she'd done in *London Affair*.

She'd taken delivery of the film canister that morning, startling herself with an unexpected excitement. They'd met the three musketeers in the large theatre hall in Spa Road Library, where Tom had erected the screen on the stage and Plum took charge of the projector. As the screen flickered to life a memory surfaced of herself sitting next to Frank in that stifling, Hollywood screening room, his body heat uncomfortable, inescapable. Only now did she understand how confined she'd felt, how she'd barely been able to breathe. The memory made her appreciate this dusty, high-ceilinged Victorian auditorium with its wide stage and generous seating, Tom sitting at a cool distance and the three musketeers intent only on whether the message of the film had got through. As the last caption rolled on to the screen there was a moment's silence, before D.M. sprang up and shook her hand.

'Thank you, my dear Miss Gilbie, you were very natural! Very moving.' He took out a large white handkerchief and blew his nose. Then, turning to Tom, he said, 'Make a note never to use Reggie again. The boy's as wooden as the skeleton-room walls!'

Tom went to turn on the lights and bent to whisper in her ear. 'You're a star.'

Matty didn't feel like a star, but she did feel an unexpected sense of freedom, knowing that the film itself was for once far more important than its leading lady.

When Tom suggested a celebratory lunch Matty was surprised. They'd only had lunch together once and she thought perhaps it had been more contact than he was comfortable with, for the offer hadn't been repeated. She was determined this time to keep the conversation work-based. There would be no personal details and certainly no tears.

When they hopped on a bus to the Old Kent Road she guessed where they were going. Beyond the Surrey Canal Bridge the Astoria stretched before them in all its white-stoned elegance. It was a beautiful cinema, and proud uniformed doormen welcomed them, before an usherette led them up the elegant staircase to a tea room in the Grand Circle foyer. Spacious and light, the foyer was bright with many angular mirror panels and geometric glass chandeliers. Round tables and wicker chairs toned down the grandeur but it was as elegant as anything in the West End. The café seemed popular – as well as cinema goers, there were suited businessmen and couples like themselves.

After they'd ordered lunch, Tom asked her if she'd ever played the Astoria.

'No, I missed out on it.' She felt a tinge of regret that she'd never been able to take up Esme's booking. 'They've got *ten* dressing rooms! It's luxury compared to the old Lah di da in Abbey Street!'

'Do you miss it?'

Matty shrugged. 'How can I miss it? I've got myself a new screen career! Didn't you tell me I'm a star?' She gave a laugh that sounded hollow even to her own ears.

'You certainly won over old D.M. He's never been keen on using professionals but it looks like he's your newest fan.'

Leaning back as the waitress placed a bowl of soup in front of him, he flicked the napkin. 'He wants us to show the film next week, we'll be in Vauban Street...'

He hadn't mentioned her meeting with Nellie and the boys at that first screening, but he'd obviously noticed it.

'You seemed a bit frosty with Nellie the other night.'

Is that what it had looked like, a frost? And to her it had felt like the beginnings of a thaw.

'Things change. People disappoint you and sometimes you just can't get past it...'

'You can say that again.' His mouth was set in a tight line and she realized that he was no longer talking about Nellie. She knew she should let it pass.

'If you mean me leaving you, then that's completely different. Nellie went along with a great big bloody lie, all those years. At least I told you the truth. I had to go, for my career.'

'Career' seemed such a cold word, when she said it out loud. But at the time, she'd chosen the thing that warmed her heart the most, her gift, her voice.

'Yes, you couldn't live without the stage. But I know you, Matty, and you can't live without your family either. *That's* why everything went wrong when you went to America.'

'Everything's always so black and white for you, Tom.' She flushed, angry that he thought he could sum up her failures and even more angry that she'd ignored her resolution to stay detached.

'Well then, don't tell me about the men who treated you badly and the choices you regret!' His raised voice drew stares from the couple at a nearby table, and he said more softly, 'I'm just worried about you, that's all.' And he fixed her with his clear gaze until she was forced to look away.

'There's no need.'

'No? Well, I think there is. Perhaps it's none of my business, but how the bloody hell did you get tied up with someone like Rossi?'

It was a good question and one she'd asked herself many times. She shook her head and let out a long sigh. How could she explain to Tom the seductive, sheathed power of someone like Frank, especially when it had seemed to be tamed by one look from her?

'His name was familiar. So I asked Sugar – my old mate from the Elephant Boys – to do a bit of digging around. Seems Rossi's got connections with the Clerkenwell mob. He's mafia.'

She stared at him, saying nothing.

'You've gone white as a sheet. It must be a shock.'

He thought she'd been surprised that Frank was a mobster, but in reality it was the Clerkenwell connection that had caused the blood to drain from her face. The henchman he'd sent to terrorize her had been an American, passing through, or so she thought. But now, like a shadow moving in the darkness, the merest suggestion Frank could be nearer than she thought had the power to freeze her blood. Tom poured her a glass of water. She took a gulp, wishing it was gin.

'I knew what he was. It took me a while to work it out and by then I was up to my neck in his business – there were things I didn't want to know about...' She gave an involuntary shudder. She was ashamed of her naivety, her weakness and most of all that she'd fallen in love with a man she now despised.

'It's easy to get sucked in, Matty. I should know – it took me years to shake off the Elephant mob, but you're never really free. Even now they come sniffing around when they want an inside man in the council. I don't want to tell you what to do, but be careful, Matty. Rossi's a dangerous man.'

Matty hugged herself unconsciously. 'Why do you think I left?' she asked.

*

Matty knew he would come. He looked even taller and skinnier, as if his new burst of growth could only go in one direction, his thin wrists poking out from his blazer sleeves and his shorts now halfway up his thin thighs. Like a fragile, leggy sapling, at ten Billy seemed to be shooting up in search of the light, and it looked to Matty as though he might disappear in the process.

He flung his arms round her and she squeezed him tightly, pulling off his cap to kiss the top of his head. She didn't ask if his parents knew he'd come.

'Want to play the old joanna?' she asked, knowing the answer, and leading him to the front room.

'Is it all right?' His fingers stroked the closed lid.

'Go on,' Matty urged, and watched as the young boy sat down at Eliza's dark brown upright.

He lifted the lid and played a chord, then looked up and smiled, his eyes bright with anticipation. 'Needs a tune!' he said.

'A poor workman always blames his tools, get on with it!' she joked. 'I'll go and make us some tea. Do you want a jam sandwich?'

He shook his head. 'No thanks, Aunt Matty, I'm not hungry.'

Matty could hardly credit that his growing body wasn't crying out to be fed. Perhaps he was just being polite, knowing, as all Bermondsey children did, that not everyone who offered a slice of bread or spoonful of jam necessarily had them to spare.

She made them tea, giving Billy an extra helping of condensed milk, but as she carried them from the kitchen she was halted by the music coming from the old piano. Holding the two cups and saucers, she listened outside the half-open front-room door and peered through.

Billy sat at the piano, head bent over the keyboard in concentration. He'd taken off his blazer and she could see the bony back and shoulder blades protruding through his thin cotton shirt. He was making a pretty good job of a difficult jazz song. 'Street of Dreams' had a changeable melody and a melancholy mood that struck her as an odd choice for a young boy. She leaned softly on

175

the half-closed door, as Billy gave a tinkling run up the minor scale and sang the incongruously world-weary lyric in his unbroken choirboy voice: '*Midnight, you heavy laden, it's midnight. Come on and trade in your old dreams for new. Your new dreams for old. I know where they're bought. I know where they're sold...*'

The floorboard creaked beneath her feet and his head shot up. 'Ain't very good, am I?' He grinned.

She pushed open the door. 'Rubbish. You're doing well! Why d'you pick that one?'

He shrugged and blushed. 'Dad was listening to it on the wireless the other night... He told Mum it reminded him of you. But I liked the words anyway...' he added, perhaps seeing her blanch at the mention of his father.

It was odd to think of Sam talking about her, keeping her fresh in his mind, when all she'd wanted to do was forget him.

'You liked the words?' What broken dreams could he have at his age? But then, she hadn't been much older when she'd made a bid to fulfil her own.

'What do you dream about, Billy?'

He swivelled round on the piano stool. His eyes were bright and two red spots burned on his cheeks. 'Oh, Aunt Matty, I want to be a piano player, more than anything in the world, and I want to go to Goldsmiths College after I leave school.'

'Goldsmiths!'

Poor Billy, she feared that college would be beyond Sam's wages. She remembered her own brother Charlie giving up his chance to go there in those hard wartime days. She wished Billy better luck.

'Play it again.'

He gulped down his tea, and was overtaken by a coughing fit that had him doubled up. As she ran to pat him on the back she realized how fragile he'd become, no longer the sturdy little boy she'd greeted on her return from America. There was a damp patch of sweat on the shirt where she patted him. A chill alarm rippled through her as she put the back of her hand to his forehead.

'You're hot, have you been feeling rough, Billy?'

He shook his head, waiting for the coughing to pass. When he could breathe again she heard a papery wheeze, like a breeze rustling autumn leaves.

'Just bit of a cough and I get achy, but Mum says that's growing pains.'

'All right now?'

Squashing down a dread she wouldn't give a name to, she sat down in the armchair. 'Off you go then, give it your best.'

But this time he stumbled over the key change.

'Shove over,' she said, sitting beside him on the stool.

'Like this.' She began to play.

'Sing it, Aunt Matty.' He leaned his head on her shoulder, watching as her fingers played over the dark and the light keys. 'Sing it for me.'

She took a soft breath in and then, with the out breath, she began very gently to sing to the young boy who had barely lived long enough to have any dreams broken. She sang it like a lullaby.

'Dreams broken in two, can be made like new, on the street of dreams. Gold, silver and gold. All you can hold, is in a moonbeam...'

She sang on, hardly daring to believe what she was hearing, marvelling at how the young boy had drawn from her the voice she thought was lost. And when she was finished, she was astonished to find that Billy had fallen asleep resting on her shoulder.

The next evening found her standing on the familiar doorstep of what had once been her home. It was late enough for Vauban Street to be empty of the usual tribe of children and she hoped that the boys were all in bed by now. Sam opened the door in his shirtsleeves. For a moment he said nothing, and she wondered if she'd even be welcome. She'd assumed, perhaps wrongly, that the injury was hers alone. Then he swung the door wide open. 'Come in, duck, come in.' He smiled and relief surged through her.

Nellie was there, and though the shock was more evident on her face than on Sam's, she was kind enough to try to suppress it. She got up and offered Matty her chair.

'I'll make us some tea,' she said and skirted Matty at an uneasy distance.

Matty couldn't blame her; she'd made herself a stranger after all. 'Are the boys in bed?' she asked Sam, who sat rather rigidly with hands flat on his thighs.

'The little 'uns have been in bed a while. Usually we can't get Billy in off the street, but he took himself up to bed with them too.' He hesitated. 'It's nice to see you, Matty.' He reached for his tobacco pouch and began rolling a cigarette. 'Nellie told me you're working with the borough films. How've you been?'

She supposed she would have to talk about herself, but she didn't want to. How could she explain to him that, in the end, it had nothing to do with her own hurt, or sense of betrayal, it had nothing to do with blame or forgiveness. It was simply her love for a child that had finally bridged the gap. She didn't care how he was related to her, Billy was an ten-year-old child that she loved and would do anything to protect. Understanding that, she understood everything she needed to about the choices Sam, Nellie and Eliza had made for herself at that age.

'I got the sack from Peek's and had to bump on for a while. But things are looking up. The job with the film department's been a lifesaver really.'

He nodded, hardly daring to look at her, intent instead on pulling out loose tobacco strands from his roll-up.

'But in a way that's what's brought me here, Sam. You see, I've learned a lot from working on the films, from the pamphlets and lectures – about all sorts, germs and teeth and looking after children's health...'

At that moment Nellie came in with tea and Matty saw a look pass between her and Sam, a look that said they had talked about this moment of Matty's return many times and had agreed not to pressurize her. That look, more than anything, unlocked Matty's heart. She simply couldn't have it, these two near strangers were the same beloved people who'd got her through the darkest days of her past and who'd supported her while she was forging her glittering future; she refused to have them frightened of her. She put out both hands, one to Sam and the other to Nellie.

She drew them into a long, tight embrace, in which she longed to glue back together all that had been shattered. Matty felt Sam's tears wet her own face and she pulled back, smudging them from his cheek with her thumb.

'Matty, I'm so glad you've come home,' he said in a choked voice and Nellie, who was always called upon to be the strong one, wiped her eyes with the edge of her pinafore.

'I'm glad to be home too, really I am,' she said. 'But there's something important I need to tell you. It's about Billy.'

*

Billy's tuberculosis was not so advanced that there was no hope. How he had caught it was not a question any of them thought to ask. TB was still thick in the air of Bermondsey, the rate of infection still one of the highest in the country, despite the borough's heroic efforts to reduce it with its slum-clearance programme, its propaganda for tuberculin-tested milk, to say nothing of the health education posters and films. All of which hadn't been enough to combat a disease that thrived in the old crowded housing that still formed the bulk of the borough's stock.

The family were ordered into the isolation mode that Matty had acted out in her scenes with Reggie. But to live separate lives in such a cramped house was almost impossible and the doctor said Billy must go to the TB ward in Guy's Hospital. The ward, situated in the oldest, grimmest part of the hospital, was actually little more than a long open-air balcony divided into cubicles. Large shutter windows built into the balcony were propped open, day and night, whatever the weather, and when Matty went to visit Billy the nurse showed her to his cubicle, gave her a mask and warned her sternly against any kissing. She sat in coat and hat, at a heartbreaking distance from the boy, who was in bed, masked and swaddled in several jumpers. He had taken the news with the resilience of youth, confident that his stay would be short and successful. But as she sat in the ward's icy draught Matty's heart quailed. His pallor had deepened to chalk white, relieved only by the brightness of his eyes and the telltale red spots on his cheeks.

'How d'you like your room?' she augmented her speech, muffled by the mask, with a sweep of her hand around the balcony.

His eyes smiled and he sang through his mask. '*A room with a view, and you! With no one to worry us, no one to hurry us...*'

'What a trouper!' She laughed.

But even such a small burst of song seemed to tire him and he let his head fall back on the starched white pillow.

'Tell me about your new film.' His large eyes showed as much eagerness as if she was working for Paramount instead of Bermondsey Borough Council.

'Well, it's all about looking after babies so I don't know if you'll be interested.'

She could see from his eyes that he was pulling a face, but he nodded. Obviously the long hours alone in the hospital had made him eager for diversion.

'We've just started filming at the mother and baby clinic down Grange Road and I play mother, demonstrating making up bottles and giving baby a bath. So there I am looking all calm, trying to keep hold of this wet, squirming, screaming baby and the chief medical officer's in the director's chair, sitting there like George Cukor, saying, "My dear Miss Gilbie, *do* try not to drop baby, there are only so many infants we can acquire in one day!"'

She heard a crackly laugh from behind Billy's mask at her expert impression of D.M.'s clipped tones.

'You know what they say in showbiz, Billy? Never work with animals or children. Well, remember – babies are the worst! I nearly ended up chucking it at him.' But she only put that part in to make Billy laugh. She hadn't wanted to throw the child at all; she'd wanted to keep it. And she hadn't really struggled; she'd been as natural with the child as if it were her own.

On the tram coming home from Guy's she allowed herself to remember the day's filming. It had been like playing at motherhood and it had been sweet and bitter at the same time. She'd needed little of her acting skill to convey maternal love, for that was something which had always run deep in her veins, this love of the small and the helpless, the urge to protect and nurture. In the family it had always been Matty who soothed the crying infants or entertained the young ones. It was an instinct she'd put on hold when she'd left for America and it had been one of the things that had caused her rift with Tom, for he'd wanted to marry and have children. Shooting the new film had stirred up too many suppressed longings and painful regrets. It had been almost unbearably painful holding the baby, which was so much heavier than her own tiny infant. She looked down at her hands now, and she could almost imagine her lost baby nestling there. Perhaps she should tell Tom she couldn't make this one, but he would want to worm out her reason, and that was best left buried, for there were only so many confidences her old lover would be able to tolerate.

She turned her mind to Billy. Sam and Nellie had been devastated by the news, but grateful to Matty. Because of her, the disease had been caught early enough for there to be hope. Nellie had blamed herself for not spotting the telltale signs, though Billy's symptoms weren't severe yet and Matty had only recognized them because of working on the TB film.

But she became increasingly frustrated at his slow progress. Her work in the public health department had taught her that there was always more that could be done, always new methods to try. The films were a case in point. Their MP Dr Salter had been the driving force behind them, even buying the camera equipment out of his own pocket. His work had transformed Bermondsey from an area with one of the highest infant mortality rates to a place where children now survived scarlet fever and diphtheria, with mother and baby clinics, immunization programmes and, above all, in Billy's case, there was the chance for heliotherapy, the sun cure.

Matty had learned the value of light. While making the consumption film she'd seen how it wasn't just fresh air, but also pure sunlight that was needed if Billy was to be saved. Bermondsey, with its huddled buildings crowding out the sky, was not a place that saw much sun. When it did poke its golden disc above the rooftops it had to compete with smoke from a hundred factory chimneys and the yellow pea-soupers that rolled off the Thames. But in an old Victorian house in Grange Road the council was using the new electrification of the borough to mimic the sun's healing rays. There it had set up an array of sun lamps in a solarium clinic, with its own generator to fuel them. Rickety or tubercular children, wearing nothing but white loincloths, powdered with talcum and looking like emaciated pale Mowglis, paraded in a circle beneath the lamps. Billy had been let out of the isolation ward once a week to take his place amongst them, and Matty had hoped that a weekly blast of artificial sunlight might see him improve. But the time had come to admit that he had not.

They were coming to the end of the outdoor screening season. They dropped off D.M. at London Bridge Station and were returning the cinemotor to the depot.

'You're looking down in the dumps,' Tom commented as he pulled out into Tooley Street. 'Is it your Billy?'

'I went to visit him yesterday, and he doesn't seem to be rallying. Surely there should be some improvement by now!'

Tom shot her a sympathetic look. 'Every case is different. He's young and strong—'

'Tom,' Matty interrupted. 'I want him to go to Leysin. I want to get him to Switzerland.'

He looked startled. 'You think he's that bad?' He knew, as

she did, that the borough funded only the worst cases to go to the outdoor sanatorium school in Switzerland.

'Not yet, but I can't wait for him to get to death's door. I'm not sitting around waiting for a miracle, not when I know there's one waiting for him in Leysin.'

Only a handful of Bermondsey children were sent each year to Leysin, and then only when all else had failed and the sunlight of the high Alps was deemed the last hope of curing their tuberculosis. She'd seen a photograph of the children there, lying on beds in the snow, wearing only white hats and loincloths, gradually having their bodies exposed to the strongest sunlight imaginable. Their pale skins, formed in sun-blocked Bermondsey, had to get used to the shock of so much light, but gradually miracles did take place. Skin firmed and muscle toned, while hair began to shine and lungs to clear. In his lectures D.M. called 'Old Sol' the greatest healer *off* the planet, which sometimes got him a laugh. But for Matty it was deadly serious and she had become convinced that Billy's best chance lay in 'Old Sol's' healing rays.

'Do you want me to have a word with D.M.?' Tom asked unexpectedly.

She shook her head. 'No, I wouldn't ask that. It should be me.'

'D.M.'s more likely to listen to me,' he said bluntly as he turned the cinemotor in through the depot gates and switched off the engine.

'You mean more likely to listen to a chap – hysterical females a bit too much for him?'

'He's just known me longer,' Tom explained, but Matty didn't believe him. She'd been a bit of a novelty in the department, and while the three musketeers had welcomed the touch of glamour she brought, she never felt that they took her very seriously.

It was well past ten o'clock and Tom helped her down from the van, offering to walk her home. 'I'll be all right. Bermondsey's lit up brighter than Broadway these days!'

Matty had actually been surprised on her return from America that the borough was still so dependent on gaslight. Sam's house in Vauban Street was lit by gas mantles as were half the houses in Bermondsey. But gradually she'd seen new electric street lamps popping up and the difference was astonishing. The light was cooler and brighter than gas, and suddenly dark alleys and courtyards had begun to reveal their night-time secrets as outdoor knocking shops and thieves' marketplaces. She knew that her route home was now well lit and she still wanted to avoid too much time alone with Tom. He was just about to protest when one of the new electric lamp posts came into view, casting its cool circle of light on the pavement ahead of them. Tom grabbed her arm.

'Blow me, Matty. I think someone's trying to nick the electricity!'

She saw two men kneeling in the circle of light, one plugging what appeared to be a radio accumulator into a lamp post that had been adapted to power the cinemotor.

'How did they get it open?' Matty whispered as Tom pulled her back into the shadows.

'Skeleton key. But I'll have 'em, Matty.' And with that Tom leaped out of the gloomy side court and into the light, shouting *'Police!'* at the top of his lungs.

Matty had never seen two men move so quickly. One ripped the cable from the lamp post and the other picked up the accumulator and ran. She could hear his puffy, wheezy breath from where she stood and he hadn't reached the corner before Tom caught up with him. Launching himself in a rugby tackle, he caught at the man's turn-ups and tugged so hard that he and the accumulator went flying across the cobbles. Tom held on for dear life, but the man was obviously used to escaping from tight spots and was wriggling like a wet eel. Matty sprang forward to help, but by the time she reached Tom, he was sitting on the fog-wet cobbles, the accumulator at his side and a pair of trousers in his hands.

He held them up. 'Wide'oh's gonna have a chilly walk home tonight!'

And they both burst out laughing. 'Was it Wide'oh?'

Tom grinned. 'It was him all right. He went off like a puffing Billy. I could hear him all the way to Tower Bridge Road.'

'Did you see the other one?'

Tom nodded and pulled a face. 'I did and if Freddie Clark's been saying he's gone straight since he got married, then he's telling pork pies! Help us up, Matty.'

She gave him a hand and something shot through her, as if she had been the one caught with her hand stuck in the lamp post, for the jolt she felt would get her into just as much trouble as a hundred volts of electricity, of that much she was sure.

Later that week Tom came to her with D.M.'s answer. 'He looked at all Billy's notes – I told you, he's a good chap. But he just doesn't think the boy's bad enough to warrant it, Matty. They've only got the money to send half a dozen a year.'

'I'm glad I never mentioned it to Sam,' Matty said, feeling more dejected than she wanted to show. It had been good of Tom to ask for her.

Her next visit to Billy was a distressing one. She'd tried cheering him up with the story of Wide'oh.

'He was only trying to nick the electric out of the lamp post! Typical Bermondsey, they'll nick anything, even the light! You should have seen him, Billy, running away in nothing but his underpants!'

Billy loved the story, but laughter had left him breathless so she had to wait patiently for him to voice his request. 'Sing us "Electricity"!' he eventually got out. It was an old music hall favourite she'd once taught him and she immediately got out of her chair and paraded up and down in an imitation of Nellie Power.

> *Moonlight, limelight and the light of day,*
> *Silber light and candlelight are not half so bright.*
> *Gaslight, bude light soon will pass away,*
> *All must take a back seat through electricity.*

Billy tried joining in with the verse, which always made him laugh, though she was sure he didn't fully understood the double entendres.

> *'Twill show us all the funny things folk did when it was dark,*
> *And let us see some spooney couples kissing in the park.*
> *Policemen down the areas then, must look-out or we might,*
> *Find where our pies and cold meat go to by electric light.*

But at the last line he fell back on to the pillows and grabbing his handkerchief from under his pillow, coughed into it till his breath was almost gone. When he lifted his face to her it was deathly pale and all his smiles had vanished.

13

All in the Family

August–September 1931

Tom's office in the town hall was bursting at the seams. As the film department's output had grown there was simply not enough space to store equipment, so they'd been loaned some space in the Fort Road Labour Institute for storing canisters of new film, archived artwork, camera and projectors. Matty was on her way to the institute to pick up some film and as she turned into Fort Road she was greeted by a solid mass of men, hundreds of them, queuing to get in. She'd read in the *South London Press* that the NUWM were planning a march to Westminster in a bid to have the means test withdrawn, and they'd asked for help in putting up hundreds of hunger marchers massing in London from all over the country. The Labour Institute had offered their premises and it was the NUWM's presence there that prompted Matty to volunteer for the errand. The crowd of men and a handful of women were waiting to be given food and somewhere to sleep for the night. They were a cheerful bunch, considering that for some of them the success of their endeavour would determine if their families starved or not. Bursts of laughter punctuated the orderly line and Matty heard scouse and geordie accents in amongst the cockney, but they all seemed universally patient as the long queue inched its way towards the Labour Institute door.

She nipped to the front of the queue, explaining why she'd come, and was let in by volunteers who were directing marchers to the basement canteen, where soup and sandwiches were being served. Matty tagged along, for the film department's store was in the basement, and after retrieving the canister she made her way up to the main lecture hall, which was set up as an operations room for the march. There was a long table where petitions, gathered from all parts of the country, were being counted and put into boxes. In the far corner was another table where organizers had co-opted the telephone; there a couple of young men were studying a map spread out on the table.

One leaned his left elbow on the table, dark hair falling across his face as he bent close to the map. Beside him a lanky young man with a floppy fringe of reddish-gold hair and round spectacles mirrored his position, leaning his right elbow to one side of the map, his left arm flung loosely round his companion's shoulder. They looked like unequal twins, the one stocky and muscular, the other rangy and fine-boned. The tall one stood up, stretching his back, thrusting his hands deep into the pockets of his black trousers, which looked like they might once have belonged to an evening suit but were now paired with a collarless shirt and a threadbare V-neck Fair Isle jumper.

The blond young man looked up at her approach, but the first carried on studying the map, his dirty fingernail resting on a street north of the river. 'I think this is the best place to join the main march. What d'you think, Feathers?'

She'd been certain she would find Will here. Since spotting him on the march down the Blue, she knew he'd thrown in his lot with the NUWM and she'd guessed he'd want to be here, in the thick of it as always. He must have told his friend about her, for she was in no doubt that Feathers had recognized her. He stuck out his hand. 'How do you do – Miss Gilbie, is it? I'm Gerald Fetherstone.'

She shook his hand and waited for Will to acknowledge her, but his dark head stayed bent to the map.

'Will, be a good chap and greet your visitor,' Feathers said, with a pleasant smile.

Matty admired the young man's courage. His ingrained good

manners obviously overrode any fear he might have of rousing Will's quicksilver temper. Will uncurled and forced himself to look at her. She'd seen him only that once, on the NUWM march, since the day he'd torn apart her world, and then his gaze had slid away, whether from dislike or shame, she hadn't been able to discern. Now, looking into the dark, coal-bright eyes, she thought she knew which it had been.

'May we offer you some tea, Miss Gilbie?' Feathers asked, looking as though he might ring for the butler at any minute.

'Thank you, that's kind, Mr Fetherstone, but I think the canteen's a bit busy now.' She looked over her shoulder through the open hall door to the vestibule where a continuing stream of men was visible, making their way down to the basement.

'Nonsense! Will, why don't you take your... umm, Miss Gilbie downstairs. I'll finish the route.'

Matty expected a growl from Will, but she'd obviously misunderstood the balance of his friendship with Feathers, for she saw nothing but a flicker of exasperated affection cross Will's face before he pulled his jacket off the back of a chair and muttered, 'Yes m'lud.'

She took that as an invitation and followed him down to the canteen. Claiming two chairs in the far corner, she watched as Will, holding mugs of steaming tea, negotiated his way round tables crammed with hungry men. The smell coming off the massed bodies added a damp mixture of dust and tobacco smoke to the predominant boiled-cabbage aroma coming from large urns of soup. There was an air of exhilaration in the room. Though experience must have told them otherwise, their faces spoke of a hope that their petition would make a difference this time. Matty understood. She felt better today about Billy because she was doing something, however fruitless it might prove. But so far, thanks to Feathers, it had gone far more smoothly than she could have hoped for. She steeled herself for the next part.

Will handed her the tea, sat down opposite and said something, but the loud chatter and frequent laughter from hundreds of marchers made it impossible to hear and she put her hand to her ear.

'Why've you come here, Matty?' he shouted at her.

She thought of how working men, presenting their petitions to parliament, must feel, surely a far more disconcerting prospect than the one before her. She took a deep breath.

'I've come to borrow some money!' she shouted back, loud enough for a few men to lift their eyes from their soup and stare at her. She heard one of them mumble, 'You'll be lucky, missus.'

Will looked uncomprehending for an instant and then to her surprise he threw back his head and laughed. 'That's a good one! You want to borrow from me? What makes you think I've got anything to give you, you've already had my money!'

'I'm not talking about your mother's money. I'm talking about your father's.'

He shook his head and then gave her a knowing look. 'You really are a little money-grubber aren't you, Matty?' He whistled between his teeth. 'You never know someone until there's money involved.'

'You can talk, Will. You're the one who took me to court and tried to blacken my name over a few hundred pounds I didn't even want.' She felt herself flush with anger at his accusation.

His face had lost its quizzical bemused expression and hardened. 'No, but it seems you've managed to spend it already without too much trouble!'

'You did get one thing right, Will, when you were rifling through my things. Frank was a wrong 'un. I wasn't in debt to him, but I've paid him off anyway because I'm frightened of him. That's where Eliza's money's gone, not on champagne at the Ritz!'

'You've given it all to him! How could you let a man like that get his grubby claws into you, Matty?'

The flash of feeling in his dark eyes was what she'd been waiting for. She'd seen a similar fire in Sam's eyes when it came to protecting his own, and now she grasped on to the glimmer of hope that her quest might not be in vain.

'I made a mistake. Haven't you ever made a mistake, Will?'

He looked at her steadily. 'You know I have...'

It was perhaps the nearest to an apology she would ever get from her pig-headed, opinionated brother, for she had begun to think of him as such, and she didn't look for more.

'I'm not asking for myself. It's for Billy. He's in Guy's with TB and I think he'll die there if I can't get him help.'

'Sam's Billy? Oh no, Matty. I'm sorry, but what help is there? If he's got TB then...' His voice trailed off and she interrupted him before he could voice the usual hopeless reaction to the disease.

'But there is help! Except it's in Switzerland. There's a sanatorium school run by a Dr Rollier. The borough pays to send a few kids there every year, but they've turned Billy down. Will...' She leaned forward, grasping his two hands in hers. 'I know you think you've got no family any more, and to be honest that's the way I felt, after you told me... it all seemed a lie. But I've found out that it's not so easy to shake off your family. They're part of us, Will, don't matter whether we call them brother, uncle, cousin, nephew... I can see Sam and your grandad in your eyes and in spite of everything that's happened between us, I can still feel what it was like to hold you as a little baby. And I can still see Billy, how he was when he was a tot... It's those things that matter, Will.'

She could see that she'd held him and it was as if he were shedding a skin in front of her eyes. The part of him that had been swallowed up by misplaced anger and hurt began to emerge like sunshine through a dense fog. His face seemed to lighten visibly and he let out a deep sigh.

'I'm sorry, Matty. I'd like to help Billy, but I really haven't got any money. Our father left me his money in trust. It only comes to me after I've completed my degree and the way things are, well, I don't think that's going to happen.'

'Why not?'

'I've been rusticated.'

'Rusticated?'

191

'Suspended.'

'What for?'

'Leading a hunger march through Trinity and draping the college quad with banners demanding the end of the means test.'

Matty groaned. 'You idiot, can't you apologize?'

He shook his head. 'No good, I can't go back until next term. Besides, I was thinking of chucking it in altogether. Other things seem more important, like the fact that a quarter of all men in this country are out of work!'

'No, Will, don't do that. My dad... your grandfather, he always dreamed one of his family would go to university. Did you know he passed through there on his way down from Hull on the old penny-farthing?'

Will shook his head.

'Well, he told me the story about when he came to London, looking for work, and on the way he stopped to have a look round King's College and imagined what it would be like to have one of his family go there... He would have been so proud of you, Will.'

'I never knew that about Grandad. Perhaps I should have followed in his footsteps rather than my father's – gone to King's instead of Trinity – then I might have got into less trouble!'

She ran her hands through her hair. 'Oh, I feel I've made such a mess of my life, Will. I had the chance to get out and now look at me... Don't you do the same.'

He looked at her with an expression she couldn't decipher, then said finally, 'I'm sorry, I'd help poor Billy if I could, but as I said, the funds aren't there at the moment.'

'I'll just have to sell the house.'

'No, not Ma's house! There must be another way we can get hold of the money.'

'Get hold of what money?'

Matty and Will looked up, startled. They'd both been so intent on their conversation that they'd failed to notice Feathers approach. Now he pulled up another chair and curled his long fingers around a mug of tea. He raised an eyebrow at Will.

'Planning to rob a bank, dear fellow? Can I come too?'

'Don't get carried away, Feathers. I know you're jealous of my Bermondsey heritage but we're not all villains, you know.'

'I'm not so sure I believe you. What was that charming ditty you taught me... *if you see a copper come, 'it 'im on the 'ead and run*?' He looked pleased with his cockney impersonation, but Matty hadn't been able to lift her deflated mood enough to enjoy it, which must have shown on her face for Feathers' expression turned serious.

'Is there some trouble?' he asked Matty.

'It's a family matter,' she replied awkwardly.

'Feathers knows everything about our family,' Will said, and then, 'he's my best friend.'

'My dear chap.' Feathers smiled in appreciation and stretched his long legs under Will's chair. 'So tell me all about the proposed heist!'

Will asked Matty to explain. When she'd finished Feathers adjusted his spectacles and reached into Will's top pocket for a packet of cigarettes.

'There seems to me only one sensible solution,' he said, offering Matty a cigarette before flipping a silver lighter he'd dug out of his trouser pocket. He took a deep draw and exhaled before finishing his sentence. 'As we're all agreed that none of us is ready to join the Bermondsey mob, I'll lend Will the "bunce" and he can repay me when he comes into his father's money.' He looked from one to the other. 'What? "Bunce" not the right term?'

Matty was surprised at how readily Will agreed to Feathers' offer. But she was grateful that their friendship seemed easy enough to counteract all Will's prickly pride. As she got up to leave, Will was called aside by one of the marchers. Feathers shook her hand and lowered his voice. 'I've told Will many times to make his peace with you, Miss Gilbie. He won't admit this to you, but he realizes what a chump he's been. I should think he'll be grateful for the chance to—'

Here Will returned and interrupted Feathers, but she

understood what the young man had meant to say. The cheque in her pocket was all the evidence she needed to convince her just how much Will wanted to make amends.

She came home to find a letter from Esme. Inside was a clipping from *Variety* magazine. The headline read *Brit Bodyguards for the Stars* and the accompanying photo showed a blonde-haired starlet in front of a flashy mansion, flanked by two fedora-wearing bodyguards. One of them she recognized: it was Frank. Matty felt a wave of nausea at the mere sight of him. Her heart thumped as she read the article about the growing need for film actors and celebrities to have their own bodyguards. Esme had highlighted the final paragraph:

> Frank Rossi, pictured right, provider of bodyguards to some of Hollywood's top celebrities, says that a bodyguard requires very special skills, not only physical strength, but a knowledge of how to protect clients from unwanted interest or an ability to blend in at sophisticated events. He's even begun recruiting from England these days, because, he says, 'Those guys have the sort of class our clients require.' Our photographer caught up with him outside the Los Angeles home of rising star Mia Morgan. She is pictured with Rossi and her new bodyguard Dan Sabini, who hails from Clerkenwell in London. Rossi says he will be visiting family in England shortly, so will be there to hand pick his next recruits!

Matty's hands trembled as she turned to Esme's letter. *I don't want to alarm you, darling,* she wrote, *but I've made some enquiries at various agencies and it seems these Sabinis are a nasty mob from Clerkenwell. If Frank's in contact with them, and he's coming here on a recruiting drive, I thought you should at least be forewarned!*

But Frank wasn't just coming on a 'recruiting drive'. She'd been an avid reader of *Variety* in their days together and she was sure the mention of his 'family' had somehow been for her. There was no family in England, apart from the child he thought he had. Perhaps she was being paranoid, but the idea that his vengeful reach might be extending all the way across the Atlantic sent a cold rush of fear coursing through her.

There was little she could do about Esme's warning, but it had backed up Tom's information and she wished she could talk to him about it. She shoved the clipping and letter into her handbag, hoping she might see him later at the Green Ginger. Freddie had invited her along to wet the new baby's head. His wife, Kitty, came from a big Dockhead family and seemed determined to keep up the tradition. The latest addition was a boy, a cause for celebration as far as Freddie was concerned for they already had two girls and his wife's family had an overabundance of them.

As soon as Matty walked into the Green Ginger, its landlady, Katie Gilbie, pounced on her. Matty knew that in Katie's mind she was a fellow entertainer, but whenever they met it made Matty almost glad she'd given up the business. It was so easy to get stuck in the past, and everything about Katie, from her piled-up hair to her thick stage make-up, fixed the woman at the time of her last great success, a spell at the Rotherhithe Hippodrome before her marriage to cousin George, which had then been followed by a lifetime of pub singing.

'You gonna do a turn for us later?' Katie's smile cracked her thick face powder. 'I heard you was bumping on, why didn't you come to me? You can 'ave as much work as you want here, darlin'. Every night of the week.'

'Thanks, Katie, but I'm working now, got a job with the borough films.'

Katie's face powder creased in disgust. 'Ugh! Who wants to see a film about the inside of yer Newington's? I couldn't stick it for love nor money. You're an artiste, Matty, you don't want to be pissin' about with all that!'

'It suits me, Katie, and if it wasn't for working on those films I don't think we'd have found out about Billy so quickly.'

'Ah, poor little bleeder, how is he? Fancy having to go to a foreign country to get a decent doctor.'

As Matty was telling her about Billy's photograph she saw Tom come in. He nodded a hello and Matty made her escape.

She pushed through the crush to the bar.

'She looked like she had you cornered,' Tom said.

'She's trying to poach me off you, says I'm wasted on films about the digestive tract!'

Tom laughed and ordered drinks.

'Listen, Tom, I've had a letter I want to talk to you about.'

He looked intrigued but said nothing until they were settled at a plush-covered bench.

'What's this letter then?' he asked and Matty handed it to him with the clipping.

His high forehead creased and his clear eyes clouded over. 'The Sabinis!' He gave a low whistle.

'What do you know about them?'

'A nasty lot, belong to the Clerkenwell mob, usually stick to their own turf, though. The only reason they come over this side of the river is to pick a fight with the Elephant Boys. But if Frank's coming over here to work with the Sabinis, then they'll help him track you down. Best lie low, unless you want to see him again?'

'No, Tom, I don't want to see him again.'

She was surprised he'd even asked, but then, she hadn't told him everything.

'Well, it's maybe not such a bad thing you lost your voice, Matty. Perhaps it wouldn't do to be plastered all over the stage bills at the moment.'

'That's typical, just when I've started singing again.'

'Really, when?'

'It happened one day when Billy asked me to sing to him. But it's all right. I like my new film career much better than the old one anyway.'

Tom looked doubtful about that and was going to say something when he stopped abruptly, his eyes fixed on the door. 'It wouldn't hurt to put the feelers out about Rossi, though… and I think the best person for the job's just walked in.'

He stood up and waved. 'Sugar! Over here.'

A man with a close-shaved, knobbly, thick-boned head, his face mostly taken up with a flattened broken nose, turned at the sound of Tom's voice. He broke into a broad, crooked-toothed grin and swaggered over, his two-tone brogues out-turned and his baggy trousers flapping.

''Kin 'ell, Tom – 'scuse me French.' He grinned at Matty. 'I didn't know you'd be here. I thought you'd give us lot the 'eave oh.'

Matty had heard Tom speak about Stan 'Sugar' Sweeting, a foot soldier in the Elephant Boys who'd stayed in the gang when Tom and Freddie had made their escape. She hoped Tom wasn't going to tell him about Frank and tried to indicate with a look that he should keep quiet.

Sugar stared at Matty. 'You ain't half come down in the world, ain't yer? Livin' in a shithole like Bermondsey, bit different to America, eh?'

He was a man whose idea of chivalry was to truncate swear words in the presence of a lady. He lowered his slick-suited, muscly frame on to a bentwood chair. He looked as precarious as a cow on a pinhead, and Matty wanted to reach over to steady him, but his splayed two-toned feet provided the necessary balance. He took a last drag on a dog-end and stubbed it out with nicotine-stained fingers.

'You still working for Nitty Nora?' he asked, pulling at Tom's hair, before cracking an imaginary louse with his thumbnail.

'No, I left the cleansing station ages ago. I'm in the borough film department now.'

Sugar's boney head wobbled from side to side as if weighing up the possible profit in such a place. He twisted a cupped palm behind his back. ''Kin 'ell, King Vidor 'im!' He gave Matty what was supposed to be a playful punch on the arm, which made her wince. 'We could always get rid of some overstock film – if you're interested in a bung.'

Tom laughed and shook his head. 'We use all the film we buy. But you can do something else for me.'

He quickly told Sugar about Frank Rossi and his Sabini bodyguards. Sugar wagged his huge knuckled finger at her. 'Playing with the naughty boys, eh? Should 'a stuck with him, lily white.' Sugar nodded towards Tom. 'Giss a snout, Tommy.' Sugar stuck out a bunch of thick, yellow-stained fingers and Tom obliged with a cigarette. While Sugar was drawing deep, he shot Matty a calculating look and sniffed through his broken nose.

'What's he got on you, this Rossi?'

Matty blushed to the roots of her hair. 'Nothing!'

'She's paid him off.' Tom thankfully lowered his voice.

Sugar narrowed his eyes as he blew out a thin stream of smoke. 'No, blokes like Rossi – they've always got something on you. Go on, you can tell us.'

'That's enough, Sugar.' Tom shot Sugar a warning look and Matty had a glimpse of the tough Elephant Boy he'd once been.

'Don't you worry, gel. I'll keep me mince pies open.' Sugar prodded two forked fingers at his own face so that she thought he might put his eyes out. 'If any Sabini bastards come over this side askin' questions I'll chuck 'em in the Thames and they can swim back to 'kin Clerkenwell.' He choked on his phlegmy laughter.

When Sugar left them to search out Freddie, Matty turned blazing eyes on Tom. 'I asked you for your opinion, not to get me involved in a bloody gang war! What were you thinking of, telling my business to someone like that?'

Tom looked hurt. 'Sugar's all right... to his friends. And he's like a bloodhound, Matty. They use him in the Elephant Boys to sniff out the police plants. It's useful having someone like him on your side. You shouldn't go by appearances.'

'Are you really telling me off for disliking one of your villain friends?' She shook her head in exaggerated disbelief.

'No, I'm just trying to help you shake off one of *your* villain friends!' Tom slammed down his glass and got up.

She put a hand over his. 'I'm sorry, Tom.'

But he wouldn't be placated. 'I could have been like Sugar. It's just he had no one to drag him out of it.'

At that moment Tom's saviour, Freddie, came over and Tom, ignoring Matty's request for privacy, repeated what he'd told Sugar. 'You should 'ave stuck with Tom.' Freddie whistled, gazing at Matty appraisingly.

'I'll leave you two to talk about old times,' Matty said, furious now with them both. 'Oh, I forgot, not such old times in your case, eh, Freddie?' She saw him glance quickly in the direction of his wife. 'I'll just go and say hello to Kitty, shall I? Tell her how lucky she is that her husband didn't electrocute himself on a lamp post last time he was nicking the electricity!'

'Come and sit over here, love,' Nellie called, making room between her and Sam. Sitting opposite was Nellie's youngest brother, Bobby, and his wife, Elsie. Elsie was one of her greatest fans, and in fact, when Elsie was only a young girl, Matty had presented her with a prize at one of the Star's talent contests. Elsie was a rather ethereal-looking young woman, who sometimes seemed to be observing events from another world than this. Not given to shows of affection, she'd always treated Matty with unusual warmth and now she got up and threw her arms round her.

'Here's our Cockney Canary!' Elsie exclaimed with undisguised admiration and Matty smiled back.

However annoyed she'd been with Tom, it had felt good just to have someone to unburden herself to and she allowed the threat of Frank to recede. Here in the Green Ginger, surrounded by people who loved her, she told herself that the Cosa Nostra was not the only family in the world.

14

Fresh Air and Fun

September 1931

Matty couldn't breathe. She was spending another day in the darkest, dirtiest, most suffocating streets Bermondsey had to offer and she was surprised at how oppressed she now felt by its close-crowded houses and alleys. The greatest sense of expansiveness she'd ever known had been on the ship sailing over to New York. The Atlantic had been so boundless she'd sometimes felt giddy with all that limitless sky and endless water. Until then she'd been used to a life bounded by narrow streets, confined by dark theatres, and it had only been since her return that she'd felt the lack of light and air. The voyage home had been as constricting as the outward one had been expansive. She'd spent it sequestered in the cabin along with her grief.

Now they were making a film about the council's slum-clearance programme and were shooting in some of the worst condemned properties at Dockhead, where they found families of a dozen or more living in a couple of rooms. Matty knew the film's intention was good. Showing the contrast between existing slums and the council's new flats was meant to be a stark demonstration of the health benefits of indoor running water, baths built into kitchens, airy courtyards and vermin-free walls. But Matty hated filming people's misery.

They arrived at Mrs Oliver's, the woman whose baby she'd bathed in the *Maternity and Childcare* film. She'd offered to let them film her two rooms in an ancient house off Shad Thames.

It was a narrow place, tilting forward towards the river with only a pub on one side and a warehouse on the other to hold it up. It looked as if it hadn't had a lick of paint since Nelson's time. It certainly had a nautical air, and when they'd first attempted the sagging staircase with all their equipment Matty could have sworn the whole building swayed as if it were buoyed up by the swell of the tide.

Mrs Oliver's baby looked different in its home surroundings. In the clinic, wrapped in a fluffy white towel and freshly powdered, the child had appeared healthy enough; now he looked pinched and sallow. The rooms were gloomy, airless. In one was a double bed and what passed for a kitchen; in the other were two more double beds. Mrs Oliver, with three children under six at home and another three at school, looked as ruined as the building she lived in, and yet she'd swept up, made the effort to put a cloth on the table and had obviously managed to home-wave her hair, which Matty appreciated was no mean feat in ideal conditions let alone surrounded by demanding children.

Dr Connan's interview turned into a stilted affair; he looked out of place in his immaculate suit and made little attempt to put the woman at ease.

'How do you find living here with your husband and six children?'

'Difficult, sir, though we don't complain.' Mrs Oliver spoke nothing but the truth.

'And tell me, do you have an indoor water supply?'

'We don't, sir, but we've got a standpipe at the back we share with the other families, so we can't complain.'

Matty could see D.M. was not getting the best out of her and quickly wrote a question on a slip of paper, sliding it on to the table. D.M. glanced at it and took the advice.

'And so how do you keep your children clean?' Here the baby cried on cue.

'My eldest helps me with the buckets up the stairs before he goes to school, but with the six of 'em, the water soon runs out, and I can't leave the little ones to get more...' And here Matty saw the woman falter. 'I hope I do my best, sir.'

Matty slipped another note across the table.

'Are all your children in good health?' The baby wriggled in the woman's arms.

'Gen'lly, sir, except I lost one to the scarlet fever since I come in these rooms. All the families in this house has had it...' she said defensively, so that D.M. would understand it was nothing to do with her housekeeping. 'And you can't keep the children cooped up in these rooms all day, the windows stick terrible and you can't get no air. So I let the children play in the street, nat'lly they mix. It was only my little Daisy that died of it, though.'

Matty could see that the fractious baby was distracting Mrs Oliver and, in a pause to change film, she offered to take him from her while they resumed the filming. She whispered to Tom as she went out, 'Do a scene with her struggling up the stairs and put one of the kids into the bed...'

She took the baby into the second room and the tightness across her chest increased; the deeper she breathed the less air filled her lungs. She fought with the sticking sash window, fearing the wooden frame would crumble away. Once it was open she held the child close, breathing deeply as air from the nearby river blew into the room. Almost within touching distance, the mast of a ship punctured the sky, and from the open window Matty could see a row of cranes in the docks. She looked up as one swung a bale full of coconuts directly over the sagging roof of Mrs Oliver's house.

She rested her cheek on the baby's soft hair, breathing in the unwashed, milky odour, which reminded her of custard creams. For a guilty moment she allowed herself to imagine this were her own child and a dragging sadness caught her, as she realized her daughter would have been a year old.

'Your mummy couldn't give you a bath, like we showed her, could she?' she asked the child. 'Show me your nails?' She examined the tiny fingers, disappointed that this perfect infant already had the dirt of the docks under its nails, almost an omen for its future. 'If you were mine I'd let you splash in the bath and you'd come out smelling like a rosebud!' She was rewarded with a smile and a giggle from the child. 'Wouldn't you like that?' she whispered. Again she felt the shameful tug of an unnamed desire which involved taking the baby home with her. What she would do with it when they got there, she had no idea, but it frightened her that such an absurd notion could have wormed its way into her heart, like an unwelcome guest that insisted on returning.

She quickly pulled down the sash, and hurried into the neighbouring room to hand over her charge to its mother. The interview was finished and it was Matty's turn to go on. She was playing the housing officer, come to give Mrs Oliver good news. Her home had been condemned and she was on her way to one of the new council flats.

This was a particularly cruel fiction, for it wasn't actually going to happen and the woman would have to continue bringing up her family in two damp rooms until the council could afford to finish another new estate. Mrs Oliver had seemed happy enough to help, but at the end of a day's shooting Matty was almost gagging for breath. She couldn't wait to get out of the crumbling old house, and with the smell of damp clinging to her clothes she refused Tom's offer of a lift home in the cinemotor and ran through the airless maze of streets until she reached the river wall. Only there, with the space of the Thames stretching before her, did she feel able to breathe once more.

That evening, she received a visit from Winnie, who as soon as they'd sat down with their tea asked her, 'Can you ride a bike?'

She put it down to the day she'd had. But when Winnie proposed she come on a trip to Winchester with the Peek's cycling club, though Matty's better judgement warned her to say no, her need for air won out.

'All right,' she said. 'I'll come!'

'Good!' Winnie beamed. 'Now all we need is to find you a bike.'

'Ah well, that won't be a problem,' Matty said with a grin. 'Drink up your tea – we're going round my Sam's!'

They found Sam in his backyard, sitting on a low stool in front of a metal cobbler's last, which Matty recognized as once belonging to their father. He was surrounded by at least a dozen pairs of children's shoes in various states of disrepair. Sam had become so upset by the sight of so many shoeless children in Vauban Street that he'd taken on the task of repairing whatever footwear they had, which were usually only the tattered remnants of uppers and no soles at all. He'd already cut out some soles from a few oddments of leather discarded by Bevingtons' tannery and was now tacking one, with quick double taps, to the smallest pair of shoes, obviously a little girl's. He had a mouthful of tacks but now spat them out when he heard Matty's request.

She wheeled the bicycle out into the centre of the yard, where she paraded it round in a little circle for Winnie's inspection.

'You can't seriously believe you're going anywhere on that!' Winnie said, open-mouthed.

'What's the matter with it?' Matty came to a halt and ran her hand down the front tyre as if it were the flank of a horse.

'What's the matter with it? It's a penny-farthing!'

'Obviously.'

'You'll never get all the way to Winchester on it! Matty, it's a bit late for us to find you a proper bike in time.'

"Bloody cheek! Are you saying my dad's penny-farthing ain't a proper bike?' Sam laughed and came over to show off the penny-farthing. 'I'll clean it up, oil the wheels, give it the once-over. If it could get Dad from Hull to London, it can get Matty to Winchester.'

'Not if she comes a cropper on the Old Kent Road it won't.'

Matty gave Winnie a sour smile. 'I won't! Anyway, I'm taller than Nellie and if she could ride it, so can I! Now get out me way.' And with one foot expertly on the back bar, she scooted with her other foot and swung effortlessly up on to the seat. Luckily, she'd been wearing some wide-legged trousers – the only ones she possessed, and perhaps a little too elegant, having been designed for a Hollywood poolside.

She took delight in nearly knocking Winnie off her feet as she circled the yard.

'See, you never forget!'

'Where d'you learn that?' Winnie seemed delighted.

'I taught her when she was a little 'un,' Sam said. 'All the kids in the family have been up on that penny-farthing one time or another, but with her height and balance she's a natural.'

Matty pulled on the spoon break and hopped off, taking a little bow.

'I don't know how you'll manage hills and rough roads? It'll be bloody hard work.' Winnie was still unconvinced.

'You'll be racing to keep up with her,' Sam said, nodding his head sagely.

'Well, I can't afford a second-hand bike, so it's this or nothing.'

Eventually Winnie agreed to a few practice runs and, being very slow on her own bike, proved an ideal cycling companion. Soon Matty had the confidence to believe Sam's predictions that she would be leading the band all the way to Winchester.

It was only when the little party of cyclists gathered outside Bermondsey Town Hall in Spa Road early one morning that she realized what Winnie had done. Tom was standing beside a bicycle and she didn't think he was there to see Winnie off. When he saw her, he looked as surprised as she felt and she nodded a hello, before pulling Winnie aside.

'Why didn't you tell me he was coming!'

She felt immediately awkward. Sharing her troubles and her worries about Frank with Tom had gone some way to reviving her closeness to him, but at work he was still her boss and she'd noticed he was careful never to let the conversation drift to their shared past. She really wasn't sure exactly how far he wanted their rediscovered friendship to go, but she did know it was impossible to imagine going away on holiday with him.

'Surprise!' And Winnie gave a mischievous smile. 'I've got my chap with me, so I thought you should have one too!'

Matty drew stares and cheerful encouragement all the way through London, and not only because of her ancient method of transport. Instead of the usual shorts and shirt, she wore the wide, high-waisted trousers with a red silk blouse and matching bandana to hold her waves in place. Just because she was on an outdoor holiday she didn't see why she had to look like a khaki sack and if she was going to draw attention, she might as well put on a good show. With her drop earrings and red lipstick she did not look the typical cyclist. At one point Tom drew level and shouted up at her. 'How's the air up there?'

'Rare, dear boy, very rare!' she said in a clipped Gertie Lawrence impersonation.

'Talk about lying low!'

The reminder of Frank's possible re-emergence clouded her sunny mood for an instant, but on a day that had turned brilliant with sunshine she refused to accept she must live her life in the shadows. Besides, the threat from the Sabinis hadn't materialized and though she knew Tom had been in touch with Sugar, no reports had come back. She so wanted to be free, and the further from London they rode the more expansive she felt. Atop her father's old penny-farthing she realized the exhilaration he must have felt, bowling along half-empty roads, making his own escape from poverty all those years ago. Tears stung her eyes, partly from the warm breeze whipping into her face, partly from the memory of Michael Gilbie, the man she still thought of as her father. How hard he'd worked for his children and how much he'd dreamed. It was only now that she understood how deeply losing Eliza had wounded him and why he'd gone along with the fiction that Matty was his daughter. She was beginning to accept that it wasn't such a bad thing, to have become his second ray of sunshine – a replacement for the one that had disappeared from his life forever.

On flat ground Matty found Sam's prediction coming true, she could outstrip the others easily, though she didn't dare for fear of losing the way, but on hills it was harder and she was glad of the strong calf muscles she'd developed through all those dancing years practising shuffle-ball changes. They broke their journey near a farm outside Crookham and Winnie immediately collapsed on to the grass.

'Me legs are killing me!' she complained, rolling over on to her front so that Matty could inspect her 'biscuit legs', with their network of varicose veins running up the calves, brought about by long hours spent standing at a bench every day.

'Perhaps they'll go down with all this exercise,' Matty said hopefully, rubbing the backs of Winnie's legs.

Winnie rolled on to her back and patted her stomach. 'I'm hoping they won't be the only thing going down,' she said, reaching for her saddlebag and the sandwiches she'd packed. 'I don't know how you do it, up on that contraption, Matty.' She offered Matty a meat-paste sandwich.

'It's not too bad when you get going – it's the starting and stopping that's hardest.'

As the others munched on their sandwiches and drank bottles of cold tea, Matty leaned back on her elbows. Gazing at nothing but a wide blue sky and green fields, listening to the buzzing of flies and the cows' baritone chorus coming from beyond the hedge, she realized she was happy. For too long her spirit seemed to have been crushed into the smallest of spaces, but today she felt able to breathe.

Her musings were interrupted by Wally, one of their party, who strolled over to where she sat.

'Giss a go on your bike, Matty,' he asked. He'd been angling to have a go on the penny-farthing ever since they set off.

It turned out Winnie had not only invited Tom on the trip, she'd also invited 'her chap' Wally. He'd been Tom's boyhood friend and someone Matty knew from her days at the Star, where he'd once been a novelty act. Known as 'Wally the Wonder Wheel', he was a trick cyclist who would ride a unicycle across a slack line stretched from one end of the stage to the other. But like herself, he'd found it hard to stay in work when the old variety theatres started changing to cinemas.

Before she had a chance to say no Wally reached for the bike, which she'd propped against a hedge. She jumped up to stop him, but he'd already started scooting away.

'Oh bloody hell, no!' she said, looking round at Tom. 'I'll be spending the rest of my holiday here unless he's improved!'

The others laughed because the thing about Wally the Wonder Wheel was that his act had always been a disaster and he spent more time on the boards than on his unicycle. In the end Bernie had kept him on as a comedy act – the more times he tumbled off the rope, the louder the laughs he got. He'd confided to Matty that he'd recently quit the stage and had found much more success in his new career as an insurance salesman.

'You'd better run after him then,' Tom said.

'Very helpful!' Matty cracked him on the head as she sprang up and trotted downhill after Wally. Unfortunately, the gradient was a little steeper than he'd anticipated and to her horror she saw him heading straight into the path of an oncoming pale blue coupé, with its cream soft top down, which was taking the bend at speed. She could see Wally fumbling to find the spoon brake.

'Swerve, Wally! Swerve!' she called. And in the nick of time, he wrenched the large front wheel to the right, veering off the road and straight into the hedge as the car sped by with a loud blast of its horn. Used to falling from heights, Wally somersaulted into a field of curious cows, leaving the penny-farthing sticking out of the hedge. The others ran up and were just in time to see Wally the Wonder Wheel sitting disconsolately in the middle of a wet cowpat.

'Walter, you idiot!'

'Sorry, Matty, is the bike all right?'

'Yes, but no thanks to you!'

Matty took possession of the penny-farthing and they set off on the Winchester road, but the episode had delayed them and it wasn't until late afternoon that the square tower and long nave of Winchester Cathedral came into view. They halted on high ground just beyond the town. Matty jumped down while the others stayed on their bikes. The day had been one of intense sunshine and the accumulated heat seemed to radiate off the surrounding fields and trees. Golden, late afternoon light gilded all the green and the cathedral tower itself seemed made of precious metal. Matty's eyes rested on a sky of rich cloudless blue, wide and seamless. She cast her mind back to Mrs Oliver, bringing up her baby in that gloomy tunnel of a street near Dockhead. At least she didn't have to watch her child growing up without space and air, or without sights that could feed a growing soul.

She breathed in deeply and suddenly Tom was at her side.

'I think we'll have company waiting for us, when we get to Winchester,' he whispered.

'Good company?' she asked, puzzled.

And he shook his head. 'That blue coupé on the road – I think I know who the driver is, and no, I wouldn't say he was your idea of good company.'

When they finally arrived in Winchester they were all weary and hungry, but as they wheeled their bikes across the ancient stone bridge that led into the town Matty stopped, enchanted at the sight before her.

'Is that it?' she pointed to an old watermill, built on arches spanning the River Itchen. A steeply pitched red-tile roof sat on low red brick walls, punctured by leaded windows. Matty could make out the massive wooden wheel churning at its heart, spewing white water down a mill race towards the bridge on which they stood. Tom had told her they were staying in a youth hostel, which she'd balked at, fearing that at twenty-eight she was too old, but he assured her that youth was fluid when it came to business, and whatever their age the youth hostel would welcome their shillings.

'Well, I can't see any other watermills about, so I reckon it is,' Tom replied.

'But you said it was disused.'

'It doesn't make flour any more, but the wheel keeps turning, just the same,' Tom explained.

Inside, the hostel was even more of a surprise. It was packed to its substantial oak rafters with bare-kneed boys and girls. Every hiker and cyclist in England seemed to have been lured out by the good weather. There was a large party of noisy boy scouts, a Methodist girls' club and several Americans, as well as themselves, and the warden informed them the dormitories were at capacity. She was a jolly woman who, as Tom suspected, hadn't asked for their ages, but perhaps had noted they were older than the other guests.

'We do have alternative accommodation which might suit you better than the dorms – the boy scouts can be rather boisterous,' the warden offered. She beckoned them to follow, leading the way through a high-ceilinged common room supported by massive beams which had once formed the lower level of the mill. It was furnished sparsely with tables and some wicker chairs, and from there a tiny back door led into a sun-dappled boat-shaped garden. Matty was enchanted. The garden was actually an island bounded on each side by the River Itchen. One stream thundered beneath the arches of the mill race and the other flowed more sedately round the mill, the two joining at the bridge in front of the mill. It was a pretty place, with a low wall all round and a central flower bed. On either side of the flowers a dozen cot beds had been set up.

'Six on this side for boys and six on the other for girls,' the warden explained.

Tom looked enquiringly at Matty. 'Might be better than a stifling dorm?'

'A lot better than a dozen noisy boy scouts!'

Matty liked the idea of sleeping under the stars and so she and Tom claimed their beds for the night, but the others, not feeling so hardy, went off to find the dorms.

'We have cooking facilities, if you've brought your own

provisions, and there are sinks for washing, but if you want a bracing bath most guests opt for the mill stream!' the warden announced before bustling off to help the others find their beds.

Tom and Matty leaned on the low wall and looked up towards the mill race, where water frothed and churned as it was forced beneath the arches and on to the great paddle wheel.

'You don't think she meant we're expected to get into that?'

'I think she did, these YHA types are a tough bunch!'

Matty shivered in spite of the late afternoon sun warming the top of her head as she leaned further over the wall, craning her neck to look into the water's depths.

The jolly warden, as well as suggesting a bath in the mill stream, had told them a moonlit walk to see the cathedral was a must and when Tom offered to go with her, Matty, taken by surprise, felt a fluttering excitement brush her, like a moth blundering blindly against her face. It seemed cruel to squash it but, ruthless, she did exactly that.

'Oh, don't worry if you're tired, I can have a wander on my own.'

But he insisted and as the moon rose they walked through the ancient town until they came to the cathedral, its long many-windowed nave stretched away from them, the moon's silver disc held aloft on the pointed tip of one of the turrets. Pale light washed down the huge west-front windows and rippled across cobbles to where they stood, looking up.

'The warden was right, it is lovely,' Matty said as they began a circuit round the old walls.

'We can climb the tower tomorrow if you like. You can see for miles.'

'Oh, I'd like that.' The thought of being on such a high perch only added to the sense of expansion and freedom she'd felt since they set off from Bermondsey. 'Can you believe we were in Bermondsey this morning? It feels like another life!'

'Well, it is. Another life, another world. But you should be used to that – you can't get much further away than America.' He hesitated. 'I never told you that I missed you.'

The heat of the day had persisted into the evening, which was hot enough for Matty to have come out without her jacket. But now a flush of heat spread up from her neck, reaching her cheeks, so that she was glad of the night to hide the effect of Tom's words.

She was aware of his clear hazel eyes turned to her and the silence hung as heavy as the heat between them. He reached out to put an arm round her shoulders and for a moment she felt the memory of his body, the exact weight of his arm and the solidness of his torso, and then she pulled away. He was right. She had been far away, in another world, another life, and though the old attraction she felt for him was undoubtedly still there, rekindling it would require facing truths about the past three years which surely were better left hidden.

'I don't think that's a good idea, Tom.'

Immediately he let go, stepping away. 'Sorry, you're right, Matty. It's just...'

'The moon?'

'Yes, the moon.' Tom gave an embarrassed laugh and looked down at her. She studied his face to see if he meant it. His finely shaped nose and high forehead were picked out by the moonlight, the laugh still lingered on his lips, but his eyes betrayed him with the sort of yearning which had once sent her flying to America with its implicit demands, but which now felt part of the unfettered delight that had swept her along on the old penny-farthing all the way from London.

'It's been such a lovely day, Tom...'

'And we don't want to spoil it...'

'No.'

They walked back in a silence which didn't feel awkward to Matty: she was grateful for its allowing her time to think. It seemed fruitless to compare her feelings now to those she'd had for Tom six years ago. Everything since then had conspired to dismantle the Matty she'd been, every certainty that had made her who she was had disappeared and the Matty who'd been put back together was a different person, and perhaps it was time to let the old Matty go.

As they approached the mill she stopped, laying a hand on Tom's arm. 'Is that who you promised would be waiting for us?' And she pointed to a blue coupé, parked near the bridge. As they drew nearer, a man got out.

'What the bloody hell's he doing here?' she hissed at Tom.

'I don't know, but I'm sure it's not for the medieval architecture, Matty,' Tom said.

'Hello, me old china, fancy seein' you here!' Sugar's brash voice boomed over the rushing of the mill race. He strolled towards them, grinning. His pale, sharp summer suit and jaunty white motoring cap seemed to glow in the moonlight, only serving to draw attention to the battered, bony face beneath. When he smiled at Matty she noticed he'd lost another tooth.

''Kin place this is to find, what are you staying in a bleeding barn for?' He shook Tom's hand. 'Can't he afford to take you nowhere decent?' he asked, giving Matty an unwanted kiss on the cheek. Sugar stared, unimpressed, at the mill.

'What's happened?' Tom asked and Matty thought he had grown paler.

'Thought you should know a feller from Clerkenwell come sniffing around – about her.'

'What did you do to him?' Matty's look of alarm wasn't lost on him.

'I didn't touch him! I just got Bernie to tell him you've left the business and gone up north where your family comes from. That was the story, wasn't it?' He looked enquiringly at Tom.

'Bernie? From the Star? How do you know him?' Matty asked.

'Cos he was the one told me about the feller in the first place.'

Matty was confused; she was pretty sure Bernie had no connections with the Elephant Boys. 'Why would he do that?'

She noticed Tom give a small shake of the head and Sugar grinned.

'Sorry, mate, put me size twelves in it.'

'Tom! Did you tell Bernie about Frank?'

He put his hands up. 'Before you jump, he already knew something went wrong with Rossi. I just asked him to tell Sugar if anyone came looking for you, that's all.'

She supposed she ought to be grateful, but she felt suddenly powerless.

'I know you mean it for the best, but can you tell me in future before you start bringing that man into my friends' lives. I don't want people I care about caught up in my mess.' Perhaps she'd spoken more sharply than she intended. Tom looked hurt and Sugar scratched the back of his head before adding, 'But there's another thing I found out. Rossi got busted for booze running.'

Matty felt a surge of relief almost knock her off her feet. 'He's in prison?'

Tom broke into a smile. 'Looks like your problem just went away, Matty!'

But Sugar gave a long sniff and Tom asked sharply, 'What?'

'Rossi done a runner, probably halfway to Canada by now, and the word is he's on his way.'

'Where, here?' Matty asked in a small voice.

And Sugar nodded his bony head.

After Sugar had sped off in his blue coupé, waking the quiet streets, Matty and Tom went into the mill through the side door and crept out to the garden, where dark mounds revealed the already sleeping forms of other guests. Matty went to one side and Tom the other, but their beds were head to head, with only the sunflowers between them. It was still so hot and muggy that she lay on top of the blanket. Listening to the rushing mill race and the endless groaning of the wooden wheel, she became aware of Tom's breathing coming from the darkness on the far side of the sunflowers.

'Tom, are you awake?' she asked softly.

'Yes,' he said.

'What I said earlier, about not wanting the people I care about caught up in my mess... that includes you.'

There was a silence, filled by the rushing of the stream, and she thought he wouldn't answer.

'I'm only keeping my eyes and ears open...'

'But it's the Elephant Boys that are doing the looking for you... it's a favour and they'll want something from you. Don't go back for me, Tom.'

15

Through the Mill

September–October 1931

It took her a few minutes to realize where she was. Then she became aware firstly that Frank was perhaps even now boarding a ship in Canada bound for Southampton and secondly that every muscle in her body was making some kind of protest. And for a moment she couldn't make up her mind which bothered her most. She attempted to move the part of her body that hurt least – her head. Pain shot across her shoulders and up the back of her neck. She lay very still with eyes closed. She was hot. She felt sun dappling her face as it penetrated the shade of a small tree growing on the island garden. If it was already this hot then it must be late. Sweat trickled unpleasantly down the nape of her neck and she felt clammy with sleep. A deep insistent groaning pierced her awareness. It was the great wheel turning. As the mill race made its roiling presence known, her eyes snapped open.

'Tom?'

There was no answer. She would have to get up. She might just manage it in stages. Tentatively easing herself up on to her elbows, a string of pain shot down her back and she cursed the penny-farthing, straightening up an inch at a time. How could this have happened? She should have known riding eighty miles on an old boneshaker must have its consequences, but she'd been fine when she went to bed. Planting her feet firmly on the paving stones and her hands on the sides of the cot she pushed herself up. Her thighs caught fire and she let out a groan that rivalled the gears of the mill wheel.

She wasn't quite straight, but at least she was standing. Every bed in the garden was empty, with blankets neatly folded on top of mattresses. Only then did she hear the splashing, shouts and high-pitched boys' laughter coming from the mill race. She leaned over the low wall, looking back to where the water rushed white beneath the arches of the mill house. She couldn't see anyone and, intrigued, hobbled towards the steeply roofed mill, stretching tight calf muscles as she ducked through the low garden door and into the mill's cool interior.

The warden had showed them the most popular place to bathe, a cavern-like spot directly beneath the mill, just where the stream forced itself through the narrowest part of the race. She made her way down some stone steps and stopped to peer over a railing. Water splashed up at her as the stream charged down the race, flinging itself into the paddle wheel. It was dim here and deliciously cool. Daylight filtered in beneath the arch, reflecting off the water. The echoing shouts grew louder and she finally saw the source of the noise. Half a dozen white-skinned, whooping boy scouts were being tossed about by the churning river. They each grasped on to ropes attached to an old beam above the race, the force of the flood lifting them almost horizontal in the water. She feared they must soon be swept on to the wheel, when she noticed that the ropes were firmly knotted around their waists.

'Fancy a dip?' a voice shouted in her ear and she jumped. She hadn't heard him come down the steps.

'Tom! Why didn't you wake me up?'

'You were sound asleep!'

'I was like an old woman when I got up!'

He put his hand to his ear and she shouted, 'Me bones was creaking!' and mimicked an old woman's bent walk for him.

'Are you coming in?' she asked.

'In there? I wasn't being serious!'

'We might as well be cool at least once today.'

217

Every bit of her felt on fire, from her muscles to her skin. And the boys frolicking in the water chute looked to Matty as cool as Antonio's ice-cream cart.

Tom looked doubtful.

'Oh, come on! The warden said she's got bathing costumes we can use.'

Tom didn't take too much persuading and by the time they'd found the bathing suits and changed, the boy scouts were gone. Tom pulled up the ropes and they tied them tight around their waists.

'You sure you want to?' he asked before they took the plunge.

'Of course! Don't forget I've flown over Never Never Land before now – when I played Peter Pan! Come on, Wendy!' She laughed up at him as she lowered herself down the rope. 'I'll teach you how to fly...'

But the shock of the cold water took her breath away and seemed to collapse her lungs, so that she could only open her mouth to draw in breath, and further speech was out of the question. Immediately the surge of water seized her feet, forcing her horizontal, so that she really did feel as if she was flying in the foam. She was gasping when Tom dropped into the millstream beside her.

'Whooo!' he yelled with exhilaration. Both at full stretch now, they appeared to be flying side by side.

'Awfully big adventure!' she shouted above the thundering millstream, but swallowed what felt like a gallon of water and immediately shut her mouth tight.

The water flung them around, spinning them on the ropes, so that they bumped into each other and their legs got tangled up. Tom somehow twisted himself round to face her and like a high-wire act on a trapeze swung himself till he was close enough to steal a kiss, which she barely felt as her lips were now as icy as the water. She certainly wasn't going to let go of the rope to push him away, but the water parted them and as it did so she felt something give. Her hands slid down the slippery rope under the weight of her own body. The fastening around her waist had loosened and she felt it uncoil and drop to her feet. Tom must have seen her expression turn to one of fear. 'Sorry, sorry!' he shouted, thinking she had reacted to his kiss.

'It's all right...' She choked, wanting to explain, but muscles already weakened by yesterday's exertions now gave into the force of the water and she was swept away from him by the angry tide that grabbed her, flinging her from the rope and into the maelstrom.

Tossed into the onrushing torrent, her only thought was that she would die soon, caught on the flailing oak paddles which had turned ceaselessly for generations. She fought the momentum, struggling to push against the water, fumbling for a handhold, but her mouth, eyes and ears were full of a drowning white foam and suddenly it seemed easier to just let go. Her mind was as cold as her lips and she closed her eyes, serene almost as she was drawn deeper into the race, not frightened of being broken on the wheel, for she knew that had already happened.

Who had pulled her hair so painfully? It must have been Tinkerbelle, jealous of a kiss between Peter and Wendy. Matty knew she'd been transported to Never Never Land, because she certainly wasn't dead and the pain where the vicious little fairy had pulled at her hair was real enough.

'Oh, thank God!' She heard his voice from far off and felt Tom's lips warm on her own.

'Did that fairy pull my hair?' she mumbled into his mouth and felt herself gathered up into wet, strong arms. 'Oh, Matty darling.' He half sobbed, half laughed with relief and squeezed her tightly. 'That bloody fairy was me!'

Then she remembered and knew why she wasn't dead. It was Tom who'd grabbed her hair as she slipped beneath the water, hauled her up and clasped her to him. Somehow he'd managed to swing them, Tarzan-like, to the edge of the gantry and had pulled her out.

Now she lay in his arms, in the cool damp cavern, water dripping from them both on to the stone floor, and when Tom's heaving breaths subsided, he turned to her.

'I'm so sorry, Matty, you could have died and it was my fault. I distracted you... I shouldn't have kissed you.'

'Idiot, a kiss never killed anyone – the rope just came loose. It wasn't your fault, Tom.'

'Still...'

She put a finger to his lips. 'Shh, help me sit up.'

When they were sitting up, with their backs to the dank stone wall, Matty said, 'Let's not tell the others, Tom.'

'All right, our secret.'

She turned her head so she could see his face. 'You saved my life. I could have dragged you under, Tom. You should have let me go.'

He put his hand to her still damp cheek and then brushed away a wet strand of hair.

'I never did let you go, Matty. Don't you know that?'

She dropped her cheek so that his hand was a cradle for her weary head. She felt tears sting her eyes. 'I never appreciated you, Tom. I didn't understand back then what you were offering me. I was so frightened if I married you I'd never be able to be me again, and like a bloody fool I ran away straight into the arms of someone who didn't even know who I was, and since I've been back... well, neither do I.'

'Oh, Matty, I know who you are. Let me remind you?'

She shook her head. 'It doesn't work like that, Tom. Everything that made me Matty Gilbie seems to have been taken away.'

She tasted salt tears mingling with the water that still dripped down her cheeks and she curled into Tom's chest, letting him hold her tight.

'You'll find out who she is. I see her every day and I promise you...' here he lowered his voice, so that she could barely hear him above the rushing water, 'she's every bit as wonderful as the old Matty Gilbie.'

'When I meet her I'll let you know.' She gave a wry smile and drew away.

'Matty, I still love you,' he said, with a tremble in his voice.

'I know.'

How long she'd known she couldn't say, but right now her heart was gripped, not with fear of what he might demand of her, but with surprise, for she found the new Matty Gilbie's feelings for Tom were totally different from the old.

'And I love you too,' she said simply, getting to her feet. 'Come on, the others will be looking for us.'

She took his hand and led him towards the stone stairs, but before they went up into the brightness of the day, she turned to kiss him. When he pulled away, the clear hazel eyes were flecked with gold, full of joy and surprise.

'You really do, don't you?'

'Yes.' And taking each other's hand once more, they went back up into the garden. Already bathed in sunshine, the flagstones were hot to her feet and warmth flooded her body. She felt a surge of joy stronger than the mill race, strong enough to wash away all her fear of Frank, strong enough to convince her of a brighter tomorrow for the new Matty Gilbie.

*

When they arrived back in Bermondsey Matty didn't feel the sense of claustrophobia in its densely packed streets that she'd suffered ever since her return from America. Perhaps she'd just got used to being home, but she suspected it had more to do with her expansive heart. It was proving as wide an open space as the Atlantic Ocean or the green hills of England. And Tom's love, far from taking up too much space as it had once seemed to do, now seemed to push up the sky and open out the river as they went for long walks in Greenwich Park or over to the Tower of London.

The Indian summer heralded another round of street screenings for the cinemotor and the heat meant even greater crowds, for everyone seemed to have abandoned their houses. Old ladies sat sentinel at their doorsteps, chatting or dozing, mothers pulled out their long tin baths into the streets, filling them with bucket after bucket of cold water, so that courts and alleys began to resemble lidos of connected zinc baths full of bare-chested children splashing around with that particular excitement brought on by open-air bathing. The heat was less fun for Tom as he operated the projector, stuffed into what was no more than a tin can with a few air slits.

They had been expecting a big crowd. As they turned into the courtyard of one of the newest council flats, they were greeted by a cheering mass of children, who ran towards the van, surrounding it in seconds, forcing Tom to slow to a crawl. They stopped in the centre of a courtyard fronted by long communal balconies which formed a natural amphitheatre. Matty jumped down from the van and, glancing up, noticed that on every floor people were already in prime positions for the show. Leaning elbows on balcony railings, craning necks for a first view of the cinemotor, the atmosphere was more like the tuppeny rush at the Trocadero than a council estate. Dr Connan stood on his stool while Tom elbowed curious children out of the way so that he could get inside the van. One of the first lessons Matty had learned was that street crowds were impatient. Any delay in setting up and they started their own entertainment, which could range from hurling insults about the films to lobbing rotten fruit at D.M.'s bowler hat. He always wore a special one for screenings, as battered and many hued as a warrior's shield.

Today the heat wasn't their friend. When Tom started up the projector it became obvious that the film had somehow stretched, resulting in a less than perfect viewing experience for the audience.

'Rubbish!' A bare-chested boy of fourteen began the heckling. 'We can't see nuffin!'

The bottom of one frame and the top of another was in view on the screen and poor Tom couldn't get the reel in synch. The film was meant to be mildly comedic, with the punning title of *Where There's Life There's Soap*, an encouragement to personal cleanliness and a warning against the perils of an unhygienic lifestyle. It featured a back view of a balding man, looking suspiciously like Dr Salter, who removed his hat to reveal a huge sebaceous cyst sitting on the top of his domed head. Unfortunately, it was now that a wit on the first-floor balcony decided it was his time to shine.

'Looks like one of my old gel's tits!'

Laughter drowned out D.M. as he tried to calm the fractious crowd, who now began stamping their feet. Matty felt a riot coming on. Poor D.M. was still appealing to the crowd's better nature, when a well-aimed stone shot his bowler hat from his head. As catcalls rained from the balconies, Matty stepped in. She banged on the side of the van and hissed through the louvres. 'Tom, I'm going on. Pull the film and sort it out for gawd's sake before they kill us!'

She jumped up on to the back platform of the cinemotor, with the screen behind her. Tom had put up a lantern slide of a tooth while he rewound the film. She lifted her arms, inviting them all to join in, and then filled her lungs. In a voice that she hadn't used since her earliest days at the Star, she launched into her famous Nellie Wallace impersonation with 'I Don't Like My Mother's Pie Crust'.

> *Tonight I'm alone, broken-hearted, to mother*
> *I've murmured "goodbye".*
> *From the home of my youth I've departed,*
> *with a tear in my bonny blue eye.*

As the crowd recognized the old favourite their heckling subsided and, encouraged, Matty soldiered on.

> *Forget all my troubles I can't tho' I try, there's*
> *only one thing left for me su-ic-ide!*

At this point she heard an exaggerated '*ci-hi-hi-hide!*' go round the balconies and yelled up to them. 'I can't hear you up there in the posh seats!' Singing over the laughter in the crowd, she flung herself into the chorus as everyone joined in.

> *I don't like my mother's pie crust. Eat it?*
> *No, I'd sooner die fust!*
> *I've tied it round me neck, and tomorrow I shall be,*
> *down at the bottom of the deep blue sea!*

When, by the end of the second verse, she had them in the palm of her hand, a part of her wanted to carry on. It was the most fun she'd had on stage in years, but this time she wasn't the star. She had to turn their attention back to the main event, so she followed with 'My Sweet Hortense', seguing neatly from the real lyrics of *'She's got two teeth in her mouth, the one points north and the other points south'* to the electric-sign version: *'My teeth are bad, my health is poor, I use no brush you may be sure!'* She glanced quickly behind her, relieved to see Dr Salter's bald head was back on screen. She brought her turn to an end with a Bernie flourish – 'I give you our own, our very own master of medical mysteries, Dr D. M. Connan!' The chief medical officer, who had never been greeted with such thunderous applause, took a bow and Matty shouted into the back of the van.

'Roll the film, Tom!'

Dr Connan was so pleased with Matty's crowd control that he insisted her little act should become a regular feature of the screenings. From then on they experienced far less panic when setting up or switching between lantern slides and films, as Matty expertly bridged the time gap, keeping the crowd occupied. Now that she had found her voice, Tom suggested another innovation.

'Why don't we go into talkies! You could sing the verse captions and we could get D.M. to record his lecture, so he wouldn't have to attend every showing. What do you think?'

'The borough could never afford it. Do you know how much sound equipment costs?'

'No, I don't, but you could find out for me.'

He was so enthusiastic she didn't like to dampen his excitement. But she knew for a fact D.M. wouldn't go for it. She'd seen the light in his eye when he stood on the stool beside the cinemotor and began engaging the crowd. He was a showman himself and could make the dullest of subjects entertaining, with his dry wit and ease with hecklers. He wouldn't want to relinquish his stage, she was sure. When Matty took the costings to the office to show Tom, it was clear why talkies were made in huge studios; the recording equipment was far beyond their yearly budget of a few hundred pounds. Tom's face fell as he scanned the figures.

'There is another way we could do it,' she offered and his eyes brightened with interest.

'Not so professional, but it might work.' She hesitated for a moment.

'Go on, tell me.'

'Well, why don't we just make a gramophone record to play alongside the films? That way we don't go to the expense of having to remake the films and all we'll need for equipment is a gramophone player, which I can wind up and keep in synch with the film.'

Tom jumped up and as there was no one else in the office he gave her an appreciative kiss. 'Brilliant, Matty. But how do we go about making a gramophone recording?'

'I've made a record before and besides, I think I know someone who'll help us with it.'

*

Matty looked round the waiting room at the new young hopefuls and the usual old troupers. Tommy Turner was still sitting there as though he hadn't moved for years, perhaps he lived here! But at least she needn't be embarrassed; she'd done what she could for him.

'Tommy!' She sat next to him. 'I heard you've got a regular spot at the Star now.'

He patted her hand. 'All thanks to you, Matty darlin'. Now what are you going to do about yourself? We miss you in the business.'

'Oh, I don't think I'll be coming back, Tommy.' She wasn't going to explain why. 'I'm here to see Esme about something else. Anyway, I like doing other things, got a new job with the Bermondsey film department.' She knew it sounded more glamorous than it was, but it might at least stop Tommy from trying to worm any more out of her. He looked impressed, which showed her he had no idea what the borough film department was all about.

'I took your advice, Matty love. I've expanded the act, do a bit of tap before the sand dancing, got meself a new partner!' Here he turned to a petite woman in her thirties, who had been sitting silently, smiling at her as if she knew her. 'In fact, let me introduce you, this is Tiny – the new Mrs Turner!'

And to emphasize the point the little lady, who wasn't much over four feet tall, got up and pirouetted. 'Tiny by name...' she said and offered her small-boned hand to Matty.

'Well, congratulations – to you both! I'm so pleased for you, Tommy.'

'What do you think?' Tommy and Tiny got up and did a few shuffle-ball changes, which brought a round of appreciative applause from the waiting artistes. They both gave extravagant bows. 'What's that about old dogs? Eh?'

'Not bad at all, Tommy.'

'But we're havin' a bit of trouble with these time steps – will you show us, Matty?' he asked eagerly. Matty glanced at Esme's door, then got up quickly to demonstrate a couple of time steps, which brought an even louder applause, causing Esme to poke her head out of her office.

'Struth! Is that the Cockney Canary treading the boards again? I never thought to see the day. Come in, darling!'

Whatever the season, Esme's office never changed, only the smoke-brown patina on the walls deepened over time to the colour of over-brewed tea. Esme dumped her overflowing ashtray into the waste bin and offered Matty a black cigarette. Before she'd even sat down a glass of Scotch was thrust into her hand. Esme was grinning, pleased to see her. She perched on the edge of her desk. 'Look at you! Have you been abroad? You look disgustingly healthy, darling.' And compared to Esme's smoke-tinged pallor, Matty supposed she did.

'Cycling tour to Winchester – there has been an Indian summer, in case you haven't looked out of the window all year!'

'No, no… it's not the tan. There's something else about you. Of course it's been a glorious summer, but you've been basking in more than sunlight.' Esme wagged a nicotine-stained finger at her and jumped off the desk.

'You're in love!'

Matty blushed.

'God, I hope you picked a better one this time.'

'I think so.' She couldn't help smiling, 'I'm back with Tom.'

'Tom? Good Lord, he's the last person—'

'We've both changed.' Matty cut her off, she couldn't bear any disparaging comment from Esme to tarnish her new happiness. 'He's been good for me, Esme.'

The woman held her hands up. 'That's all I could hope for, darling. It's heaven to see you happy again.'

'I am happy, Esme – very, and what's more I want you to help me make a record!'

'A record! I'd love to, but to be honest,' Esme said, blowing out a long plume of smoke, 'after the clipping in *Variety* I sent you I thought you'd want to stay out of the public eye for a bit longer.'

'Well, I have been.'

'Doesn't look that way to me. Here, have you seen this?'

Esme plucked a newspaper from a small mountain of papers stacked on the sideboard. She flung it across the desk.

Matty read the headline aloud: '*Cockney Canary Quells Near Riot in Bermondsey Street Screening.*' Then she silently scanned the rest of it. *Our reporter was on hand to witness*

*the comeback of a much loved local star, Matty Gilbie, as she
captured the unruly crowd with her magnificently amusing
version of 'Mother's Pie Crust', thus saving Chief Medical Officer
Dr Connan from much embarrassment, not to say serious injury,
at the hands of five hundred boisterous denizens of Bermondsey.*
The health propaganda campaign was given a cursory reference.
But then it went on to describe in good journalistic fashion the
exact location and date of the screening, along with further
handsome praise for Matty's impromptu performance. Could
it be, the journalist wondered, that the Cockney Canary would
soon be gracing a much larger screen than the one at the back of
Bermondsey Borough Council's cinemotor?

Matty let out a long groan. If the penny-farthing ride
wasn't enough to announce her whereabouts to the Clerkenwell
underworld, then the *Daily Express* had just done the rest.

16

Blood Ties

November–December 1931

'I didn't know anything about a journalist being there, but, Esme, this is *not* good, not when Frank's put out the word to the Clerkenwell mob to find me... so he can look me up when he arrives.'

'He's coming to England? How can you be sure about that?'

'Oh, I'm sure. Tom knows someone in that world. He got inside information.'

She stood up and went to the window. Lunchtime crowds hustled through the courtyard below – a short cut to Charing Cross Road.

'I want you to be careful, Esme. They might be watching your office, and I know there've been people snooping around the Star, asking questions about me.'

Esme looked shocked. 'I'd sort of hoped he'd lose interest.'

'I hoped that too, but Frank... I should have known it. He never lets go...'

'What are you going to do?'

'Tom's asked this old friend of his to keep an eye out, but there's nothing I can do, except lie low and hope.'

'So why on earth do you want to make a record?'

Matty had almost forgotten her purpose in coming here, but the mention of it catapulted her back to a world where death could reach out from the bug-infested walls of your home, and that made the threat from across the Atlantic seem small in comparison.

She hurried back to the office with the news that Esme had agreed to help them make the gramophone recordings and though she wasn't intending to mention the newspaper article, she spotted a copy of it on his desk.

'D.M. brought it in,' Tom said. 'He's happy as a sandboy about it.'

Apparently the chief medical officer didn't mind cutting a slightly ridiculous figure, considering that the propaganda benefits outweighed any personal ridicule.

'I've already seen it, at Esme's. We might as well have sent Frank a telegram.'

'No, I'm not worried about it, Matty. It's not front page and chances are no one'll notice it...'

Tom was a bad liar. Those too transparent eyes had never been able to hide much from her.

'But you got on to Sugar?'

'Oh yes.'

'And all the others in the know?'

He blushed. 'Just a precaution.'

She went behind the desk and draped her arms round him. 'Tom, you can't protect me from everything.'

'I'm not trying to, Matty – just from him. But there is one thing...' He looked away for an instant, his blush deepening.

'What?'

'Matty, you've got to trust me. It's better if I know everything. You told Sugar that Frank had nothing on you, but if there is something, you would tell me?'

She looked steadily into his eyes. 'No one can know *everything* about someone else, Tom, and even if I told you all the facts, you still wouldn't know everything...'

He kissed her and said, 'You always liked to be a woman of mystery, didn't you?'

'Oh, it's not that. I'm just trying to forget that part of my life. Anyway, the good news from Esme's is that she'll book us studio time and get us a good deal. Bermondsey borough's going into the talkies!'

'And I spoke to D.M. He loves the idea of a gramophone recording, though you were right about him not wanting to give up centre stage, Matty. It'll just be you singing his verses and slogans, getting the crowd warmed up, and we might have a few other experts from the health department doing sections. He's keen for you to put his Grade A TB-tested milk verse to music.'

Matty smiled ruefully. 'It's a good job I like a challenge then.'

She worked on the material for the recording through until the leaves in Southwark Park turned slowly to gold they were almost ready to cut the vinyl. As she walked home from the town hall one afternoon, clouds covered the sun for the first time in months and she was feeling the shadow of her past hanging over her. There had been no immediate consequences from the *Express* article, but still she worried. Tom had said it would be better if he knew everything, but of course there were things she would tell no one, especially not Tom. Besides, she suspected he would be less keen to take on the role of protector if he knew everything.

But tonight she was determined to finish off the blasted Grade A Tuberculin-Tested milk song, which had proved by far the hardest part of the exercise. So after she'd eaten her solitary tea she went to the piano and began to polish the tune she'd composed to match the opening words of D.M.'s doggerel:

> *Poor Jimmie's gained the heavenly prize,*
> *his spirit soars beyond the skies,*
> *Beneath this stone his body lies, and*
> *it will cause you no surprise,*
> *Since we in Bermondsey are Wise,*
> *to know that such a sad demise,*
> *Was due to the appalling lies, told*
> *by the milkman who supplies,*
> *The poison which his firm disguise, as milk!*

The doctor's verse went on to berate the popular practice of 'sterilizing' milk, which amounted to boiling it within an inch of its life while giving bacteria a good soup to grow in. He'd added a dollop of what he referred to as 'sob stuff', with Jimmy's death due to TB. He gave the verse an upbeat ending with Jimmy's dad educated about the dangers of poor milk, saving the rest of his children from Jimmy's fate.

> *And so he says, "I will arise!", and off to Bermondsey he hies,*
> *And soon he knows what we advise,*
> *Banished his sorrows, gone his sighs,*
> *with joyful voice aloud he cries:*
> *"Blind was I once, but now I see,*
> *henceforth I drink Grade A (TT)!"*

The words brought Billy painfully to mind and she doubted that switching to tuberculin-tested milk at this stage would fill Sam and Nellie with any sort of joy, nor wipe away their grief should the worst happen. The tune she was playing had turned into something more like a Scottish lament and she shut the lid of the piano. She told herself that Billy was in the best place and she had no reason to think he'd taken a sudden turn for the worse, but still D.M.'s verse had set her worrying. She'd heard nothing from Switzerland for a while. Not since Nellie had shown her a photograph of Billy with several other children, sitting at wooden desks ranged in a classroom formation, but unlike a normal classroom this one had no walls. The desks nestled into deep snow. Behind them an alpine peak fell away to a pretty village of wooden chalets with an onion-domed church. Billy was sitting near the front of the 'classroom', and like all the other children he wore sunhat, socks, walking boots and a loincloth. The risks of pneumonia obviously outweighed that of TB in the sun-cure sanatorium, but Billy had looked happy enough. She'd scrutinized his face and frame for any signs of improvement. Tanned and smiling, he held an open book in one hand and a small bottle of milk in the other; at least Dr Rollier was feeding the minds as well as the bodies of his charges. To Matty, any improvement in Billy's health would have been worth the struggle to get him to the clinic. She'd convinced herself he looked more robust on the outside; she only hoped the sun was doing as much good on the inside.

Will, who had recently earned his reviled degree and come into his father's money, had, in celebration, gone off on a walking holiday in the Alps with Feathers. He'd promised to visit Billy at Leysin and send word back.

Billy had become a sort of bridge between her and Will, a safe ground to meet on, and she'd been touched by his continuing interest in Billy's progress. But she'd not received the expected postcard from Will, who'd been gone over a fortnight. It might be the continental postal service; on the other hand, perhaps there was something happening in Leysin that the doctors were keeping from them. She determined to write to the sanatorium that evening. She found pen and paper in Eliza's old desk and turned on the lamp.

But as she went to close the front-parlour curtains she jumped back in alarm, a cry escaping her lips. She let fall the curtain and ran to bolt the front door. Normally she did it automatically, as soon as she came home, but tonight she'd forgotten. Her heart thumping, she was fumbling with the top bolt when she felt a pressure on the other side of the door. Had they picked the lock? She shoved back with her shoulder, leaning in with all her weight, shouting, 'You'd better go away, I've rung the police! They'll be here soon!'

But the opposing pressure suddenly stopped as she shot home the bolt. Her breath came in short, painful gasps, her heart was drumming, temples thudding. She was about to run to the telephone when a cultured voice called through the letterbox.

'I'm terribly sorry, Miss Gilbie, there's absolutely no danger. I didn't mean to startle you.'

It didn't *sound* like one of the Clerkenwell mob.

'Who is it?' She steadied her voice.

'It's Feathers… Gerald Fetherstone.'

She didn't understand why Will's friend was here without him, when they were both meant to be halfway up a mountain in Switzerland. She flung back the bolt and as the door swung wide, she saw that Feathers was not alone. Slumped at his feet was Will. He sat on the doorstep, leaning against his friend's legs as if for support, and Feathers was resting a protective hand on his head.

'I'm afraid we need to impose upon your hospitality, Miss Gilbie. Might we come in?' he said, as though he were inviting himself for afternoon tea.

'Of course you can, you daft 'apporth! Let me help you with him.'

She put a hand under Will's arm and Feathers took the other side. Together they dragged him into the passage, for he didn't seem able to support himself.

With an effort Will lifted his head, looking at Matty with glassy eyes. His grey face was covered in a sheen of sweat and pain was written all over it. 'Don't jaw me,' he whispered hoarsely, and she was reminded of a day when as a boy he'd played truant from Dulwich College and she'd caught him in Tower Bridge Road with a few of his schoolfriends going into Manzi's pie-and-mash shop. His face had reddened with guilt and embarrassment at the sight of her. 'Just showing my pals how well we dine in Bermondsey!' he'd said loudly, then as he ushered the boys into Manzi's white-tiled steamy warmth he'd whispered to her, 'Don't tell Mother, she'll jaw me!' She had kept his secret then, but this looked a far more serious matter than hopping the wag.

'Let's put him in here.'

They lowered him on to the sofa in the front parlour and she watched as Feathers gently took off Will's shoes and raised his legs.

'Feathers, will you get a blanket from one of the beds upstairs?'

The young man looked at Will, as if loathe to leave his side, but Will nodded briefly.

Once alone with him, Matty sat beside him. 'What happened, did you fall off the mountain?'

He gave a short laugh, which made him wince and clutch his stomach. He shook his head and let out a long hissing breath. He pulled his hand away, revealing fingers painted red with blood.

'Oh my God, what have you done? Will, you need a doctor.'

'I'm all right, Matty, don't fuss.' He took a laboured breath. 'Anyway, I saw a doctor in Germany.'

'Germany? What the bloody hell were you doing there? I thought you were in Switzerland! I've been expecting a card from you about Billy and when it didn't come…'

She realized that ever since he'd left for Switzerland she'd had a nagging feeling that something was wrong. She'd thought her concern was for Billy, but now she knew it had been for Will.

Feathers was back with the blanket. 'I think it's time to come clean, Will. Tell your sister where we've been, there's a good fellow.'

But Will was incapable of telling her anything, for at that moment he cried out in pain, clutched at his stomach and raised his legs. Matty dropped down beside the sofa and lifted his jacket. His shirt was caked in day-old blood and now a new dark red stain was announcing a fresh flow.

'Feathers, how could you have let him travel in this state?'

The young man looked stricken. 'I'm sorry. I did my best, found a medical student to patch him up, but we had to run for our lives, Matty. The stitches have ripped open.'

He put out a trembling hand, which she noticed was wrapped with a makeshift bandage, then he gently lifted Will's shirt, easing off the places stuck with blood, to reveal a jagged wound, hastily stitched and obviously infected. She was ready to lambast Feathers, but saw tears welling in his eyes. How young he looked – for all his sophisticated, worldly air, he was not much more than a boy. They both were, two boys who'd been on an adventure that had obviously gone horribly wrong. Explanations would have to wait.

'All right, Feathers. Let's stay calm.' She put a hand on his shoulder, thinking rapidly. What would be the quickest way of getting Will to a hospital? She dashed to the telephone and, trembling, dialled the town hall. The phone rang several times. 'Be there, be there,' she prayed softly to the ringing phone. She was about to hang up when there was a click and a familiar voice answered.

'Hello?'

'Thank God you're still there! Tom, I need your help. Will's been hurt. I need to get him to hospital – now!'

She waited, trying to concentrate on his words, while he explained what he thought was best. 'Just make sure you're ready. I'll be there as soon as I can.'

She went back to Will, enveloping him gently in the blanket, then threw on her coat and hat before gathering a few things she thought he might need. Will was still insensible, so she turned her attention to Feathers, who was kneeling by the sofa, head in hands. 'You're right.' He looked up, his face a ghastly white. 'I should never have gone along with it! Oh, Will, stay with me.' He put his arm round his friend, who stirred and moaned.

A rapid knocking came at the door and Matty ran to let Tom in.

'What happened?'

She led Tom into the parlour. He went straight to Will and lifted the blanket, peering beneath his shirt. 'Dear God, I saw plenty of these when I was in the Elephant Boys. It's a knife wound, and a nasty one. Let's get him up.'

Matty eased Will gently into a sitting position. 'Feathers, help Tom carry him. Careful! He's lost a lot of blood.'

The two men lifted Will and, ignoring his cries of pain, carried him outside. In the street Matty exchanged an enquiring look with Tom. 'We're going in that?'

'Sorry, this was the best I could do at such short notice! Here, get the keys out of my pocket.'

Matty reached into Tom's jacket as he and Feathers supported Will.

'Side door,' Tom said.

Matty unlocked the side door of the cinemotor and slid it open. It wouldn't exactly be a comfortable ride, but they managed to lie Will flat on a blanket. As Feathers attempted to get inside with her, Matty stopped him. 'I'll stay in the back with Will. You get in the cab.'

Matty sat on the van floor, holding Will tightly as they took off. She blessed the extra suspension that Tom had installed in the cinemotor, designed to keep the projector as stable as possible on their journeys. He'd told her that in the early days they spent half the show time recalibrating the equipment and had lost many a bored audience in the process. But still she tried to shield Will from the jolting sharp turns and stops as Tom sped towards Guy's Hospital through Bermondsey's darkened streets.

'It's all right, I'm here,' she soothed each time Will moaned. Smoothing his cheek, she felt a two-day stubble, testament to his long flight home.

When Matty reached over to let some air through the vents, Will's eyes snapped open, wide with fear, and he hardly seemed to see her.

'Did they catch us at the border, Feathers? Where are they taking us?' He tried to get up, but collapsed back on to her lap almost immediately.

'Will, it's Matty. You're safe now. We're taking you to hospital. It's all right, love, you're home.'

But he was shaking his head. 'No, not home, got no home.' He spoke through chattering teeth and she could feel his whole body trembling with the exertion.

'Yes, you are, you're home in Bermondsey, Will. I won't let anything bad happen to you now, I promise.'

And she gathered him up in her arms, mourning the child she'd loved so much and seemed to have failed so badly as an adult. It might not have been her that had caused the rift, yet she couldn't help comparing him to Billy. She had moved heaven and earth to save her nephew; had she tried as hard to save Will?

She had known full well what a headstrong nature he had, that he would always go the hard way, and this was a combination which, as she'd learned from her own mistakes, could prove as deadly as any disease.

The young doctor who first examined his wound winced. 'Nasty. Looks like he's been sewn up with fishing line.' He looked round accusingly and Matty saw Feathers pale.

'We were nowhere near a hospital,' he explained. 'I found a medical student...'

The young doctor raised his eyes. 'Hmm, he'll go far,' he said dryly, then briskly organized a trolley. 'We'll have to do our best. First things first. Who's the next of kin?'

He looked instinctively at Tom and Feathers, but then Matty said, 'I am. I'm his sister.'

The brusque young doctor nodded and took down her details, then ordered them to go away while they operated on Will and to come back the next day. But Matty knew none of them would be sleeping that night, so they went instead to the canteen to wait. They crossed the courtyard to the basement of a grim old Victorian building, on the way passing the isolation wards where Billy had been. Matty instinctively glanced up, feeling a rush of disappointment that Billy hadn't had the promised visit from Will, which he'd so been looking forward to.

The canteen was at the bottom of some worn stone steps, hot-water pipes ran round green and cream tiled walls, and steam seeped from a tea urn. The place resembled a sauna. Soon they were seated with cups of mahogany-coloured tea. Matty noticed Feathers' bandaged hand, still trembling as he tipped in three spoonfuls of sugar.

'We should have got someone to put a proper dressing on that hand.'

'It's nothing,' Feathers said as he put the cup to his lips.

'Feathers, how did Will get a knife wound?' Matty asked finally.

The young man grimaced as he carefully lowered the cup.

'From a Stormtrooper's blade.'

'A Stormtrooper? For God's sake, what have you two got yourselves involved in?' Tom exclaimed.

The cup rattled in the saucer. Matty took it from Feathers. She put a comforting hand on his and gave Tom a warning look. She sensed Feathers was blaming himself just as she had blamed herself. 'Take your time, Gerald,' she said, letting him compose himself. He took in a deep gulp of air.

'Will so wanted to do something. He said he couldn't live with himself if he stood by and let the Nazis' bully boys imprison our comrades and kill innocent Jews. He wanted his money to do the most good.' Here he hesitated, and lowered his voice. 'Really, what he did to you was inexcusable, but it was the idealism of youth, you see...' Matty had to smile at Feathers returning now to his world-weary veneer of sophistication, but she had seen the boy lurking there and was not fooled in the least.

'Go on, Feathers, that's all in the past...'

'As I said, he wanted to use his inheritance for the cause, and it will do so much good, Matty, it will save hundreds of innocent lives—'

'And it might cost him his,' Tom said grimly.

'It was risky, but nothing many other comrades haven't done before us. The cell in Berlin had appealed for contributions, said they needed bribe money for the underground refugee work – there's always some petty official willing to turn a blind eye, not pass on a tip-off, lose the relevant bit of paperwork. Will's money was enough to get hundreds of communists and Jews out of the country to safety.'

Matty was getting frustrated. 'All right, if that's what he wanted to do with his father's money, I understand, but why not just telegraph it – why did you have to take it into Germany? Why put yourselves in such bloody danger?'

But she knew why. A telegraphic transfer was not heroic

enough for him, he would have to be in the thick of things, on the front line, waving his damned red flag for all to see.

'Transfers can be intercepted; they leave a trail. The money is always in cash, and couriered personally. It has to be put into the hands of a member of the cell. Will didn't think it was honourable to let someone else be the mule.'

Matty could see it now, the allure of cloak-and-dagger playing at spies. Will would have loved it, but she suspected Feathers had only gone along for the sake of his friend.

'When we left England our instructions were to meet someone in a Paris café and we'd be told what to do. We got there with no trouble and a French chap passed us a suitcase and the address of a hotel in Berlin where we were to be at a certain time. He told us to put the money in the case and just leave it with a hotel porter there. That was it. It should have been simple.'

'But it went wrong?' Tom interrupted.

Feathers nodded, taking another gulp of hot tea. 'When we arrived in Berlin, there were Brownshirts everywhere, strutting about the train station, pushing people around, singling out communists and Jews. One man protested and they pulled him out of the queue and kicked him to the ground. We hadn't realized the Brownshirts had got so much power. Anyway, they were checking everyone who'd come off our train and I didn't know what we were going to do – we had the money in the suitcase, far too much for two students on a walking holiday. But before we reached the barrier Will said I was to go through and he would meet me at the hotel. He took the case and jumped back on the train... I didn't want to leave him, but I couldn't make a fuss. Will knew that... He took the case because he knew I would panic...'

'So you got through the barrier all right?' Matty asked. 'But what about Will?'

'He hid on the train for a bit, then crossed to another platform, and later that night we met at the hotel. We'd just handed the money over when they barged in, three great brown-shirted brutes. The porter told us to run and disappeared with the case – we were left being bounced about from one Neanderthal to another.'

'So they knew you were coming?'

Feathers shrugged. 'Seems like a bit of a coincidence they were searching our train when we arrived, and they knew we'd be at the hotel.'

'Is that when Will got injured?'

Feathers' gaze seemed to be following the large hot-water pipe behind Matty, so that he wasn't looking directly at her when he said, 'It should have been me. Never was very good with my fists and they got me on the ground pretty quickly. Will has a good left hook, and took his man down, then the other, but the one sitting on my chest pulled out a blade, long, wicked-looking thing. I thought I'd had it, would have done if Will hadn't jumped him. It wasn't until we were three streets away that I realized how badly he was injured. God.'

He covered his eyes with the bandaged hand. 'I wish I'd never agreed to go with him.'

'Then he'd have gone alone and what chance would he have had then?' Matty covered his hand with her own, tracing the dirty bandage with her fingers. 'You fought for him, Gerald, and you got him home. Stop blaming yourself.'

Tom went to get them more of the canteen's dark brew and some yellow, knobbly rock cakes, which Feathers devoured like a starving man.

'So there never was a walking tour in Switzerland and Will never intended visiting our Billy?' She felt particularly hurt by this part of the deception.

Feathers swallowed the last of the rock cake and held up his hand, hastily feeling around in his inside jacket pocket.

'There was no walking holiday, no, but Will was adamant, he insisted we go via Switzerland. We stopped there first. Here, Will entrusted this to me on the way home…'

Feathers handed her a letter.

Her hand flew to her mouth. The envelope was splashed with brown, dried blood.

'We did manage a brief visit with your nephew.'

'You saw him? How was he?'

'Brown as a berry and Will said he'd grown at least two inches.'

Matty felt a wave of relief at the news.

'But,' Feathers went on, 'the poor boy was disappointed when we had to rush on. We promised him a second visit on our way home... sadly not to be.'

Feathers described their flight home, with a stop at a safe house on the way.

'One of our comrades risked his life, went out to find a medical student friend of his who stitched Will up and then drove us to a small station outside Berlin. When we arrived at the border, the guards got suspicious of us so we nipped off the train and made a run for it. That's when Will's wound opened up again... he was bleeding all the way home.'

Feathers rubbed his eyes with dirty fingers. 'I was terrified he'd bleed to death.'

She had been gripping Billy's letter all through Feathers' story of their escape and now she looked down at the boy's careful handwriting. He had addressed the envelope very properly to *Miss Mathilda Gilbie*, but her name had been almost obliterated by the rusty telltale stain of blood that had seeped from Will's body as he'd fled back to a place he still could not call home and a woman he had never wanted to call sister. She let her tears fall on to the envelope, watching as they mingled with the faded stamps of her brother's lifeblood.

17

Cocktail of Lies

December 1931

Their long wait was in vain, for the matron in charge of Will's ward would not let them in to see him again, saying only that he needed rest after his operation. When Matty pressed her for details she pursed her lips at her presumption.

'I can assure you that the young man is in the best of hands and *if* he is improved tomorrow, you will be able to see him then. But *only* during visiting hours!' She stabbed at a sign next to the ward doors which stated the visiting times.

'I wonder if I might have a word in private.' Feathers tipped his head to one side and gave her his most urbane smile. Her starched rigidity seemed to melt at the sound of his cultured voice and she meekly showed him into her office. Within minutes Feathers had returned with a smiling matron.

'We've been granted five minutes,' he whispered.

They followed Matron along the rows of slumbering patients until they reached a screened-off bed. She pulled aside the curtain and there was Will, pale-faced, hair plastered across his forehead, but apparently sleeping calmly. Matty noticed his arms were bandaged. There had obviously been more wounds hidden beneath his jacket. She hurried to his side and smoothed back his thick hair. She didn't care if she upset Matron; she wanted Will to hear her.

'Will dear, it's Matty. Feathers is here too, he's told us everything... You silly sod, just like you, but he got you home,

Will, and you'll be fine. And when you're stronger, I'll come and get you, hear me?'

She kissed his forehead and he stirred, eyelids flickering. Then Feathers was beside her. He took Will's hand and put it to his cheek. 'Dearest, brave chap. You'll be up and about in no time.'

'Matron's coming,' Tom warned as he tweaked aside the bedside screen. With a parting squeeze, Feathers let fall Will's hand and they left him, Matty looking back all the time at the pale figure, praying silently that Matron would soften her fierce protective care with some maternal tenderness.

Matty linked her arm through Tom's, glad to lean on him. Weary to her bones, she asked, 'So, how did you do it, Feathers?'

'Do what, Miss Gilbie?' he answered.

'Get us past that dragon in a matron's hat?'

'I simply told her my mother is a trustee on Guy's governing board. Rank has its uses.'

'Says the young communist,' Tom muttered under his breath and Matty elbowed him in the side.

The following morning, Tom called in on the way to work. It wasn't something he'd ever done before. She was still in her dressing gown, finishing off a piece of toast when she answered his knock.

'Tom! What's happened?' Her immediate thought was that the hospital had telephoned him, rather than give her the bad news.

'No, nothing. I just wanted to make sure you're OK – you had such a shock last night and I was worried about you.'

As she shut the front door behind them he took her in his arms, and they stood together, swaying slightly in a long embrace. She felt tears prick her eyes and taut muscles relax, realizing that his arms felt like home. Eventually he stood back.

'Stay for breakfast?' she asked quickly, and not waiting for an answer she led him to the kitchen where she busied herself making him tea and toast.

'When I saw Feathers through the window last night, you know I thought he was one of Frank's men. Stupid, but I really was terrified, Tom. I thought I'd had my taters. Then when I saw the state Will was in, I was sure he'd bleed to death in the parlour...'

'That's what I meant by a shock! Don't come to work today, Matty, stay home. You won't be able to settle till you've been to Guy's anyway.'

'But we were supposed to be finishing the record material!'

'Another day won't matter. Besides, it's only D.M.'s damn milk song to lay down. I'll get his OK on the rest of the material – you just go and see your brother.'

She leaned over the table to kiss buttery lips and wiped a crumb from his chin.

'Who am I to argue with the studio boss?'

Glad that he had suggested it, she left the house soon after Tom, but before going to Guy's she had an urgent errand to carry out. Sam had already left for work, but she knew Nellie would be back from her early morning stint cleaning the offices at Pearce Duff's. Matty never failed to admire her stamina – she was now doing three part-time jobs as well as looking after the family. To her afternoon shift at Pearce Duff's she'd added an evening shift. For though Will was covering most of the sanatorium bill, Nellie and Sam had insisted on putting something towards Billy's stay in Leysin.

'Matty, love, come in!' Nellie's look of delight at seeing her was almost immediately replaced by concern, as it was an unusual time for Matty to visit. But she led Matty to the kitchen, where she was clearing away the breakfast clutter.

'Find a place to sit if you can. I'm running late, getting the boys off to school.'

Nellie swept laundry off a chair and then whisked plates and cups off the table and into the scullery. 'What's brought you here so early, have you heard anything?' she called in a casual voice which Matty knew disguised her constant worry about Billy.

'I've had a letter.' Matty followed her into the scullery. 'Come out the way, Nellie, and let me make you a cup of tea. You can have five minutes sit down, surely.'

'A letter? From the sanatorium?'

Matty nodded. 'From Billy.'

'Well?' Nellie looked at her expectantly.

'He's coming home!'

Nellie threw wet hands round Matty and jumped her up and down in a dance of excitement. 'Home!' Nellie held her at arm's length. 'Are you sure, Matty?'

'Would I get your hopes up if I wasn't? Here, read it, while I make your tea.' And she pushed Nellie out of the scullery.

When Matty took her the tea she found Nellie with the letter on her lap. She smoothed it out and handed it back to Matty with tears in her eyes. 'His lungs are clear! Oh, Matty, he's cured... thanks to you, love.'

Matty shook her head. 'It's thanks to our Will, really, Nellie.'

'It was you spotted the TB. But give him his due, it was his money and that boy's surprised me. I don't suppose I'll ever fathom what he did to you, but he's always welcome here. One thing I don't understand – why didn't the sanatorium let me know about him coming home?'

'Ah well, your letter's probably in the post. I had mine hand-delivered.'

Matty saw the light of an impossible hope in Nellie's eyes. 'Is he home already?' she asked.

And Matty laughed. 'No, love. I'm not that much of a fairy godmother, he's not waiting in the wings! It's Will we've got to thank again. He brought the letter back from Switzerland last night.'

Nellie looked at Matty with a puzzled expression.

'That's the other thing I've come to tell you, Nellie. It's about Will.'

Matty made sure she was waiting outside the hospital well before visiting hours began.

He was lying with his arms resting on top of a bedspread white as his face. She eased herself quietly into the bedside chair, feeling it was impossible to breathe until she knew that her brother still had breath in his body. He looked like death, but as she gazed intently at the cover, she saw a small rise and fall, and only then let herself take in a deep draught of air.

She sat silently, realizing that she didn't need him to be awake. She didn't even need him to be her friend. She just needed him to be alive. As she sat vigil, studying the man's face, she wondered how it had emerged from that of the child who'd come barrelling into her legs and her life one day. Determined, in a hurry, intent on going where he wanted to go and never deviating, he had instantly bestowed on her an unearned affection, latching on to her like a small tethered hawk. Now she understood the hidden origins of that bond, the close family tie, closer than she could have imagined, and out of all that she couldn't see how or when that bond had begun to chafe him so much that he'd lashed out in the cruellest way and ripped it apart.

She became aware that his eyes were open and that he was looking at her. He said nothing for a long moment and she thought she saw a resigned sadness in his eyes.

'Looks like you saved my life...' he croaked. 'Don't know why you'd want to, after what I did to you...' His voice trailed off and he closed his eyes.

'But you knew enough to come to me. You knew I'd never turn you away.'

With an effort he opened his eyes again. 'Yes, I knew that.'

His breathing was shallow and harsh, but she could see some colour returning to his face.

'Matty, I've wanted to say I'm sorry—'

She interrupted him. 'It doesn't matter now, Will.'

But he went on. 'You deserve an explanation, but I'm not sure I understand it myself.'

He was attempting to raise himself in the bed, but she put a hand on his shoulder and eased him back down. 'Will, stay calm, that old witch of a matron will jaw me if you get upset.'

He gave a weak smile. 'You'll sort her out. There's something a little bit scary about you too, you know. But let me say what I need to.'

He turned his face towards her and she could see the painful effort it was to speak, but part of her selfishly wanted the answer to the questions that had been tormenting her.

'Remember you told me you felt you'd wasted your chance – to escape Bermondsey, the factories and the docks and the dirt, all of it? You said to me "I had my chance to get out and I wasted it, don't waste yours"... But, Matty, what if I never wanted the chance to get out? What if all I ever wanted was the chance to get in?'

At first she didn't understand what he meant, but then she saw with painful clarity how hard it must have been for him, always longing to be fully part of a world where his difference branded him an exile.

She reached out for his hand. 'Is that where it all came from? You resented me for belonging here when you couldn't?'

He blinked, seeming to consider. 'I think so. You never had to try. Bermondsey was home for you, Matty. Everywhere people loved you and you belonged... and me, I was always outside. And then I saw things, heard things that made me think you were taking away from me what really was mine – my mother.' He let go of her hand and she was astonished to see him wipe a stray tear from his cheek. She looked at him in wonder at so much hurt, running like an underground stream, out of view, undermining the person she thought he was, until it had emerged in one destructive burst.

She grasped his hand again. 'Surely you know that's not true. Listen to me, Will. I could never have taken Eliza from you. Don't you understand? She didn't feel any more love for me than you, she just felt more guilt! That's what made her change the will. For God's sake, it was *you* she kept! You think you never belonged to your Bermondsey family because of your rich father and your posh school, but that's not it at all. Belonging's nothing to do with

248

where you're born, it's more about what you do. When Nellie took me and Charlie in as kids, that was belonging. When you forgot about hating me and helped Billy, that was belonging... Don't you see, Will?'

He let his head fall back on the pillow, let out a deep sigh and squeezed her hand. 'I do see,' he said, his eyes brimming. 'Matty, when I get out of here, can I come home?'

*

He was the worst of patients. It should have come as no surprise that Will immobilized would resemble the boiler in a train held at London Bridge Station. Stoked, fired up, ready to go but with the signal still firmly at red, he was spouting steam and she was in the direct firing line of all his pent-up energy. After a couple of weeks of Matty battling to keep him in bed, Nellie offered to stand in as nurse while Matty was at work. They portioned out his care around Nellie's shifts and by the end of his third week home they resembled jailers, giving each other an update on his attempts to escape. His latest foray had nearly worked, but there he'd had an accomplice.

'For God's sake, Will, get back up those stairs! The doctor said you'd need at least a month's bed rest.'

She'd caught them, like a pair of surprised burglars on the stairs, guilty-faced and frozen. Will was in his slippered feet, with his shoes underneath his arm.

'And you! You should know better.' She pointed an accusing finger at Feathers, who was following with Will's jacket and hat.

'Matty, you're a terrible nurse. You've got no bedside manner. If I ask for water it takes half an hour to get here. I might as well be shifting for myself,' Will grumbled jokingly.

'Ungrateful brat!' Feathers stood on the stair above and cracked Will's head with his knuckle. 'Matty has been the embodiment of patience and the only reason I agreed to assist your escape was to give her a rest! Of course we weren't going to leave without asking first, but we thought rather than waiting for

Christmas, Will could come with me to Fonstone now for the rest of his convalescence?' He turned his charming smile on Matty.

Fonstone was Feathers' family home, a place where Will had always been made welcome and had spent his last couple of Christmases. But she wasn't to be so easily won over.

'How can I trust that you two are actually going where you say you are? You could be going to Berlin again for all I knew.' She saw a look pass between them and Feathers burst out, 'Well, come with us then! Stay Friday to Monday, and you can see him safely tucked up in bed by my old nanny.'

Matty shook her head. 'No. It's too early for Will to be travelling all that way.' She addressed her brother. 'Do you want the wound to rip open again?'

Will pulled a face and he muttered, 'I don't have to go to Fonstone to be nannied. You're doing a pretty good job of it right here.'

Matty sighed. 'Well, now you're out of bed, Will, you might as well stay up for tea, but I'm not letting you out of the house and I think this Christmas had better be a Bermondsey one for you.'

She saw a look of disappointment pass over Feathers' face and felt sympathy, but the deep and jagged knife wound had almost killed Will and she preferred him to be where she could keep an eye on him.

Matty went to prepare their tea. She might complain about him but she'd been secretly grateful for the chance to nurse Will. Whatever blame she'd heaped upon herself for his lostness had dissipated in these last weeks when she'd helped him back to health. The old jokes and easy banter had slowly returned, but with a depth that had never been there before. Now, with his growing impatience to be out of bed, she had to admit she could do with a rest and would secretly have liked a trip to Fonstone. She smiled to herself, imagining a lazy weekend being looked after in the grand, ancient house, wandering the parkland full of old trees and hedged gardens. But it wasn't her world and she couldn't imagine fitting in. She could see the attraction for Will.

It was obvious that Feathers was as sure of his place in the world as Will was unsure of his.

As she pushed open the parlour door with a tray of tea things, she heard Will speaking under his breath to Feathers.

'What possessed you to ask her to Fonstone – the whole point was to go to the rally on the way!'

'I panicked,' Feathers hissed.

'I *knew* you two were up to something else!' She set the tray down so firmly the cups rattled. 'What rally's this?'

Will groaned and passed his hand across his eyes. 'It's the anti-fascist rally at Trafalgar Square. We were only going to listen to the speeches before we got the train up, weren't we, Feathers?'

'Don't look at him!' Matty was furious with them both. 'For university chaps you're both as thick as two short planks. Where's the best chance of getting a beating from a fascist this weekend? You might as well just get the train back to Berlin and find another couple of Stormtroopers to open up that wound for you! Feathers, make yourself useful, be mother,' she ordered in exasperation.

'I wouldn't have been able to come to Fonstone anyway. But thanks for the kind invitation, Feathers...' she said tartly. 'I'll be at work with Tom. We'll only have the studio till the end of next week, so we need to go in on Saturday to finish the recording.'

Their original recording project had evolved since Esme had booked the studio. D.M. and Birdy liked the idea so much they'd commissioned more recordings to accompany three other films.

'So, as I'm going to be busy, I suppose it might be a good idea for Feathers to stay here and keep you company. But you've both got to promise me, no sneaking off to rallies while I'm out.'

Both young men grinned, nodding their heads as if they were no older than Billy. Feathers poured the tea like a butler and then offered round the sandwiches. She knew Will was getting better when he polished them off – there was certainly nothing wrong with his appetite. He picked up a newspaper report on the annual exhibition of Bermondsey Health Propaganda Department, which Matty had been reading.

'Feathers, have a look at the statistics in this report?' Will tossed the paper to his friend.

'Infant mortality halved, TB and fever rate almost down to the national average… very impressive.' Feathers cast an approving glance in her direction.

'It seems these films of Matty's are actually doing some good!' Will said.

'Don't sound so surprised. It's not just the films. Birdy – Mr Bush – has been working like a Trojan setting up displays of dental laboratories and sun-ray treatment at the exhibition. But the films seem to make the most impact. Tom's had an idea for a new series just for women. *The Modern Woman and Work, Modern Woman and Home*… that sort of thing. Guess who'll be playing the modern woman?'

'Matty, that's brilliant. I admire what you're doing with your talent,' Will said, so earnestly that she had to smile.

But she felt a bit of a fraud, knowing that her motives in joining Bermondsey's health crusade had more to do with saving herself than saving others. But the truth was, she'd changed during the months she'd worked on the borough films. Going into the darkness of Bermondsey's poorest housing had opened her eyes to the misery and disease lurking down every backstreet, and she'd found herself embracing the health propaganda gospel with as much zeal as Tom and the three musketeers. They all saw themselves as guardians of public health, helping to eradicate and educate disease out of existence, and she found it amusing and sometimes touching that they'd adopted her as a sort of Boadicea to fight alongside them.

'Dr Connan thinks we'll be lucky to get the funding, though,' she said, breaking off her musing. 'Our budget's being cut.'

'Mother might be interested,' Feathers said.

'*Your* mother?'

'She's very progressive. I suppose I take after her.' Feathers popped the last of the fruitcake into his mouth. 'Really, Matty, your films are every bit as important as the work Will and I do for the NUWM, don't you think so, Will?'

His friend nodded, his own mouth full of fruitcake. 'More.'

Matty instinctively offered him another slice, which made him giggle. 'Not more cake! I meant more important, the films are life-and-death stuff.'

'Just Ma Feathers' thing, she's been looking for a new charitable project. You really must come to Fonstone and meet her, Matty. Come when we go up for Christmas – bring Tom!'

'No, I meant it. Christmas is too soon for Will to travel. Perhaps we'll come up in the New Year,' she said, with no belief that it would ever happen.

Matty never dreamed she'd be included in Will's earnest world of social reform. Although it had seemed to happen naturally, looking back, she could chart the sea change in herself. Her undoing had begun with that terrified flight from Frank and the shattering emergence of Eliza's secret. But her re-emergence as a new creature, she owed to Tom. From the day he'd offered her the job it had been him, steadily helping her to gather up all her unravelled self into a new person.

*

When Esme telephoned to invite her for lunch, she'd assumed they'd be talking about the recording studio hire which Esme was handling for them, but which would be paid for by Bermondsey Borough Council. D.M. had authorized a certain amount and no more, which was why she and Tom had been going through the schedule, cramming as much into their studio time as possible. But when she'd arrived at Esme's office, her agent's face told her something was wrong.

Esme said nothing until they were settled in a small Italian restaurant in St Martin's Lane. Then she pushed an envelope across the table.

'Not that I want to spoil your appetite, darling. I always seem to be the harbinger of unwanted news, but this can't be ignored.'

The envelope contained a picture of Matty. A still taken from a film. It took her back to a time in her life she'd hoped never to revisit and its resurrection caused an instant cold rush of nausea, forcing her to take in a deep breath.

'Was the film ever distributed?' Esme's low voice broke into Matty's thoughts and she let out her breath slowly. She was alarmed to find that her hand was trembling as it held the photograph. She nodded, laying the photo face down on the table as the waiter brought them bowls of spaghetti. If it were only as easy to turn the truth over and lay it face down, out of sight, if only she could erase it by ignoring it. That had been her strategy so far and it had failed time and again. The photograph showed her seated on a bar stool, a long silk kimono loosely draped around her naked shoulders, falling open to reveal one bare breast, before being caught in at the waist by a single fastening. Her long legs parted the silk and left not much to the imagination as it flowed artfully to the floor. Matty looked at the steaming pasta, heaped with tomato sauce, just like Mama Rossi made, just the way Frank loved it. She retched and covered her mouth.

'Oh, darling, I'm sorry.' Esme pushed a glass of water towards her and Matty breathed deeply again. She didn't trust herself to pick up the glass; instead she dropped her shaking hands to her lap and gripped them so tightly the fingers turned white.

'Where did you get it?'

'Someone stuffed it under the office door one evening. I didn't see who, but I presume it was one of Frank's minions. The *Clerkenwell* mob, I believe you said they're called?' she said with obvious disgust. 'And it came with this grubby semi-literate missive.'

Matty read it. *This gose in the pappers if the canary sings.*

'It took him long enough to dig this one up.'

'But I don't understand, Matty. Why on earth would he want to stop you singing?'

Matty almost burst out laughing, but it wasn't funny. 'He doesn't mean on the stage, Esme. He means talking to the police. There are things I know which could land him back in jail.'

'Back? I didn't know he'd ever been in!'

'Not for long. He's on the run, could even be in the country for all I know.' She picked up the photograph. 'Frank's just letting me know he can still hurt me – wherever he is, Canada, middle of the Atlantic, it doesn't matter...' She studied the pose in the photograph, feeling embarrassed by her sultry stare – gazing through half-closed eyelids in imitation of Greta Garbo. 'Stupid!' she muttered, then looked at Esme. 'I've been dreading this thing coming to light ever since I got back with Tom.'

'Matty, I'm sure you had your reasons, but tell me, why make a film like this? You had a perfectly legitimate career!'

Matty rubbed at her face. How could she explain to Esme the impossibility of crossing Frank.

'Esme, I was still in love with him and, at the time, I believed he felt the same. It's hard to explain, but it was as if we were a team of two against the world, and he made it obvious that everything he asked of me was a test of how much I loved him. He said that the Crash had wiped him out, all he wanted was to make enough money to launch the new film. It was all for me, he said, and besides, he told me, everyone did it these days, it was just for a private distribution – he swore the negative would be destroyed...'

'I bet he did.'

'You're right. I was such a bloody fool! It wasn't long after that I realized just what sort of man I'd fallen for. He'd always had that raging temper and sometimes it scared me, but I thought he'd never touch me.'

'But he did?'

Matty instinctively clutched at her stomach, the painful memory had been buried so deep in a dungeon of her mind that the merest chink of light stung her eyes with tears.

'When I first met him I thought he'd die for me.' A bitter laugh escaped her lips. 'I never expected I might have to die for him. Yes, Esme, he hurt me badly and that's when I ran.'

'Poor darling. If I'd known...'

'You couldn't have done anything. The only one who could get me out of it was me.'

'So, what do you want to do now?'

Matty groaned. 'I don't know.'

*

They walked briskly along the Charing Cross Road. A grey November day had turned to a drizzly, foggy evening. The pavement was slick and patterned with reflections from illuminated shopfronts. Some of the second-hand booksellers were taking in their trestle tables, but others had lit lamps and pulled out awnings against the rain. As they passed a brightly lit musical instrument shop Tom stopped, wanting to show her a baby grand piano, the keys pristine black and white, the glossy ebony lid raised to reveal silver and gold strings.

'How would you like that one, Matty?' he asked as she slipped her arm through his. 'It beats Eliza's old upright. Not sure if I'd dare play "*Henceforth I drink Grade A TT*" on it, though!'

After a long day in the studio, they had finally completed the recording of three gramophone records and they were going to the Astoria Ballroom in Charing Cross Road for a night's dancing and celebration. The Foyles bookshop electric sign came into view and they dodged window shoppers standing beneath awnings the length of its illuminated frontage. Lamps suspended like glowing lozenges bounced light off wet bowler hats and mackintoshes, while women hurried along in the lea of shopfronts, conscious of losing their marcel waves in the mizzling rain. It was as if all London wanted to be somewhere else. Fuzzy headlights announced the arrival of a bus, which disgorged passengers into their path, and as they waited for them to disperse Tom took her hand and smiled. 'Happy?' he asked.

'Of course.' She leaned in close and held on to his arm. She wasn't lying. These had been some of the happiest weeks she'd ever known – working closely with Tom, both of them part of something she'd come to see as important. Before America their worlds had been poles apart – the only thing he'd known of her singing career had been what he'd seen on the stage. The work and grinding hours of rehearsal had been hidden from him. All he'd seen was the illusion, the swan gliding along while its feet paddled wildly under the surface. These past weeks, he'd seen the hard graft behind her polished performance.

But there was still a part of her that wasn't happy. She had put off talking to Tom until their recording work was finished and now, with the prospect of what she had to tell him weighing heavily on her mind, the last thing she felt like was dancing. They passed the shuffling queue for the Astoria cinema, which disappeared in the fog as it snaked back round the corner into Oxford Street, and made their way to the ballroom entrance. The dance floor was fitted into the basement of the cinema, which was one of the new lavish Roman-style palaces, with seats for two thousand. It had been built while she was in America and Matty had never visited it, but she'd read about the opening night in a *Variety* magazine. After they'd checked in their coats they walked through to the sprung dance floor, where hundreds of couples were already whirling in a synchronized, quickstepping current. She was astonished at the size of it. A vast octagonal space, which looked big enough for over a thousand dancers, it was surrounded by a gallery, with tables and a bar. When she'd read about the place, she hadn't been that impressed – a ballroom in a basement wasn't her idea of a glamorous venue. But this was like descending into an Aladdin's cave of music and light. The band members were surprisingly good too, and were already in full swing. It was just the choice of song that she could have wished different. They were playing 'Little White Lies' and the singer was cheerfully vocalizing the very thoughts that had been plaguing her. '*Heaven was in your eyes, but the devil was in your heart, when you told me those little white lies.*'

Her lies had certainly been white, lies of omission to protect Tom, or so she told herself. Now her hand had been forced and she would *have* to tell him. But for now she pushed the inevitable conversation to the back of her mind, giving herself up to the dancing and Tom's arms, letting herself be swept up in the swift, mesmeric movement. The band seemed to enjoy playing at breakneck speed and Matty thought the band leader would poke his own eye out with the baton, he was so vigorous. But eventually she had to give in and plead tiredness.

'I'm sorry, kid. I've worked you too hard lately. I bet you really wanted to go home and put your feet up. I just thought this place would be a bit of glamour after all those weeks of concentrating on cockroaches and bedbugs!'

Tom put his arm round her shoulders and led her off the dance floor, up to the gallery. He found them a table at the back, where the strains of the band were low enough to allow conversation.

'Drink?'

'I'll have a Gibson.'

Tom looked puzzled.

'Gin, vermouth and a silverskin onion. I used to have them in America – they'll know how to make them at the bar.'

He called the waiter and ordered two Gibsons, and when they came lifted his glass.

'Here's to Matty Gilbie's new screen career, courtesy of Bermondsey Borough Council!'

They clinked glasses and she took a sip. As she twirled the silverskin onion she found herself thinking of all the opaque layers that formed it, just like herself, with layer after layer of secrets to unpeel. She wondered if, when every layer was stripped away, there would be anything left of her.

'Did you know this place used to be a pickle factory?' she asked suddenly.

'You're having me on.'

'It's true, Crosse & Blackwell! I read about it in *Variety*. They kept the old shell and ripped out the interior. Worst job of my life, that pickle factory.' She gave a shudder.

'There's me thinking I'd bring you here for a bit of glamour and it's just a reminder of all those weeks you spent dripping in vinegar!' Tom looked disappointed.

Matty grinned and raised the dripping onion to her lips. 'Well, you know what they say, you can take the girl out of the pickle factory, but you can't take the pickle out of the girl!' She popped the onion into her mouth and crunched. Then she took a gulp of Dutch courage; it was now or never.

'Tom, there's something I've been meaning to talk to you about...'

18

Fonstone

December 1931–January 1932

Out in the street the contrast with the brightly lit ballroom was stark. Although the rain had stopped, the fog was damp on Matty's face and a chill dankness cloaked her as they walked in silence towards Trafalgar Square. Nelson was invisible atop his column and the lions were brooding dark sentinels in the shrouded square. Cars crawled along, smudged headlights only emphasizing the surrounding opaqueness. Tom took her elbow, guiding her across a fog-draped crossing into the Strand. He had greeted her revelation about the blackmail with a disconcerting tight-lipped impassivity and she wished he'd said more. Now the silence between them felt as impenetrable as the fog.

As they passed the stone cross outside Charing Cross Station, Matty looked up at his stony face. 'I'm sorry, Tom. I know you'll hate me now. I'll hand my notice in on Monday.'

He looked sharply at her. 'What are you sorry for?' he asked.

'I'm sorry for letting myself down, for letting you go, for letting Frank into my life. Ohh, I'm sorry for lots of things, Tom.'

He stopped mid-stride, and looked into her eyes. His tone was reasonable, which Matty found more worrying than if he'd been shouting. 'I can understand all that, Matty. I've seen how blokes like Frank operate. They can make strong men do as they're told, never mind a woman on her own in a strange country. But what I can't understand is...' He broke off and turned away.

'What, what don't you understand? Talk to me, Tom.'

'Now you want to talk?' he said, and his voice had a bitter edge. 'Let's just leave it.'

'No, I've done my talking, and that was bloody hard enough...' She was breathless, trotting to keep up with him. 'It's your turn to talk.'

'All right then, why the hell didn't you trust me when I asked you to tell me everything?' He turned a rigid face to her. His eyes, half shadowed by the trilby brim, were harder than she'd ever seen them. 'How can I protect you when I don't know what the threats are?'

'There's nothing you can do to protect me against this. If he wants to go to the press he can, any time.'

'There's always things you can do – if I'd *known*! A bloke like Frank has always got plenty of enemies.'

Their bus ride home was a sombre affair and when Tom said goodnight, he gave her the barest brush of a kiss. She had expected outrage, disgust, but not this impervious anger. He'd not mentioned the salacious role she'd played in the film, but she knew him: the things that he spoke of least were the things that bit the deepest. Her lack of honesty was what he could talk about, but she knew that hadn't been all that had angered and hurt him. Had her reticence about her life with Frank come from lack of trust, or had it come from love? The only truth she was sure of was that the less Tom knew about Frank's affairs the safer he would be.

*

Tom flatly refused to accept her resignation when they were back at work. But his frostiness towards her had, if anything, deepened. Being in the office alone with him became almost unbearable. He initiated no conversation unless it was necessary for work and his replies to her were either grunts or monosyllables. Perhaps because he'd had time to think about what she'd done.

During the autumn they'd begun to show films in the library halls, and now they were accompanying them with their own recordings. She thanked God for the arrival of the gramophone records, which was the only thing that softened him. For a moment he almost forgot to be angry with her, becoming excited and caught up again by the work they'd done together. But Matty had no idea how to reassure him and perhaps she never could. Part of her reason for leaving him in the first place had been that his idea of trust between them was that she reveal all, even down to the thoughts in her head. He had only been comfortable if there wasn't a space between them and she had only been comfortable if there was. When she'd returned she'd appreciated his new coolness and distance. But now she feared the line between protection and constriction would become blurred and she began to wonder how much he really had changed.

But Matty was determined that nothing should mar Billy's homecoming. The bulldozers had been making a steady assault on Vauban Street, clearing the dilapidated terraced houses to make way for new council flats. But they had stopped their relentless advance in a Christmas truce, halting at the top end of the street, sparing the Gilbie's old house long enough for Billy to have a proper homecoming. It was a magical time for Matty, with all the family packed once again into Nellie's tiny kitchen. There was not an inch of elbow room round the table, so that Matty was thrown vividly back to the days when she and Nellie's brothers would cram round this very table, pasting matchboxes so that Nellie could afford the rent. It was Will's first Bermondsey family Christmas since Eliza's death.

'Come on, Will, you sit there between Matty and Sam.' Nellie ushered the young man in, but Billy wanted to sit next to his cousin and swapped places with his father. Will had always been a hero in Billy's eyes, now even more so since he'd heard the story of his cousin's dramatic, wounded flight from the Nazis.

Billy had changed. He seemed to have left his childhood behind. A seriousness had come over him, a consequence of facing grave illness perhaps. But Matty also noticed that his Bermondsey accent was less thick and he'd obviously assimilated

Swiss propriety and manners. Now, sitting next to Will, the similarity between them was undeniable. The three of them sat in a row, Matty, Billy and Will, the most widely travelled of their family, and all in their different ways overwhelmingly glad to be back here.

When Matty slipped away to the scullery to help Nellie with dinner, she put an arm round her. 'Thanks, Nellie. It's so nice to be home.' And Nellie, red-faced and flustered with the heat, turned a smiling face to her. 'Always, darlin', the bulldozers can pull it down around our ears, but this is always your home – and Will's.' She nodded towards Will and Billy, 'They're like two peas in a pod, never seen it before.'

'Will was nervous – coming here today.'

Nellie raised her eyes. 'Silly sod, he's always welcome.'

There was a knock on the door and in came Nellie's sister, Alice, who had made the journey up from Croydon with her husband in order to see Billy. Small and fragile-looking, she was well turned out in a fashionable fur stole and long coat, cutting a rather affluent figure. Matty hadn't seen her since coming back to England and she was overwhelmed by the warm greeting Alice gave her. She'd always admired how Alice just seemed to get on with life. So quiet, so steady, she had surprised them all when she'd progressed from powder packing to the offices of Pearce Duff's custard factory and had within a year married one of the managers. Later that evening the party was complete when Freddie and Bobby, Nellie's brothers, turned up with their wives and children.

While they all made a fuss over Billy, Matty took the chance to escape into the backyard for a cigarette. She was happy to brave the frosty night for a moment's peace in which to think about Tom. She hated this coolness between them, but she felt now that it was up to him to end it. She walked over to where the old penny-farthing was stored and, leaning against it, she looked up at the stars. Frost sparkled on the cobbled yard, which was lit with a warm glow from the scullery window. She hugged herself and stubbed out her cigarette; they would be missing her. She was just about to go in when Nellie emerged from the back door.

Coming to her side, Nellie leaned her back against the large wheel of the penny-farthing. 'Remember the night we spent in that shed when the Zeppelins bombed Courage's?'

Matty laughed and nodded. 'Then Freddie "found" a few barrels of beer washed up on the foreshore and rolled home blind drunk!'

They were silent for a moment, then Matty shivered.

'Are you cold?' Nellie put an arm round Matty to keep her warm.

Matty sighed miserably. 'No, I was thinking about Tom.'

Nellie gave her a long look. 'Don't tell me you've given him the elbow again! Matty, he's a lovely feller! I was half expecting to hear you'd be getting engaged. He's waited long enough for you.'

'No, we're not engaged! I *would* have said we're happy as we are, but the truth is lately we haven't been getting on... he can be a bit over-protective.'

Nellie sniffed her disapproval. 'If that's all that's wrong with him, then think yourself lucky. You only have to remember that feller Rossi you left behind in America. Give me protective any day!'

She leaned her head on Nellie's shoulder. 'You're right, as usual. You'll miss this old place, won't you?' Matty smiled up at her in the moonlight.

'But not the rats...' Nellie said. 'Nor the stink of the glue factory. But Will was telling me you're off to somewhere a bit grander for New Year.'

Matty lifted her head and pulled a face. 'I haven't decided yet.'

'Why not? You need to get out of Bermondsey, Matty. You've been used to a different life. You go.'

'Truth is, Nellie, I've got nothing to wear and the council pays me less than Peek's. I don't know how I'm going to afford any new dresses.'

264

Unnoticed, a pale shadow had joined them, and both Matty and Nellie jumped when a small voice said, 'Don't worry, I'll ask my sister Milly to make you some if you like. She's a lovely seamstress.'

Bobby's wife, Elsie, always seemed to gravitate towards Matty. She was a lifelong fan and Matty found her adulation touching. She was going to refuse when Nellie pronounced decisively, 'If Milly Hughes makes your dresses you wouldn't look out of place in a palace!'

*

Will had described it as a jumbled mixture of medieval castle, Elizabethan manor and eighteenth-century mansion, a history of England in linked wings, with some rooms furnished like Hampton Court, and others decked out in Lady Fetherstone's choice of stark, angular modern furnishings, looking more like the Savoy Hotel. She was intrigued by what she'd heard of Feathers' family: their ancestors had come over with William the Conqueror and an unbroken line of Fetherstones had lived in Fonstone since then. But his mother had injected a strain of modernity, taking over the decoration and entertaining. It was rumoured she'd had many lovers, mostly from the theatre world, though her current favourite was Neville Piper, a playwright and songwriter, who would be among the New Year guests.

They had been collected from the station by the Fetherstones' car, which was now negotiating the steep, winding drive. They reached a break in the screen of trees and Matty had her first glimpse of Fonstone, spreading proudly across the brow of a hill. The sight drew a simultaneous intake of breath from both her and Tom.

The central russet-brick mansion was flanked by two grey stone wings, each with a terrace reached by a flight of curved stone steps. The house was fronted by a long, striped lawn the size of Southwark Park, with green columns of clipped yews lining the final stretch of drive. As they mounted still higher she could see beyond the main house, where another two-storey building, pierced by pointed windows, formed a cloistered courtyard. The fourth side of the courtyard was a turreted wall ending in a massive circular tower, with arrow-slit windows. The arms of the Fetherstone family fluttered on the tower and Matty thought the castle Douglas Fairbanks had stormed in *Robin Hood* must have been modelled on it.

'Impressive, isn't it?' Will asked, obviously proud of his friend's home.

Tom shifted uncomfortably in his seat next to her. 'I can't see why Lady Fetherstone would want to get involved in our little operation,' he said with an audible swallow.

Tom hadn't been keen to come, but she'd persuaded him they'd be more likely to secure Lady Fetherstone's support if he were there to argue the case. Now she wondered if she'd done the right thing to push him. At least she'd had some experience of being wined and dined by high society in America. Frank had taken her to the best hotels and restaurants, although now she doubted he'd ever had to foot the bill. With Will sitting between them, she'd had no chance to talk to Tom on the train journey and their estrangement was stripping her nerves. She wasn't going to apologize again. She'd confessed to him all that she wanted to, all that she dared, and if it wasn't good enough, then she'd have to live with that. If he wanted an open book for a companion he could go to a library!

They drew nearer the house and just as the car crunched gravel the heavy front door was flung open and a butler appeared on the front steps. Barrel-chested and grim-faced, he was soon joined by two uniformed footmen who began unloading their luggage. The chauffeur helped her out of the car and for a moment she didn't know where to go. Should she follow the footman and her suitcase or approach the unsmiling butler?

'He looks a friendly type,' Tom hissed into her ear and she grabbed his arm. Will hopped out of the car. 'Don't mind Daring. He likes to think he owns the place,' he said under his breath.

'Dear chap!' Matty was relieved to see the familiar, gangly figure of Will's friend hurrying out to meet them. He was dressed differently than he'd been in Bermondsey, in a smart tweed suit and tie, and he'd obviously made an effort for his guests, but the floppy hair and broad smile were the same. He greeted her with a warm handshake.

'Follow me. Ma Feathers is desperate to meet you. I've been given instructions to take you straight to her sitting room!' He took Matty's hand and led her past Daring, the butler, who fortunately was shorter than Matty, so couldn't look down his nose at her, though she suspected he would have liked to.

Lady Fetherstone was a tall, thin woman, with an almost concave figure. Long-limbed like Feathers, she was otherwise very different from her fair-haired, round-faced son, who must have taken after his father. Her dark hair, parted on one side, shone in rippling waves to her drop earrings, which dangled with sparkling brilliance. She flowed elegantly towards them, hands outstretched to greet Matty as if she'd known her all her life.

'My dear Miss Gilbie, Gerald has told me so much about you. And this must be Mr Roberts.' She shook Tom's hand and he smiled nervously. 'Will, tiresome child, I should lock you in the tower for daring to drag my son into Herr Hitler's lair!' She tried to frown at Will, but then her smile and kiss belied the stern words.

'You'll have to lock me up too then. I've told you, Ma, I'm as much to blame.'

Matty saw a look pass between mother and son, and guessed that the discussions between them had been heated.

'I've beaten you to it, Lady Fetherstone, Will's already been imprisoned with me in Bermondsey for a month,' Matty said.

'Which was punishment enough...' Will muttered.

'Enough recriminations! Come and have some tea.' Lady Fetherstone rang a bell and sat down near the blazing fire.

The room was furnished in the latest art-deco style. A coffee and cream circular rug filled the centre of the room and curve-backed sofas and chairs in cream leather were placed round the fire. On the walls, black ebony panelling was inlaid with lighter wood, each panel seeming to tell a pictorial story. Matty was intrigued by the panel above the fireplace, showing stylized images of industrial machinery, which, if she hadn't known better, Matty would have taken for the belt-driven machines that carried the biscuits from the bakeroom in Peek Frean's.

'Ah, do you like my tribute to Great-Grandfather's model production line?' she asked Matty, spotting her interest. 'My father's family made their money in biscuits!' she said proudly.

'A bit like Matty really!' Will whispered to his friend mischievously.

She was relieved to see that the remark had gone unnoticed, for Lady Fetherstone tucked her long legs to one side and leaned forward, elbows on knees, chin propped on hands in an attentive attitude.

'Now, Miss Gilbie, may I call you Matty? Will you tell me all about these wonderful films you are making in Bermondsey? I'm fascinated to hear how you became involved.' She glanced at Tom. 'And where did you find Mr Roberts?'

Matty saw Tom raise an eyebrow and begin to open his mouth. Before he could say anything clever, she said, 'Oh, he found me!'

Once she'd launched into a description of the public health films she felt on safer ground, and invited Tom to talk about the cinemotors and their MP Dr Salter's vision for a borough full of the latest health centres, maternity clinics and a purpose-built solarium.

'In fact we've brought along a film to show you,' he said. 'Feath... Gerald tells me you've got a projector.'

'Yes, mostly for our holiday films, but it would be marvellous if we could have a screening. Now tell me about the new talkies you intend to make with Matty as the "Modern Woman". These are where I think I can help. I'm on the committees of various women's charities, which may well want to support them. I'm sure I could steer them in the right direction.'

Her gaze strayed to one of the long windows with a view of the front drive. She sat back and began playing with her long string of pearls. 'Ah, Neville,' she said, almost to herself, and stood up. 'One of my other guests. Would you excuse me? We'll talk more this evening!' She gave Matty a lingering smile, as if she genuinely couldn't bear to drag herself away, and glided out of the room.

'A promising start,' Feathers said, and only then did Matty realize that he'd been nervous about introducing her and Tom to his mother. However progressive Ma Feathers might be, she'd been elevated well beyond her great-grandfather's biscuit-making roots.

They stood up and Matty glanced out of the window. She recognized the man getting out of the car as Neville Piper, toast of London's theatre land.

As Feathers came to join her at the window, they watched his mother greet Neville with a very unmaternal kiss. Matty felt herself blushing, but the young man looked on impassively and said, 'You'll find that we are that rarest of things – a family without secrets.'

She was delighted to find that her room was in the older, cloister-like wing at the back of the house. A stone-mullioned arched window gave her a view of the gardens and the park beyond. Hedges divided the garden into separate rooms, with a rose garden nearest. In the fading light, black bare-stemmed bushes were outlined in crusted frost with only the large red hips giving any colour. Beyond the rose garden, Matty could make out a rectangular pool surrounded by the interwoven hedges of a knot garden. She was trying to imagine the scene in summer when a knock came on her door. It was Tom.

'Are you sure you should be here?' she said, letting him in anyway.

'There's bound to be some rule against it, but what would your charming little oik know about that?' He shoved his hands in his pockets and went to the window.

'Tom! What's the matter?'

'Where did you *find* me?' His pale eyes flashed irritation.

'Oh, she didn't mean anything by it. What's your room like?'

'Better than yours.'

'Don't let it go to your head, and remember why we're here. Just be your usual charming self and you'll win her over in no time. It's the films that matter, after all.'

'I'm not sure she's really serious, Matty. I feel as if we're her latest hobby.'

This wasn't like Tom. Whatever his faults, lack of enthusiasm wasn't one of them. She suspected it had more to do with her own trustworthiness than with Lady Fetherstone's.

She joined him by the window. He was staring towards the line of trees in the park, which had now turned black against a violet sky. If things had been easier between them, now would be the time he'd take her in his arms, in laughing defiance of propriety.

'Tom—'

He interrupted her. 'Better get dressed for dinner.'

But at the door, she wouldn't let him go without a kiss. He pulled away as a maid appeared at the end of the long corridor.

'I'll come and knock for you,' he said and disappeared in the direction of his room.

She went to the wardrobe where the new silver-grey evening dress had already been hung up for her. Elsie's sister, Milly, had lovingly crafted it, cleverly bias-cutting the satin so that its fluid folds enhanced Matty's slim figure. She had been impressed by the woman's quick understanding of exactly what was needed – maximum impact for minimum cost. Milly Hughes certainly had an eye for style and knew better than Matty what hemlines and colours were in fashion. But she felt guilty at the many hours it must have taken her to sew on all those beads, and also at her insistence she only charge Matty for materials. 'Because you're family,' she'd said with finality.

Matty dressed carefully, finally draping a black velvet wrap over the low-backed dress. When Tom called for her, she was rewarded with a wide-eyed look of appreciation.

'You really do look like a screen goddess!' he said, but this time, when he didn't bend to kiss her, she understood the depth of his hurt. She was certain she had lost him.

The dining room was the opposite of Lady Fetherstone's sitting room. It was an ugly confusion of coloured marble, the floor chequered with russet, black and white, and the walls panelled in turquoise and ivory. A heavy marble sideboard held silver dishes and the chandeliers bounced light along the dining table. She was glad to be on Tom's arm, unsure of who else would be among the party. But she needn't have worried. She'd been placed next to Neville Piper, who it turned out was, apart from Elsie, her greatest fan.

'I saw you at the Hippodrome before you went to America and I have your recordings, my dear – and there are far too few of them! Of course I adored *London Affair*. But I have a bone to pick with you! How could you deprive us of the Cockney Canary? You're far too young to have gone into retirement. Can't I persuade you out of it?'

Will, who was sitting opposite, came to her aid. 'Oh, she's doing far more important things now, really making a difference.' And though Neville Piper didn't seem impressed to have been interrupted, she was grateful for the distraction.

The dinner was proving less daunting than she'd expected. It seemed that Lady Fetherstone was a widow and the only other member of the party was Frances, Feathers' sister. She was a hearty-looking young woman of about eighteen, conspicuously without make-up, with hair bound loosely in a Grecian loop, and dressed in a wide-shouldered voluminous garment that looked more home-made than Matty's own.

'Look at Miss Gilbie's divine dress, darling,' Lady Fetherstone remarked to her daughter at one point. 'Perhaps you could give Frances the name of your dressmaker in London,' she asked Matty pointedly.

'Man-made fibres are anathema to me, Mother,' Frances said fiercely. 'You should know that.'

'Our dear Frances is a keen member of the Kindred of the Kibbo Kift,' Feathers explained. 'She'll give us a demonstration of wood craft later, if we ask her nicely.'

'Oh, shut up, Gerald, it's more than just camping and wood carving.' She addressed Matty. 'We're working towards a better world, you know, one where your Bermondsey factories would be made redundant – surely that would make your work a lot easier?'

'Well, Frankie, if it weren't for Great-Grandpa's biscuit factories you might never have had the leisure to handcraft your delightful costumes and walk barefoot in the dew!'

Frances shot her brother a venomous look and Lady Fetherstone suggested they retire to the drawing room. It was only when the men came in from drinking their port that Matty began to feel awkward. Neville made a beeline for her and she wasn't sure that Lady Fetherstone enjoyed being deprived of his attention. He insisted on taking her on a tour of the room, which was vast and high-ceilinged and covered in the most deceptive *trompe l'oeil* paintings on walls and ceiling. The illusion was of a Roman villa, with recessed arches and niches housing stone vases and statues. And the curtains weren't real curtains at all, but painted drapes that Matty felt the need to reach out and stroke.

'It's like a film set!' she exclaimed. 'None of it's real!'

And Neville Piper seemed pleased. 'Hideous, isn't it, darling? Painted by a former favourite of Lady Fetherstone,' he said tartly. 'And now, of course, they can't get rid of it without tearing the bloody walls down.'

To Matty it was as magical as any Hollywood studio, but she said nothing. Their circuit of the room ended at a cocktail table. A table lamp glowed through various exotic-looking bottles, their gem-like colours of green and ruby red splashed on to cocktail glasses and the tall silver shaker. Feathers was mixing drinks.

'Tom's been showing me how to make a Gibson. Here, try this,' he said, pouring the drink from the cocktail shaker and adding a silverskin onion.

She took a sip. 'Perfect!' But before she could drink any more,

Neville Piper whipped the glass away and took hold of her hand.

'Come with me, darling. I'm determined you *shall* make a comeback and there's no time like the present!'

He led her to a gleaming black grand piano, sat down and struck a chord. Matty wanted to run. This was not why she'd come. She looked appealingly at Tom. Either he didn't want to see her or he really was engrossed in his conversation with Lady Fetherstone about the 'Modern Woman' in films. She heard the words 'biscuit factory' and hoped to God he wasn't elaborating on her stint at Peek Frean's. Will and Gerald were lounging together on the sofa, cocktails in hand, ready to be entertained. Her only hope was Frances. She was sure the girl would prefer an evening of folk songs, but now she surprised Matty with a request.

'Oh, do sing "Love is the Sweetest Thing", Miss Gilbie. It's my absolute favourite!'

Neville played the introductory bars, there was a pause and some automatic response drew the sound up from deep inside her. For Matty, it was as irresistible as breathing. She opened her mouth and sang in a low, reflective tone. So low, that it would force those who were speaking to fall silent, if they wanted to hear. She matched the style to the audience, letting the words emerge, almost reluctantly, as though she were having a conversation with herself.

Love is the sweetest thing, what else on earth could ever bring
Such happiness to ev'rything, as Love's old story?

And the conversation could not help but be a sad one, for as Tom turned an intent face towards her, she felt powerless to stop 'love's old story' from turning into a tragedy once more. Whether he wanted to hear or not, she sang on, meeting his gaze.

Love is the strangest thing, no song of birds upon the wing
Shall in our hearts so sweetly sing, that love's old story?

The end of the song was greeted with applause, but Neville wasn't to be deterred, running the end of the first song into another, assuming she would know them all. She saw that Tom had recognized the opening bars of 'I'll See You in My Dreams' before she had. But there was no way she could refuse to sing it without making a scene. She was aware of a stillness. Perhaps it was the presence of attentive listeners, but it felt more as if it were a stillness inside herself, as though all the mistakes and clutter of her life counted for nothing and only one thing held any importance – that Tom's eyes should not turn away as she came to the final words of the song.

> *Lips that once were mine, tender eyes that shine*
> *They will light my lonely way tonight,*
> *I'll see you in my dreams.*

19

A Family Without Secrets

New Year 1932

Neville monopolized her for the rest of the evening. He was full of praise for her singing style. 'You really can do intimate spaces very well, Miss Gilbie. If we couldn't tempt you back on to the stage, what about performing at soirées such as tonight's? Or I could introduce you to a few select private clubs where I'm sure you'd be in great demand!'

'That's kind, but—'

'Don't say "but"! If you're nervous about your performance skills being a *little* rusty in places, I'd love to help coach you. In fact...'

Here he drew nearer and shielded her from the rest of the room. 'I have a bijou bolt-hole in your neck of the woods, overlooking the river, near the Angel pub. An old sea captain's house, I believe.' He leaned even closer and whispered into her ear. 'It's such a romantic little spot, nothing but a passing Thames barge to interrupt us.'

'The Angel? Of course, it's by Cherry Garden Pier,' Matty said in a stage whisper which had the desired effect of catching Lady Fetherstone's attention. She left Tom with a word of apology and glided over, her concave figure leaning proprietorially against Neville's.

Matty smiled at her, half with relief, half with mischief. 'Lady Fetherstone, Mr Piper was just telling me about his little "bolt-hole" in Bermondsey – it's such a small world!'

Lady Fetherstone raised first her cigarette holder and then an eyebrow. Turning deliberately to Neville, she said, 'A small world indeed. In fact, that's given me a marvellous idea. Perhaps, Neville, you'd invite me to stay in your little "bolt-hole" so that I can see Mr Robert's pioneering film work on the spot!'

Neville didn't answer Lady Fetherstone. Instead he kissed her lightly on the cheek and said, 'Time to toast the New Year, Marjorie darling. Champagne for your guests?' He plucked a bottle from the ice bucket and popped the cork, sending a foaming fizz over the silver tray as he filled glasses. 'Come on, everyone,' he addressed the room, 'let's drink to 1932!' Neville kissed Matty as he handed her the champagne glass and she pulled away, flustered. The only New Year kiss she was interested in would come from Tom, but when Matty looked around the room for him, he was not there.

The following morning was taken up with showing Lady Fetherstone the films they'd brought with them. The projector was set up in her sitting room, which had been blacked out for the purpose, with the shutters and heavy curtains drawn. She proved surprisingly knowledgeable about the benefits of childcare and sunray treatment and seemed genuinely moved when Matty told her Billy's story. By the end of the screenings, she had virtually guaranteed them the funding for the new series of films featuring Matty.

After lunch, Matty stood on the terrace watching the boys traipse off to shoot at clay pigeons. As she was about to go in she spotted the bizarre figure of Frances disappearing down the drive, dressed in an even more outlandish outfit than the day before – it reminded Matty of coalmen with their improvised coal-sack hoods. Frances' sacking garment reached only halfway down her thighs and she wore thick woollen stockings held up by cross garters. On the front and back of her wide-shouldered tunic she had appliquéd a lightning bolt.

'Poor girl, she does look ridiculous, but she won't listen to me. I'm told she's organized a very important gathering of the local

Kindred of the Kibbo Kift in Fonstone Wood.' Lady Fetherstone's brow creased as she followed her daughter's progress. 'I'm not sure which of my children I'm more worried about.'

'They both want to make the world a better place,' Matty offered and Lady Fetherstone smiled suddenly. 'Come for a walk in the park, Miss Gilbie. It's such a beautiful day.'

Matty was certain the cherry-red two-piece Milly had made for her was unsuitable for a country walk, but it was all she had and the detachable fur collar meant that at least the jacket was warm. She went to put on her oval black hat, setting it at a fashionable angle and adding a pair of black gloves. Lady Fetherstone was waiting for her on the terrace, dressed in tweeds and sensible shoes. A flicker of surprise crossed her face at the cherry-red outfit and Matty, smiling brightly, pulled up the fur collar and crossed the terrace as if it were a stage. The woman set off with a long, brisk stride, but Matty was a match for her. They walked through the gardens towards a small lake, with Lady Fetherstone pointing out specimen trees and a folly on the way. It was a bright, crisp afternoon and Matty was beginning to enjoy the walk when the woman stopped.

'This is the heart of Fonstone, Matty. May I call you Matty?'

They had come upon a tall block of weathered stone, sticking out at a drunken angle from the level grassy area.

'The story is that it's a stone from the original castle, dislodged by a trebuchet in one of the many sieges. But it's actually much older than anything else on the estate, probably just one of a stone-age circle. There are others scattered around the area, but this is the largest. No one could ever move it, there's far more stuck below the ground than on top of it, see?'

'We have a stone in Bermondsey, but a tenth smaller! They say it's the only relic from our old abbey. Did you know that kings and queens stayed in Bermondsey Abbey?' Matty said, running her hand over the smooth stone.

'It's certainly a place that attracts a motley assortment. Speaking of which – I do hope Neville wasn't bothering you too much yesterday evening,' Lady Fetherstone said suddenly. 'He is quite naughty. I don't expect fidelity, but I do expect good manners, and if he put you in an embarrassing position...'

Matty smiled and shook her head. 'I've been on the stage most of my life. I had to learn how to deal with – attention at an early age.'

'Well, my dear, you dealt with it admirably last night, and I appreciated your tact. I was teasing Neville slightly, but I really did mean it, about coming to Bermondsey to see your work. You see...' she gave an almost imperceptible sigh and her tall figure caved in a little more, 'I lost one of my own children to scarlet fever.'

Matty's surprise must have shown on her face, for she had only ever thought of it as a disease of the poor, spread in crowded, unhygienic, poor housing.

'Privilege is not always a protection, but it's a help. At least I didn't lose all my children, as some of those poor mothers in your films have done.' She heard Lady Fetherstone's voice break and her heart immediately went out to the woman. Ignoring polite convention, she took her hand. 'It's a terrible thing, to lose a child,' she said softly and Lady Fetherstone nodded, squeezing Matty's hand.

They walked on in silence till they reached the almost circular lake and sat on a bench, watching a pair of swans glide towards them.

'Now tell me about your handsome Mr Roberts – he's obviously head over heels. So what's the trouble between the two of you?'

Matty blushed and pulled at the fur stole.

'Have I shocked you? I'm sorry, my dear, but I have an antenna when it comes to matters of the heart, and I can spot one that's breaking a mile off.'

It was strangely comforting to unburden her heart to this virtual stranger from another world. Matty would have thought she'd have nothing in common with Ma Feathers except her son and her philanthropy, but she soon discovered the woman had an uncanny knack of drawing her out. She seemed genuinely interested.

'The truth is, I kept something a secret from him for a long time and then I told him, and now he doesn't trust me...' Matty confessed.

'Ah, secrets, yes. I've always found them a great inconvenience.'

'Your son told me you were a family without secrets,' Matty said and Lady Fetherstone gave a short ringing laugh that caused the swans to look haughtily in their direction.

'It's true, I try to do without them. But sometimes it is tempting – to avoid hurt.'

Matty nodded vigorously. 'That's what I thought, but that only seemed to make Tom angrier.'

'I don't think you need worry too much about him, Matty. Last night he was manfully trying to stay focused on our conversation, but his eyes gave him away. They were always on you, my dear.'

That evening another guest joined them, a former tutor of Will and Feathers, who'd been researching Hadrian's Wall. He had been invited to stay the night on his return south. He was a short, roundish man, with a benign face and tufts of white hair crowning his bald head. Will told her Professor Dubbs was a fearsomely intelligent and respected academic, though he looked to Matty more like a grocer. Even the addition of an evening suit didn't eradicate the impression. But the boys both seemed in awe of him. Matty had never seen Will quite so deferential to anybody and Feathers' nonchalance had deserted him.

The professor exchanged a few pleasantries with Matty after dinner, but she felt oddly as though she were in the presence of a character actor. Each of his pronouncements was followed by a short, hearty laugh, and though his smile was broad and the corners of his eyes crinkled, the gaze that held her was pinpoint sharp. She felt like a butterfly impaled on a pin, held up to the light and impassively studied. Perhaps that was what a fearsomely intelligent mind did, but Matty didn't like it and she was glad when he turned his chilly attention back to the boys.

She went instinctively to the fire, which was ablaze with logs brought in from the park. Whether it was the flames or the dazzling light from several huge chandeliers hanging in the room, the unsettling exchange with Professor Dubbs had left her feeling exposed. She realized he'd found out much more about her in those brief minutes than she had about him.

Tom came to her side and she turned to him with a smile. They were going home tomorrow and Matty felt disappointed they'd had no chance to talk.

'Come out for a bit of air?' she asked, indicating the doors leading to the terrace, and he followed her.

Tonight she was wearing a midnight-blue velvet gown and matching wrap which, once outside, she pulled more closely around her shoulders. The stars here were more numerous than she'd ever seen – even in America. The thin northern air and lack of London fog seemed to boost their brilliance against the deep black night.

Tom lit them both cigarettes and she waited for him to speak. He looked at her with eyes that seemed to catch the starlight.

'You look beautiful.' He sighed. 'But it's no good, Matty...'

She held her breath, a dread, colder than the night air, clutching at her stomach.

'I was an idiot to expect you'd come home from America without a history. I'm sorry.'

What was he sorry about? Sorry that he couldn't live with her secrets? Sorry he had expected her to trust him enough to reveal them? She had no idea.

'It's all right, Tom, I understand. You can't ignore my past. It's a lot to expect of any man.'

'I've tried to make myself not care what happened between you and Rossi, but I do. Sometimes when I look at you all I can see is you in that photo. I don't think I even blame you. I just can't get the picture out of my mind, and I want to smash his face to a pulp. But he's not here, so all I do is get angry with you.

I know it's not fair, but I keep thinking about what you said at Winchester.'

She was trembling, not from the cold, but from fear of what he would say next. She wrapped her arms tightly around herself.

'What did I say?' She heard her own voice, shaky and thin.

'You said, *Don't go back for me*, and I know you meant the gangs, but perhaps you were right in another way... I shouldn't have gone back for you.'

At that moment Neville Piper stuck his head out of the terrace door. 'Ah, I'm sorry to interrupt,' he said, looking anything but sorry. 'But Lady Fetherstone requires your presence. She wants to try one of those Gibson cocktails and apparently I'm making a mess of it. Could we borrow Mr Roberts to be our barman?'

Tom shot her a miserable look and murmured, 'I'm sorry', leaving her to the terrace and her tears, which she found impossible to stem. It was only gradually that hushed voices made their way into her consciousness. They were coming from below the terrace and she instinctively moved back from the balustrade, not wishing to eavesdrop – until, that is, she recognized Feathers' voice. She knew she shouldn't be listening, but the young man's tone was high-pitched with urgency.

'It's not just myself I have to think of. I'm part of a family with many responsibilities. There are certain duties, expectations, of someone in my position.'

'And that is exactly why, my dear boy, you are perfectly placed to play this role. Who would suspect someone in your position? You will have access to certain information that will further our cause. You wanted to make this a fairer, more just world, didn't you? You told me you have felt the burden of guilt all your life, for your privilege, your unearned right to all the things denied to most of humanity. Now is the moment in history when you can make that difference. You only need the will. You've made a start – albeit an abortive one, but what we are asking of you would be a lifetime commitment. Putting the comintern cause above country, family, friends, personal happiness, *that* is what is required of a young man in your position, *that* is the expectation, *that* is responsibility.' It was the mesmerizing voice of Professor Dubbs, and tonight there was no hint of the grocer in it. It was both forceful and reasonable, so that Matty realized with disgust that she was almost willing Feathers to agree to the 'great enterprise', which would undoubtedly ruin his life, if not end it. She felt sick. Had Dubbs given the same speech to Will? If he had, she didn't doubt what his reply would have been. She'd been naive to think the two boys had acted alone in their foolhardy trip to Germany. Wasn't there always someone who stayed safely at home and pulled the strings? She gripped the balustrade, her heart thumping so loudly she thought the sound must reach the two below and give her away.

She heard Feathers clear his throat. 'I do, most sincerely, wish to do my bit, Professor, and I think I'm up to the challenge. What is it you had in mind for me...'

She heard shuffling feet and she saw the two glowing tips of their cigarettes move slowly along the lower terrace. Professor Dubbs' answer was lost to her as they moved out of earshot. She realized she'd been holding her breath, and now before Tom could come out and reveal her presence she hurried inside.

She bumped into Will, who was on his way out to join her. He took her elbow, leading her back into the warm bright room.

'Bit uncle willy out there, ain't it?' he said, in his other voice, which for some reason tonight she found endearing rather than irritating. She slipped her arm through his. 'I've been thinking, Will. You should really get a proper job.'

He threw back his head and laughed. 'Now you do sound like our mother.'

'I'm not joking. You want to give your father's money away and International Red Aid might be a good cause, but have you ever thought about working in Bermondsey? Can't you make a better world starting there?'

'What's sparked all this off? Seen too much privilege this weekend?'

She steered Will towards the gramophone, which was playing a version of 'Ain't Misbehavin''. Then, lowering her voice, she said, 'Has Professor Dubbs made you a proposal?'

The beginnings of a blush spread up Will's neck and she could see him fighting with surprise. 'What on earth could old Dubbs propose, apart from a dusty life in the groves of academe – not for me, Matty.' He gave a strained laugh and she knew he'd accepted.

'Don't give me that old flannel, Will. You bloody well tell him to shove his comintern cause up his arse, hear me?'

This was the last thing he expected from Matty and his eyes widened with what looked almost like terror. The greatest secret of his life, probably less than an hour old, had been blown to the four winds by his sister, the faded music hall star, and for once Will was speechless.

'I've just heard him having a go at Feathers too. And the silly sod's going along with it! Please, Will, our mother was all for changing the world, but what that feller's asking sounded like treason! Don't have anything to do with it,' Matty urged fiercely.

Will glanced at the others seated now round the fire. 'Don't you have any idea what's going on in Germany?' he hissed. 'Well, I've seen it first hand and our government's doing *nothing* about it! Believe me, those Nazi bully boys will take over the world unless we organize ourselves to stop them. At least Dubbs and the other comrades are trying!'

Their whispered exchange had caught the notice of the others and Neville, with a nose for gossip, strolled over to them.

'Family tiff?' he asked almost gaily and, without waiting for a response, said, 'Shall I change the record, or will you sing for us, Miss Gilbie?'

Matty pretended to flick through the sleeved gramophone records sitting on the table and picked one out at random. 'Here, this one. I don't really feel like singing tonight,' she said, looking at Will's stricken face and following his gaze to the terrace door, where Feathers had made his entrance with Professor Dubbs. The two boys exchanged looks of flushed excitement, which only she and Dubbs could possibly interpret.

'So much,' Matty thought, 'for a family without secrets.'

She decided that for the moment she could do nothing about Tom, but the following morning, after a sleepless night, she thought she could at least try to help Will and Feathers, and there was only one person she could turn to. If Feathers could be dissuaded, then she suspected Will would not want to carry on with Dubbs' plan alone. Part of the attraction, she was sure, was that both boys were in it together. She took her chance after breakfast and made her way to see Ma Feathers.

Lady Fetherstone looked up from her desk, a chunky black and brass affair with fan-shaped ends.

'My dear, Matty. I would have come to see you off! Have your things been brought down?'

She showed Matty to one of the cream leather armchairs. 'I hope you think your visit has been worthwhile?' she asked, sitting opposite.

'Oh yes, very,' Matty said, aware she sounded breathless.

'I was a little worried last night when you left us early. Neville—'

'No, as I said, I'm used to dealing with that sort of attention,' Matty interrupted her. 'It's not Mr Piper, not at all. In fact he was kind enough to suggest introductions to a few private singing venues. It's something else. It's about your son.'

'Gerald? What's he been up to now?'

Matty licked her lips, dry-mouthed at the accusation she was about to make.

'You remember we were talking about what a special family you are... one without secrets?'

Lady Fetherstone nodded.

'Well, I think Gerald's just broken with tradition.'

How Ma Feathers had managed to do it, Matty didn't know, but that it had been done she was certain of when Professor Dubbs caught hold of her arm as she emerged from her room about half an hour later. She'd been checking to make sure nothing had been left behind.

'Miss Gilbie, I'm glad I've caught you before you leave,' he said smoothly. 'Let me assure you that the idealism of youth is in endless supply. These two have been lost, but there will be others.' She felt his breath cold on her cheek. 'I do not appreciate your interference in our work. It has resulted in a waste of very valuable assets and I abhor waste – as I'm sure a person of your background would agree, it's... criminal...' He fixed her with unblinking eyes and gripped her upper arm with surprising strength.

She yanked herself away.

'Oh, I beg your pardon, Miss Gilbie. Other people often comment that I am stronger than I look...' The oily smile was constant and the tone pleasant, but the stare pinned her to the spot more firmly than his hand had. 'I'm deeply sorry you felt it necessary to jeopardize my activities. It would have been better for you if you'd never come to my notice at all. But now you have, I suppose I should warn you that as a historian I excel at uncovering the secrets of the past, and a woman such as yourself has almost certainly acquired some of those.'

'I've got nothing to hide,' Matty said, sounding more certain than she felt. 'And besides, you don't know anything about me.'

He let out a short, metallic laugh and his tone hardened. 'What I do not know I make a point of finding out. Because I am thirsty for knowledge.' His lip curled unpleasantly with the effort of maintaining his smile and his face was now inches from hers. Trapped between him and the door, she began to panic. She hadn't been aware of the silent approach of Daring.

'Is there anything I can help you with, Miss Gilbie?' He gave her the pleasantest smile she'd had from him since she arrived. He turned to Dubbs. 'Professor? I believe her ladyship has arranged a car to take you to the station.'

Professor Dubbs made no move to go, but Daring paused slightly and continued with emphasis, '*Now*.'

The professor turned abruptly on his heel and Matty wrapped her arms around herself, determined to disguise her trembling, watching as he descended the stairs. He looked somehow taller, stronger, the avuncular veneer peeled away, a trick of smoke and mirrors abandoned now to reveal the menace behind the actor's cloak of meekness.

'Would you like me to accompany you to the car, Miss Gilbie?'

Matty nodded. 'Yes, please.'

Daring glided along the corridor beside her and down the stairs. 'I doubt the professor will have any more to say to you today.' He dropped his voice. 'Her ladyship has seen him off, and may I say, Miss Gilbie, we owe you a debt of gratitude for what you did for Master Gerald.'

'How did you know about that?'

Daring smiled slowly. 'Ah well, Miss Gilbie, there are no secrets in this house.'

Outside by the waiting car she and Tom said goodbye to Will, who was staying on for a few more days with Feathers. The boys' hangdog expressions confirmed what Dubbs had told her. He had lost them. She managed to whisper a quick thank you to Lady Fetherstone before getting into the car with Tom. As they drove away she was full of gratitude that Ma Feathers had saved their precious boys from becoming pawns in some great game, but she couldn't shake the venomous barb of doubt that Dubbs had launched and she feared that their freedom might have been bought at the cost of her own.

20

Cards and Knife

February–March 1932

Matty yawned, stretched her arms above her head and rubbed sleep-filled eyes with her knuckles. She reached out for the ringing alarm clock, slapping it off the table, so that it skittered under the bed, then she turned over, snuggling deep beneath the candlewick bedspread so that only the top of her head was visible. A cold wind was blowing through the room and she was shivering beneath the bedclothes. Today, she would be returning to Peek Frean's and she was not looking forward to it. The insistent ringing of the alarm eventually forced her to throw back the covers and go in search of the irritating clock. She squirmed under the bed. First she pulled out a rose-patterned chamber pot, then, crawling further in, she threw out an unmatched stocking, a dried bouquet of flowers and a mewing kitten, before finally emerging triumphant with the clock. But in her groggy half-asleep state she knocked her head on the iron bedstead. Rubbing her head vigorously, she waited for her vision to clear and peered intently at the clock.

'Oh no, my first day and I'm late!' she groaned, and flung the clock at the wall. In a frenzied hopping dance, she circled the room, pulling out stockings and skirts from a chest of drawers, shoving on whatever came to hand. She was finally dressed in an absurd mish-mash of summer and winter clothes – a too heavy sweater and a too light summer coat. She stuffed her feet into her gold leather dancing shoes, grabbed her handbag and dashed out, slamming the door behind her so that the walls shook.

'Cut!' Tom called, and Plum stood up from the camera. 'One take?' He gave a nod of appreciation to Tom. 'Gosh, she's good!'

Matty stuck her head back through the door of the skeleton room and scooped up the kitten. 'Too much?' she asked, looking from Plum to Tom.

'Perfect!' Tom said. 'Are you all right to go straight into the next scene?'

Matty came back into the skeleton room, feeling the door hinges for damage. The set was fairly solidly built, but she'd given the door a hefty slam, partly in true anger at being made to return to Peek's. She'd begged Tom to choose another local firm for the *Modern Woman and Work* factory sequence. She almost felt he was punishing her, but he insisted it was D.M.'s idea. Apparently their medical officer knew Peek's owner and approved of the firm's high moral standards, seeing their provision of dental and eye checks for workers as the sort of enlightened philanthropy that should be rewarded with free publicity in the borough's films.

The late-for-work scene was meant to show how the modern woman should *not* begin her day and would be intercut with the caption that Matty would eventually record for the voice-over:

> Think ahead to get ahead! The modern woman
> starts her day in a calm, organized manner, clothes
> and overalls freshly laundered and laid out the night
> before. Women who slack, quickly get the sack!

This would be followed by a contrasting scene showing Matty, having learned her lesson, dressed in modern, practical clothes arriving at the factory gates, with a skyline shot of Peek's clock tower emphasizing her early arrival for work.

D.M.'s input into the scripts had sometimes felt a little too preachy for Matty's liking. She wondered how often he'd had to launder his own shirts before turning up in pristine collar and bowler to the town hall. But Tom had been entrusted with the direction of the whole 'Modern Woman' series and D.M. had given them carte blanche to inject as much tongue-in-cheek fun into the films as they could.

Tom and Plum covered the skeleton room set with tarpaulin while Matty went to return the kitten to its owner, an elderly lady who lived next door to the TB dispensary. The three of them set off in the cinemotor for Peek Frean's. With a letter of authorization from the directors, they were waved through the gates along with a cart delivering churns of milk and a lorry packed high with sacks of flour. Tom parked the cinemotor between two Peek's delivery vans in the loading bay.

'Ready to go back to making biscuits?' he asked brightly.

'Can't wait,' Matty said and pulled a face at his back as she followed him out of the van. The mingled smells of cocoa and vanilla baking together hit her. 'Oh no,' she groaned, 'it would have to be a Bourbon-cream day!' She sighed and helped Tom and Plum unload the camera and lights. Their first scene was to be a panoramic shot taken from the top of the van, showing the endless surge of workers coming through the gates, with Matty one small drop in the ocean of labour. While Tom fixed the camera on to a tripod on the roof of the cinemotor, she ran back to the gates, getting in position for the opening shot. The hooter blew and a mass of workers jostled forward. Plum panned the camera down from the white clock-face, zooming through the crowd to pick out Matty, looking lost and hesitant as she gazed up at the rows of identical windows. This time there was no curious welcoming committee for Matty – the workforce had been primed to cooperate with shooting and told to act as normally as possible whenever the cameras were around.

With the first scene done, Tom went to report their presence at the office and find out where they'd be allowed to shoot that day. They'd been promised someone to guide them round the factory to ensure the cooperation of all departments.

Matty tried to tell herself she was back here on her own terms, but there was something about the toasting smell and the heat wafting over from the bakehouse which stuck in her throat and instantly depressed her spirits. How on earth she was going to inject any humour into these scenes she didn't know, but when Tom returned with their guide for the day, Matty gave up any hope of lightening her mood.

'This is my colleague, Matty Gilbie. I believe you two know each other.' Tom grinned mischievously. 'Matty, the works manager has kindly given us Edna for the day – I suppose you could say she's our runner!'

She might not know what a runner was but from Edna's sour expression it was obvious she'd deduced the lowly position she'd been assigned, and was clearly looking forward to the day even less than Matty. She folded her arms and gave Matty a curt nod.

'The works manager says we can start filming on the packing line,' Tom explained. 'Would you lead on?' he asked Edna, with a charming smile for Matty's former enemy.

Cheers rang out along the Bourbon-cream packing line as they advanced and Winnie waved furiously at her. Matty saw Edna's sharp eyes note the Bourbon creams piling up into a little mountain at Winnie's station.

'All right, keep the line going. You're meant to be acting normal!' she ordered.

Tom whispered something to Edna, who looked as if a whole Bourbon cream might be stuck in her throat. She coughed and nodded, then beckoned to Winnie.

'The gentleman wants you for a special shot.'

Matty could see Winnie biting her cheek, trying not to laugh as she stepped boldly up to Tom and gave him a kiss on the cheek.

'That's no gentleman, that's me brother!' She laughed, though Edna didn't appear to find it funny.

'Who else shall we take?' Tom asked Matty. And when she proceeded to pull every one of the Tiller Girls off the packing line, Winnie's giggles overcame her.

'Right, we want to do a few scenes showing health-and-safety issues,' Matty explained, drawing the girls to one side. 'Let's have a look at your plates, girls.'

Obediently the girls formed a line, turned side on and raised their knees as one, in the Tiller Girl high step. A passing machine minder gave a wolf whistle and the whole packing line erupted in laughter.

'Well, none of you've got sensible shoes on your feet. This is what you're all meant to be wearing.' Matty did her own high step and, flashing her brown, wide-fitting flats, pointed her toe.

'Borrowed 'em off Nurse Rayon from the solarium! All I need now is someone with biscuit legs,' she said, looking round. 'Any volunteers? We need to show what standing at a packing line in tight shoes and garters will do for your pins.' Matty eyed the girls hopefully and then Winnie put up a hand.

'Well, Edna was on the line twenty years before she got promoted,' she said meekly, and Sophie chimed in, 'Your veins is terrible, ain't they, Edna?'

'Would you mind, Edna?' Tom asked. 'Just a quick shot, all in the cause of improved health and safety, which I understand the Peek's board is very keen to promote...'

But Matty found herself feeling sorry for the woman as Edna, smiling rigidly, sat on a stool and obediently raised her overall above her knees. Plum zoomed in for a close-up of the raised blue tributaries of varicose veins marbling the woman's calves and Matty thought of all the years of hard graft that had caused them.

'OK, Matty,' Tom said. 'Let's have a shot of your legs then!'

'Do I need to?' she asked, feeling awkward.

'We need a comparison shot, and it's not anything you haven't done before,' he said, turning away to set up the shot with Plum.

Matty sat next to Edna, and reluctantly lifted her skirt slowly to the knees, pointing the toes of her sensible shoes and revealing her unblemished legs.

'Don't be ashamed of them, Matty, let's see a bit more of those lovely legs...' he said pointedly.

'That's all you're getting,' she said tartly. 'Besides, neither of us has got anything to be ashamed of. Edna's veins come from twenty years' hard graft!'

Edna shot her a surprised look of gratitude, but Winnie smiled victoriously and said, 'Matty's pins go on forever and not a vein on 'em.' As she returned to her station she whispered to Matty, 'Revenge is sweet,' before popping a Bourbon cream into her mouth.

But though Matty couldn't share Winnie's glee at Edna's discomfort, she did enjoy the next part of the filming, a section on the need for motivation during the working day. Tom had rolled out to the managers the latest research, which showed productivity soared when workers were able to sing along to music. The final shot of the production line showed Matty, leading her fellow workers in a chorus of 'When You're Smiling'.

After three days' filming they had all the shots they could use: Matty had undergone a series of misfortunes, playing the part of a fainting young worker in the bakehouse being revived by pints of lemonade generously provided by the firm, illustrating the need to stay hydrated, delivering an agonized performance as a burn victim whose fingertips had been blistered while picking up biscuits still red-hot from the oven, had a hand caught in a machine belt and been almost crushed by a poorly secured sack of flour falling from a loading bay.

After they'd packed up the cameras on the last day of filming, Matty waited at the factory gates for Winnie and the Tiller Girls. She had invited them for a drink as a thank you for working as extras. When they arrived at the Concorde pub the girls were full of Matty's unlikely return to Peek's.

'Did you see Edna's face when the works manager took down the *No Singing* sign? Looked like she'd choked on a raisin out of a garibaldi!' Winnie said to her as they moved chairs and tables to accommodate half the Bourbon-cream production line.

'Before I forget.' Winnie reached under the table for a voluminous bag, which banged against Matty's legs as her friend pulled it up on to the table. 'Mrs Peek's finest, we're sick of 'em.' Matty peered into the bag, which had at least half a dozen Christmas puddings packed into it.

'Gawd sake, Win, how much pudding did you think you'd need last Christmas?'

'Well, I might have gone over the top, but they'll help Nellie out, feeding those three boys. I know it's been a struggle for her, helping to keep Billy at the sanatorium. I bump into her sometimes, running from one job to another. She never stops.'

Matty leaned over to plant a kiss on her friend's cheek. 'You're a diamond. She'll be grateful.'

'And there's a bag of broken in there for the boys, and tell 'em to make the most of 'em cos they're the last I'll be able to get.'

'Why?'

'I'll be getting me cards.'

'Oh, love, I'm sorry. What happened?' Matty was puzzled by the undeniable twinkle in Winnie's eyes and barely concealed smile. 'You don't look too unhappy about it.'

'I don't want to lose me job, love, but it could be worse.' She banged on the table. 'Shhhh, everyone. I've got an announcement to make.' The chattering and laughter went on. 'Shut yer cake'oles, you lot!' Winnie bellowed and finally the Tiller Girls stopped their conversation, putting down their glasses, attentive faces turned to Winnie.

'Well, gels, I shall be getting me cards and me knife!'

The girls jumped up as one, eager to congratulate Winnie, and finally Matty was able to hug her friend. For when Peek's presented a woman with her cards and a knife it meant only one thing: she was getting married. These days, the 'Modern Woman at Work' could never include a married one and the firm sacked every woman for the sin of matrimony. They sweetened the pill of losing an income with the gift of a knife to cut the wedding cake.

'Winnie! You're getting married to Wally the Wonder Wheel? When did all this happen?' Matty said, admiring Winnie's ability to keep a secret.

Winnie laughed. 'Walter proposed at Winchester – he fell arse over tit off your penny-farthing and I caught him! You was too busy with our Tom to notice.'

'Oh, Win, I'm so happy for you. But what'll your mum and dad do without your wages coming in?'

'I reckon they'll be better off. They'll get more relief when I move out and Wally's lovely – he says we'll help them out. Lucky he's good at selling, eh?'

Winnie knew all the jokes about Wally being good at everything but his specialty act.

'Win, you do know all about his selling?' For Wally supplemented his work collecting for penny insurance policies by offering clients whatever contraband was doing the rounds of the Bermondsey pubs.

'That's what I meant, you silly mare! You didn't think I was talking about insurance, did you?'

*

Matty and Tom sat at a table with a view of the dark Thames flowing beneath the window. A string of lamps on the far embankment spread flickering pathways of light, which reached long fingers of flame across the river. The old Angel pub was full of nooks and crannies, where dimly lit tables and high-backed benches provided some seclusion away from the noisy bar. Matty imagined him reaching across the table, taking her hand and raising it to his lips. It was what he would have done, once, but now she dropped her hands to her lap.

'Were you jealous?' he asked.

'Don't be an idiot. Why would I be jealous? I don't want to get married...' Matty paused, as Tom's expression froze. She didn't respond well to game-playing. If he wanted just to be friends, then he should learn to steer clear of asking about her feelings.

'Of course you don't,' Tom said, giving his white tie a vigorous tug.

'Leave it alone, you look very dashing. You're spoiling the suave look.' Matty relented. He'd at least been trying to be civil, and he'd been the one who'd offered to come along tonight for moral support. Straightening the tie, she sang a snatch: *'I'm tying up my white tie, polishing my nails...'*

'I was pleased for them,' she went on. 'I just wondered why you hadn't told me about your own sister getting engaged.'

'I only found out the day before you, and besides, we never have time to talk at work.'

Though they spent each day together and they'd managed to maintain a civil relationship at work, still, she missed talking with him. She felt cheated as she tried to stifle her rekindled love, and now she remembered that old excitement of being courted by him. Tonight he looked especially handsome. He wore the same evening suit he'd hired for the Fonstone house party, for tonight they were going to Neville's private club in the West End, where Matty was making her debut as a torch singer.

'Come on, we should go. Neville will be waiting,' Matty said, and allowed Tom to drape her black feather-trimmed stole across her shoulders.

The streets around the pub were narrow, cobbled and dark, a canyon of warehouses and quaysides. The pair should have been out of place in evening wear, but there were others in the pub dressed, like them, for a night in the West End. While Matty had been away, the few habitable houses directly fronting this stretch of the river had been taken over by a select group of bohemians and theatrical types. The roughness of the dirty riverside streets, coupled with the ancient flow of the Thames, seemed to provide the sort of romance that couldn't be bought in Mayfair.

Neville Piper's bolt-hole was an ancient, narrow, steep-staired maritime house, with a bow window on the upper floor jutting out over the river, giving a spectacular view of the wide sweep of the Thames up to Tower Bridge. The room was ablaze with candlelight that bounced off piano and mirrors, reflecting a hundred flames in each bottle pane of the window. Neville greeted them with cocktails and warm words of encouragement for Matty.

'You aren't nervous are you, darling? It will be a very intimate crowd. They'll adore you!'

But Matty wasn't nervous; she was buzzing with excitement. She'd loved singing to crowds of five hundred or a thousand from an upturned stool beside the cinemotor, getting them to join in, being swept along by their exuberance and banter, yet Neville had spotted something she'd barely admitted to herself: the old hankering for the spotlit glamour of a proper stage, however small, had returned. Tonight's venue, the Blue Lotus, was a private cabaret and dining club near Piccadilly, where Neville often performed his own songs. An appearance there was bound to get her noticed again in theatre circles, but she'd stressed to Neville that publicity should be at a minimum and he'd promised to limit it to word of mouth.

River fog rolled around them as they dipped into the warmth of the taxi.

'How did you get a cab to come down here?' Matty asked Neville as they set off along Bermondsey Wall. 'Normally taxis won't come near this place.'

'Oh, they know me by now, darling, and I always pay them danger money!' Neville had a high tinkling laugh; he was an odd mixture of toughness and sensitivity. Anyone looking as he did would be a target for verbal if not physical abuse in these rough backstreets, but he seemed oblivious.

As the taxi crossed Tower Bridge, she went through her set with him and he advised changing a few of the downbeat songs to cheerier ones.

'You don't want to have them too depressed, my darling. They like to be made blue, but by the time they stumble out into the night they should also believe in the power of true love to conquer all!'

Matty gave a small smile. 'But surely they'll only believe that if I do, Neville.'

Tom shot her a look in the dim interior of the cab and she turned her own gaze to the murky river, feeling the disconcerting bump as they passed over the small gap between the two bascules of the bridge, a place that had always made her feel slightly queasy and unstable.

The club was half empty when they arrived. Double glass doors led into a gallery bar that overlooked the restaurant and stage area, where a single pianist was playing softly. They descended a curving chrome and glass staircase to the restaurant, where a few diners, couples mostly, sat at booths round the edge. But the tables in the centre of the floor, facing the small stage, were still empty.

'Don't look so worried, darling.' Neville put a guiding arm round her shoulders. 'You won't be playing to an empty house. We attract the after-theatre crowd here. You'll have plenty of time to settle in before the place fills up.'

Neville led them backstage, where Matty was surprised to find a smart dressing room, far better than some of the cupboards she'd been used to in large theatres.

'I'll leave you to freshen your war paint, Matty darling.' He kissed her as if she were his oldest friend and let his hand linger a little too long in the small of her back.

'Now don't forget what I said about your set – true love conquers all at the end!'

After he'd left with a waft of expensive brilliantine and cigarette smoke, she saw Tom's eyes on her.

'I suppose all theatricals are over-friendly,' Tom said reasonably, and she could see he was struggling to mask his jealousy. 'I'm so happy for you, Matty,' he said finally. 'Something's changed – your eyes, they've come alive. All this, it gives you something our films never could...'

'It's exciting, Tom. But it's not the "everything" it used to be. What we're doing with the films feels solid, as if it will last.

This...' she blew on the black feathers of her stole, 'could be blown away tomorrow and no one would know the difference, but our work's saving lives. Look at our Billy.'

'Perhaps you can have both?' Tom suggested and she loved him for it. Wanting nothing more than to fling her arms around his neck, instead she held that yearning in her throat. Not so much that it would rob her voice of power, but just enough to give her the edge required to draw up a performance that would move her listeners. This was what she'd missed, the emotional dance with an audience set in motion by her own voice. The Bermondsey street crowds reflected back humour, sometimes frustration, but rarely deep emotion. Mostly Matty's task was to educate and Dr Connan's verses sung to the tune of 'My Sweet Hortense', though it might give her satisfaction, could never feed her soul.

And as she discovered, Neville hadn't lied. By eleven thirty, the place was packed. The members had downed their first cocktails and been served with food, and now a purple cloud of cigarette smoke hung over the tables. Tom wished her luck and went out into the restaurant. She walked into the spotlight on the stage and was revealed in a swirl of smoke. She smiled to herself as she began low and even, with a new sultry torch song that she'd only just learned, called 'Smoke Gets in Your Eyes'. Gradually she sensed the chatter subside and felt the attention of the room turning towards her, as she moved on to *'You've got me crying again, you've got me sighing again'*, and segued into *'Call it woman's intuition but it can't go on like this'*. She went through the repertoire of newer songs she'd been learning ever since Neville invited her to sing at the Blue Lotus. At one point she dipped into an even darker mood with an English version of 'Mack the Knife', but she could see the lyrics about Macheath's flashing shark's teeth and his hidden knife were not fitting the crowd. The song was weakening their attention so she tugged on their strings with some lighter more romantic songs and ended with 'The Clouds Will Soon Roll By'. When she sang

'*Somewhere the sun is shining. So, honey, don't you cry. We'll find a silver lining. The clouds will soon roll by*', she hoped she'd done enough to heed Neville's warning and convinced her listeners that love would indeed conquer all in the end.

The applause was instantaneous and when people started jumping to their feet, she felt Neville at her side. He was hissing in her ear, 'They want an encore, darling. Have you got something?' She hadn't expected this, so asked the pianist for the first song that came to mind: as she sang 'I'll See You in My Dreams', she was aware only of Tom's face shining up at her. She felt a surge of life and energy as she left the stage and joined Tom at his table. Perhaps she had done enough.

'You were sensational, Matty,' he said.

'Thanks, Tom. I really need a gin, though,' she said, resisting the impulse to kiss him and instead pulling the stole up around her shoulders, for now she was out of the spotlight she felt suddenly chilly. Left at the table while Tom went to get drinks, she dropped her chin into the black feathers. Something other than the normal after-show anti-climax was niggling, like a pearl in an oyster, and a sick feeling threatened her sense of triumph. She probed for a reason and as she mentally ran through her songs she realized that all, bar the final two, reminded her of the way she'd felt with Frank. That simmering unease, which she'd once mistaken for excitement, now gave her an unsteady feeling, the sort she got when she crossed Tower Bridge and felt an instant of danger as the bascules just failed to meet, revealing the river far below. She remembered 'Mack the Knife'. She'd only included the song at the last moment, thinking it might please the sophisticated crowd, but only now did she realize with a shudder that the lyrics too reminded her of Frank, with his sharp white teeth and, of course, his knife.

Resenting Frank's power to invade the most precious moments of her life, she shook her head to rid herself of him.

'Penny for them?' Tom handed her the glass. 'Neville asked us to join him. Lots of his friends want to meet you.' He smiled, his first genuine smile for her in a long time. 'You should enjoy the moment, Matty. I'm so proud of you.'

And Matty felt the cold draught of Frank's memory receding.

They didn't leave the Blue Lotus until the early hours, for she hadn't wanted the night to end. Walking down Piccadilly, they reached the Strand, passing the odd group of early morning revellers. At Covent Garden they stopped while Tom went to hail a taxi. Porters were already unloading vans in side streets and transporting fruit baskets on their heads to the market. Matty noticed a group of down-at-heel men hanging around the lorries, leaning on walls or lounging in doorways, seemingly idle. Their papery faces had a wary look and their idleness was taut with watchfulness. Matty realized why when one of them approached a porter.

'Got any specks, mate?'

'Sorry, it's all good stuff.'

'Nothing for the kids?' the man persisted, but the porter waved him away, not unkindly, just intent on getting his load transported to the market.

The man pulled his cap down and retired with a resigned look, but then the porter missstepped, sending his load of fruit tumbling to the cobbles. The men were on the scattering fruit in a wasp-like frenzy, stuffing as much booty into their pockets as they could, some running off, others settling back to wait for the next windfall.

Though she'd been on relief herself, Matty felt the contrast between those desperate men and her own good fortune. Her stage finery felt like an accusation and she went to join Tom at the street corner, grateful that he'd found them a cab.

By the time Matty and Tom were approaching Tower Bridge in the taxi, dawn was breaking. A sky of pale rose and gold hung over the Tower of London, its once white walls black with the soot and grime of ages.

'Tom, let's get out here and walk across,' Matty suggested.

'It's chilly,' Tom warned. 'Are you sure?'

Matty nodded and he asked the driver to stop the cab at the foot of the bridge. Tom quickly paid the cabbie and they hurried on, Matty drawing up her stole against the cold wind whipping up from the river. As they reached the central span, she stopped and walked to the thick wooden railing. Deliberately she made for the gap between the bascules and when Tom joined her, he gave her a puzzled look. 'What's brought this on?'

'Did I ever tell you I was always frightened of walking over this gap?' Matty asked.

'No, you never did.' Tom looked doubtful. 'Not that I'd have believed it. You always seemed like you could take on the world back then, Matty.'

Matty was silent for a while. 'Well, I couldn't and I found out there were far worse things to be frightened of than the middle of Tower Bridge.' She turned a serious face towards him. 'But I don't want to be frightened any more.'

He looked down at her and now his eyes brimmed with undeniable love.

'Matty, I'm sorry I forced you to tell me about that film. I swore to myself when you went away that if you ever gave me another chance I'd just let you be yourself...'

'You didn't force me to tell you.'

'Perhaps not, but I've put you through the mill since you did. I've not been fair. Give me another chance, Matty, and I promise... I'll let you keep your secrets.' He drew her into a tight embrace and she shivered in his arms. 'I don't need to know everything he did to you, Matty, but I do know you need never be frightened of him again. I'm going to look after you. I love you.'

They kissed on the central span of the bridge and Matty allowed herself to believe that Tom's love could save her from her past. She forgot about the long drop to the fast-flowing current below, she forgot the ever-swaying span beneath her feet as traffic started to rumble past, she forgot the cold wind chasing up the Thames – she forgot everything but the sweetness of his lips and the warmth of his arms, and when she finally pulled away from his embrace, the morning had turned from gold to pale turquoise and her eyes were fixed only on the brightening sky.

21

Moving On

March–April 1932

Matty became a regular at the Blue Lotus, singing there once a week or sometimes at club members' private parties. The low-key nature of the work fitted in with their continuing filming of the Modern Woman series. Tom had given them a tight schedule of producing three films before the summer screenings began. Sometimes Tom would come with her to the nightclub, but when a deadline loomed he would spend his evenings planning storyboards and organizing shooting schedules. Their first film, *The Modern Woman and Work*, had already been edited and they were waiting for the final print from the film company. They'd made the voice-over recording and D.M. was delighted with her take on 'He's Only a Working Man', which she'd turned on its head, making it into a song about the ideal working woman.

It seemed that Tom's prediction had come true. She could have both – a life on stage and a life on screen. She could sing her heart out by night and by day she could produce films that made a difference. They were in the middle of planning *The Modern Woman and Home* when an idea came to her.

'Why don't we film a move from one of the old condemned streets to a new flat?' she suggested to Tom. 'We could show a woman coping with the evils of the old houses – rats, bedbugs, damp, overcrowding. And then we could show her in one of the new council flats – plenty of room, electricity, running hot water, a bath – paradise on earth really!'

'It's a good idea, Matty,' Tom said, 'but we'd have to persuade someone to let us into their old house and their new flat.'

'Oh, that won't be a problem. I know just the family!'

*

'I don't know about that, Matty,' Nellie said, as she boxed up her best bone-china tea set, a lilac-patterned fluted affair that was rarely allowed out of the cupboard. 'I don't think I could do any acting. Besides, we've got enough to do getting ourselves to Grange House without having a cameraman getting under our feet!'

'We won't get in your way, I promise. Tom's doing the filming and you won't have to actually be in it. I'll be playing the mother. I've got to look worried and frazzled, which you, try as you might, could never do, Nellie.' She gave Nellie a winning smile, but she knew Matty too well.

'Don't give me all the old soft soap,' she said curtly.

Matty tried a different tack. 'It'd be good if the boys could be in it. I bet they'd love it, especially Billy, and it might keep them out of your way.' Nellie continued to silently box up.

'We really need to show a family going from an old place into a new flat – so we can show what an improvement it is and how excited you all are...'

'Well, the boys wouldn't need to put *that* on for the cameras. They're driving me mad. The first thing they want to do is get in a proper bath with taps. It'll cost us a fortune in hot water! Here, wrap these photos while you're standing there.'

Nellie pushed a pile of framed photographs across the table and Matty started to wrap them in newspaper. She held up one of her dad, Michael Gilbie, astride the old penny-farthing just after his long cycle down to London in search of work. Another showed her as a toddler with her parents, Michael and Lizzie; they each held a hand and were obviously helping her with her first steps.

Nelly caught her lingering over it. 'They would have been so proud of you, Matty.'

'Do you think so?'

'I know so! The way Lizzie used to get you to stand in the middle of the kitchen and sing for me when I came round! She knew what you were meant for. She'd have been glad you've started singing again, you're just like your old self.'

Matty reached out for Nellie's hand. 'It wasn't easy finding out Eliza was my real mother, but now I know... well, I've realized I've got a lot of her in me too.'

'Oh, I'll tell you one thing for a start – you've both always managed to get your own way!'

She laughed. 'That's true! But not *just* that. Since I've started working with Tom, I understand what made Eliza give up everything for her work. It's heartbreaking some of the things I've seen. We filmed a homeless family last week, living under Gedling Street railway arch. The woman had the tiniest baby and no milk.' Tears pricked Matty's eyes at the remembrance of the infant that had searched in vain at her own breast while she held it, feeling an irrational desire to provide the milk its mother lacked. But as its wizened face creased in distress, so dehydrated it cried without tears, the old pain tore at her heart and she relinquished the baby, whose mother soothed it with a rag soaked in condensed milk. 'In the end the mission took them in, found them a couple of rooms. Not much, but it was better than a railway arch.'

'I do know how lucky we are, going into a new flat,' Nellie said.

'That's what I mean. This film will be seen by high-ups in the LCC. Perhaps they'll start giving us a bit of money for some new houses for a change, instead of leaving it all to the Bermondsey borough to pay for...'

Nellie sighed with a mixture of exasperation and resignation. 'Oh, all right then, we'll do it. See what I mean, you *always* get your own way!'

Before the Gilbies finally moved out of Vauban Street, they filmed scenes showing Matty struggling with the weekly wash, heating up the copper and transporting buckets of water to fill the tin tub in the yard. A contrasting scene in the new flat would show the hygienic and time-saving value of running hot water. The night before the move Matty and Tom went to film some more 'before' scenes. Nellie had always kept her homely house spotless, but it had been a losing battle over the years with damp lifting any new wallpaper Sam hung and bugs hiding in the crumbling old walls. Now bare of ornament and mementos it looked a suitably grim example of old Bermondsey. Billy, Sammy and Albie obligingly snuggled up in bed together under a blanket, while Matty, playing their mother, sat vigil with a candle, ready to chase away any bold rats making their way into the house from the nearby knackers' yard.

'Stop giggling now, Albie,' Nellie admonished her youngest. 'You're meant to be fast asleep.'

And Sammy pinched him to emphasize the point. Once the boys were quiet, Matty sat on a kitchen chair at their bedside and moved her face into the candlelight, a picture of haunted worry. The caption was to be *A mother guards her children.* Tom had already gleaned plenty of footage of rats coming out of the boneyard into the night-time streets, to be shown with her recorded script: *How can I sleep when my children could be bitten by rats in the night? If only I could get on the list for a council flat.* Suddenly Matty jumped up, knocking over the chair. Waving her shovel, she chased away a rodent invader. Now the boys' acting skills came into play as three heads poked up from under the covers, eyes wide with terror.

'Cut!' called Tom and the boys leaped out of bed.

'What's next?' asked Billy, who'd been the most eager to appear in the film.

'I've got a special part for you later,' she said. 'But that's enough for tonight. You've got to be up bright and early tomorrow to help Mum and Dad!'

She and Tom joined Nellie and Sam for a farewell drink in the old kitchen.

'I'll be singing "My Old Man Said Follow the Van" tomorrow,

Matty,' Nellie said, raising her glass. 'Sam's borrowing the horse and cart to move us!'

'Well, we won't get it *all* on the cart. Freddie's bringing his lorry too,' Sam said.

'We could get some lovely shots of the boys on the back of the cart, waving the old place goodbye.'

'Good riddance, more like,' Sam said and shook his head indulgently. 'How's that song go, "*I dillied, I dallied*"? I guarantee we won't be in the new place before midnight by the time we get this lot out of here.'

But Sam was wrong. At the end of the following day there was still enough light left for them to film the final outdoor shots of the move. They filmed the boys being porters, ferrying chairs and boxes up the stone staircase to the new flat, and then Billy's special scene, which Matty had choreographed.

'I want a shot of you dancing along the balcony to your new front door,' she explained. 'Imagine you're so happy you can't help but dance, imagine it's to the tune of "Happy Feet". Do some shuffle-ball changes and side-swing your arms as you go, then when you get to the door we'll have some scissor steps? OK?'

Billy nodded and Matty sang so he could get the rhythm. '*Happy feet, I've got those happy feet, give them a low down beat, and they begin dancing...*'

He performed the routine just as she'd instructed.

'That boy's got to go on the stage!' She grinned as she ran to sweep him up and in through the open front door to join the others.

After a long day's filming and unpacking, Freddie offered to give them a lift home in his lorry.

'Fancy stopping off for a drink at the Red Cow first?' he asked them. 'It's thirsty bloody work this moving lark.'

'Won't Kitty be expecting you?' Matty asked. She knew that Freddie didn't get out much these days. His growing family and business left him little leisure time, and he'd surprised them all by settling down to be a model husband and father, in spite of his odd skirmish down memory lane with Wide'oh and a few boxes of hooky.

'She does give me a night off now'n again!' Freddie winked at Matty. 'Come on, I'll stand the drinks. Besides, I wanted a word.'

It was a quiet night in the Red Cow and they found an empty table easily. When Freddie went to buy them drinks, Matty asked Tom, 'Do you know what he wants to talk about?'

'No idea, family news?'

Matty shrugged. 'Could be another baby on the way. Kitty's Catholic.'

But when Freddie returned, he didn't look like a man who'd come to impart good news. His handsome face clouded as he lowered his powerful frame on to the seat next to Matty's. He leaned in and dropped his voice.

'Bit of news about that business of Matty's. I saw Sugar yesterday. He'd been looking for you, Tom, but you was out so he come over the yard to me.'

'We were filming at Vauban Street all yesterday,' Tom said. 'What was the news?'

Matty felt the hairs on her arms lifting. Sugar had become a little like an unpredictable guard dog in her mind. She never got any sense of security from knowing that Tom had set him to keep his ears open for news of the Clerkenwell mob doing Frank's dirty work. Whenever she saw Sugar, his squashed, bulldog features signalled danger, and she was never sure if that danger came from him or what he was reporting.

'It might be nothing, but you know there's already been business between Frank's outfit and the Clerkenwell boys – they've supplied him with a few bodyguards, usually they're boys that need to get out of this country quick. Anyway, now there's a rumour one of 'em's helping Frank get out of Canada – hands across the pond and all that. Seems Frank wants some of what they've got going over here and they think he can add them a bit of clout...'

Matty swallowed as a heavy silence fell over the table.

'I don't want to frighten you, Matty. It might come to nothing, but...'

'It's not like I haven't known it might happen,' she said firmly, remembering her vow to herself as she'd stood over the gap in Tower Bridge. 'But I'm not frightened.'

'Good,' said Tom, squeezing her hand. 'If he comes at least we'll all be prepared.'

Matty was about to say that no one could really be 'ready' for Frank, but instead she asked 'All?', looking from Tom to Freddie. 'What do you mean, *all*?'

*

It wasn't until Winnie's springtime wedding that she got an inkling of the extent of Tom's 'protection programme'. They were waiting with the other guests outside St James's Church. The borough beautification department had filled the flower beds with daffodils and primroses, and though they hadn't put on the show solely for Winnie's day, it did make a pretty setting for a wedding. Winnie had managed to ignore the temptations of Peek's for the last few months and had lost the weight she'd gained since working there. Matty had helped her choose the dress and was now excitedly waiting for her to arrive. But the bride had turned up and promptly been sent away in her hired Bentley. The Peek's Tiller Girls were all there, dressed in matching bridesmaids' dresses. Matty could see them bobbing up and down, trying to get a glimpse of the bride's progress along Frean Street. The Bentley came into view a second time and, turning in through the park gates, it drew up outside the church steps.

The driver was about to hop out and Matty could see Winnie's eager face staring out through the window.

'Bloody hell, where's he got to?' Tom said, waving the car away again, and Matty blew Winnie a kiss, mouthing, 'Don't worry, he'll be here!'

Winnie's car left to do another circuit of Spa Road, and it was then Matty spotted the groom approaching through the opposite churchyard gate.

She nudged Tom.

'Oh my God, no, he's not. Tell me when it's over, Matty.'

Tom covered his eyes with his hand. For Wally, beautifully dressed in wedding suit and white carnation, was wobbling precariously towards them atop his unicycle.

Encouraging shouts echoed round the churchyard. 'Here he is, Wally the Wonder Wheel! Come on, Wal, you can do it!'

Staying upright had always been a problem for Wally but today proved the exception. Waving to his well-wishers, he managed to keep his seat and was looking very pleased with himself. But braking was also a problem and now it appeared that the stone steps of the old Waterloo church were the only impediment to Wally's progress. The crowd parted as he came to a crashing halt on the bottom step. His one wheel buckled and Wally leaped off, somersaulted and somehow landed on the top step, giving an extravagant bow to a burst of applause. Wally was a better acrobat than he was a cyclist.

'It's over,' Matty said. 'You can look now.'

'Stone me, I just hope he hasn't persuaded our Winnie to leave with him on a tandem.'

'Well, he did ask me if I'd sing them out with "Daisy, Daisy"!'

'Are you kidding me?'

'*But you'll look sweet upon the seat of a bicycle made for two!*'

'My poor sister.'

'I'm joking, you idiot!' Matty giggled as Tom picked up Wally's unicycle and stowed it out of sight.

On her third circuit, Winnie was allowed out of the car and into the church to be married. It was the unlikeliest of unions and yet, as he stood beside Winnie at the altar, Wally's face lost all its usual bumbling clownishness and Matty saw an intensity in his eyes that she thought boded well for them.

Bernie had offered the bar at the Star for the wedding reception. The place had been smartened up and decorated for the occasion and Winnie had asked Matty to sing later on.

'How's me darlin' Cockney Canary?' Bernie put his arm round her. His moustache tickled her cheek and as usual he smelled of cigars and whiskey, a smell that could take her back in an instant to her fourteen-year-old self and her early days on the stage in this place. 'I hear you've gone up the 'Dilly on us,' he said, laughing.

'I'll have you know I'm a reputable artiste in a private club!' she said, and swiped the back of his pomaded head for his cheeky reference to Piccadilly's other more disreputable claim to fame. He sat beside her, looking on at Winnie and Wally's first dance. The piano player was the regular cinema organist, but his technique was not the best.

'He spends all his time playing that Wurlitzer. You'd think he could remember how to play a bloody piano!' Bernie complained. 'Anyway, how are you, kid? Still making your bedbug films?'

Matty nodded. 'We've gone into talkies!'

Bernie looked impressed. 'But you're back singing.' He put an arm round her. 'That's the important thing, couldn't be more pleased to hear it. I'll have you back on that old stage...' He nodded towards the Star's auditorium and Matty smiled, feeling a moment's sadness for the excitement of those old times.

'The clubs suit me better nowadays, Bernie.'

'Look, I know why you've been staying off the circuit.' Bernie lowered his voice. 'We all do, all the old crowd – every hall in London and the provinces... Anyone comes asking after our canary, we know to tell your Tom. Your feller's even recruited him.' Bernie nodded towards the dancing couple.

'Wally? What, to protect me?' She threw back her head and laughed, so that she caught Tom's attention, who smiled back. But Bernie was looking deadly serious. 'You do know where that silly sod's true talent lies, don't you?'

Matty shook her head.

'Well, me darlin', let's just hope you never have to find out,' Bernie said, tapping the side of his nose.

The Modern Woman films were to be launched with more than the usual fanfare, with a special first screening at the Spa Road Library hall, with the mayor and other local bigwigs in attendance, as well as special invitations for the Bermondsey 'extras' who'd played so many parts. They had also booked showings in fifteen factories and twelve mother and baby clinics, as well as Goldsmiths College. They had high hopes for this third film, *The Modern Woman and Health*, as D.M.'s feeling was that if a woman looked after her own health, then it followed her family would be healthy too.

Matty had found it hard when it came to portraying a sickly woman, for she had never felt healthier, nor happier. She wasn't entirely sure when the corner had been turned, but whenever she considered the contentment that she felt in Tom's arms or the satisfaction she got from her film work or the excitement of her nights singing at the Blue Lotus, the image that flashed into her mind was of standing with Tom in the centre of Tower Bridge at dawn. When she'd declared herself unafraid, it hadn't only been Frank she was thinking of. It had also been the fear of giving her heart to a man again. Tom had offered her protection from Frank, but not from love. And over time she'd gradually come to see that it was as impossible to protect herself from either. They were both coming for her, so she'd decided to stop running from both.

The only sadness was that Tom's father was failing. Tom thought it had less to do with his health than his pride, for he'd never fully accepted that the end of his working life would be spent living on the grudging handouts of the state. In his mind it was 'outdoor relief' and as demeaning as the workhouse. He'd managed to attend Winnie's wedding, but had then retired to his bed.

One evening Tom came to Reverdy Road, more upset than she'd ever seen him.

'What's the matter?' she asked as soon as she opened the door.

He came in, pulling off his trilby, raking his fingers through his hair. 'It's the old chap. I think he's given up, Matty. Win's had the doctor out, but he said Dad's heart's failing and there's not much to be done. I'm sorry, love, I don't think I can come with you tonight.'

She was booked to sing at the Blue Lotus and Tom had said he would go too.

'Oh, that's the least of your worries, Tom. Neville will take me. You go to your dad.'

'I just wish I could have done more for the old feller. I tried to help him out, but he hated taking anything from me. I ended up giving it to Mum on the quiet.'

'You've done everything you could. Don't start blaming yourself, Tom.'

She knew how much he hated seeing his once strong father fade away, chased out of his job and his dignity by the deepening Depression. She held him for a long time, wishing she could make it easier for him, but there was no ease to be had. His father was dying for reasons beyond any of their control. The Crash of twenty-nine had certainly sent Matty's life into a spiral, but over the past three years the effects had rippled out, reaching every part of the globe, including the small corner of the world where Tom's father was its latest casualty.

Much as she would have liked to stay and comfort Tom, Matty had promised Neville a performance and was reluctant to let him down. As she'd told Tom, Neville was happy to share his taxi with her. He'd promised to perform songs from his latest play and Matty was to accompany him, part of Neville's growing campaign to chip away at her enforced semi-retirement. Tonight the place was packed as always, but she could see there were more than the usual after-theatre crowd. There was a large contingent of Neville's theatre friends, but also a table of non-regulars that Matty hadn't seen before, wearing expensive suits and extravagant jewellery. Neville said they were here to listen to her.

'Soon the Blue Lotus won't be able to hold all your fans, Matty dear, and you'll have to let Esme book you bigger venues. It's criminal for that lovely voice to remain so closeted.'

She'd grown fond of Neville. She believed his interest in reviving her career was genuine and the truth was she enjoyed singing with him. His light, clever songs were a welcome contrast to the heavier torch songs she'd been performing.

Once they'd begun, the chattering diminished, apart from the table where the new crowd sat. Matty hadn't played the Star for so many years without being able to sing to noisy audiences. She shut them out of her mind and out of her sight, focusing on the intent faces of those she could see, lit by the footlights of the tiny stage. But a movement caught the corner of her eye, distracting her so that she fluffed a lyric, which only Neville seemed to notice. Someone had joined the rowdy table and a flicker of recognition jolted through her brain like an electric shock. Something about the tall figure, the tilt of the head, the effortless gliding walk, the easy way he slid into his seat and crossed his legs, all in a second had impacted her attention and frozen the blood in her veins.

22

Protection

April–May 1932

She was trapped. She couldn't run from the stage. Pinned by the spotlight, she carried on singing. Only Neville could tell that the power had drained from her voice and only she knew that her stomach had turned inside out, that her heart was bursting through her chest and that the air was raking at her lungs. Her legs were not supporting her; they were water. Only her tight grip on the microphone stand was keeping her from falling off the stage. She allowed herself the briefest glance in Frank's direction and found his dark, fathomless eyes fixed on her. The room lurched and she thought she might throw up all over the elegantly dressed young couple seated at the front table. Instead she looked desperately at Neville who, she could hear, was winding down from the final chorus, bringing the set to an early end, with a look of gaunt incomprehension on his face. But she didn't want the set to end, for the stage was now both her prison and her protection. While she was up here, he could not touch her.

Neville played the final chords of 'I'll See You Again', and the applause told her the crowd hadn't noticed that during the last song she'd been entirely absent. Neville grabbed her arm for the final bow, hissing in her ear. 'What was all that about, Matty darling, you *never* have stage fright!'

She took his hand, using it to steady her trembling. She smiled broadly and leaned to kiss him, whispering, 'It's not stage fright. Someone just walked in that I don't want to see.'

They bowed together and headed for the door to the dressing room. She gave a backward glance and saw Frank get up and cross the floor in a few easy strides. In seconds he was standing between her and Neville. She had forgotten how tall he was. Now he filled her vision, a broad-shouldered, powerful-looking man, muscles evident beneath the immaculate cut of his sharp suit. She saw his Adam's apple rise and fall, the square chin, cleft darkly shadowed where he could never quite reach with the razor. She knew that her only protection against this man had been his infatuation with her. The minute that had vanished she'd become little more than prey.

'Hello, Frank,' she said, surprised that her voice sounded so normal.

'Matty.' His smile revealed sharp edges of pearl-white teeth. 'I really have missed you.'

The eyes were meant to reveal the soul, and now she wondered why it hadn't troubled her more that when she looked into Frank's dark eyes she'd only ever seen passion or anger.

Neville glided back into view, an ineffectual bright bird, unaware a hawk was circling the sky.

'Introduce us, Matty darling.'

Frank turned a straight face to him. 'We're having a conversation.'

Neville smiled nervously. 'I do beg your pardon,' he said, retreating, leaving Matty alone with Frank.

'Yeah, let's talk, why don't we?' Frank said affably, as though the idea had just occurred to him. 'Talk about old times, eh, Matty?' But his grip was vice-like on her arm and he steered her to the bar, where he ordered her a Gibson and a bourbon for himself.

'So, people tell me you're doin' well.' His teeth snapped shut, Adam's apple bobbed as the bourbon went down. 'I have to hear it from other people. I have to hear it out of the blue from some nutty English professor called Dibbs, Dobbs, whatever, 'cause I don't hear it from you. Two years, I don't hear nothin' from you. Why is that, Matty?' He tipped his head to one side, and pushed the cocktail towards her. 'Drink it, don't insult me.'

Her hands were clasped in her lap. She wrenched one free and picked up the glass, which trembled slightly and knocked against her teeth. The oily drink coated her throat and she stopped herself from gagging. All her fine vows to be unafraid, where had they gone? And then she asked herself, what could he do to her? He could kill her, but would that be so bad? Would that be worse than living her life stalked by his shadow?

'You know why, Frank.'

'No, I honestly don't.' He brushed a piece of lint from his trouser leg. 'I want you to tell me, why, after I give you everything, you think you can walk out on me, leave me without a word?' His voice was even and low, with a stabbing intensity that deepened with every iteration. 'You never wrote, you, never called me... You hurt my feelings.' He gave a wounded little-boy look, which she once might have thought was genuine. But in an instant it turned to stone. 'Nobody walks out on Frank Rossi. I thought you understood that.'

She understood. She understood that his pride would never have allowed him to leave her alone to live her life. There was always going to be a reckoning. And today was that day. She nodded her head.

'I invested in you, Matty. It was good business for a while, you and me, some very profitable films we made, remember those?' His leering smile told Matty he was not referring to *London Affair*. 'But the speakeasy days are numbered. We still got protection rackets goin' on, but I'll be honest, Matty, business is bad.' He spread empty palms in front of her, like an apologetic businessman looking for a bank loan. 'So – I need you back.' He reached up and ran a perfectly manicured fingernail down her cheek. 'I *want* you back, Matty.'

She realized that the rowdy, expensively dressed crowd in the corner had gone quiet, watching their exchange. Some of the men had turned towards them, sitting on the edge of their seats. Clerkenwell mob probably, or his own boys, brought with him from America. She had no choice. She stood up to go with him. There was nothing else she could do.

Frank looked over in the direction of his boys and gave a small smile of triumph.

'Don't worry about those clowns. They took it too far. Really, Matty, I don't want to make it hard for you, with all your high-class friends and your good works. I read in the paper about one of them films you made. *Fresh Air and Fun*? Your do-gooder friends don't need to know what sort of fun we used to have, eh, Matty? I told the Sabini boys they shouldn't have threatened you. It's not necessary, is it, Matty?'

She shook her head and swallowed. 'No, Frank, it's not necessary,' she said meekly.

She laid her beaded evening bag on the bar. 'I just need to go to the ladies.'

He stood up, a look of smug certainty on his face, knowing that she'd do as she was told. His eyes followed her as she pushed through the door leading to the dressing room.

Neville was waiting for her in the passage, white-faced. 'Is that Frank Rossi?'

Matty nodded. 'How do you know about him?'

'Tom told me to look out for him, to let him know if he ever turned up. Surely you're not thinking of going off with him?'

'Am I buggery! Can you get me out of here, Neville?'

'I certainly can, darling.' Neville grabbed her hand. 'Out this way, come on.'

'No, not the back door. Frank's bound to have someone there. Is there a window?' She was panicking, Frank wouldn't wait for long.

Neville nodded his head decisively. 'Through here, now!'

He led her to a small salon, used for private parties. A heavily shaded lamp was suspended above an oval table covered in green baize cloth.

'The poker room,' Neville explained, leading her to a sofa set against the back wall, which he quickly shoved to one side. 'Sometimes our members need a quick getaway.' She was looking at a low door, which Neville pushed open. 'It's not a cupboard,' he answered her puzzled look. 'It actually leads into a side alley, go to the end and turn left into Piccadilly. I'll let Tom know. Go now!'

She kissed him quickly and ducked through the door. A short passageway led to another door which was bolted. Quickly slamming back the bolt, she pushed open the door, peering up and down the alley, making sure no one had been posted there. It was empty. She saw the lights of Piccadilly and dashed towards the end of the alley. Traffic was still fairly heavy and black cabs cruised past, touting for custom. But she had no money for a cab. She'd left her bag on the bar, thinking it would seem more convincing to Frank if she went without it. Standing in Piccadilly, wearing her long silver evening gown, without coat or hat, she began to attract attention. Passers-by stared and a drunk in evening dress blocked her path. She pushed him away and walked hurriedly towards Piccadilly Circus. She saw a short, dumpy figure in a trilby and dark suit coming out of the side street leading to the Blue Lotus. It was one of Frank's men and he had spotted her. She broke into a sprint. Weaving in and out of the late-night crowd, she dashed across the road, heedless of traffic. Her long legs were impeded by the narrow gown, so she picked it up above her knees and raced towards Haymarket – if she could only reach Leicester Square first, she might have a chance of reaching a safe haven.

As she ran, she allowed herself a quick look back – the short-legged man was lagging well behind. He had obviously been no match for her. She didn't let up her pace, but careened into Leicester Square, careless of the odd looks she attracted. The square was still crowded with people coming out of late film shows and restaurants. Here she could blend in and slowing down a little, she ducked down a side alley and into a little courtyard, her chest heaving. She stopped outside a narrow door, panting for breath and trembling. She slammed the knocker loudly and continuously. 'Be in, be in,' she prayed in rhythm to the knocking.

The darkness of the little court was suddenly relieved by a glow from an upstairs window. Matty knocked even louder and finally the door was flung open mid-knock.

'For Christ's sake, I'm here!' Esme stood open-mouthed with shock. She looked a fright, her hair frizzed into a ball, bare of make-up and wrapped in an old dressing gown, which looked as if it had belonged to her grandfather. 'Good God, Matty!'

'I'm sorry, Esme. Can I come in? I really need your help.'

Esme ushered her quickly up the narrow staircase to her top-floor flat adjoining the office, where Matty explained what had happened. Esme sat her down and threw a blanket across her shoulders, for she was shivering with shock and the effort of her flight. Esme handed her a brandy.

'It was only a matter of time.' Esme was pacing the floor, taking occasional sips of her own brandy. 'Listen, Matty, I don't think it's safe for you to stay here. If he tried to abduct you, or whatever it was he intended, I can't see him stopping now... and they know where I am.'

Matty jumped up. 'You're right, Esme. I don't want to put you in any danger!'

But the woman laid a restraining hand on her arm. 'I'm not frightened of that. I just think we should get you somewhere they wouldn't think of looking. Not your brother's... What about Tom's, would they know about him?'

'I don't think so.'

'Best go to him tonight.'

There was a sound in the courtyard below and both women froze, but the clattering of a dustbin lid and a long miaow followed. Matty knew Esme was talking sense and she'd certainly feel safer with Tom tonight. He'd obviously been rallying the troops behind her back for a very long time, setting up his very own 'protection' operation, with her as its object. Perhaps he'd have a better plan in place than her own, which at the moment was simply to run and hide.

'All right, I'll go to Tom's. But, Esme, I'll have to borrow the fare. I haven't got a penny on me.'

Within minutes she was leaning back in the safety of a black cab, wearing Esme's coat.

'Where to?' the cabby asked.

'Bermondsey,' she said.

'Sorry, love, I'm just going home for the night, other way,' he said apologetically.

'London Bridge then?'

Seeming satisfied with the less threatening destination, even though it was still south of the river, he flicked the meter. 'Right you are,' he said and pulled out into the line of cars streaming down towards Charing Cross. He kept to the north side of the river, shooting along the Embankment, strung with lamps that sent pillars of light rippling across the dark Thames. Eventually they came to the heavy-set, darkened banks and offices of the City and turned southward across London Bridge.

When the taxi pulled into London Bridge Station forecourt, she chanced it. 'Could you take me a bit further, just as far as Tooley Street?'

The cabbie raised his eyes and shook his head.

'Oh, come on, you'll be all right there, it's hardly Hickman's Folly!' she said, naming one of the more notorious streets along the river with a reputation for housing criminals.

The cabbie reluctantly took her on and she tipped him generously for his trouble with Esme's money, thinking of the next poor stranded traveller who needed to get home south of the river late at night. Tom lived in the basement of a house behind Devon Mansions, a large tenement block stretching along Tooley Street. She hurried down the basement steps, shivering in spite of Esme's coat, and praying that Tom would be home from visiting his dad. But there was no answer to her knocking and the only sounds were of a couple arguing in the flat above and the howling of a dog from further down the street. She leaned her back against Tom's door, sinking in despair to the front step.

She didn't feel that she could push her body another inch and she contemplated curling up in the shadowy trench of the airey, grateful at least for its sheltering walls. But then an idea struck her. She had mentioned Hickman's Folly to the taxi driver as a less than salubrious destination. She wasn't that far from it now and it occurred to her it might be an unlikely place of sanctuary for her tonight. Besides, she needed to keep moving and it was worth a try.

As she hurried away from Devon Mansions, towards Dock-head, she realized she wasn't sure what number she was looking for, but she was pretty certain if she knocked at any house in Hickman's Folly she'd be pointed in the right direction. In the moonlight she rounded the long finger of stagnant water that was St Saviour's Dock and passed the Swan and Sugar Loaf pub on the corner of Hickman's Folly. She knocked on the first house in the long narrow alley. A young man answered the door.

'I'm sorry to trouble you at this time of night, but could you tell me which house Stan Sweeting lives in?'

For an instant she thought he would close the door in her face. 'Sugar?'

Matty nodded.

'Who are you?' The young man licked his lips. 'I don't want no trouble.'

'It's all right, I'm a friend of his. I just forgot his house number.'

'If there's any trouble, don't tell him it was me told you where to find him, will ya?'

Matty promised there would be no trouble and the young man pointed her to Sugar's house. She felt sorry for the boy. She wouldn't like to get on the wrong side of Sugar either.

The house was towards the end of Hickman's Folly. It looked one of the least cared for, with a couple of panes in the front sash window blocked up with cardboard. The door had been kicked in at one point, for planks of wood were nailed across it at odd angles. There was no knocker, so Matty banged on one of the more solid panels with her fist. She heard a scuffling sound coming from the window and thought she saw curtains move and a figure peep through one of the dirty panes. Soon she heard the unlocking of bolts.

''Kin 'ell gel, get in here, you'll draw attention!'

Sugar pulled her into the unlit passage, slammed and bolted the door, and with a jerk of his head indicated that she should go into the back room. She was immediately struck by the contrast to the outside of the house. The room was as smart as the outside was shabby. The amount of light hurt her eyes, The room was full of lamps and modern, garish furniture, a fan-shaped radio gramophone in one corner and a black and brass cocktail cabinet in the other. Then she realized that the table was aglitter with jewellery: silver and gold bracelets, necklaces strung with precious gems, diamonds and ruby rings glowing yellow and claret. It was like an Aladdin's cave and the shock must have shown on her face.

'Shut your cake hole, gel, you'll be catching flies in it.' Sugar broke into a crooked-toothed grin.

'Just been checking the merchandise. It ain't staying here for long. Sit down, Matty. Want a drink?'

Matty nodded, moving a black velvet box containing a string of pearls from the chair and sitting down at the shimmering table.

Sugar looked towards the scullery. 'We got company!' he yelled. 'And she needs a drink!'

The scullery door opened to reveal one of the most handsome women Matty had ever seen. Her hair was a lustrous black, set in marcel waves, and her large blue eyes were accentuated by kohl and darkened lashes. She was all of six feet tall, big-boned, but perfectly proportioned. She wore a coffee-coloured cashmere two-piece, set off by several belcher gold chains. Glittering drop earrings hung from neat ears. Her large hand on the doorknob displayed a ring on every finger: plain gold, diamond-studded, ruby-lozenged, the rings were all massive and those hands looked powerful enough to pull the door off its hinges. Her long, silk-stockinged legs were shapely and her rather large feet, shod in expensive brown leather shoes, looked quite capable of kicking the front door in.

'You ain't met my Queenie, have you? This is my fiancée, Queenie Quex.' And then in explanation to Queenie, 'This is Tom's Matty.'

'I know who it is, you silly bleeder – it's the Cockney Canary!' Queenie said and walked over to plant a kiss on Matty's cheek.

'Fancy anything, love?' She indicated the treasures on the table. 'We'll give you first dibs, you're practically family! But you ain't come for a social call. Tell Queenie all about it.'

And she gathered up a handful of enamelled gold powder compacts from another chair so that she could sit down at the kitchen table. 'Get the gin out, darl',' she ordered Sugar, who meekly went to the corner cupboard and brought out a bottle and three cut-crystal glasses, worthy of Fonstone. But Matty could have been drinking from an old jam jar, she didn't care. The shock of seeing Frank and her unthinking flight had begun to sink in and she felt her hands trembling again as she accepted the gin from Sugar. She gave an involuntary shiver as the fiery liquid burned in her throat.

'It's Frank Rossi.' She looked up at Sugar. 'He found me at the Blue Lotus. Asked me to go back with him.'

Sugar jumped up, suddenly not domestic at all. His fist was balled and held ready to punch someone. 'I'll have him.'

The fist he held to the ready was an odd dark colour compared to his florid complexion and Matty remembered Tom telling her he pickled his hands in brine, to harden them.

'Hold up, Sugar,' Queenie said, taking hold of one of the pickled fists and leaning forward eagerly to Matty. 'If Rossi still loves you, there's no problem, gel. You can use that against the bastard.'

But Matty shook her head. 'He wasn't really giving me a choice, and the only reason he wants me back is so he can use me in the sort of films he sells privately.'

Matty felt herself blushing and Sugar gave a low whistle. 'Does Tom know?' he asked.

'Shut your row up.' Queenie shot Sugar a stern look. 'Not all women's tough enough to stand up to bastards like that. I'd give him a right hander, but Matty's not been drug up like me, have you, gel?' She gave Matty's hand the sort of squeeze that would have crushed it had it lasted a minute longer. 'Do you want my Sugar to go an' give him a tap on the head with a mallet? He wants to, don't you, darl'?'

''Course I do, but Tom don't want it handled like that.'

'Tom? It ain't what Tom wants. It's what Matty wants.'

'Thanks, Queenie, but I don't want to get anyone into trouble. If I could just get him to leave me alone...'

'But they don't, his type, think they own you. I don't go with anyone if I'm not the boss.'

Sugar raised his eyes. 'She ain't lying, she's in charge,' he said to Matty. 'Anyway, best thing is you go with my Queenie. She's got places all over the Elephant and Castle where she can hide you. Just while me and Tom work out what to do about your Italian.'

'Here, love, put this round ya, it'll keep you warmer than that thing you've got on.' Queenie said, pulling out a plush velvet evening coat from a pile stacked on the sideboard.

Matty had no idea of the time, but as they left the house she saw that the moon had moved across the sky and all the lingering night sounds from pubs turning out and late-night traffic had died down. Queenie led her back down Hickman's Folly to Dockhead, where she stopped at a car that Matty recognized as the blue coupé Sugar had driven in Winchester. Queenie surprised her by unlocking the car and getting into the driver's seat.

'Hop in, love.'

Matty got in beside her. 'Won't Sugar need the car himself?' she asked.

'It's mine, not his!' Queenie said, putting her foot to the pedal, so that the roar split the silent dockland streets as they sped towards the Elephant and Castle.

On the way it became apparent to Matty that Queenie hadn't exaggerated when she'd called herself 'the boss'. She was, it seemed, one of the brains behind the most notorious girl gang in London. Once, she told Matty, they'd been known as the Forty Thieves, but some wag had rechristened them the Forty Elephants because their home turf was the Elephant and Castle and the girls usually emerged from a shoplifting spree twice the size they went in, with stolen goods packed into concealed pockets under their clothes.

Tonight, Queenie said, Matty had found her and Sugar sorting through a single day's haul. Matty could scarcely believe it as it seemed to her the accumulation of a lifetime's crime.

'Me and the girls did a raid up the West End, went in mob-handed. Twenty of us piled in, half of us lifted everything we could from the jewellery department, the rest did evening wear. Well, we was in and out in fifteen minutes. Them dozy shop assistants didn't know their arses from their elbows. By the time they works out what's going on we're halfway up Regent Street and the gear's in the back of three vans all going in different directions. The hardest bit's getting rid of it, to tell you the truth. But Sugar's got his contacts for that.'

Queenie drove very fast, with one hand on the wheel while the other held a cigarette in a holder. It seemed only a matter of minutes before they were pulling up in a side street near the Elephant.

'You'll be safe as houses here, love.'

Matty got out, her legs shaking with fatigue. She eyed the building in front of them, which certainly seemed more respectable than Sugar's from the outside. It had an ecclesiastical air to it and looked a bit like a convent, with steps up to an impressive pointed arched door beneath the porch.

'Welcome to the C of E mission hostel for respectable single girls.'

Matty looked shocked and Queenie gave a booming laugh. 'Only kidding. I try to keep my girls out of the nick, so you could call us respectable, or you could say we're just bleedin' clever!'

Queenie explained the place used to be a vicarage, but the church had fallen into disrepair and the vicar long departed. Matty didn't care if it was a nunnery or a prison. She was so tired she was sure she'd sleep anywhere and as Queenie let herself into the building Matty followed, almost asleep on her feet. Queenie showed her to a small, cell-like bedroom.

'What better place to hide a load o' tea leaves than somewhere that looks like a Christian hostel!' She chuckled. 'We try not to keep stuff on the premises. That's all farmed out. Me girls love it here. I don't get no complaints from any of 'em – apart from the prayers at teatime.' Again she gave her low, hooting laugh.

'You get some kip, love.' She put a heavy arm across Matty's shoulders. 'While you're here, you're under my protection and no bastard touches one o' mine, understand?'

Matty smiled. For all the woman's tough veneer, Matty heard a definite maternal concern in her voice. 'Thanks, Queenie, I really appreciate it.'

She gave Matty a squeeze. 'Sleep tight, love, no bugs to bite you in this gaff.'

And laughing, she left Matty to fall on to the narrow single bed, where she slipped between clean white sheets and soft blankets, falling immediately into a deep sleep. During the night she woke with a start, hearing the front door opening, but the muffled voices were undeniably female, girlish, high-pitched, excited and so full of expletives Matty doubted they would last five minutes in a respectable hostel for young Christian ladies. After that her sleep was fitful, plagued by thoughts of Frank's next move and worries about Tom. Why had his flat been empty? Why hadn't he come home last night?

23

The Forty Elephants

May–June 1932

When Matty awoke the next morning she felt safe, for an instant, and then she remembered Frank. His presence in the country changed everything. Wherever her thoughts stretched his malevolent intent seemed to have got there first. If she thought of Tom and why he hadn't come home last night, she worried that Frank had somehow got to him. When she thought of the health department films, she heard Frank's threats to expose her part in films she'd rather stay hidden. If she thought of Will, she remembered the insidious power of Professor Dubbs, who had followed through on his promise to ferret out her secrets and alerted Frank to her whereabouts. There was nowhere she could rest her thoughts and so she got up.

Although it felt foolish in the dull light of day, she was forced to dress in her evening gown, throwing Esme's day jacket over it. Thinking Queenie would want the velvet evening coat back, she folded it over her arm and padded down the corridor till she found a kitchen. Queenie was seated round a large table with half a dozen other women; they'd obviously just finished breakfast and some were leaning back smoking cigarettes.

'Ah, here's our escaped little bird! Come in, darlin', meet the family,' Queenie said.

She was introduced to the girls, who all greeted her warmly except one. She wore her hair in a severe black bob and stared, unblinking, at Matty with kohl-rimmed eyes.

'Say hello, Dolly, don't be bloody rude to me guest. She's a friend of Tom Roberts,' Queenie said.

The girl slid her gaze away from Matty to Queenie. 'I know who she bloody well is and why she's here, and I don't think it's too clever of you, Queenie, taking her in. She'll bring the Sabinis sniffing around, and what if they want some of what we've got?' Dolly stood up, pushing the kitchen chair back so hard it toppled over. But with a speed that surprised Matty, Queenie lunged across the table, shot out her big-boned hand and grabbed Dolly by the neck. The girl's kohl-rimmed eyes widened with fear as she was almost lifted off her feet.

'I'm doing my Sugar's friend a favour and if you don't like it you can sod off!' She let go of Dolly, who put a hand to her throat.

'I've had enough of this,' Dolly said, tossing her plate of toast into the sink so that it shattered, before brushing past Matty out of the kitchen.

A girl who'd introduced herself as Ruby got up to clear the sink, as if such incidents were a common occurrence, and asked Matty, 'Want some tea and toast, love? Never mind Dolly dark-eyes. She's just jealous, used to go out with Tom when he was one of the boys, didn't she, Queenie?'

But Queenie waved her hand in dismissal. 'Tom was another class. He wasn't interested in Dolly.'

But Matty wasn't sure she believed her.

A younger girl with platinum hair and a tinkling high-pitched voice said, 'Hope we didn't wake you up coming in. We'd been havin' a bit of a celebration.' Matty recognized the voice from last night. 'We had a lovely day's shopping up the West End!'

'Show her how it's done, girls,' Queenie ordered, sitting back with an indulgent smile upon her face.

Ruby put Matty's breakfast on the table, then walked out into the centre of the room and lifted her skirt to reveal the most voluminous pair of bloomers Matty had ever seen. Like a stage magician, she plucked the edge of a piece of black velvet cloth from a concealed pocket in the knickers. And as more and more velvet appeared, it soon became clear it was Queenie's evening coat.

Matty, who hadn't seen the coat disappear from the back of her chair and certainly hadn't seen Ruby stuff it into her knickers, laughed with delight, clapping her hands, for a moment forgetting that this wasn't a stage act, but well-practised thievery.

'How did you get that great thing inside those?' Matty laughed, pointing to the bloomers.

'Our Ruby can get anything in them knickers of hers – size no object!' Maisie, the platinum blonde, said to roars of laughter from the other girls.

'Show her another one,' Queenie said, proud of her girls' accomplishments.

An older woman with grey-streaked hair, who looked like a typical housewife in her sensible frock and cardigan, stood up and brought the black velvet coat to Matty.

'Hello, darlin', I'm Esther.' She gave Matty a warm smile. 'I loved that film of yours. We all did, didn't we, girls?'

The others, nodding enthusiastically, turned smiling faces towards Matty, and it was only when they all burst into laughter that she noticed Esther pulling Matty's own necklace from a deep pocket inside the black velvet coat.

'How did that get there?'

'Must've fallen inside – accidentally,' Esther said, while dipping down into another deep pocket in the coat's lining. 'Same time as these!'

'My earrings!' These she absolutely knew she'd left on the bedside table in her room.

'Esther's the best.' Queenie nodded approvingly. 'Looks so innocent, like everyone's mum. You see, Matty, you've got to trick their brains as well as their eyes!'

'Well, you certainly tricked both with me,' Matty said.

Esther handed her the jewellery. 'Don't worry, love, we don't take from our own,' she said. 'Best be getting off to work – I got forty elephants to feed!' And she looked affectionately at the girls sitting round the table.

Queenie got up, the game over, changing from mother to boss in an instant. 'You lot, don't sit there on your arses all day neither,' she said, and the girls obeyed, some clearing up breakfast things, others leaving the kitchen to get on with their day's shopping up the West End, Matty supposed.

'Come on, Matty, let's get you something to wear. You look like you've been dragged through a bleedin' hedge backwards in that get-up.'

Matty looked down at herself, shocked at the effects of her late-night escape on her dress, which was ripped from hip to toe where her long legs had broken through its constriction. The hem was filthy and her shoes scuffed. Esme's jacket had fared better and Matty made a mental note to keep a tight hold on it, as it was certainly good enough quality to appeal to one of the Forty Elephants.

Queenie took her to her own bedroom, a large, double-windowed corner room on the first floor. Matty recognized the hand of the same interior designer as in Sugar's home: the furniture was obviously all brand new. Looking like the entrance to an Egyptian temple, a heavy bedstead dominated the room. Carved and gilded stylized wings spread out across the headboard, while a frieze of angular figures marched across the footboard and a gold satin quilt billowed around it, all very different from Matty's nun-like room.

Queenie threw open the double wardrobe. 'Anything'd look good on you.' She glanced over her shoulder, assessing Matty's size. 'It'll need to be something that's a bit tight on me, though!'

She picked out a light wool skirt and paired it with a loose, knitted silk V-neck top and cardigan.

'Very elegant, very *respectable*.'

Matty noticed Queenie often used the word *respectable*, her tone almost regretful, perhaps aware respectability was something she'd never possess. Matty looked for the label before slipping the skirt on. It looked very good quality.

'It's a Jaeger,' Queenie said, 'but you won't find no label. We take 'em off soon as they come in. We have our little sewing-circle evenings – all sit round the table, picking the labels off the day's takings, gives us a chance to have a nice chat. I quite enjoy it.' She stood back to assess the outfit on Matty. 'Ohhh, don't you look lovely in that. See, I knew you could wear anything, looks better than it ever did on me.'

Matty was surprised at how natural it felt to be having a girly exchange with this hardened criminal, while feeling totally comfortable in what was undoubtedly stolen clothing. She wondered what Tom would say, and felt a pang of anxiety.

'Do you think Sugar will get hold of Tom this morning? He should be at the town hall.'

'Sugar won't hang about, him and Tom have been planning what to do if Rossi turned up. Tell you the truth, the Clerkenwell mob have been getting a bit too big for their boots anyway, coming over our side, muscling in. The Elephant Boys have been looking for a way to teach 'em a lesson and your Italian might just have handed it to them on a plate.'

'Queenie, I don't want Tom getting involved with the Elephant Boys again, not over me. I'd never forgive myself if he got dragged back in – he's not made for it.'

Queenie looked at her pityingly. 'Your constitution don't matter, love. If they can find a use for you, they will. But I'll have a word with my Sugar, make sure he looks after Tom. Which he will anyway, 'cause he thinks the world of him.'

She was holding up a cashmere three-quarter length coat against Matty. 'Very kind to him, your Tom was, when they was nippers. Tom used to take him home for tea, even when his own mum and dad didn't have a pot to piss in. 'Cause you know, my Sugar didn't get no upbringing. His mother got her money hitchin' up her skirts under the arches at Waterloo. Don't tell him I told you. But she used to send him out on the streets to shift for himself all day.' Queenie shook her head sadly. 'Your Tom had a heart of gold as a littl'un and Sugar don't forget that.'

'Tom's a kind man,' Matty said, realizing it perhaps for the first time. 'When I got back from America, I really was on my uppers, Queenie, though it didn't look like it to everyone else. And he got me a job, helped me sort myself out, even though I'd broken his heart.'

Queenie sat on the bed, indicating that Matty should sit beside her.

'I don't want to ruin his life again.'

Queenie leaned forward, elbows on knees. 'Well, you don't have to. You can always sort it out yourself.'

'What do you mean?'

'I mean these.' And Queenie held up her hands, twirling them in the light that slanted through the ecclesiastical-looking windows. 'You should learn to fight your own battles, like me.'

Matty laughed. 'If you'd seen Frank, you wouldn't say that. Besides, you're as strong as any man. I'm not. I may be tall, but these weren't made for hard graft.' She held up her own fine-boned long fingers.

'You don't need a lot of brawn. I've seen a strong man beaten to the ground with one of these.' She reached down a hatbox from the wardrobe and pulled out a chic woman's fedora.

'A hat!' It hardly seemed a promising weapon to Matty. But Queenie tossed it to her and as Matty caught it she realized this was no ordinary hat. 'It feels like it's lined with lead!' Matty said, hefting the hat from one hand to the other.

'That's 'cause it is! If you get a wallop over the head with one o' these you don't get up too quick, I can tell you that.'

Queenie gripped the hat and demonstrated a sharp downward slice of the brim into the billowy gold quilt, which caused an impressive dent.

'Have a go.'

Matty clutched the hat.

'Careful!' Queenie said, pointing to the front brim, which she peeled back to reveal a small razor blade. 'Wouldn't kill ya, but gives a nasty sting.'

Matty carefully grasped the brim at the side and copied Queenie's downward and sideward slicing motion. Her first attempt sent the hat rolling under the bed.

'Let the hat do the work, you just sort of let it go,' Queenie advised, and after a couple more tries Matty perfected the action.

'Have a look at this.' Queenie pulled at the small side feather tucked into the hatband. As she did so Matty gasped, for the feather's quill was actually a small steel stiletto with a vicious-looking tip.

'Now, if you want to sort that bastard out yourself, all you got to do is meet 'im in your new outfit!' Queenie handed her the hat and hooted with laughter, pleased with her gift.

Matty was about to refuse but Queenie pressed her. 'You keep it, love!' I got plenty more. Now all you need is yer rings. They don't have to be real gold, like mine, just heavy. Esther's got a load, we'll kit you out so if you end up having to give him a right-hander his face'll look like a nice juicy steak by the time you're finished.'

Queenie gave another whooping laugh and followed up by demonstrating a ju-jitsu throw on Matty, which had her on her back every time. Matty didn't like to insult Queenie by appearing ungrateful, so she accepted the martial arts advice and the weapons with good grace. But she couldn't imagine ever having the presence of mind to use them.

Later that morning when Tom still hadn't been in touch, she suggested to Queenie they go in search of him. The woman looked doubtful.

'Not a good idea. There's a reason they call this a safe house. If Rossi's got the word out, his boys'll be all over Bermondsey looking for you.'

'But I can't stay in hiding forever!'

'It won't be forever, darlin'. You'll be back on your cinevan before you know it... if that's what you want to do, though I think you're wasted on them health films.'

Matty was going to disagree when there was a loud knocking from downstairs. Queenie sprang over to the bedroom door with a surprisingly light-footed agility, her face still, her head cocked to one side. The sound of front-door bolts being slammed back reached them and Queenie relaxed slightly. Whoever had opened the front door obviously trusted the visitor enough to let them in. She followed Queenie to the stairs.

'Matty, stay up here till I'm sure.'

But the voice coming from the hall was familiar, if bizarrely out of place.

'I'm afraid I must insist on seeing Miss Gilbie. I have a rather urgent message for her.'

Queenie shot her a puzzled look. 'D'you know that geezer?'

Matty nodded and rushed past Queenie down the stairs. 'Feathers! What are you doing here?'

Feathers wore his usual calm expression, but when he saw her a look of relief passed across his face. 'You're safe! Thank God. Will was desperately worried, wanted to come himself, but of course I convinced him it should be me – not so likely to arouse suspicion if any undesirable should care to follow!' He pulled a face, but Matty could imagine he'd enjoyed the cloak-and-dagger trip to the den of the Forty Elephants.

'But why've you come?'

'Because, dear Matty, Tom could not.'

She stifled a cry with her hand. Her instincts had been right. There *was* something wrong with Tom. 'Is he hurt?'

Feathers shook his head. 'Not exactly. I'm afraid his father died last night. He was desperate to come to you, of course, but he needed to be with his poor mother. Besides, Mr Sweeting persuaded him you were in excellent hands.' He smiled charmingly at Queenie, who didn't seem impressed.

'I must go to him,' Matty said, already making for the door.

'I was to deliver a message.' Feathers restrained her. 'Tom knew this would be your response, but he said on no account should you leave here. I believe his "spies" have reported sightings of suspicious characters asking questions today at the Star and at the town hall.'

'I don't care. I'm going to him.' She shrugged off Feathers' hand.

'Let her go,' Queenie ordered Feathers and turned to Matty. 'I wouldn't stop you going to Tom, but just be a bit cute—' the woman tapped the side of her head – 'and make sure you wait till tonight before you go to his house.' She waved a disdainful hand in Feathers' direction. 'I suppose you'll attract less attention if he takes you rather than me. I'll stick out like a tart in a nunnery.' Queenie barked a laugh and Feathers flinched.

'You've been so kind, Queenie, thank you.' Matty kissed her new protector.

'Perhaps I could take you to the Labour Institute first, Matty,' Feathers offered. 'It's hardly the place anyone would be looking for you today, and we'll do as your friend suggests – visit Tom later under cover of darkness...'

Matty heard a faint snort from Queenie, who no doubt didn't trust Feathers' amateur bodyguard abilities.

'Hang on a minute, before you go!' Queenie turned and took the stairs two at a time. In seconds she came thundering back down.

'Don't forget yer titfer!' She winked and handed Matty the weighted fedora. 'And you, make sure you get her back here safe tonight!' she warned Feathers as they hurried down the front steps to his waiting car.

'Never fear,' he muttered, as he pulled out into the New Kent Road, 'this particular carriage won't be turning into a pumpkin at midnight.' He shot a glance at Matty. 'And the glass slipper would never fit on her size tens, would it?'

'Feathers! That's not very kind.' Matty stifled a smile. She'd never seen the barbed side of the young man.

He looked suitably chastened. 'I apologize. I didn't meant to be rude. To be honest, Matty, it's pure fear on my part. That woman was terrifying!'

Matty thought of Queenie's kindness and how all her soft side had been masked by a lifetime fending for herself among the toughest men in London.

'Feathers, I know we promised Queenie to wait till tonight, but actually, I'm *not* frightened of her, and I want to go straight to Tom.'

'You're as stubborn as your brother! All right, but we'd better stop off to see Will first. He's been terribly worried about you ever since that alarming trick cyclist came to give us Tom's message this morning.'

'Wally?'

Feathers nodded. 'I was rather disappointed he'd left the unicycle at home!'

Feathers drove the car along Tower Bridge Road, expertly negotiating the crowds spilling out into the road as they milled about the market stalls lining the street. He hooted his horn and a young boy gave an obscene gesture before hopping out of the way.

Matty felt herself sitting rigidly to attention, her focus on getting to Tom, all thought of her own danger driven from her mind. But it occurred to her again that Feathers shouldn't be here. Since the boys' narrow escape from being recruited as Dubbs' agents, Lady Fetherstone had kept her son on a tight rein.

'What are you and Will doing back in Bermondsey? I thought you were both writing articles about unemployment in the northern towns?'

'Slipped Ma Feathers' leash so we could join the NUWM hunger march to Westminster. We've been drumming up support from a few of our Bermondsey comrades. Talking of which, I never thanked you for your intervention with comrade Dubbs – the old fellow just got his claws into us and wouldn't let go! I admit that was a narrow escape. It's one thing to fight for a fairer world, but quite another to turn spy on your own country.'

'Dubbs hasn't been back in touch?'

'Good heavens, no! Ma Feathers had a word with the vice chancellor and I don't think Professor Dubbs will be influencing any other impressionable youths. Your dear brother and I are the last of our kind...' he said with mock regret. 'Why do you ask?'

'I think it was him tipped off Frank in the end.'

'But how would he know about Frank?'

'Spies are meant to know everything, aren't they?'

'Oh, Matty, I'm so sorry. It's our fault.' His face fell. 'I would do anything to help.'

'You already are, and it's not your fault. Frank would have found me eventually. He was just biding his time. Never heard of the cat and the canary?'

They pulled up in front of the Labour Institute in Fort Road and Feathers ran round to open Matty's door. As she got out, Will hurtled down the steps of the institute.

'Thank God you're all right.' He flung his arms round her. 'Quick, Feathers, get her inside.'

'No, Will. I'm not staying. Did Wally say anything about Tom?'

The young man took a step back. 'Only that he was worried about you... I am too.' His dark eyes flickered with hesitation. 'You're always fussing at me to be careful – well, now it's my turn.'

'All right, I promise,' she soothed. 'I'll just visit Tom quickly and then go back to my Forty Elephants.'

Will still looked unwilling to let her go and the reason for his reluctance struck her: without Eliza she was the closest family he had. She resolved to be careful, if only for his sake.

It was Winnie who opened the door of Tom's mother's house. Her friend's tear-streaked face lit up at the sight of her.

'He'll be cross with you for coming,' she whispered, 'but I'm glad you did. He's been breaking his neck to see you, but he thought someone might be following him.'

Tom sat next to his mother, holding her hand. His face broke into a smile when he saw her, but then anger flickered in his eyes.

'Matty, can't you ever do as you're told?'

She ran to him. 'Shut up, Tom. You should know by now you can't boss me about.'

Throwing her arms round him, she felt resistant muscles in his back and arms giving in as he hugged her tightly. She broke away.

'I'm so sorry, Mrs Roberts.' Matty took the woman's hand.

'Oh well, love, the best of my Sid was long gone, truth be told. I swear if he'd only been able to get out to work, he'd still be alive today...' And the woman buried her face into an already saturated handkerchief.

'You two go in the front room. I'll stay with Mum,' Winnie said, pushing them into the passage.

Once they were alone, Tom kissed her as though he might never kiss her again. 'Oh, Matty, I'm sorry I wasn't there. I've been going crazy with worry ever since Sugar turned up here this morning.'

'And I'm sorry I wasn't here with you. I know how much you loved your dad.'

His eyes brimmed and he turned away. 'I didn't want to be like this in front of you.'

'Tom, you haven't got to pretend to be strong with me.' She pulled him back into her arms and brushed the tears from the corners of his eyes.

'Did he hurt you?' he asked, looking intently into her eyes.

'No. Neville helped me get away. But, Tom – Frank wants me back. I don't think he'll stop till he gets his own way.'

His grief-filled eyes hardened. 'Not while I've got breath in my body. I've got to see Sugar – I'm not sitting in here doing nothing. Mum's got Winnie.'

'No, Tom. Sit down a minute. I need to talk to you.' She forced him to sit in his father's old chair by the fire, while she kneeled in front of him. She had been rehearsing what to say to Tom and now her words tumbled out in a rush.

'I've been hearing things about you planning something with Sugar and the Elephant Boys. Tom, please, please promise not to go up against him. He's so dangerous – you don't know. And you shouldn't be going anywhere near the Elephant mob. They'll drag you down. I can't be responsible for ruining your life twice over.'

'You never ruined my life. Matty, my darling, I'd be nothing without you. Your leaving forced me to change. Even though I knew I'd never have another chance with you, you made me want to be worth something.' He dropped his eyes. 'There's never been any one else for me, never will be. What sort of a man would I be just to give you up to him?'

She didn't reply and the room resonated with her silence. It was thundering in her ears – her silence, her secrets. She took in a deep breath; perhaps there was only one way to convince Tom. Her theory had been that the less he knew, the less danger he'd be in, but now he was rushing in as if Frank was in the same class as a Bermondsey wide boy.

'Tom, listen to me. Before you go anywhere, before you make any more plans, it's time you knew just what sort of man you're dealing with.'

'All right, tell me then,' he said, unafraid.

She began to draw the story up from the deep cave of memory she'd hidden it in and it was as if she were pulling out a part of her heart on a long, fine cord. Up to the surface it came, white and shrivelled, unused to the light of day. It was a poor, neglected thing, blighted by the memory of Frank, in a back alley in New York.

'There was this night, when I finally found out what he was. I'd been singing in Frank's club and after my set I went out the back door for a cigarette. It was pitch-dark in the alley but then something moved, a shadow but in the shape of a man, and he was sort of uncurling from the ground. He was black as the night, and I wouldn't have seen him if it hadn't been for this orange light coming from a window. When the shadow stood up I could see it was holding something. It looked like a flame, but then I saw it was a knife, with a long blade shining in that orange light. Then I realized there was another shape, a man sprawled out on the alley floor.' She looked to see the effect of her words on Tom and he was leaning forward, straining to hear, and she realized she'd been whispering.

'I was too terrified to move. I wanted to scream... but I couldn't! Then, so fast I couldn't follow him, the man with the knife sort of pounced, just like a cat on a mouse, and there was this horrible gurgling sound that seemed to go on forever, and then nothing. I should have shouted for help – done something. Then the man with the knife got up. He just strolled over to the window and held the blade up to the light, almost like he was admiring it.' Her voice seized up altogether and she felt Tom squeezing her hand. 'My God, Tom, the blade was just dripping with blood, great black spots of it on the cobbles...' Matty leaned forward, retching, and Tom caught her. Every inch of her body was trembling and though he gripped her as tightly as he was physically able, not all his strength could stop that trembling.

'You don't have to go on, Matty.'

But she wanted to pull the last festering splinter of this memory from her and be rid of it forever.

'No, I want to, because then you'll understand.' She pulled out of his arms and went on. 'It was then I realized that I wasn't the only one watching. There'd been an audience all along – Frank's boys, standing back in the shadows, so I hadn't seen them. And he strutted over to them, all cocky, holding up the bloody blade, and you know what he said?

'*Ah, look, boys, the kid's broken-hearted!* And he stood over the boy and stuck the knife in his chest till all you could see was the handle. That's when I must have made a noise – I felt like I was choking. He saw me. He looked at me and I thought I was dead. And then he smiled, the same smile he used to give me when he would meet me after a show or collect me from the station when I hadn't seen him for a while, as if he was pleased to see me. But what makes me so sick with myself is that I smiled back... I smiled back, Tom.'

Then she bent over double, hugging her stomach, protecting the idea of herself as an independent woman who'd gone to take

America by storm, though she had ended up no more than the canary in the paws of the cat. She allowed herself tears of shame, remembering how she'd slunk back into the shadows, sickened by a sight so horrific she couldn't even equate it with the action of a human being, let alone someone she'd loved.

Frank never spoke of the murder. He didn't need to. From then on she'd been little more than his prisoner, and he was as sure of her silence as he was of his own power to hold her. She shuddered at the appalling risk she'd taken in leading him here, exposing everyone she'd ever loved to his lethal will.

Dashing away her tears, she said, 'I'm so ashamed of myself.'

'No!' Tom took her by the shoulders. 'You're not to blame! How could you have tackled a monster like that?' Tom was fervent in her defence, but he had just made her point for her.

'Then how could you?'

He got up, and though she clung to his arm, he prised her hand away. 'It's time that man was dealt with so we can get on with our lives. My dad sat in this room and let other people decide how his life would be and how it would end. I won't do the same, Matty. So maybe Frank is a dangerous man, but Bermondsey's got her own Italians...' He reached for her hand and rested it on the nape of his own neck. 'I reckon I might need a haircut – what do you think?'

'You're going to Minetti's?'

Minetti had been the local barber for as long as Matty could remember. His shop with the red and white striped pole outside had been a regular port of call for all the men and boys in her family. 'Ask for a tuppeny all off' was her mother's injunction to Sam and Charlie, and then later Nellie's to Bobby and Freddie, before sending them off with the two brown pennies to wait their turn along with all the other little Bermondsey boys sitting on Minetti's bench. As they grew older, Minetti offered them much more than a haircut – everything from advice on how to look after themselves on the tough Bermondsey streets to explaining the mysteries of a 'packet of three', which she remembered Charlie divulging to her in whispered guilt one day when she'd found them in his pocket.

Minetti told them stories of 'back home'. Its hard men, much harder, he said, than the Elephant Boys, hinting that he'd once played his part, using the razor for more than cutting hair in his misspent youth. But if any of his young customers ever threatened to join the gang's ranks, he would frighten them half to death with tales of dead men he'd once known who'd followed a similar path. Now, Minetti in his old age was an affable man, with thinning dark hair and a still pronounced Italian accent. He was fond of saying his wife had tamed him, but to look at him you'd hardly think he'd ever needed taming. These days, he insisted, he was retired from all but barbering. But today, Matty was sure of one thing. Tom didn't need a haircut and he wouldn't be going to Minetti's to ask for a tuppeny all off.

24

The Cat and the Canary

June–July 1932

Matty went back to 'the vicarage' that night and Queenie assured her she could stay under the protection of the Forty Elephants for as long as she needed to. Matty had no idea what Tom's business with the barber Minetti would mean for her, but he'd asked her to trust him and to wait for him to send word. She almost felt as if she'd taken the veil and been banished to a cloister for criminal nuns. For though the girls liked a drink, they seemed too frightened of Queenie to be so raucous as to draw attention to the household. To the outside world, they passed as respectable hardworking single women, who were well enough off to own smart cars and dress in expensive clothes. They went off to work in the West End every day and never had gentlemen staying overnight. Queenie kept strict house rules, with them all taking turns for housekeeping and cooking.

She patiently spent the following day in cloistered seclusion while the girls were out working. But by the time they came home Matty was so bored that she asked to be let in on the sewing circle, which Queenie at first refused.

'You could get nicked just for taking the labels out, you know,' she warned.

'I'm already in the nick!' Matty complained.

'All right then,' Queenie said reluctantly. 'You can join in, but you'll have to sing for your supper.'

So that evening Matty sat unpicking labels and singing the girls' requests. They had a taste for the more sentimental old tunes, which Matty remembered from her music hall days. 'Mother I Love You' and 'Pal o' My Cradle Days' were special favourites, and Matty felt her heart warm towards her unlikely audience, none of whom, she suspected, had ever had the kind of mother who might deserve such paeans of praise.

The only one she couldn't warm to was Dolly dark-eyes, as she was known by the girls. Matty was unsettled by the kohl-rimmed eyes staring at her as she sang and she hoped she never found herself alone with the girl.

After another day with no news from Tom and nothing to do, Matty began to feel the same sort of confining panic she'd experienced during her final months with Frank. What good was it to have struggled so hard to escape him, only to allow him to force another incarceration upon her? In the early hours of the morning, she woke to a weight pressing on her chest and a pair of kohl-rimmed eyes staring into her face. She opened her mouth to cry out, but Dolly's hand stifled her. Matty had drunk enough gin in her life to recognize the smell and when Dolly spoke, her voice was slurred.

'Tom was my feller, a long time before you set your cap at him... woulda got back together an'all if it weren't for you, you stuck-up bitch. I saw him after you pissed off and all of a sudden I wasn't good enough.' She shoved the hand on Matty's chest down, till the breath was forced from her lungs. But as she gulped in air, Dolly's other hand clamped even more tightly over her mouth. 'Shut your fucking cockney canary gob—' Dolly shoved again 'and listen to me. I want you out. Sod off back to your Italian and leave Tom alone, and if you say a word to Winnie, I'll carve up your face so no one'll want ya!' She shook Matty like a rag doll and stumbled out of the room.

Matty lay perfectly still until she heard the slamming of Dolly's door. Then, shivering, and certain sleep would not come, she got up and prowled the draughty old house, finding herself at the high arched windows of the octagonal front room. She sat on the window seat, looking out at headlights flaring off early morning traffic in New Kent Road until the sky lightened to pewter and silver. She couldn't help wondering what Tom had told Sam about her sudden disappearance – he would be so worried. And what about the film work? What would Tom say to the three musketeers? They were meant to be launching the Modern Woman films next week with a special screening in the Spa Road Library hall.

Her new life had been brought to a screeching halt by Frank's emergence from the shadows and all the light she'd fought to let in over the past few years seemed to have dimmed. So much light had returned to her: the light in Tom's eyes, the light of the flickering cinemotor screen, the spotlight at the Blue Lotus, all darkened now by the shades of her past mistakes. He'd even managed to subdue the renewed joy in singing. Frank had robbed her of so much, more than she'd ever admitted to anyone, but most of all he had stolen the light of her life, her child. She pressed her forehead against the glass and began slowly, softly, to beat her fist against the leaded windowpanes.

Queenie found her there, when she came down for breakfast. Matty, barefoot and shivering in a thin negligee of pink silk from which she had personally removed the Harrods label, looked up blankly as Queenie sat beside her on the window seat. The woman untied the cords of her own velvet dressing gown and draped the garment around Matty, who lowered her eyes, transfixed as Queenie tucked the velvet around her with gentle, huge hands, the strength of which she'd demonstrated to Matty only last night when she'd taken an apple and with a quick twist broken it in two, offering her half.

'You're climbing the walls, ain't ya?' Queenie said.

Matty nodded.

'Why should it be me in prison?' she asked. 'I need to get out.'

'I know what it's like. First time I went inside, I wasn't much more than a kid. I don't shout about it much, but my gawd, I ended

346

up banging me head against the cell walls. I'd a done anything to get out and I've made damn sure I never went back in. That's why I'm so careful when I'm on a job and why I make sure all my girls are careful too.' She studied Matty's grey face and bruised eyes, then seemed to make a decision.

'All right then, one trip out, but you'll have to come over the other side with me and work, just like the rest of the girls do! Well, not *exactly*, 'cause I ain't having Sugar blaming me for getting you banged up.'

Matty's heart leaped at the chance of freedom, however short-lived and however dangerous. That morning she dressed, as Queenie instructed, in a chic belted dogtooth-check suit, and finished it off with her lead-brimmed black fedora, perched at as jaunty an angle as she could manage given the weight. She found she rather liked wearing the reinforced hat – she imagined it gave the sort of illusory protection that Sam must have felt when he was issued a tin helmet during the war.

Matty, Queenie and six other of the Forty Elephants walked round to the back of the vicarage, where Queenie's blue coupé was parked along with two other powerful-looking cars. Queenie pointed to Ruby, Esther and Maisie, who all looked larger than they had at breakfast that morning. Their added girth wasn't due to an excess of sausages and bacon, but because they were wearing coats double-lined with several deep pockets. They'd shown her how one elephant could fit a dozen dresses into these pockets, adding a fistful of jewellery into each leg of their bloomers. So what amount of booty seven of them might return with, Matty could only imagine. She knew Tom would be furious with her for going along with the escapade, but the part of her that was rebelling against constraint silenced her doubts.

'You three go in the Humber. Me and Matty's in the Alvis. Dolly, you take the others in the Vauxhall.'

Dolly glared at her. She looked the worse for wear, and her voice was husky with booze and cigarettes. 'What's she coming for?' she challenged Queenie. 'She'll get us nicked!' In two strides

Queenie was on her, slamming her face against the side of the Vauxhall. When Dolly looked up, Matty saw dark rings blooming beneath her eyes.

'Satisfied?' Queenie asked, unruffled. 'Now you're Dolly effin' black eyes, so leave her alone.' She nodded towards Matty and opened the door of the blue coupé. 'See you there, girls!'

Queenie drove at a sedate pace until the vicarage was out of sight and then put her foot down so suddenly that Matty's head was thrown back against the seat. She zoomed past the Elephant and Castle Tube Station, heading for Waterloo Bridge, and on the way puffed at her cigarette holder, explaining the day's 'outing'. It appeared that Matty was joining the Forty Elephants on a steam raid in Oxford Street.

'It all happens quick once you're there, so keep up, stop when you're told and move when you're told!' Queenie told her, adding that Matty would only be acting as lookout today and that when they reached the vantage spot where she was to stand, she would give Matty a sign. Her only job would be to alert the girls if a policeman came through the store's revolving brass and glass entrance doors.

When they reached Selfridges, the day's target, they parked the cars at the back of the shop and then walked in boldly through the front entrance, the girls fanning out, each heading for a different department. Queenie pointed her ruby-ringed index finger at a perfume counter nearest the main entrance and muttered, 'Stand there. If you see a copper come through them doors, break the glass on that fire alarm with your hat. Got it?'

Matty nodded.

'We'll only be fifteen minutes, so when you see me beltin' down them stairs, you grab on to me coat tails and don't let go. Enjoy your shopping – I know I will!' She winked and was gone, moving towards the staircase with easy strides, unbuttoning her coat as she went. Matty strolled over to the nearest glass-topped counter, picking up a small sample bottle of Atkinson's Black Tulip. It was a scent that often wafted over from Atkinson's factory to her house in Reverdy Road. She dabbed some perfume on to her wrist and inhaled. The intense sweet smell was like a distillation of home. She felt almost dizzy with longing and had the oddest sensation of being out of place and time. What was she doing here? She should be back in Bermondsey with Tom. But that wasn't possible. Displaced from all that was familiar, anchorless, she realized that this escapade with the Forty Elephants was a case of allowing the tide to take her. And yet part of her had certainly wanted to come. She might not approve of her line of business, but she certainly admired Queenie's tough independence and the way she took charge of everything in her life. She couldn't ever imagine Queenie running away from Frank.

Matty glanced nervously at the entrance doors, relieved that the only uniformed figure in sight was the commissionaire ushering people in from Oxford Street. She strolled to the make-up counter. Politely refusing the help of a young assistant, she picked up a pretty enamelled Atkinson's compact. Bright red poppies on a green background meant the fragrance must be California Poppy. Taking a deep breath, she noticed her hand trembled as it held the compact. She glanced at her watch. Queenie had only been gone ten minutes. Now Matty was regretting her stupid recklessness, wishing Queenie and the girls would hurry up. It was as she moved over to the lipsticks that she heard the commotion coming from the staircase – loud shouts and a woman's shrill screaming. 'Stop thief! Stop her!'

She wasn't sure what to do. Queenie's orders were to wait for her, but Matty's legs were turning to water, and if she waited any longer she might not be able to walk out of here, let alone run after Queenie. The nearest sales assistant was now on the alert and Matty heard her shout across to the perfume counter. 'Oh God, it's the Forty Elephants. I've just seen a bobby pass the front doors, run out and get him!'

Then, turning a terrified face to Matty, the girl said, 'I'm sorry, madam, but I'd advise you to move out of the way if you don't want to get trampled in the crush. They'll punch your lights out if you get in their way.'

Matty decided it was time to play her part. She ran to the fire alarm and taking off her fedora, smashed it into the glass. As she pressed the bell the store erupted around her, with customers and staff running off in all directions, tumbling over each other in an effort to reach the fire exits.

At that moment thunderous feet on the staircase announced Queenie's arrival. She came into view pursued by a rotund young salesman who had no hope of keeping up. Matty saw the other girls converging from different areas of the store with almost military precision. Ruby was running towards her, grabbing handfuls of perfume bottles, stuffing them into her pockets without breaking stride. Esther emerged from the lift, her increased girth and the trail of taffeta frills revealing that her inner pockets were stuffed full of dresses.

'Come on, Canary, move your arse!' she shouted.

Matty needed no encouragement and as Queenie pounded past she sprinted after her, barrelling through the revolving doors straight into the arms of a truncheon-wielding policeman.

'Excuse me, madam,' he apologized, and before he could realize his mistake Queenie landed him a punch with her knuckle-dustered fist, quickly side-stepping round him.

The punch floored the constable, but he shot out a hand just as Matty scooted past. He grabbed her ankle and she tumbled heavily to the pavement, grazing hands and knees as she did so. Queenie, Esther and the other girls were already disappearing into the Oxford Street crowd by the time Matty lifted her chin from the pavement. But then Queenie stopped and looked back. On her command the girls halted as one and doubled back. Charging the constable, they threw themselves at him in a rugby scrum of flailing stockinged legs and stolen petticoats. Strings of pearls and gold chains dropped from Queenie's pockets as she pinned him down with her knee, gasping instructions at Matty. 'Mortimer Street... van waiting. Walk... don't run!' She pushed

Matty in the right direction and when she hesitated, barked, '*Go!*', galvanizing her into action.

Matty sprang up and off. Hugging the shopfronts, head down, she walked as quickly as she could against the tide of shoppers towards Oxford Circus. But it wasn't long before she heard shrill policemen's whistles and saw several constables running towards Selfridges. When Matty looked back a policeman was sitting on Queenie, who, bucking like a mule, was trying to kick him off. Matty was horrified to see several other burly uniformed figures surrounding the girls. It appeared that the stampede of the Forty Elephants' elite brigade had been well and truly thwarted.

At Mortimer Street, Matty could see no waiting van. She walked up and down the street several times before giving up. The driver had probably realized the steam raid had gone wrong when the elephants missed their rendezvous time. She decided the only thing to do was to return to the Forty Elephants' den.

She took the Tube, standing all the way, holding on to the strap and rocking gently in the smoke-filled carriage, feeling sick and drained of all strength. At every stop she was expecting the transport police to board and cart her off. Once at the Elephant and Castle, she stumbled the short distance to the house, reaching it just as the late afternoon sun dipped below the steeply pitched gables. There was no answer to her knocking and she let fall the heavy metal knocker, resting her head against the solid oak door in despair. She had hoped that at least some of the girls might have escaped to make it home. Just as she was contemplating breaking in through a window, the front door was flung open and she was face to face with Dolly dark-eyes. Her severe bob was dishevelled and the two black eyes that Queenie had inflicted gave her an even more frightening stare. She said nothing at first and then took a step forward. Matty flinched and the girl laughed. 'Some fucking lookout you was. Queenie's been nicked, thanks to you. I'm the only one got back.' She drew her fist back and launched a punch at Matty, who dodged aside. 'What, don't want to come in? Then piss off!' Dolly shoved Matty so hard that she stumbled back down the stone steps, and by the time she righted herself the front door had been slammed tight shut.

Without Queenie there to protect her, the place had lost all feeling of sanctuary and she began walking along New Kent Road. She scanned for Frank's men, just as Queenie had told her she should, but saw only some schoolchildren on their way home for tea, a pair of tramps, no doubt walking up to the Methodist Central Hall soup kitchen, and a raddled young woman dressed for a night's work under the arches at Waterloo. It seemed safe, as safe as anywhere while Frank was in the country.

She headed for Tower Bridge Road, wondering how Queenie was. If she hadn't come back for Matty she'd have been snug in the vicarage by now, removing labels. But she had an odd maternal protectiveness towards her girls and Matty supposed when she'd moved in with the Forty Elephants she'd become one of them. In spite of her situation, she had to smile. 'How many mothers does one person need?' she thought ruefully.

*

She noticed the maroon and black Austin parked outside the town hall in Spa Road. It was a popular model, the type D.M. drove, and she thought it was his. If he was still here, then there was a good chance Tom was too. She ran up the steps and bumped into Plum, who was finishing for the day. He looked surprised to see her.

'Matty! How's your aunt?'

'My aunt?'

'Tom told us you'd be up north looking after her at least another week.'

'Oh, she's better,' she explained, and asked Plum if Tom was still in his office.

Plum looked even more surprised. 'No, he's taken the day off. It was his father's funeral.'

'Oh yes, of course.'

Plum apologized for having to rush off, wishing her goodnight, leaving her there on the town hall steps, feeling utterly empty because she'd not been with Tom to bury his father. She wanted to run across the road to Sam and Nellie's in Vauban Street, but with tears blinding her, she realized that their old house no longer existed. It was rubble dust, along with every other house in the street. In a daze, she'd almost stumbled down the steps.

It happened so quickly. She hadn't registered the two men in dark suits and fedoras sitting in the front of the Austin. One of them flung open the car door into her path, knocking her backwards, the other ran round the car, grabbing her from behind, covering her face with a cloth that made her retch and choke as the light failed and she was lost in darkness.

Matty shivered. Her teeth buzzed with the cold. Surrounded by impenetrable blackness, she put out both hands and felt freezing metal. Her fingers followed the chill curved womb that enclosed her till they reached a sharp protrusion. It was a lock. She pushed against it, straining every muscle to force open whatever door was confining her, but it was immovable. Panicking, she opened her mouth to scream, but instead an icy terror grabbed at her throat, preventing any sound from escaping. Then she became aware of pain tearing through her spine and legs as she tried to stretch out. She couldn't move more than an inch in any direction. Her wrists and ankles throbbed in protest at the rope ties that burned into her skin. Her head felt clamped in an iron vice, with the heavy weight of Queenie's fedora, still jammed on to her head.

Images surfaced, playing out on the flickering screen of her memory, but she couldn't make sense of them. It was the smell of ether, in her nostrils, on her lips, permeating the confining space, which brought her back with a jolt. She didn't remember it, but they must have bundled her into the boot of their car. It was a small car and a tiny boot. No wonder her very bones were screaming.

She'd once seen the strong man on Tower Hill lock himself inside a trunk not much smaller than this. He was able to dislocate every joint in his body, but she couldn't, and her long limbs had been tortured into impossible angles in order to stuff her inside. Now it occurred to her that she might have been left here to die. The car wasn't in motion, so they must have arrived at their destination, wherever that was. A whimper escaped from her throat as she understood what was happening. She hadn't been left to die. It was much worse than that. There was only one possible place she could be and only one possible person who would be coming to let her out.

Fear coursed along her veins, pounding in her temples, throbbing in her stomach, seeming to replace her lifeblood, robbing her of consciousness. She blacked out, though for how long she didn't know. When she surfaced she remembered having dreamed of her mother, Lizzie Gilbie. It was an old recurring dream, of her mother's last day on earth. Matty, still only a child, had never left her side. She'd been the only one home, keeping vigil over the person who meant most to her in all the world, praying that one laboured breath would be followed by another, and knowing with a certainty beyond her years that when her mother had asked Matty to sing 'My Love is Like a Red, Red Rose', this beloved person would leave her. But this time the dream had changed subtly and Eliza's face replaced Lizzie's, looking up from her deathbed, saying, 'Goodnight, my angel'. And then in the dream Nellie's arms were round her, warming her in this freezing place, and finally Queenie's voice, brash and bold and disembodied, echoed out of the dream: 'All your mothers are with ya, little Canary, but it's time to get up off yer arse and look after yourself...'

Matty awoke from the dream with a sob, which was interrupted by the click of the lock turning. A harsh electric light flooded her prison and she blinked against the blinding glare.

'Why the hell d'ya shove her in here? Did I tell you to damage the merchandise? Get her outta there.'

Two men lifted her like a trussed chicken and dropped her on to a stone floor. Her face grazed the gritty surface and she smelled petrol and oil.

'Sit her up, sit her up!' the voice ordered, and she found herself dumped on to a wooden chair.

The man dropped to his haunches in front of her and hooked a finger under her chin, forcing her to look into his coal-black eyes. The stare was unblinking and his expression unreadable.

'Didn't I always say you were mine? Why don't you never believe me, Matty? You can't run out on me and expect nothing to happen. There ain't no one out there for you. Nobody's coming to get you. Understand?'

Frank's finger forced her head up.

'Got nothin' to say to me?' He shook his head almost indulgently. 'Was a time I couldn't get you to shut up, chattering away in that cute accent, telling me how much you loved me.' Again his face was inches from hers. 'Remember? Are you telling me now it wasn't true?'

He made a quick gesture to his two henchman, the ones from the maroon and black Austin. As they came closer, their bad teeth and inferior suits betrayed them; they weren't Americans. They must be the Sabinis' men, in which case she was probably somewhere in Clerkenwell. They untied her hands and feet, which was more torture than relief as her muscles went into spasm. Frank jerked his head to dismiss the men, and when they were alone he straddled a chair opposite her. He sat just out of range of the single unshaded light. All she could see of him was the occasional glint from his white teeth and black eyes as he spoke to her in low, reasonable tones.

'What do you want me to do, eh? You know I can't let you go. These English guys, how'll they ever respect me if I let a broad give me the run around? So, here's the thing, Matty – I'll take you back.' He slapped his thigh. 'What, you think I would've tossed you in the damn Thames? Why would I do that to the mother of my child, Matty?'

The breath was sucked from her body as if he'd thrown a punch, deep into her gut.

He sat silently, waiting for her to recover.

'Why would I do that, *il mio piccolo canarino*?' He lunged forward, grabbing her chin. 'You're mine, but you got something else that's mine, and I want both back. It's family, you understand?'

She heard a fly buzzing and burning on the electric light above them. She tossed her head, trying to shake off his hand. 'There is no child,' she gasped finally, and then with what felt like her last breath spat out, 'You killed it!' Her head fell to her chest. She sobbed and the words rasped in her throat. 'You killed my baby.'

She didn't see his swift hand shoot out, but she felt the crack of his fist smash into her jaw.

'Liar! My bitch of a sister told Mamma. You think I don't know you ran away with my kid in your belly?'

Matty tasted blood and leaning forward saw it splash scarlet on to her skirt. She resisted the agonizing memory of that other day on the ship coming home, when she'd woken to the telltale bloodstain on the sheet. The memory of the excruciating pain had faded, unlike the intensity of grief that had filled her as she held her little girl, so tiny that Matty could cradle her in one hand, and whose perfect minute fingers she could still sometimes feel, gripping one of her own. That secret pain had never faded and every night when she closed her eyes, she saw the tiny heart, visible through translucent skin, beating like a fluttering bird until it finally faded away.

'I lost the baby.' Her voice sounded like a cracked bell. 'I lost it... on the boat home.' She lifted her head, bitter bile rising to mix with the blood in her mouth. 'It was your parting gift to me, Frank. Don't you remember? That last kick in my stomach? That's what killed your child.'

'You lying to me?' He slapped her softly across the cheek. 'You think you can keep my kid from me?' He slapped again, harder, and as she pulled back he stood up, kicking his chair aside.

'I didn't want it to be like this, Matty. But you gotta tell me where the kid is and then we can be a family. I got plans for you, like I said. You were always a good investment with that body of yours...' He whistled slowly through his white teeth.

356

He came up behind her, his hands running over her breasts down to her stomach. But his touch there fired her anger. She said nothing, but let it burn, picturing the tiny baby who'd never even opened her eyes to look upon the world. She summoned all the nights she'd mourned her lost child, all the times she'd held other people's babies and imagined they were hers. She had rebuilt her own life, while silently mourning all the landmarks of her child's life, all those stolen birthdays, all those unseen first steps, unheard first words, all the missed days of motherhood.

What was it Queenie had said in her dream? *Your mothers are all here, but it's time to get off yer arse...* Perhaps it was the dream that prompted her, perhaps it was sheer survival instinct, but she had been given an idea. She imagined her body strong, stronger than Queenie's. She saw herself as she had once been with Frank in the early days, confident in her power to dazzle him. She must look a mess now, but she knew that a part of him meant it. He really did want her back.

She let her head fall back on to him as he stood there behind her.

'All right, Frank. I can't give you the child, but you can have me instead. I'll come back. I'll come back with you to America.'

He walked round to face her, and gave her a long look, suspicion vying with vanity, his deep weakness – born of an over-indulgent mother – the conviction that he was irresistible. She matched his stare, willing adoration to appear in her eyes. She made herself think of Tom and some flicker of devotion must have flared in her gaze.

He nodded, reaching out to stroke her cheek. 'Of course you will, *il mio piccolo canarino*.' A slow, smug smile curled on his lips, creasing his inky eyes into a travesty of love.

He reached down to untie her bonds, kneeling before her as he fought with the tight knots until she was free. She yelped as blood pulsed back into her hands and feet, then, before he could rise, she grabbed her hat, bringing it down in a side-swipe to his temple. The momentum knocked him sideways and before he could recover, she stood over him, slashing the brim with its concealed blade across his heavy-lashed eyes, so that he seemed to cry tears of blood. Unsteady on her swollen feet, she knew her survival depended on making sure he couldn't follow. She smashed her fist, still adorned with Queenie's rings, into Frank's face and dropped to her knees at his side. Drawing the small feather from the hatband, she whispered, 'This is for my baby,' and she plunged the steel deep into his neck.

25

The Modern Woman and Murder

July–August 1932

There was blood, a lot of it, coating Frank's face and neck, but she wasn't hanging around to see the effects of her handiwork. She ran to the garage door, swung it wide open and glanced back at the Austin. Lupe Velez, her fiery Mexican film-star friend, had taught her more than how to roller-skate in those days on the studio lot. Lupe's red sports car had been lying as idle as the two young women and had beckoned to the mischievous starlet, who insisted on giving Matty driving lessons. Matty remembered that giddy afternoon, propelling the car around in jerky circles, learning to drive – after a fashion.

She hesitated. The choice was stark: either run out into a Clerkenwell full of Sabinis or chance that she'd remember her brief driving lesson. She turned back, taking heart from the fact that she'd been able to get back on the penny-farthing without a wobble and cycle all the way to Winchester. A sickening gurgle of blood bubbling from Frank's throat decided her. She wrenched open the car door, turned the key and prayed.

But the engine coughed, spluttered and died. Turning the key again, she despaired at the prolonged wheeze and final cough. If it didn't work this time, she would have to run. She put her foot down on the pedal and held her breath. The engine bucked suddenly to life and the car shot forward into the street. Frank's men would soon realize what had happened, so she would have to move fast. She stamped on the accelerator, sending the car slewing round in a circle, spinning back the steering wheel, then aimed the Austin towards the main road at the end of this little side street. Speeding up to the junction, she swerved on to the main road, searching for a street sign. It was the Farringdon Road, which she knew would take her straight to Blackfriars Bridge and south across the Thames to Bermondsey. It was then that she saw a bus in front of her heading for Islington Green. Frank's henchmen would no doubt expect her to drive south to the nearest river crossing and the safety of home, but it occurred to her there was somewhere else she could go. In fact, if she thought about it, she had homes all over London, and Collins Music Hall on Islington Green had been as much a home to her as anywhere during the early days of her career. Week after week she'd played there alongside the likes of Tommy and Timmy Turner or the Naughty Nightingales, a risqué trio of singing sisters whose lack of vocal ability was offset by the large amount of flesh they revealed each night. She yanked the steering wheel and nestled the car in behind the bus, following it all the way up St John's Road. It was a straight road and the traffic was light, for which she was grateful, for she was unsure what she'd do if she was required to change gear. As it was, the engine was roaring like a caged lion, but so long as she was heading away from Clerkenwell, she didn't care.

When she arrived at Islington Green she recognized the familiar old music hall but drove straight past it, pulling up in Essex Road by the stage door. She wrenched the handbrake and sat very still, gripping the wheel, her breath coming in shallow gasps. This street was one still illuminated with gaslight and in the flickering orange glow from a street lamp, she examined her bruised hands, noticing how Queenie's rings were now painted with Frank's blood. She wiped the rings on the car seat, then, spitting on her fingers, scrubbed as much of Frank off her as she could. She checked her face in the rear-view mirror. Bruises already bloomed around her neck and cheeks where the Sabini thugs had grabbed her. There was not much she could do about that. She wiped spatters of blood from her face and tucked her hair under the black fedora, now battered out of shape and minus its feather.

Matty got out of the car and walked on unsteady legs to the stage door. She judged it must be just before the end of the second show, for through the open stage door she could hear laughter rippling down from the auditorium. She stopped outside for a moment, getting up her courage, and noticed the playbill. A familiar name, low down and in small type, jumped out at her. The Collins had been a lovely place to play. It welcomed anyone who wanted to put on a show – you didn't necessarily have to be much good, but anyone who wanted to be an entertainer and spend their lives making other people happy for a few short hours was given a chance here. And it seemed that their policy hadn't changed over the years.

'Percy?' she called, sticking her head through the window to the stage doorkeeper's little cubby-hole. 'Have you got that kettle on?'

She flashed Percy the doorman a stage smile and hoped he would remember her.

A red-faced, elderly man with a military moustache, wearing a smart brass-buttoned coat, stuck his head out of the window.

'Well, stone me, if it's not the Cockney Canary!' he said, his accent betraying his origins in Kerry. 'Who let you out yer cage?'

She leaned through the window to kiss the old man on the cheek.

'Where's your manners, Perce, I'm gasping.'

He threw open the door of his cubby-hole, which contained two chairs and a shelf on which was a gas ring and a kettle, boiling its contents away, just as it had when she'd last been in Percy's 'office' as he liked to call it. A cup of tea had always been on offer while he telephoned for a taxi home or saw off unwanted stage-door Johnnies for her.

'Jeezus, Matty, it must be what, five years since I seen ya? You done well for yerself. I took the missus to see yer talkie. Very good 'twas too.'

He poured her a brown brew, thick with condensed milk, which she put to her lips, shaking so much that she dribbled some down her chin.

'Sit down, God love ya, you're all of a tremble. State o' them knuckles. Been in the wars?'

This was Percy's euphemism for a night on the tiles.

'Something like that, Percy. I was passing this way and I had to come and have a look at the old place. I thought you'd still be here...'

''Course! Place'd fall apart without me.'

The old man's expression turned serious. 'You know me, darlin', soul o' discretion, stage-door secrets don't go no further than this room.' He tapped the bench with a thick, ridged nail. But word's out in the business you might be in a spot o' trouble, and anythin' I can do to help – you just tell old Perce.'

She covered the old man's leathery hand with her own. 'Thanks, Percy, there is something. Can you get a message backstage for me? Could you tell Wally I'm here?'

For the name Matty had recognized on the playbill was none other than Winnie's husband, Walter. Wally the Wonder Wheel was obviously a filler act, judging by the minsicule typesize of his name on the playbill, but Matty was surprised to see him there at all. As far as she knew he'd last ridden a unicycle at his wedding, and after that spectacle Winnie had ordered him to make it his final appearance. She'd told Matty he'd given in and was happily pursuing his career as an insurance salesman.

'I think he's still here. He went on earlier.' Percy wrinkled his nose. 'The boss is a soft touch, still gives him the odd spot, you know, for old time's sake. I'll go and get him, love, you help yourself to another cup o' tea.'

When he'd gone she hugged herself tight, praying Wally would still be here. She'd had no plan in coming to the Collins, other than finding somewhere safe to wait while throwing the Sabinis' men off her trail. She could have just asked Percy to get her a taxi, but now she knew Wally was here she'd feel safer going home with him.

In a few minutes Percy was back, with Wally, who was struggling in the narrow corridor with his unicycle packed away in its carrying case. Before he could ask any questions, she explained she'd been out with her Italian friends in Clerkenwell and needed an escort home. His eyes widened with understanding.

'And your friend from America?'

Matty nodded, grateful that he'd understood.

'Can you flag us a cab, Perce?'

When they were safely inside the taxi, Matty slumped against Wally, leaning her head on one of his sloping shoulders. She let out a groan. 'Thank God you were there tonight, Wally. I was just about done.'

He made her recount the day's events, listening without comment until the part where she stabbed Frank with the stiletto, when he let out a long whistle.

'Matty, love, you was lucky, very lucky. He sounds a nasty bastard and it looks like he's got the Clerkenwell mob in his pocket too. But you're all right now, love, I'll get you back to Tom. At least now he won't have to sort Rossi out.'

Matty didn't have the strength to argue. She just said, 'Tom's an office worker these days, Wally. Frank would have ate him for breakfast.'

Wally patted her hand. 'There's more to Tom than you know.'

'I know he's not a villain.' Matty let the swaying taxi cab lull her into a numbness that she hoped would drive away the memory of Frank's last gasps.

'Did you know my old dad used to run the Elephant Boys?' Wally asked.

'No, I didn't! I can't imagine that.'

'Well, he did. Retired from that game now o' course, but he wanted me to follow in his footsteps. He kicked me up the stairs when I told him I was going on the stage. We came to an understanding in the end, though. But you know who he tipped to take over from him one day?'

'Who?'

'Your Tom.'

Matty gave an incredulous laugh. 'Well, if that's true I've got a bloody bad taste in men! I've just killed one gangster boyfriend and you're telling me the other's just as vicious?' Matty could barely believe it.

'No! Not *vicious*. No, my old dad said Tom had the brain for it. Your Clerkenwell and Whitechapel mobs – they've got plenty of brawn, but they ain't got the savvy, not like the Elephant Boys, and that's what Dad saw in Tom. He said to me, that boy'll run rings round the other mobs, given a bit of training.'

'But him and Freddie got out,' Matty said, sure that her faith in Tom hadn't been unfounded.

'Dad let them go. Usually you're not let go. Once you're in, you're in for life.'

'That's what Frank said, you can't walk away, ever. So why did your dad make an exception with Tom?'

'Said he'd got too much heart, it'd get 'em all killed one day. But he always had a soft spot for Tom.'

'And you walked away too? I never heard you talk about it, Wally.'

And then Matty realized that her friend Winnie must know, though she'd never mentioned it.

'Walked away? Cycled more like.' He chuckled and patted the unicycle in its case beside him. 'I remember that day, all three of us – me, Tom and Freddie – walking past the Elephant theatre and Dad calling after us, *Go on, fuck off, useless bastards the lot of yer.* Broke his heart and all I could think of was going round the stage door of the Elephant to get an audition!'

Matty had to smile. Wally was a born trouper.

'But if Tom's so soft, what makes you think he could have handled Frank?'

'He told me at his dad's funeral. He had a plan to see off Frank. He never said what it was, just that I'd need to be on call and that we were all going back to being Elephant Boys.'

'Didn't he say any more than that?'

Wally shook his head. 'Couldn't talk much.'

'How did he seem? I should have been there.'

Wally put a hand over hers. 'Nothing much you could've done, love. You know what funerals are like.'

They were driving through the deserted City now, passing darkened banks and blank-windowed offices, weaving down past the Monument to London Bridge and finally across the inky Thames.

'Wally?' she said suddenly. 'What were you doing at the Collins tonight?'

'These days the old insurance lark ain't much cop. Who's got any spare money for the insurance man? I'm lucky if I pick up a penny policy here and there to bury 'em. 'Course I make a bit from the knocked-off stuff, but with Win's mum to look after we can do with the extra. But to be honest, love, I'd do it for nothing. I love it. Get's in your blood, don't it, darlin'?'

'It does, Wally, it does. But I'm wondering now, if I hadn't started singing again in the Blue Lotus whether Frank would have found me so easily.'

'Oh, he would have found you, sweetheart.'

'I suppose so. He wasn't the type to let go.'

'Well, Matty, I think he's let go now.'

Matty had never been happier to cross the river. Entering Bermondsey felt like returning to the safety of a walled fortress. Wally kept the taxi running and she heard his whispered brief explanation to Tom that she'd had a run-in with her 'American friend'. But she felt he must be talking about someone else. Was she really the one who'd slashed and stabbed and caused so much blood to flow? The taxi pulled away and Tom gathered her up into his arms, carrying her straight to his bedroom. He tried to lie her down, but her arms were looped about his neck and she found herself unable to let go. With her head buried into his chest, she clung on tight, waiting for her trembling to subside.

'Oh, Tom, I think I've done something terrible, I need to—'

But he put a finger to her lips. 'Shhh, don't try to talk, you can tell me everything later, I just need to clean up these wounds, my darling, and then you can sleep. All you need to do is lie here for a bit while I get some hot water.'

He prised her arms away and laid her gently on the bed. His face was drawn and grey, his brow etched with anxiety. 'Lie quietly, sweetheart,' he said softly. 'I'll be back in a minute.'

He came back with disinfectant and a bowl of warm water. Taking one hand and then another he gently eased off the rings from her swollen fingers. Light from a bedside lamp revealed bruised knuckles swollen to twice their size. She winced and cried out as each ring came off, exposing the grazes and cuts she'd suffered while pummelling Frank. He examined the torn nails and bloody fingertips, which she supposed she'd got from scrabbling at the car-boot lock. Taking each finger, he first bathed and then with soothing sounds covered the cuts with salve, before bandaging her hands.

Then he began tracing the bruises on her neck and chin and she saw his mouth tighten.

'My poor darling. I'll kill the bastard...' He choked.

Matty shuddered and in a hoarse whisper replied, 'You won't need to, Tom. I already have.'

'You've killed him? How?' Then before she could answer, he said, 'Good. If he's dead... good.'

He lay on the bed and held her so tightly in his arms that her bruised body rebelled and a cry escaped from her lips.

'Matty, I'm so sorry. What did he do to you?'

Tom's voice sounded small and faraway. She knew he dreaded hearing the answer, but he would have to know. So in the soft light from the lamp, grateful that she could lean her head on his shoulder and not have to look him in the eyes, she unfolded her story.

When she'd finished, he kissed her tenderly. 'Oh, Matty, to think I could have lost you. If you've killed him, then you don't shed a tear, hear me? It was you or him.'

'Tom, should I go to the police, before they find out?'

For a moment he was silent. 'Chances are they won't find out, Matty. He's on the run, can you see the Clerkenwell mob reporting it? For now, let's just be glad you're alive. We can worry about what to do next tomorrow.'

She nestled more deeply into his arms and he stroked her hair until she fell into a sleep deep enough to escape her own warring terror and relief at what she'd done.

In the morning she awoke alone. It took a few seconds to register where she was. She felt the space next to her in the bed. It was cold. Where was he? She propped herself up, noticing new centres of pain across her shoulders and along her shins, grazed when they'd dragged her into the car. She looked down at herself, still fully clothed in Queenie's ruined dogtooth-check suit, then her eye fell upon the fedora, which had saved her life. Tom had placed it on his chest of drawers. Blood caked the brim.

Matty groaned at the enormity of what had happened. She had killed a man. No matter that he would have done the same to her in a heartbeat, had she not cooperated. She thought back on all the innocent trail of decisions, beginning with that fateful one to go to America, which had added up to the horror of last night, and which she could never now escape.

A loud drumming interrupted her thoughts. Rain hurled itself at Tom's basement window. The room darkened as the heavens opened and a leaden light descended over her. She shivered and then froze, suddenly alert. She'd heard a noise coming from outside the bedroom door.

'Tom!' she called. But there was no answer, just muffled sounds. Her heart was suddenly drumming along with the rain. Senses fizzing, she sat on the edge of the bed. 'Tom? Is that you?' She jumped as a loud clatter was followed by an expletive. Launching herself out of the bed, she scrabbled for the key to the bedroom door, but there was none. Like a trapped, hunted animal, she hadn't stopped to think or reason – instinct was motivating her. She'd even forgotten that Frank was dead, that he was in a place where he could no longer harm her. She stood with her ear to the door and heard a tinkling noise. Was it breaking glass? There was no escape but out of the basement window. She ran to it and shoved up the casement. Putting one leg through, she straddled the sill and was about to slip over into the airey when the door burst open.

'Gawd's sake, get yourself back in here, you're getting drowned!'

'Nellie!' Matty sat astride the sill, soaked by the pounding rain. 'You frightened the life out of me! What are you doing here?'

She curled herself back into the room, feeling foolish and relieved.

'Tom's got the big show on at the library hall, showing your Modern Woman films, says he couldn't miss it. But he asked me to come and keep an eye on you. Looks like a good job he did.' She put the tray of tea and toast she was holding on to the bedside table and opened her arms wide. 'Come here.'

Matty ran to Nellie, who enfolded her in that familiar, long-remembered safe embrace.

'He's told me what's happened,' Nellie said simply.

'Everything?'

'Yes, love, everything.'

'But I didn't want you and Sam involved! The less you both know the better.'

'Perhaps you'd have done better to tell us more and protect us less. What good's it having a family if you don't let them help you, eh, Matty, love?'

But Matty shook her head. 'I couldn't be responsible for bringing someone as dangerous as Frank into your lives. If I'd put your boys in danger, well...' She shuddered.

'Life's full of danger, you can't protect them forever,' Nellie said matter-of-factly and urged Matty back into bed.

'Here, drink your tea while it's hot. I'll get you a towel. I've brought you some of your own clothes and I never forgot your war paint!'

Trust Nellie to realize how Matty relied upon her 'armour'. A fine frock and a carefully made-up face could always boost her courage, on stage and off. Nellie was one of the few who knew the person buried deep behind the facade. She needed no reminding that little Matty Gilbie of Beatson Street was still in there somewhere and that today she would need all the guns in her armoury to face what was to come.

With her tangled hair combed out and styled as best she could, she dressed in the green and white print dress Nellie had chosen for her. Mercifully she'd brought a white scarf too, which Matty wrapped around her throat to hide some of her bruising. The green edge-to-edge jacket with long sleeves and a pair of white gloves would cover up the rest of her wounds. Once she'd dusted her face with powder and rouge most of the outward signs of her ordeal had disappeared. She tried to squash the sick fear that the police would come knocking at any moment and turned as bright a face to Nellie as she could.

'Well, Nellie, love, I suppose I'm ready to face the world. What do you think?' she said, presenting herself to Nellie.

'You look lovely, but Tom said you wasn't to go out!'

Matty shook her head. 'Oh no. I've had just about enough of men locking me up lately. I worked bloody hard on those Modern Woman films and I'm not missing their first screening, I don't care what happens afterwards,' she said firmly. And, turning to the mirror, she adjusted her close-fitting green hat, then pulled on her gloves.

'Come on, Nellie, you can be my bodyguard.' Matty smiled. Then, suddenly aware that she no longer needed one, she felt a guilty relief flooding through her. Frank was dead. Frank was gone. Whatever consequences came, at least she'd enjoy her freedom while it lasted.

Nellie had taken the day off from the various jobs that she juggled during the week. It couldn't have been easy. Some were cash in hand and Matty knew the money was necessary to bolster Sam's wages.

'Nellie, if you need to get to work, I'll be all right,' Matty offered, as they walked along Tooley Street.

'I'm not letting you out of my sight! Besides, I wouldn't mind going – they sent me and Sam an invitation to the film premiere.'

When they entered the large library hall it was almost full. There was an excited bustle and chatter. She looked for Tom, but could only see D.M. and Birdy in conversation with the mayor. Then she spotted Tom. He was setting up the gramophone that would provide the commentary for the film. Tom jumped down from the stage and Matty saw him checking the extra speakers brought in for the occasion. He glanced up and a flush of what she knew was anger was the only sign that he had seen her. He turned his back to her and, after a few words with Plum at the projector, he strolled over to where she and Nellie were looking for seats.

'Don't blame me!' Nellie told him before he could say anything. 'You know what she's like.'

Tom laid a hand on Nellie's shoulder. 'Don't worry, Nell.' He turned a stony face to Matty and said in a tight, low voice. 'What do you think you're doing, Matty? You came home half dead! You should be resting – to say nothing of who might be on the lookout for you!'

'Who? He's gone. Why would they come looking for me now?'

Tom raised his eyes. 'Matty, there might be consequences.' He shot a look over his shoulder. 'The Sabinis might not take kindly to you bumping off their partner!'

But at that moment the lights dimmed and D.M. made his way to the stage. She and Nellie found seats near the aisle as D.M. praised the work of his film team in 'bringing the Bermondsey health films into the talkies era with their innovative and relevant films for single and working women'. He went on to scatter some impressive statistics at his audience. How the public health gospel spread throughout Bermondsey halved the infant mortality rate, slashed the TB rate and radically reduced instances of preventable diseases. 'Due in no small part to the Bermondsey borough's health propaganda films!'

Here he was encouraged to end, with sustained applause and a stamping of feet from the Bermondsey extras worthy of the tuppeny rush at the Star. D.M. laughed good-naturedly and held up his hands. 'Let the films, quite literally, speak for themselves!'

The hall went dark, the screen flickered to life and there was Matty in bed, yawning and rubbing her eyes, looking convincingly reluctant to get out from under the warm covers and begin her first day at Peek Frean's. Matty got a reassuring amount of laughter in all the right places and when they reached the scenes inside Peek's Matty heard cries of recognition. 'Look, Win, that's us!' And looking round, she spotted Winnie and some of the Peek's Tiller Girls, enjoying their screen debuts.

She caught Winnie's eye and waved, and when her friend mouthed, 'You all right?' Matty knew Walter had told her everything. She sank back into the seat. She wasn't all right. She was a murderess. And if she wasn't facing hanging, then, as Tom had pointed out, the Sabinis might want to inflict their own form of justice. She could see the headline now. *Cockney Canary Slain in Gangland War!* Perhaps she should just go to Tower Bridge police station and hope they believed she'd killed Frank in self-defence.

It was impossible for her to concentrate on the films she'd worked so hard on. But their effect on the audience was palpable – not only on those who'd appeared in them, but also on the officials sitting in the front row. Matty could see them engrossed in the storylines, which were something quite different from the usual educational approach. These films had characters who tugged at the heartstrings and drew on the audience's sense of familiarity. The women in the audience were thinking of their own struggles in keeping a home and family going.

Although most of her was absent, her thoughts returning again and again to Frank's bloodsoaked face, in the middle of the *Modern Woman and Home* film there came a scene that completely disarmed her. It was the one they'd filmed with a homeless family living underneath the railway arches. Matty was holding the baby, a tiny, wizened little boy with an old man's face, wrapped in the thinnest of blankets. She was looking down into its large sunken eyes and she remembered now the feeling of connection, the impossibility of giving the child back to its homeless mother, and how she'd wanted only to walk off camera and take the baby with her.

Matty was horrified. Her face was raw with an emotion she'd assumed was well hidden in her everyday life. She hadn't been acting. It was here for the world to see, her longing, her loss, as she raised the tiny child to touch its cheek to her own, and her own eyes stared out of the screen with such haunting sadness that she felt the tears brim, then roll in an uncontrolled stream down her cheeks. Nellie's hand covered her own and she felt the woman's concerned eyes on her.

'It's all over now, love,' Nellie whispered. 'You're safe and sound.' Nellie squeezed her hand and Matty squeezed back, thanking God that her tears had been misunderstood. She dabbed at her cheeks with the back of her gloved hand. Safe, yes, but not sound. She took in a shuddering breath and turned her gaze back to the screen.

26

Brown Bread and Bomboloni

August–September 1932

The first factory showing of *Modern Woman and Work* had taken place in Peek Frean's canteen earlier that day. Tom and Matty were sitting at a corner table in the Concorde, toasting its success, when Sugar walked through the door with Queenie on his arm.

When Queenie spotted them she threw her arms wide. 'Come 'ere, me lovely canary!'

Matty leaped to her feet, running to her as if the woman really were her long-lost mother. Queenie's muscular arms encircled her and with the strength of a man she lifted Matty off her feet.

'Queenie! How did you get out of prison?'

The woman planted a firm kiss on the top of her head and lowered her to the floor. With her arm through Matty's, she swept her across the pub to where Tom and Sugar were already in conversation.

'Detective Sergeant Praah of Tower Bridge nick, darlin', that's how,' Queenie drawled in answer to Matty's question. 'Bent as a nine bob note, do anything for Sugar and me. Well, do anything for anyone so long as they bung him and remember to call him DS Praah – never Pratt!' She hooted with laughter. 'Sugar slipped him a pony and Pratt got me and all the girls off – insufficient evidence! Ha!' Queenie's foghorn laugh drew curious glances from the other drinkers. 'Them coppers was cuddling me and the girls all the way to the nick. I don't know how all that stuff up our knickers managed to disappear by the time we got there, but when it come to it, love, there wasn't a frill, a flounce or a fuckin' furbelow between us. No stuff, no charge. Get us a gin, Sugar darlin', I'm dry as an Arab's arse.' She settled herself down next to Matty and took her hand.

'So, darlin', I hear my titfer come in very handy?'

'It saved her life,' Tom said and Queenie stared at him for a moment.

'Oh no, that's where you're wrong. She saved her own life, didn't you, sweetheart? Not many would have had the guts to do it, not when it come to it. But you did.' She looked at Matty with undisguised admiration. 'You ain't got the muscle on you, but I'd have you in the Forty Elephants tomorrow if I thought you wasn't made for better things.'

'I'll get the hat back to you,' Matty said. 'I've cleaned it up as much as I could, but the feather...' Matty gulped. 'The feather's lost.'

'I daresay it is. Some bastard swallowed it, I hear. No, you keep the hat, I'll get you another "feather" for it.' Queenie winked. 'And keep the rings, seems you remembered what to do with them an' all.' She gave a satisfied nod.

'I hope I don't have to use them again – ever. But I'm grateful, without them I'd be dead or on my way back to America with Frank by now.'

At that moment Sugar came back with drinks. Beer and gin slopped on to the table as he sat down, jamming his thick legs under it.

'So, have you heard anything?' Tom asked.

Sugar had been charged with keeping his ear to the gangs' bush telegraph. 'Nix. It's like the geezer was never here. Suits the Clerkenwell mob, though. Less trouble for them if he's just "disappeared". He come into the country on the quiet as it is. They might just let it go...' Sugar looked uncertainly towards Matty.

'But, as far as the police are concerned, there's been no crime committed,' Tom mused.

Matty gave him a long stare. 'But, Tom, his family will have to know eventually. A person can't just disappear.'

Queenie snorted. 'Listen to the innocent! Half of Thames mud's made up of people who "just disappeared"!'

Matty put her head in her hands. The sick feeling she'd had since killing Frank was like a worm slowly boring into her gut. She'd barely eaten or slept. The man was still ruining her life even from the grave. She rubbed her face.

'I don't think I can live like this, waiting for the Sabinis or the police to turn up on my doorstep. Wouldn't it be best to go to Tower Bridge nick and just tell them it was self-defence?'

'Silly as a sackload o' monkeys!' Sugar blurted out. 'You'll be walking up the stairs to Jack Ketch before you know it!'

'What's the matter with you, frightening her like that, Sugar?' Queenie thumped him on the arm. 'She's gone white as a sheet!'

The mention of the hangman had hit Matty like a blow to the chest. She sat in miserable silence until Queenie nudged Sugar. 'Come on, Shug. I got an early start tomorrow. Goin' for an early morning dip!' She stood up, giving Matty a reassuring squeeze on the shoulder.

'You're always welcome at the vicarage, love, and if you need me to have a word with our bent copper any time, you just come and see me. Night darlin'.' She kissed Matty and grabbed Sugar's elbow, steering him out of the pub.

'Matty, let's just wait a bit before you rush to the police. Sugar's right, you know. They could charge you with murder. Do you want to hang?' Tom's voice was urgent and taut with fear.

She didn't want to hang. In fact it was a recurring dream of hers, that she was standing beneath the scaffold in a line of condemned prisoners, watching as each one walked up the steps to be hanged. And the paralysing terror she felt at just waiting for her turn to come was usually strong enough to wake her up. Now she felt that terror every waking minute. 'Tom, you don't understand. It's the waiting that's the worst...'

*

She tweaked the lace curtain and scanned the street of terraced houses. Matty was looking out for Tom. The house stood in almost accusing silence behind her. She was in the sedate parlour, still full of Eliza's pictures and books and photographs. Matty had placed the two childhood pictures of her and Eliza at the same age on either end of the mantlepiece. They stood like two silent sentinels, reminding Matty of the bitter power of hope hijacked by regret. And now it seemed she had made the same mess of her life Eliza had. All the dreams for escape, for a better life, shattered for love of the wrong man.

Tom had insisted he go with her to Tower Bridge police station. He'd promised to be here early and now her heart leaped at the sight of him, walking towards the house, dressed in his best suit and trilby. His eyes were fixed on the pavement, and he looked lost in thought. Whatever encouraging words he was preparing for her were belied by the anxiety plainly written on his face. As she found herself wishing she'd been able to share more of her secrets with him, he looked towards the window, spotted her and broke into a reassuring smile. She wasn't fooled, but at least the waiting was almost over.

She let him in and he slipped his arm round her waist, drawing her in close and kissing her. 'Ready, my darling?'

'Ready.' She paused. 'Tom, I'm so glad you'll be with me.' She gripped his hand. 'Shall we go?'

He nodded silently. It seemed he'd used up all his arguments. 'Come on then, sweetheart.'

They walked together to the bus stop in Southwark Park Road. But after only five minutes, Tom, seeing Matty's increasing agitation, suggested they try for a taxi. Before she could answer Matty heard the roar of a speeding car. The flashy blue coupé with its cream soft top came to a screeching halt at the bus stop.

'Hop in!' Sugar ordered, leaning over to push open the passenger door.

Matty gave Tom a hesitant look and whispered, 'Is this a

good idea?' She didn't think it would help her case to turn up at Tower Bridge police station in the unmistakable motor of a known criminal.

'Get in the jam jar!' Sugar ordered.

Tom turned to Matty. 'It's OK, Matty. He can drop us off before we get to the nick.'

She agreed and squeezed herself into the tight back seat, while Tom sat next to Sugar. She was grateful the soft top wasn't down today, as there was a chilly breeze blowing and a fine drizzle in the air. Sugar roared up Southwark Park Road but soon executed an inexplicable and dangerous U-turn.

'You're going the wrong way!' Tom said.

But Sugar ignored him, halting at the stretch of Southwark Park Road known as the high pavement. Here the buildings were elevated and reached by two stepped pavements.

'What's the point of picking us up just to drop us here? We could have walked if we wanted a pint and a fish and chip dinner!' Matty said, for the high pavement boasted a pub and a fish and chip shop.

Sugar turned round, his battered face unusually serious. 'There'll be no nick for you today.'

'For God's sake, tell him, will you, Tom. I've made up my mind.'

'Sugar—' Tom started, but his friend held up a brown bony hand, knuckles freshly grazed.

'Listen! She's no need going to the old Bill...' Sugar said, 'because the geezer ain't brown bread!'

Matty felt as if someone had poured ice down her back. 'How do you know? Are you *sure*?'

She couldn't believe Frank had survived her attack. 'I saw him die. That steel was buried in his neck – if you'd seen the blood...' She shuddered at the memory.

'I wouldn't say it if I wasn't sure. I see him meself. Right mess you made of his boat race!' Sugar grinned at her and Tom grabbed her hand.

377

'Don't worry, Matty, don't worry,' he said, breathless and white-faced, shocked out of his normal calm response to any crisis.

Sugar got out of the car. 'You two comin'? Queenie says I need an 'aircut,' he said, brushing his hand over an already severe short back and sides. He began walking towards a shop on the high pavement with a red and white striped pole outside.

They followed Sugar to Minetti's barber shop and, as Matty entered the white-tiled, mirrored interior, she noted that every one of the black leather chairs, with their silver pedestals, was empty.

Minetti raised his head. He'd been studying the *Sporting Life* and now folded it slowly. 'Hello, boys, ah, and lady.' He got up and brushed off a black leather seat, which needed no brushing off. 'Bella, have a seat.' He smiled at Matty.

'Tony, this is the friend I told you about – the one that's been having a bit of trouble with her Italian,' Tom said cryptically.

Minetti shook her hand. 'Need a translator, eh? I can help with any Italian problem you got – it's my native tongue after all.' He gave a shrug and spread his hands.

Matty felt she'd landed in some boys' convoluted game, the sort her brother Charlie and Nellie's brothers had liked to exclude her from when they were kids, with secret rules and hidden passwords and obscure outcomes. Except this wasn't a game.

'But didn't you tell me the lady's Italian friend had gone home?' Minetti said, his brown eyes suddenly sharp as the cut-throat razor hanging by his chair.

Tom nodded thoughtfully. 'We made a mistake. He's extended his visit.'

Minetti walked to the front window and turned the shop sign to *Closed*.

'It's a slow day. I got nothing better to do than talk about the old country. Come in the back. Mrs Minetti's just making coffee.'

When they entered the little back parlour Minetti's wife gave him a puzzled look, but welcomed them as if they were family.

'Come in, sit down. You're just in time – I've made Bomboloni!' she said and disappeared into the kitchen.

Minetti smiled at his wife's back as the kitchen door closed behind her, then he leaned forward, speaking soflty. 'She don't like the idea of me coming out of retirement. I can tell you, she was relieved when I told her the problem had gone away...'

Tom nodded sympathetically and Matty felt like the elephant in the room. 'Can I say something?' She put up her hand. 'I don't want you getting into trouble with your wife, Mr Minetti.'

'Trouble? No trouble!' The barber waved his hands. 'She's like a lamb... my Anna. A lamb. I tell her, we been here so long in Bermondsey, it's like family now. What else should I do when one of my boys asks for help?'

Soon the aroma of roast coffee and sounds from a bubbling coffee pot reached them.

'No, I think we should involve as few people as possible,' Matty insisted.

Tom ignored her. 'So, you're still in, Tony? We go back to the plan?'

'Hold on. I'm sitting right here, Tom. What's going on and why don't I know anything about this plan?' Matty glared at him.

The tinkling of coffee cups announced Mrs Minetti's return. Sure enough, as if she really had been expecting them, she carried a plateful of golden, doughnut-like cakes oozing yellow custard from their tops and dusted with icing sugar. Matty thought Mrs Minetti's welcome remarkably warm for someone who had cause to wish them a hundred miles from her husband's shop.

They all waited in silence as the barber's wife poured coffee. Sugar shovelled four teaspoons of his namesake into the fine china coffee cup, which he gripped with thick fingers. His eyes lit up as Mrs Minetti handed round the Bomboloni and he stuffed an entire fluffy ball into his mouth, avoiding the fuss of a plate.

'Mmm, good as Edwards'!' he said appreciatively and Mrs Minetti smiled at the compliment, for Edwards' bakery in Tower Bridge Road produced the best doughnuts in London, more sugar-dusted clouds than confection, and Sugar regularly walked around with a white paper bag full of them.

'Let's ask Mama what she thinks,' Mr Minetti said, after she'd sat down at the head of the table. He spoke to her in very fast Italian. Her neat head, a silken black cap of dark hair drawn back into a tight bun, nodded as she considered each point her husband made.

Matty could only recognize a few words, one of which was *mafia*, which made her shift uncomfortably in her seat. Eventually the barber's wife said, 'Si, si,' gave another decisive nod and then turned to Matty.

'I'm so sorry, Matty, for what happened to you. My Tony, he ain't been in no trouble since we left Italy, I made sure of that.'

Mr Minetti rubbed his chin and nodded. 'S'true. I'm just a barber these days.'

'*But,*' Mrs Minetti went on, 'what I think is this, you got to fight fire with fire and like he says, Bermondsey is family now, and we help our own... fire with fire.'

She placed her hand over her husband's and Sugar reached out for another Bombolone. Cramming it expertly into his mouth, he plucked a blue silk handkerchief from his top pocket to wipe away a drip of pale lemon custard from his chin. 'So, we're wheeling out the Bermondsey mafia then?' he said through a mouthful of Bombolone.

Matty laughed. 'What are you talking about? There *is* no Bermondsey mafia!'

Matty knew that as well as anyone else sitting round this table, with its pretty cloth and delicate china. Those Bermondsey boys wanting to be career criminals generally gravitated to the Elephant mob. What Bermondsey had in abundance was wide boys, small-time villains in every street, tipsters, touts and dippers working the race courses, bookies' runners and fences aplenty who would move on anything from cigarettes to coconuts thieved from the docks and warehouses. Well known for their cunning in outwitting or co-opting the law, they were more mischievous than vicious.

Whatever organization Mr Minetti had once had dealings with in his youth back in Italy, Matty believed his wife when she said there'd been no contact with them in forty odd years.

Mr Minetti spoke. 'I don't like the sound of your friend, this Rossi. He got what he deserved. People don't usually get what they deserve, Matty, but they always get what they expect! And if this Rossi expects a Bermondsey mafia, that's what we'll give him.'

She shook her head. 'I don't want any more violence, Mr Minetti.'

Sugar snorted and Tom said quickly, 'Don't worry, Matty, there won't need to be any.'

'But you want to be rid of him, don't you?' Minetti asked, dropping his voice so that Matty could almost imagine the neat little parlour was in a whitewashed house, perched on a sun-striped hillside in Italy rather than on the high pavement in Bermondsey. She wasn't sure what he meant.

'I want him out of my life, but not—'

'Brown bread,' Sugar said, lifting another Bombolone from the plate.

Matty swished the curtains closed against a leaden early evening sky. The fine rain which had fallen all day was still soaking the slate roofs to black and the sandy brick to green. She ached as if the damp had seeped into her bones and her heart felt as heavy as the sky. She was tired. She and Tom had walked back to Reverdy Road largely in silence and were now seated in the parlour, where Tom was coaxing a fire into life against the damp.

'Pour us a gin, love,' she said as she came to sit down in the armchair nearest the fire.

He got up, brushing coal dust from his hands. 'It's not exactly the end to the day you expected?'

She switched on the shaded standard lamp next to her chair and rested her head on the old-fashioned antimacassar. There was so much of Eliza still here that she couldn't bring herself to let go, as if answers to all the unasked questions of a lifetime resided in these domestic objects that had been handled, chosen and touched by her real mother.

She closed her eyes until she felt Tom placing the drink in her hand. He sat opposite, sipping at his whisky while the fire crackled and spat its light around the two of them.

'What was it that Mr Minetti said? People always get what they expect? Perhaps a part of me knew Frank wasn't dead... and didn't want him to be?'

'You haven't got it on your conscience, at least.'

The gin and the fire began to warm her. 'It would have been a lot to live with, Tom. And now I've got a second chance, whatever we do, I don't want it to end up with him...'

'Brown bread,' Tom finished, using Sugar's slang, forcing a smile from Matty.

'Not him, not anyone.' She put the empty glass on to the side table, knowing that she needed to pull herself out of the lethargy that had descended on her. It would have to be one step at a time.

'All right, tell me this plan you've been cooking up behind my back.'

'Basically it's a sting. We're going to convince Frank to sideline the Clerkenwell mob and come into business with the Bermondsey mafia. We've got a scam going to lift a fortune in silver and gold ingots off a boat coming into Surrey Docks.'

Matty looked alarmed but Tom held up his hands. 'Don't worry, we're not really stealing it. It's just a way of getting Frank to double-cross the Sabinis, then we'll tip them off when the exchange takes place.'

Tom repeated his promise that the plan wouldn't involve more violence. 'We'll just hand him over to the Sabinis, let them deal with him – believe me they won't take kindly to being cut out. After that, I don't think he'll be troubling you any more, Matty. I've not wanted to tell you about it, until I knew I could get all the players. It would have been a bit like starting to film a 'Modern Woman' without the extras... or the star. Wouldn't do, would it?'

She shook her head.

He explained that they would need the cooperation of quite a few of the Bermondsey wide boys and confessed he'd already recruited Nellie's brother, Freddie Clark, and his friend George Flint, more commonly known as Wide'oh.

'Is he the one we saw nicking electricity from the lamp post with Freddie?'

'That's Wide'oh. Anyway he's agreed to let us use his lock-up on Bermondsey Wall for the first meeting with Frank. He's got the place stacked to the brim with hooky stuff, booze and cigarettes. Runs a dodgy drinking club there too. Just the sort of place to set up a meeting with the "Bermondsey mafia".' Tom grinned and again she felt she was in the middle of a boys' game.

The Italian contingent necessary to complete the illusion would be made up of the barber Minetti and their local grocer, Joe Capp, who like Minetti had come to Bermondsey from Italy forty years earlier and considered it his home.

Tom hesitated, a frown creasing his forehead. 'There's just one thing, Matty. It's hard for me to ask... But to make sure Frank goes for it, we'll have to offer him some bait he can't refuse – you'll have to see Frank again.'

Though his face was ruddy in the firelight, she thought she saw the colour deepen as a blush passed over it. She paused for a beat and said, 'I'll do it.'

27

'Gold, Silver and Gold'

September–October 1932

When Tom walked into the Angel, Matty knew something was wrong.

'Didn't he go for it?' she asked, as he slipped into the seat beside her.

He'd been at the first meeting of the newly formed 'Bermondsey mafia' with Frank and his men at Wide'oh's lock-up. It had taken some delicate secret negotiations, with Sugar as the go-between, but today they had put their plan to Frank.

'Oh, he went for it,' Tom said, with an edge to his voice that made Matty uneasy.

'You don't seem very pleased. Did something happen?'

'It went perfectly.'

'Tell me, Tom! What did he say?'

Tom raised his eyes, as if struggling to remember.

'Well, his exact words were *I'll pay your price for the ingots, but her I don't pay for... I never did before, so why should I start now.*'

Matty's face burned and she put cold hands to her face. 'I'm sorry, Tom.'

'I'll tell you the rest later. I'll walk you home.'

Outside she slipped her arm through his, wishing he would speak. Eventually the silence was like a cord tightening around her heart. She had to break it and she blurted out, 'Tom, what he said about paying...' She felt his arm stiffen. 'Do you want to talk about it?'

'No.'

'I want to explain.'

'What's to explain? He was pretty clear.'

'Tom, please.' She pulled him round to face her and they stopped by the river wall. He turned away, leaning his elbows on the parapet. She stood silent now, waiting for him to say something. She couldn't look at him. Instead she gazed out over ranks of moored lighters, across the inky river to the lights on the Wapping side.

'Matty, it's better if we just leave it. We need to concentrate on seeing this through and making sure you're still alive when it's done.' His voice was tight with hurt.

'If I could do it all again, Tom, I would never have left you. I would never have gone with Frank... believe me.'

Even as she said it, she knew it wasn't true. She'd often wondered why she'd so resisted becoming Tom's lover before going to America. It was something she'd never regretted, until now. For Tom would have been forever and, back then, forever felt like too long a time.

He sighed. 'You believe it. But I don't. None of us get to do it all again. If you *could* have stayed with me, you would have. You had to fly, I know that. But what I'll never understand is why *him*?'

He was right. It was the Matty of today who would give herself to Tom in a heartbeat, not the Matty of yesterday. She struggled to remember the person she was when she first fell in love with Frank. How could she explain why she'd so easily fallen into his bed? She knew the irony of it now, but at the time it had felt somehow safer than being with Tom. For her heart had known that however fierce Frank's passion, it would one day burn itself out and she would be free again. Or so she'd thought. It seemed impossible now that she hadn't been able to tell what he was, that all her instincts had so completely deserted her.

'I thought he was someone else,' Matty said finally. 'He was charming, he said words that made him *seem* kind and did things that made him *seem* thoughtful. He looked like a film star and

I was going to the land of dreams to meet film stars, wasn't I? I know it sounds stupid, but I *was* stupid and I believed him. It was like all my dreams coming true.'

It wasn't enough, she knew it, but it was all the explanation she could give. She stood beside him, mesmerized by the swift running tide. If only she could toss all the faded flowers of her past mistakes on to its oily stream, like an offering to the river god, who would float them away, down the wide estuary and out to the all-forgiving sea.

*

The SS *Artemis* docked, carrying its load of silver and gold. River mist curled in pewter wreaths about its bows so that the top of the crane high above the cargo hold was almost invisible. When the first coiled rope basket landed on the quayside the dockmaster was waiting to check its contents. Bright silver ingots were tumbled haphazardly inside it. They might as well have been a bushel of bricks for all the care that had been taken in loading them. But however they were unloaded, they would be counted and double-checked against the manifest and then checked on the lorry by the dock police as they went out of the main gates.

They were virtually impossible to steal, but somehow the Bermondsey mafia had convinced Frank otherwise. And the ship's arrival at the docks signalled the final part of their plan.

Tom had closed the subject of her past and along with it his heart, or so it seemed to her, and she felt his coolness like an icy knife in her own. He'd concentrated on going over the details of her handover. He'd told Matty she would only need to see Frank once and then it would be over. It would be at Neville's bolt-hole by the Angel that she would finally come face to face with Frank again. They'd persuaded him the best place to exchange Matty was when she was feeling safe and unsuspecting at one of the soirées Neville often hosted before they left for the Blue Lotus. Tom had insisted she'd be in no danger, that the Sabinis were interested in taking Frank, not her. But though she put on a brave face to Tom, she made a mental note to wear Queenie's hat on the night – just in case.

*

The night was thick with fog and the dockside business of daylight hours had been replaced by an echoing silence as they made their way along unlit cobbles to Neville's bolt-hole. Bermondsey Wall was a long canyon of a road, hugging the meandering Thames on its way through Bermondsey. On one side of the street, a low river wall punctuated with piers and river stairs was faced with slab-sided warehouses on the other. He took her hand as they hurried up the dark street. Splashes of light spilled from occasional riverside pubs or ancient houses like Neville's, remnants of a time when sea captains made their home along this stretch of the river. She shivered and hugged herself as they walked, feeling a slick veneer of damp river mist on her evening coat. As they entered the house, she heard a piano and recognized the snatch of a song Neville was playing.

Dreams broken in two can be made like new,
on the street of dreams.
Gold, silver and gold, all you can hold is in a moonbeam…

It was from 'Street of Dreams', one of Billy's favourites.

'Oh good, we've got a soundtrack!' Matty announced as she and Tom entered the room. 'We let ourselves in. Thanks, Neville – thanks for leaving the door ajar, not as if there's any dangerous men on the loose tonight!'

'Matty, darling!' Neville greeted her. 'With all the visitors I'll have tonight I thought it would save me endless trips to the front door! Don't worry I'll shut it before our guest of honour arrives. Champagne?'

He left the piano and gave her a glass of champagne and a kiss, as if this were no different from any other night they'd met up before going to the Blue Lotus. As Neville took her black cape and fedora, he joked nervously, 'I'll have to be careful with this, I hear it's deadly!'

'I'm not planning to use it! It's my lucky charm,' Matty said.

'We won't need luck,' Tom murmured.

'Ah, Tom, I think you're meant to stand over there by the drinks cabinet, aren't you?' Neville said, taking charge as if he were the director rather than Tom, who had planned every step of the operation with meticulous care. 'I believe you're supposed to be one of my friends tonight, so you might as well help yourself! I'll take care of Matty.' He put his arm round her and she noticed Tom bristle slightly. Tonight he was hardly recognizable as the respectable council employee that he was. He'd dressed in a flashy suit, which Matty thought must have been hired for the purpose, and had slicked back his hair with Brylcreem so that it looked almost black. He had, to Matty's surprise, an almost sinister air as he took up his planned position.

The room was illuminated by a couple of small table lamps and its usual exuberant amount of candles. Their flickering light bouncing off the deep bow window exerted its magic on Matty, in spite of her nerves. Neville had staged the scene well.

'So, Matty, you come here with me, let me pose you in the window seat.'

Two chairs in the bay were placed either side of a delicate side table, in the centre of which was a slender silver candelabra. Matty sat still, allowing Neville to arrange her long evening dress so that its silver and gold brocade fell in folds around her legs. The ill-fitting windowpanes let in a cold draught that Matty's spun silver stole did nothing to shield her from. Neville stood back admiring his work.

'Now you look suitably composed – and irresistible, my darling... as always, don't you agree, Tom?'

Tom was pouring himself a glass of water and nodded stiffly, but she could see the slight tremble in his hand as he lifted the glass to his lips. She wished she could go to him; instead she smiled encouragingly, though she doubted she looked less nervous herself.

She shivered, glancing out at the dark river. The opposite bank was invisible tonight, veiled in a shifting silvery brume that hung above the waters. Smudged paths of golden light from the Angel pub's windows unfolded in rippling columns over the fast-running river. She imagined carefree drinkers inside the pub, warm, safe and unaware, wishing for a moment she could be one of them. She turned away. She would have preferred to sit by the fire, but that place had been reserved for Minetti and Frank.

They had gone over the scene again and again, as closely as if it were to be played out in the skeleton room under the watchful gaze of Plum's camera. Tonight she was playing the role of sacrificial lamb, supposedly unaware that she was about to be betrayed by Neville and her Bermondsey friends. The story they had spun Frank was that she would be meeting Neville for a drink at his bolt-hole, as they usually did before going to the Blue Lotus. Matty would suspect nothing wrong and all Frank had to do was come along and pluck her like a piece of ripe fruit.

As if on cue, Minetti and Wally arrived, and they brought with them the smell of river fog. Minetti was a slim, tall man, but whether it was a trick of light and shadow or that he was already inhabiting the part he was playing, he seemed to Matty bulkier now, more imposing, and all his usual mobility of features had turned to stone. When Wally greeted her, his mouth was dry and she sensed a whiff of stage fright, noticing a telltale sheen of sweat on his forehead. The two took their places by the fire, Minetti seated, Wally standing to one side of him. Wally wiped his forehead with a handkerchief and caught her eye.

'Break a leg, eh, Matty?' he said, with a fixed smile.

When Sugar arrived Neville closed the front door and then ushered him into the bedroom. Sugar would stay there out of sight just in case anything went wrong. The plan was for the Sabinis to take Frank as he emerged with Matty from Neville's. Freddie was outside, tasked with signalling the Sabinis' arrival and making sure the handover went smoothly.

Tom looked at his watch and Neville gulped his champagne. Minetti straightened his tie and Wally unbuttoned his coat. The room was silent, apart from the ticking of the elaborate rococo-style clock perched on the mantlepiece. Matty looked round at the men, all here taking risks with their lives – for her. Matty broke the silence.

'Thank you.' She looked at each of them in turn. 'I don't know what I've done to deserve such good friends, but thank you.'

Minetti, taking the role of godfather to heart, answered for them all.

'Like Mrs Minetti said, Matty, you're family.'

The others nodded in agreement as a loud knocking came from the front door.

Neville smiled at Matty, put down his champagne glass and said brightly. 'Curtain up!'

She had ruined his beautiful heavy-lashed eyes. His face was shadowed by a wide-brimmed fedora, but the array of candles scattered about the room offered no hiding place for Frank's destroyed features. A raised, livid scar sliced through both eyelids, crossing the bridge of his prominent nose in an unbroken, angry line.

Her gasp of fear as Neville showed him into the room was unfeigned, for Frank had always been so vain about his good looks and Matty could well imagine what venom had been stored up for her each time he'd looked in the mirror.

'This gentleman says he's a friend of yours, Matty darling.' Neville played the innocent party very well. 'I wish I'd known he was coming!'

Neville offered to take Frank's hat, but Frank shrugged him off.

'Let me offer you a glass of champagne!'

'I ain't stopping. Where is she?'

Frank's henchman whispered something into his ear and Matty realized what other damage she'd inflicted with Queenie's fedora. Though she was sitting in a blaze of candlelight, dressed in glimmering gold and silver brocade, he was obviously having trouble seeing her. Now he lifted his chin, tilting his head, squinting from beneath his slashed eyelids.

'Ah, there she is, *il mio piccolo canarino*!' His feigned delight at her presence was chilling. 'I don't see too good no more, Matty.'

'Neville! What's he doing here?' She loaded her voice with shock and terror. 'Who told him I'd be here?'

'Sit, Rossi! Let's have a drink to seal the deal,' Minetti invited Frank from his place by the fire. He glanced at Neville's ormolu clock. 'Besides, your second consignment ain't even ready to collect yet.'

'OK, gentlemen. I'll drink to our new business arrangement.' Frank looked over his shoulder and his bodyguard stepped in front of him. Frank followed with that deliberate, light-footed walk she would have recognized anywhere, almost like a dancer's glide. Today, however, his progress was more hesitant than usual. He halted, feeling for the chair next to Minetti's. Tom poured him a drink with a steady hand that Matty could only admire. He handed the drink to Frank and moved deliberately to one side.

'Cheers, gentlemen.' Frank raised his glass, then looked in Matty's direction. 'What d'you know? Your Bermondsey friends ain't so friendly when it comes to business!' Frank gave a mirthless laugh. 'They threw you in free with a couple crates of silver and gold!'

For a moment the room was a frozen tableau. Nobody stirred, nobody spoke; only the shimmering candle flames moved, guttering as chill river air blew in through warped windows and lopsided doors. Each of the men kept their appointed place as if waiting for a signal. Then Matty stood up, looking ready for flight.

Frank raised a hand to his henchman. 'Get her.'

The man took two lumbering steps across the room and grabbed her arm. Tom gave the smallest nod towards the clock. It was too early to leave. She had to stall until Freddie gave the signal that the Sabinis were waiting outside to take Frank.

'It's cold outside,' Matty said quickly. 'Let me at least put on my coat and hat.'

'Bring your coat, leave the fuckin' hat,' Frank said, holding his glass out to Tom to be refilled. Matty shrugged off the bodyguard's beefy hand.

'Neville, would you get my coat? It looks like the Blue Lotus will have to do without me tonight.'

'I'm sorry, my dear,' Neville said, helping Matty on with her coat.

As Frank drained the champagne glass and picked up his hat, Matty saw a worried look pass between Tom and Minetti.

'What's the rush? Have another drink,' Minetti said.

'You got a reason you want me to stay?' Frank asked, a look of suspicion on his scarred face.

Minetti shrugged and spread his palms wide. 'Suit yourself.'

Matty's legs were turning to water. If it hadn't been for Neville's hand beneath her elbow she would have sunk to the floor. It was all going wrong. The signal from Freddie should have come by now. She felt Neville's hand tighten and then she heard it. A faint whistle, two tones, as if Freddie were piping an admiral aboard a ship. Wally reached inside his jacket, Tom moved to her side and now they would hand her over to Frank. Her body was rigid with fear, but she could do it. She wouldn't be with him for long, just the time it took to walk out of Neville's and into the Sabinis' waiting arms. But just then the door was flung open with such force that it came loose from its hinges.

A man charged through the door, bellowing, 'Rossi's ours!' He was pointing a gun at Frank and was followed by three others, dark-suited, broad-shouldered and all armed. They hadn't waited. Tom wrapped his arms round her and Matty watched the scene play out, almost in slow motion.

Frank jumped up, unseeing and vulnerable. He groped for his own gun. 'What the fuck are you doin' here?' he shouted.

'Work it out! You don't double-cross the Sabinis.'

Frank's mouth twisted in fury as realized he'd been set up by the 'Bermondsey mafia'. He delivered a vicious back-handed swipe at the nearest target, which happened to be Minetti. Frank's bodyguard tossed aside a delicate chair and charged across the room, head down, straight into the path of a Sabini gun, and was felled with a single downward chop of the barrel. He didn't get up. Now Frank was on his own in a room filled with Sabinis.

He pulled his own gun and lunged at Matty, firing wildly in her direction, blinding her with a burst of flame. A ringing deafness gave way to a high-pitched buzz as he fired again and a bullet whizzed past her ear, shattering a pane of the bow window. Another shot rang out, and she gagged on the smell of cordite and burned flesh. She felt Tom's arms let go of her as his body thudded to the floor. 'Tom!' she screamed and fell to her knees beside him.

The gunshots had brought Sugar from the bedroom. 'You was meant to wait outside for 'em! Just grab Rossi!' Sugar ordered the Clerkenwell mobsters, who were focused on ducking more of Frank's misdirected bullets. But Frank now had Matty in his sights, her shining dress a beacon in his benighted world. Slumped across Tom's inert body, she didn't see Frank coming and he reached her before either Wally or Sugar could. Frank grabbed her hair and all the men froze, guns poised.

Frank waved the gun in a frenzied circle. He yanked her up in front of him. 'Walk!' he ordered. Smoke from gunfire and river mist curling through the broken windows seemed to have fogged her reactions. She couldn't move her feet. 'Move!' Frank hissed into her ear. Then another voice, from another world, another time came to her. Almost a stage whisper, but very insistent. 'Don't block me, dear!' the voice said and she was instantly transported back to her early days on the stage, when she'd unwittingly stood in front of an old trouper, blocking the audience's view of him.

'Don't block me, dear!' he'd whispered, giving her a good dig in the back to emphasize that he wasn't going to be upstaged.

The cardinal stage rule had become so ingrained in her being that as soon as she heard Wally utter the words 'Don't block me, dear,' she dodged to one side. Wally fired and the bullet thudded with precision into Frank, smashing him against the elegant table and sending candlesticks flying in all directions. Now Matty understood why Bernie had insisted it was better she never find out the thing Wally really was best at.

Flame from scattered candles spilled along floorboards dust-dry with age, painting Neville's Persian rug in new colours of russet and gold as fire folded it into embers. Sparks caught a faded tapestry hanging above the fireplace and soon a blaze was licking up dry plaster and lathe walls, reaching searing fingers to where Matty lay, groping the burning floorboards, searching for Tom.

'Leave Rossi, he's had it. Just get out!' she heard one of the Sabinis shouting. The old house had caught like a tinderbox and whichever way she looked furnishings and fabrics were ablaze. Then she heard a long, agonized groan, the old captain's house death cry, as burning timbers collapsed and the entire river frontage, including the massive bow window, detached itself and fell, crackling and hissing into the Thames below.

She heard screams, shouts, as black billowing smoke engulfed them. She thought she heard Neville sobbing and Sugar shouting for Freddie. But all she could think of was Tom. She couldn't see him, couldn't feel him. He was gone. She lifted her head and, as she cried out for help, was hit by a blast of heat so intense that she heard her hair crackle and singe. A wall of flame sprang up, barring her way to the door, as figures like ineffectual demons danced behind the flames, powerless to help her.

'Matty, Matty!' she heard Freddie half scream, half sob. 'Get her out! Chrissake, Sugar, help me get her out!'

Holding her stole to her face to block out the searing smoke, she tried to make herself heard. 'Freddie, I've lost Tom!' she screamed. But her words were drowned out by a loud crack. She looked up to see the plasterwork ceiling crumble to ash and fall.

There was nothing left of Neville's bolt-hole by the Angel except a pile of charred timbers and a mound of rubble. There would be no more intimate champagne suppers for two, no more clandestine visits from Lady Fetherstone, no more high-society entertaining along Bermondsey Wall. Neville had collapsed at the sight of what the conflagration had done to his hideaway, and was now being tended to by a local doctor who'd left his pint on the bar of the Angel pub and come running when the fire broke out. Freddie, Sugar, Minetti and Wally watched like four silent minstrels, soot-blackened and red-eyed as firemen scoured the debris.

'Keep back!' a fireman warned Freddie as he walked forward into the steaming pile, stepping on to a charred, smouldering beam. 'It ain't out yet. It could flare up again any minute!' he warned.

Sugar pulled him back. 'Come on, mate, there's nothing else you can do.'

'Did you see Matty get out?' Freddie asked Sugar, his normally strong voice, hoarse and faint. He cradled his hands, burned raw from battling through flames to reach Matty.

Sugar shook his head. 'Nah. I see her dress catch fire, then the whole ceiling come down. I didn't see her no more. I'm sorry, mate.'

'What about Tom?'

'He was with Matty, then Rossi shot him and I see him go down…' Sugar scrubbed at his face, smearing soot-like war paint over bony cheeks.

'I got Rossi,' Wally said, his voice exhausted and hollow.

'Dead?' Freddie asked.

'Dad always did say there was only one thing I was good for. Rossi can't touch our Matty no more,' Wally replied, his face etched with sadness.

'She's free now,' Freddie echoed in a dull, husky voice, staring at the blackened hulk of a house, and the even blacker Thames beyond.

When the ambulance arrived to cart off Neville and Minetti to St Olave's Hospital, the three ex-Elephant Boys refused to leave. They stayed through what remained of the night, until the last red-hot brick had cooled enough for the firemen to sift through them all. They moved methodically from what had been the front door, to what had once been the back wall but which was now a precarious precipice jutting out over the river. When the first body was brought out, Sugar put his massive arm round Freddie and squeezed him till his friend's bones crunched.

Wally said. 'Stay here, mate. I'll go and find out.'

He was allowed to view the charred remains and came back in seconds.

'It's Rossi,' he said.

'Are you sure?' Freddie turned haunted red-rimmed eyes to his friend.

Wally jerked his head towards the firemen. 'As far as they're concerned he burned to death, but I knew what I was looking for.' Wally pointed to the centre of his forehead. 'That's where I aimed and that's where it went. It was Rossi all right.'

Sugar nodded. ''Kin good riddance.'

'Did they find—' Freddie began to ask, but Wally interrupted him.

'No, no one else. Fred, they think Tom and Matty are in there somewhere, but the fire was so fierce, there might not be a lot left...' Wally looked towards the firemen, who were rolling up their hoses. 'They say they'll come back when it's light, look some more.'

'No!' Freddie dropped to his knees and the two friends hunkered down beside him. 'No, I ain't having it.' Freddie's big frame seemed suddenly shrunken. 'I ain't going nowhere, not till I find her.' Tears coursed down his cheeks, carving white rivulets in their sooty coating. 'How can I go home and tell Sam and Nellie our Matty's gone?'

'You can't.' A voice came from out of the smoke-filled half-light and all three men looked up sharply at the intrusion.

Will stood, ashen-faced and bare-headed before them. A breeze off the river blew pale cinders around his head, which settled on to his dark hair like fat snowflakes.

'Will! How did you find out?' Freddie sat back on his haunches, wiping a sleeve hastily across his eyes.

'Neville telephoned Ma Feathers at her London flat. We're staying there. Feathers drove me here.' He looked over his shoulder as his friend joined them.

'We dropped Mother at St Olave's Hospital and came straight here. Is there anything we can do?' Feathers asked.

Freddie turned bleak eyes towards the smouldering ruins. 'Tom and our Matty are still in there, somewhere, but the firemen couldn't find them…'

'But we're not giving up, are we?' Will drew back Freddie's gaze to his own, which at that moment bore all the fierce determination of his mother and all the stubborn intransigence of his father.

Freddie's eye brightened briefly. 'No, we're bloody well not giving up.'

'Well, I'm not telling Winnie her Tom's gone neither,' Wally said.

'All right then. If they're packing it in,' Sugar stared with disdain at the retreating backs of the exhausted firemen, 'we'll just have to find 'em our fuckin' selves.'

He put his massive hands under Freddie's armpits and hoisted him up as if he were light as a child. 'Come on, Fred. Let's get crackin'.'

The men picked their way through what had been Neville's drawing room. Bending low, they sifted plaster dust and turned over sooty bricks, rooting around blackened candelabra, which reached out of the rubble like fossilized branches of ancient trees. When they had swept the entire remains they converged cautiously at the edge of the back wall, which was now little more than a jetty, jutting over the Thames. Freddie looked over the edge. There was a slow groan as a part of the floor tipped forward, sending all the men off balance for an instant.

'Back up!' Sugar shouted and they all retreated.

Freddie lay cautiously on his stomach so that he could peer over the edge of what was left of the house. 'You hold me legs, Sugar, in case the whole bloody lot goes!'

'What, do you think they've gone in the water?' Sugar asked, taking hold of his friend's feet.

'Maybe,' Freddie answered just as a loud crack rang out. The floor beneath him jolted and the remains of the front wall fell into the river with a hollow slap that reverberated among the pilings beneath them.

'You're too heavy, Freddie! Let me do it, I'm the smallest,' Will urged.

'No, you stay where you are!' Freddie shouted.

But Will kneeled down beside him. 'You'll be no good to Matty if you bring the lot down. I've got more chance!'

'He's right, mate. Let shorty 'ave a go,' Sugar said.

As the floor joists moaned again, Freddie gave up and eased himself slowly backwards. Will took his place and edged out on his elbows until his torso was hanging over the river. Though he was shorter and lighter than the others he was athletic and well-muscled, so that his own upper-body strength supported him, suspended in mid-air above the swift-flowing river. Some of the foreshore had been exposed by the ebb tide, but the river ran so swiftly down to Limehouse Reach and the estuary beyond that anyone who had toppled into its irresistible stream at this point would by now have been swept far beyond Greenwich.

'Can you seen anything?' Freddie asked.

'Just a bit further...' Will snaked forward. 'Give me the torch.' He reached back a hand and Freddie slapped the torch into it.

Bleached fingers of weak early morning light reached between the algae-draped wooden piles that supported this part of the house as it jutted out over the foreshore. Will shone the torch between the dank struts.

'I think I can see something! I'm going down!' He handed

the torch back to Freddie. 'Shine it down there.' Will pointed to a place where two beams about a foot thick had intersected, forming a fork just above the water line. He swung himself round and began to lower himself over the edge. Freddie took a step forward. 'No! Stay back, Fred, your extra weight could bring it down. I can just reach a beam with my foot.'

Freddie froze and they all watched in silence as Will lowered himself down. All that was now visible of him were his fingertips. And then they disappeared.

After a tense minute Feathers called to his friend. 'Will? Are you there yet?'

'Nearly there!' came the muffled reply, and then, 'Oh my God!'

'What?' the others shouted in unison

'Something moved... I think it's Tom! He's wedged between the pilings!'

A shout went up from the waiting men, but Freddie voiced the question that followed their elation. 'What about Matty – is she there too?'

28

From the Ashes

October–November 1932

She had lost Tom. That had been her last conscious thought, before fire consumed her every sense. Incandescence robbed her of sight, roaring flames deafened her, stifling smoke filled her nostrils and her hands lost all feeling as, skin melting, she had searched the flames for Tom. Then her dress of silver and gold brocade caught fire, and in a moment's clarity she knew what she had to do. She had no choice. She gave herself up to the fire and let herself fly.

Diving through the gaping hole where the bow window had been, her one thought was that death by water was preferable to death by fire. The flight, which in real time was a matter of seconds, felt to her like a slow eternity. From the corner of her eye, she was aware of a comet-like tail blazing behind her, the remnants of her dress in flames, turning her into some mythical burning bird. She ended her flight with a stinging slap into the unyielding embrace of water, which hissed around her like a thousand snakes as filthy Thames water extinguished the flames. She swallowed mouthfuls of the stinking river and immediately felt the tide tugging her, expecting any moment to be snatched away by the current. But something impeded her progress, hammering at her ribs. It seemed the tide had carried her into the path of an algae-covered piling. She wasn't on fire any longer, neither was she drowned, so where was she? Disorientated in the green-black shifting darkness, she grabbed the slippery piling and began to tread water. Suddenly her feet found slime, the yielding sludge of Thames mud. She was in the shallows! The ebb tide had left a thin strip of foreshore and now she began to half swim, half trudge through the muddy shallows towards it.

She grasped the slippery wooden beams to help pull her forward through the water. She reasoned that these must be the pilings that supported the old captain's house, in which case she was not far from help if she could just get to the beach. She was about to shout for help when something caused her to stop. Had she heard a sound? She froze. There it came again and she whirled round, setting up a ripple that splashed and sucked at the beams. And then she saw it, a lighter shape nestling in the black geometry of angles made by the beams. Finding a looped mooring rope attached to an iron ring, she grasped on to it and inched back out into the stream. Immediately her feet were taken from under her, and then as she managed to pull herself upright, a hand brushed her cheek and she screamed. The scream echoed around the cavern made by the river wall and what remained of the old captain's house above her. She reached up. Her fingers touched fingers. She looked up into Tom's pale face. His cheek was pillowed on a tangled mass of algae and he had been caught, like her, between the crook of two pilings. Unlike hers, his perch was further out into the stream and he was not holding on for dear life. With each slap of a wave, the tide was easing him inch by inch off the pilings and she could see him slipping slowly into the water.

She didn't consider that he was dead. She thought she'd lost him, and now she'd found him again. She wasn't going to let him go. She remembered the time when he'd hauled her up out of the mill race; perhaps she could do the same. She grasped his hand and attempted to pull him further into the angle of the two pilings, but he was too heavy and she was below him, with nothing to brace herself against. She would simply have to climb up to where he was and hold him there till the tide went out further. She gripped the cross-beam with two hands and, like a trapeze artiste, swung herself up so that she was sitting astride the beam with Tom in front of her. Encircling him with her arms, she pinned him with her body into the cleft where he had come to rest and laid her head on his back.

'It's all right, my darling. I've got you now and I won't let you go. We'll just stay here, me and you. We're safe now.'

It didn't matter that he hadn't heard her, nor answered her. She hadn't expected him to.

She became aware of sounds above her, the shouts of men, the rush of fire, the gush of water pouring from hoses into the conflagration. There was no way anyone could see them from the house; she would have to attract their attention. She screamed as loud as she could, but all that emerged was a hoarse whisper. The heat and smoke had scorched her throat and burned her lungs. She saw the irony. 'What do you think of that, Tom?' she whispered into his back. 'The one time I need my bloody voice and it's gone!'

She knew she was talking to herself. His body was so cold. She curled dryad-like around him, but half naked and shivering with shock, she had little heat left to give to him. She tightened her hands round his body, realizing for the first time that the skin was gone from them.

'Don't worry, love. Once the tide's gone right out, they'll see us then.'

She had a sudden overwhelming desire to sleep. She closed her eyes and felt an imaginary warmth surge through her. Her head fell forward and she jolted awake, stopping herself just in time from slipping off the beam. 'No, no, you've got to stay awake!' she told herself. And then so that she wouldn't sleep, she started to sing, in a rasping, gravelly whisper. *I'll see you in my dreams, hold you in my dreams. Someone took you right out of my arms, still I feel the thrill of your charms. Lips that once were mine, tender eyes that shine. They will light my way tonight, I'll see you in my dreams...'*

It was their song, but it wasn't the right song, and its lullaby quality had exactly the opposite effect to the one she wanted.

So when Will finally managed to clamber down the moss-slick pilings to where he'd seen Tom, he found Matty asleep there, curled around Tom's inert body.

'Yes! She's here!' he shouted up to the men above, and Matty woke with a start, her eyes clouded, struggling to focus.

'Oh hello, Will. I'm so glad you're here, love,' she said sluggishly. 'I dreamed I was the bird that catches fire, but I can't remember its name. You're the clever one, you'll know what it's called.'

And Will's voice caught in a sob. 'It's called a phoenix, Matty.'

*

There were nights and days that followed, full of pain and absent of colour. White faces, staring down at her, speaking in hushed voices; white bandages on her hands, which lay on white sheets. But whitest of all, was the mist of memory, which swirled as she lay half conscious. It was as if she were constantly searching for someone she'd lost in the fog. She might look as if she were lying still beneath the starched sheets, but she wasn't, she was flying through a pearl-thick fog or was it smoke? No, no that wasn't right, the smoke had been charcoal-black and when the pain shot up her arms and legs, then she would emerge from out of the mist, wings on fire, eyes blinded by a flame-red light and she would reach for his name, the one she'd lost, but always she would sink back into sleep before she could name him.

Then one day the whispers grew more distinct.

'Why won't she wake up?' It was a man's voice.

'She doesn't want to and can you blame her, after what she's been through?' the woman answered. 'She'll come back to us when she's ready.' She felt the woman's hand cool on her forehead. 'She's burning up.'

'That's what she said, when I found her. She said she was burning up. Oh, Nellie, she's got to come back. I can't bear it if she doesn't. I need to say how sorry I am, every day, for what I did. She'll never know if she...'

Now Matty knew who the man was. Not the one she'd lost, but Will, the brother who'd come back to her. She wished she hadn't heard him, for now she'd have to speak, let him know she'd long ago forgiven him. Now she'd have to make sounds and she knew the fire had robbed her of her voice, robbed her of the man she loved. So there was no reason to come back. But Will was in pain; she could hear it in his voice. She drew in a deep breath. A grating cough bounced off white ceilings and walls. Then she spoke. Her voice rasped like a crow's. 'Trust you not to let me sleep. You always were a torment.' She opened her eyes to see Will standing at her bedside, with Nellie next to him.

'I tried to tell him, but he's never had no patience.' The familiar, kind face leaned forward to kiss her and the feel of the kiss brought tears to her eyes. She reached a hand up, but it was wrapped tight as a mummy's and pain shot through her as she tried to lift it.

'I heard,' she croaked, focusing as much reassurance into the harsh sound as she could. 'There's nothing I haven't forgiven you for, Will. You ought to know me by now. I've always loved you, you little bugger.'

Will's laughter mingled with his tears as he kissed her forehead. And at the touch of his lips she remembered the name of the other man, the one she'd been searching for in the mist.

'Tom? Where's Tom?'

Nellie paused just an instant too long before answering.

'No.' Matty breathed her denial and closed her eyes again. The unknowing mist was better than the red-hot pain of certainty.

But there came a morning when the sun penetrated behind her eyes, a golden disc that followed her whichever way she turned her head to avoid it. Will and Nellie were gone, replaced by a brisk presence that Matty felt an immediate resentment towards. She was the one responsible for the burning disc that wouldn't leave her alone. Curtains that had screened her from the world were swished open, blinds lifted.

'It's time you were back in the land of the living, Miss Gilbie!' the nurse said brightly, as Matty peered from beneath half-closed lids. 'It's visiting hour. Shall we let in the light?'

Matty groaned a hoarse reply. 'Go away. I like the dark. Let me sleep.' There was only one visitor she wanted and he wasn't coming.

The nurse turned her head quickly to look at Matty. 'Ah, then you don't want to see your nephews? We don't normally allow children on to the burns ward, but in your case the doctor said we could make an exception...' She waited for a response and when none came she began to gently brush Matty's hair. When she'd finished she straightened the bedclothes. 'I'll send them away, shall I? Such a shame, they've been looking forward to seeing you so much.'

She turned to walk out of the ward.

'No! Don't do that, Nurse. Let them come in.' She lifted her bandaged hands. 'Do I look all right? I feel like King Tut's mummy. I don't want to frighten them.'

The nurse approached the bed. 'You won't frighten them. They know you've been injured. But if you're worried, let's tuck them away.' The nurse lifted the sheet and carefully covered Matty's hands.

They came in with the other visitors. She spotted Sam first, then the three boys, all carefully dressed in Sunday best. They approached her bed shyly. Sam held Albie's hand and Billy stood close to his father, in awe of the imposing matron who had swept through, checking the number of visitors per patient. She stopped at Matty's bed.

'Wonderful to see our Cockney Canary is awake! Not that we have favourites,' she lowered her voice, 'but Doctor is a great fan...'

'Say hello to your aunt, Billy.' But Billy, a newly self-conscious eleven-year-old, simply smiled nervously. Suddenly Matty wondered for the first time about her face. Had the fire taken that too?

'Nellie's give 'em all the gypsy's warning about behaving,' Sam explained. 'They're frightened of talking too loud in case they get slung out. Give them a couple of minutes.' He smiled and sat down with his arm round Albie. 'Matty, love, it's so good to see you awake. You've had us worried.' He kissed Albie's curly head of hair, hiding the tears that pooled in his eyes. 'Didn't she, Alb, have us worried?' And the little boy nodded.

'Mum promised us you'd get better. She said you was tough as old boots.' Billy had found his voice.

Matty smiled at her nephew. 'She knows me too well, love.'

'What's the matter with your voice, Aunt Matty?' Sammy, the quietest of the boys, asked a rare question.

'Do I sound terrible? My voice got burned, same as the rest of me, I think, Sammy.' she said in the husky whisper which she felt belonged to a stranger.

'Will it get better?' he asked

'Of course it will,' Sam answered for her.

Billy approached the bed and touched the sheet. 'What about your hands? Mum said they got burned too and there was a shoot-out!'

'Shhh, Billy, what did we tell you!' Sam said.

'You kids! Can't have any secrets, can I?' Matty drew the mummy hands from beneath the sheet, so the boys could feed their curiosity about Aunt Matty's mysterious injuries. She could imagine the whispered conversations they'd had about her at bedtime.

Billy gasped. 'Will you still be able to play the piano?'

She looked down at the bandages. 'Maybe, but it won't sound very good.'

He nodded in agreement. 'Then I'll play for you.'

'Thanks, love, that'll be nice...' she closed her eyes briefly, imagining a future without hands to play or voice to sing. With a pang of regret she remembered the days she'd been unable to sing after finding out about Eliza.

'All right, boys, can I trust you to wait outside and not make a noise? The nurse said you could only stay five minutes.' Sam shooed them gently away from the bed.

They nodded and kissed Matty goodbye. She watched them walk on tiptoe out of the ward.

'You can tell Nellie the gypsy's warning worked!' She smiled and shifted uncomfortably in the bed, unable to use her hands to prop herself up.

'Can you help me sit up?'

Sam lifted her carefully and fluffed the hard hospital pillows. Matty sank back against them. 'How long have I been in here, Sam?'

He hesitated, seeming reluctant to tell her. 'It's been almost two weeks, Matty.'

'Oh! That long.' But the truth was she had lost all concept of time while she'd been lying in this hospital bed. It felt as if she had been striving to find Tom for a lifetime in that fog of forgetfulness before she'd come back to herself.

'I need to ask you something...' Her heart thumped in her ears and blood rushed to her temples. 'No one's talking about Tom. I need to know what's happened to him.'

His face fell, and she felt almost sorry for him – sorry that he'd be the one to have to answer her question.

'Tom?' He shook his head and she felt her hands clenching painfully in their bandages.

'He's gone, hasn't he?'

'Gone? He's gone away, but he's not dead, Matty!'

'Oh, thank God.' Matty drew in a long breath. 'I've been lying here all this time, thinking he was dead.' She grasped Sam's hands with her bandaged ones and kissed them with gratitude. 'Oh, thank you, thank you. He's not dead!'

'Don't thank me, Matty duck. It was you saved his life, not me. But he's got a long way to go, love.'

'What happened, did Frank shoot him? It's all a fog. I felt him fall and he disappeared and I couldn't find him...' Her heart was beating faster and she was aware that the breath in her lungs was running out, her chest heaving. She had to get out of the bed.

'Where is he? I'm going to find him...'

Sam was at her side, holding her firmly by both arms. He spoke clearly and slowly as if she were a child. 'No, Matty, you can't see him now. It was a bad gunshot wound and he nearly died, he lost so much blood, but they did marvels and now we've just got to be patient. Do you understand, Matty?'

She lay back, defeated. She was too tired for this fight. 'But he's nearby?'

'He's gone away... to the country. The doctors said he needed peace and quiet. But you'll see him when you're up and about again. You just have to...'

'Be patient?' she finished for him.

'Yes, love, and concentrate on getting yourself better.' He stroked her hair. 'My little canary, why didn't you come to me? If I'd known what sort of trouble you were in...'

She had tired herself out and now even her croaky voice seemed to desert her. She whispered, 'I couldn't come to you, not without putting the boys in danger. Frank would've hurt them... hurt anyone I loved.'

'Well, he can't hurt anyone ever again.'

She closed her eyes. 'Dead?'

Sam leaned in close to whisper in her ear. 'Yes, thanks to Wally the bleedin' Wonder Wheel, though the police have put it all down to the Sabinis.'

She opened her eyes again. 'Of course it was the Sabinis. Bermondsey's got no mafia, has it?'

Sam gave a wry smile. ''Course not – but the barber sends his best wishes and he gave me these for you... from his wife.' Sam felt inside a bag that he'd placed beside his chair and brought out a cake tin. He lifted the lid so she could see the contents. 'They look a bit like doughnuts,' he said.

Matty smiled as she looked in the tin. The Bombolini looked even better than the last batch. It reminded her of the 'Bermondsey mafia', and after Sam left, she allowed herself to think about Frank. She had been so intent on discovering what had happened to Tom that she'd almost forgotten Frank, which seemed strange as all this pain and mayhem had been set in motion by him. She tried to recall the events of that night, remembering how she'd dodged out of the way on Wally's order. She'd known Frank had been hit and remembered feeling surprise that Wally's expertise should turn out to be sharp shooting. But she couldn't know how good a shot he'd been. How strange it should be her old music hall friend that had saved her.

She looked out of the window at what remained of the afternoon light. Beyond St Olave's Hospital was Southwark Park and from her window she could see rows of old chestnuts, lining a path. Russet leaves glowed as the sun began to set. And, like the end of a long day, she felt the sun go down on that part of her life that had been ruled by fear. She stared out of the window until the red sky turned to mauve and then indigo. She would let fear sink into the night, along with every memory of Frank and the harm he'd done to her and the child that should have been hers.

*

Sam had told her to be patient, but that had never been one of Matty's virtues. She lived for visiting hours. A steady stream of friends, old and new, had made their way to see her. Bernie from the Star came and had heard from Wally the crucial role of *Don't block me, dear* in saving Matty.

'Secretive old devil, that Wally! Rubbish unicyclist but shit hot with a gun! I warned you, didn't I, that you never wanted to find out what he was bloody good at,' he said in a rather loud voice, the one he used to introduce acts from his podium.

'Shhh, Bernie! We don't want Wally having to walk up the stairs to Jack Ketch, do we?' Matty said. 'Winnie would never forgive me.' Which made Bernie laugh.

Esme came, bearing gifts of cotton gloves and cocoa butter for Matty's burned hands, which, when the bandages were removed, had made the woman cry at the sight of angry burns spoiling their long fingers. When Esme leaned over to kiss Matty she'd whispered, 'Don't block me, dear!'

'How did you find out?'

Matty's shock must have been evident.

'Don't worry, it stays with me, darling. But I can't pretend I wasn't ecstatic when I found out the bastard was dead.' Esme never did pull her punches.

But the most unexpected visitor arrived on one long, dull afternoon when Matty was beginning to think she must discharge herself. Now that her wounds were healing and her voice was almost back to normal, she was desperate to see Tom. She'd heard nothing from him and though she'd been told that, like her, he was still healing, the silence was beginning to weigh on her more heavily than her own injuries. She began to suspect Sam and the others were hiding something from her.

The woman's concave figure was unmistakable, though oddly out of place, and it took a moment before Matty could believe she was really there. She glided elegantly between the rows of beds, in stark contrast to the purposeful half-run of the nurses, who scattered before her approach.

'Lady Fetherstone!'

'Forgive me, my dear. I should have let you know I was coming.'

Matty covered her confusion and attempted to sit up, but Ma Feathers put a hand on her shoulder. 'Lie still, my dear. I don't want to disturb you.'

She sat down and rested her expensive-looking handbag on her lap. 'As I was in town I thought I'd see how you're getting on and, of course, I thought you'd like news of your young man?'

'Tom? Yes, of course I would! All they've told me is that he's at a convalescent home.' Matty was confused as to how Lady Feathers could know anything about Tom's condition. 'But if you know anything more...'

Matty was surprised to hear the woman laugh. 'I should hope so – he's staying in my house!'

'Tom's at Fonstone? I thought he was at Fairby Grange,' she said, naming the borough's nursing home.

'When I heard the poor young man would need a protracted convalescence I invited him to come to us. Neville's been staying with me since the dreadful fire and two invalids are less trouble than one.' She gave a conspiratorial smile. 'At least I've found that to be the case when Neville is one of those invalids! He needs constant conversation, my dear, and Tom is taking him off my hands. My doctor comes in regularly, of course, so Tom has the best of care. He's finally begun to show some signs of improvement...'

Matty heard an unspoken 'but'. 'Tell me everything.'

'Physically, he's made a fairly good recovery, the wound's healing nicely and he's started to walk around the gardens... but my doctor says his progress could be better. The thing is, Matty – he's very low. Not acting at all like a man who's been spared death. Perhaps Neville shouldn't have told me this as it was a confidence, but it seems Tom blames himself for your injuries.'

'But why would he think that? He was trying to help me... free me!' Matty said with unintended vehemence.

'You've no need to convince me, my dear. Of course we know that's the case, but he told Neville about a promise he made to you, that the scheme would involve no violence and that no one would come to any harm... least of all you.' She paused for an instant. 'My doctor says his low spirits are a factor in his slow recovery.'

Matty groaned. 'I need to see him.'

'Exactly so.'

'But they won't let me out of here like this.' Matty held up her hands.

Lady Fetherstone tilted her head to one side, so that her diamond drop earring caught the weak autumn sunlight glancing through the hospital window. 'That might depend upon who asks.'

29

New Dreams for Old

December 1932–Summer 1933

It hadn't taken Lady Fetherstone long to convince Matty's doctors that a stately home in the middle of the peaceful English countryside, under the care of a personal physician, would be preferable to another day in the bleak burns ward at St Olave's. Shades of the workhouse infirmary that it had been only a few years earlier still hung about the hospital. The nurses and doctors bravely tried to counteract it and Matty had valued their solicitude and expertise, but she couldn't wait to leave.

She walked with deliberate care towards the hospital gates, which spanned the two sooty Victorian wings. Heaving a sigh of relief, she passed beneath the hoop-shaped wrought-iron gate, topped by its massive lantern. The pain surprised her. The burns on her legs had been superficial compared to those on her hands, but still, her first walk had been an ordeal. The doctors credited her dunking in the Thames for lessening the severity of all her burns. But even so, tender skin stretched along her shins and calves as unused muscles flexed. She tried hard not to hobble, God forbid anyone should stop her now. If they did, she thought she might reach for her hat.

She had said her goodbyes to Sam and the family the day before and Lady Fetherstone had promised she would send a car to take her from St Olave's to the station. No doubt Matty could have waited in the ward, but the anticipation was even more painful than her healing skin. Soon she would see Tom, soon everything that had been so muddled and impossible would become clear. He blamed himself, he felt guilty, he thought she would not want to see him – he had confessed as much to Neville. The Tom who waited in Fonstone was obviously a very different man from the one whose jealousy over Frank the week before the fire had made him so cold to her.

She waited outside the hospital gates in the company of a small group of dockers who'd obviously failed to be called on that morning at nearby Surrey Docks. Dressed in identical flat caps and white chokers, they were lounging on the wall, hands in pockets, exchanging the odd comment. Either they couldn't bear to go home so early to their wives without a day's pay, or they were waiting to pick up a few hours' work in the afternoon. Matty thought she could tell those who were ashamed from those who were hopeful and she counted herself in good company, for she felt both.

Matty didn't consider herself a manipulative person, and yet the years had taught her that people were far more likely to forgive the mistakes of another when they were living amidst the consequences of their own. If all was to be clear between her and Tom, then he would have to be convinced that she forgave him, and he would have to find forgiveness in his heart for her. For the ghost of her lost child had come back to haunt those mist-filled dreams when she'd evaded consciousness in the stark hospital ward. She had carried the secret for so long that she had built a world apart for her and the baby to live in. She had conjured a fictional life of first smiles, first words, first steps, in an imaginary world that excluded the real. Her secrets had been prised from her one by one by fear alone. Tom had promised he would demand no more of them from her. But this last one she would have to give up freely, if they were ever to have a life together.

She became aware of a little girl skipping towards her. The child's dress was a grubby, once-white hand-me-down, and she wore no shoes. She ran straight past Matty, the little black soles of her feet kicking up behind her. She could have been the spectre of a Victorian orphan running from the workhouse gates. But Matty heard her shouting, 'Mum sent me to find you!' And then came a joyful shout as one of the shamefaced dockers swept her up and whirled her round. Matty felt a pain like a fist in her chest. How many moments like these had she secretly imagined in the past few years? It was as if she had wrapped up all her dreams for that lost child and put them into a genie's lamp. Now, witnessing this moment of simple joy forced the stopper off, let the dream out of the lamp, and in its emergence she realized it had never felt good; it had always been just an illusion. Looking at the living child caught up in her father's arms, Matty understood that in the keeping of her secret she had denied her child its existence. Its brief life had been barely formed, yet it was still a life and needed to be acknowledged. It was time to let her little girl go free.

*

'Mr Roberts is taking a walk in the gardens, Miss Gilbie. I could send someone to let him know you've arrived, if you would like?' Daring, the butler, welcomed her and had already sent her bags up to her room. He had greeted her like a beloved family member; her saving of Feathers from Dubbs' clutches had made her a heroine in his sight.

'Oh no, thank you, Daring. I think I'd like to surprise him.'

'I'm sure he'll be very happy to see you, miss. He usually walks to the stone and back. You're likely to find him there.'

She thanked Daring and set off for the ancient megalith that lay at the heart of the estate. She wasn't sure if she really did want to surprise Tom, but she simply couldn't wait any longer to see him. She remembered the way to the stone, through the formal gardens with their low hedges and bare rose bushes, out on to the long striped lawn, past the circular lake. The tall slab came into sight, smoothed by the ages, pointing like an accusing finger in her direction. And there was Tom, sitting on the grass leaning his back against the stone. He faced the lake but his eyes were closed. She thought he might be sleeping. She walked softly towards him, but the grass was deep here and she could hear her own feet brushing the sward.

His eyes stayed closed as she lowered herself softly beside him. She waited for him to wake. Easing her back up against the stone, which was wide enough for both of them, she watched as scimitar-winged birds curled and dipped across the lake, then rose in wheeling arcs before returning for another pass across the fly-dappled water. She turned at a sound beside her and found herself looking into his pale hazel eyes, liquid as the wintery lake in front of her. She waited for them to catch fire. Such a strange alchemy, how his eyes became flecked with gold whenever he looked into hers, like a secret small signal that only she could read. There they were, she saw them, small sparks of amber that told her he loved her still.

'You're here,' he said simply.

'I'm here.'

'You're so beautiful, Matty.' He looked down at her hands. She wore the soft white gloves that Esme had given her and a spasm of pain crossed his face. 'I'm sorry,' he said.

'You've got nothing to be sorry about, Tom. I'm free.'

'You could be dead, and if you were, it would have been my fault.' He dropped his head into his hands. 'I let you down, Matty. I promised you no one would get hurt and I was a fool.'

She peeled off her gloves and reached for his hand. She laid her scarred fingers across his palm. 'See these?' She pointed to the red raised burns that striped her skin. 'Each one's a reminder of what you saved me from. If Frank had got his hands on me I would have had more to worry about than a few burns.'

But he shook his head.

'Tom, you know I'm right! You saw what I did to his face. Do you think he wouldn't have repaid me ten times over?'

She felt his finger begin to trace the scars. 'You saved my life, Matty. I felt you there, holding me, keeping me from falling into the river. I even thought I heard you singing to me. It kept me alive. And if you can forgive me, there's something I want to ask you, something I should have asked a long time ago...' His eyes were now wide with hope and it hurt that she had to stop him. She put a scarred hand up to his cheek.

'I forgive you, Tom, though there's nothing to forgive. But before you ask me anything, there's something I need to tell you and after you've heard it, if you still want to, you can ask me... whatever you like.' She smiled and felt her lip tremble.

The birds were still tracing curves across the lake and she concentrated on their flight, the hypnotic rhythm of the endless arcs seeming to calm her.

'Remember when you told me I was entitled to my secrets? That you didn't need me to give them all up?'

Tom nodded. 'I meant it.'

'There's one last thing you deserve to know...'

He opened his mouth to interrupt but before she could lose her courage she sped on. 'Tom – there was a child and I lost it.'

His expression turned to stone. Immobile as the granite block they leaned against, it had frozen at the point where hope had turned to bewilderment and she couldn't bear to look at him any more. She spoke to the wheeling birds and the mirrored lake.

'Frank never knew about the child. I was going to tell him, but I wasn't showing and something made me wait. I was four months pregnant when I saw him murder a man and I knew I had to get my baby as far away from that monster as I could. It was my fault I lost the child. All I had to do was keep my mouth shut, but I couldn't even do that for my baby. Always chattering, you know how I got the nickname as a kid, always singing, always prattling. Ask Sam and Nellie – they had to put up with me. I'm sure I used to drive them mad. Frank liked it, said he loved hearing me chattering away in my cockney accent, it made him laugh. You think monsters don't laugh, but they do. If only for once in my life I'd kept silent. I knew that what I'd seen could be the death of me, but I couldn't keep it to myself. I told Maria, Frank's sister. She was good at *omerta*, that's what they called it, keeping your mouth shut. But then one day, she slipped up, one small slip of the tongue and he knew I'd told her. And that's when it happened. He wanted to teach me a lesson, what happens when you break *omerta*. He beat me black and blue, kicked me around that posh apartment till there was blood all over the cream rugs, and then he finished it off with a kick to my stomach. I thought I'd die, but it wasn't me who died. Me and Maria, we'd already made our plan to get me and the baby I was carrying away from Frank. But it was too late. He'd already killed my poor little baby. That last kick I'm sure is what did it. I thought we'd escaped. It was on the boat home... that's when I lost my little girl.' Matty had been holding the scrunched-up white gloves and now used them to wipe away her tears. Tom had listened in silence and she didn't look at him, frightened at what she might see – hurt, disappointment, disgust.

'So, now you know, and I don't expect you'll want to ask me anything now.'

She went to get up, but felt Tom's hand grasp her arm and pull her back down.

'Look at me.' He turned her face towards him, but she resisted.

'Matty, look at me.'

When she did, she saw that tears had wet his cheeks and she wiped them away with one of her white gloves.

'My poor, darling Matty,' he said, taking the glove and kissing it. He pulled her close, and he placed her head on his shoulder, while she sobbed in his arms. He waited until her tears had subsided and whispered, 'There's still something I need to ask you...'

She raised her head to look him full in the eyes. 'Yes.'

'But I haven't asked you anything yet.'

'Tom, you've been asking me for years, I just couldn't hear...'

'Well, you're not doing me out of this, Matty Gilbie.' He took a deep breath. 'Will you marry me, Matty?'

'Yes, Tom, I'll marry you,' she said, and it was as easy and natural to her as singing her favourite song. There was no struggle left in her heart, nor question left in her mind that this was right,

417

and Tom's radiant smile convinced her that he felt the same. There were no shadowy secrets that could darken their happiness any more, and he kissed her so passionately that for Matty all the past, and all the future too, was resolved into one eternal moment of love so intense she felt it must be as timeless and enduring as the ancient stone that had been their only witness.

It was Will who broke the spell, though Matty couldn't have been happier to see him. The silent stone had been a fine enough witness, but now she was ready to share her news with the world. She had seen him approaching, swishing a stick as he walked towards them through the long grass. He spotted her and waved the stick.

'Come on, you two. Daring wants to serve lunch and I'm starving!' he called to them.

'Will! I didn't know you'd be here!' She beamed at him, pushed herself up and ran to greet him.

'Feathers' idea – he thought you and Tom might find undiluted Neville and Ma Feathers a bit of a strong brew... Besides,' he continued, leaning to kiss her cheek, 'Sam asked me to keep an eye on you.'

'Oh, I'm fine... more than fine!' she said, looking at Tom.

'What's going on?' Will said, looking from one to the other. 'Come on, Matty, you know you're useless at hiding anything – what's the secret?'

She laughed, marvelling at how light she felt, then smiled at her brother. 'There's no secret, Will. Tom's asked me to marry him and I've said yes.'

Will whooped and caught her in his arms, then shook Tom's hand. 'About time too, talk about drag your feet. I thought you'd never ask her!'

Lady Fetherstone insisted they turn their lunch into a celebration. Daring was despatched to find a bottle of champagne and Neville made the toast. 'To Tom and Matty, may we soon hear our Cockney Canary singing for joy once more!'

It was the first time that Matty had seen Neville since the fire and after lunch she took the chance of speaking to him.

'Neville, I'm so sorry about your beautiful bolt-hole. I feel responsible.'

'Nonsense, darling!' he said cheerfully. 'It's not as if I had no other home to go to – there's the Kensington flat and my little place in Cap Ferrat. But in many ways, the whole affair did me a kindness.' He dropped his voice. 'Lady Feathers was shocked into an uncharacteristic declaration of love and I am permanently ensconced in the lodge! I'm a fixture, Matty darling – immovable as a dowager duchess!'

'Or the Fonstone stone?'

He flashed her a smile. 'Even better! But, Matty, there's a business matter I need to talk to you about...'

At that moment Tom came to find her. It was as if an invisible cord of happiness had been strung between them and each of them felt the tug of it. Though the room was full of people and she was conscious of needing to speak to all of them, she felt a magnetic pull which inevitably led her back to his side. She knew he felt the same way as he put his arm round her.

'Can I have my fiancée back, Neville?' he asked.

'For a while, dear boy, for a while,' Neville replied enigmatically.

At cocktail hour in the scene-painted drawing room that had so caught Matty's imagination on her last visit, she discovered the meaning of Neville's remark. She and Lady Fetherstone were sitting on the sofa in front of the fire.

'A Gibson for you, Matty?' Neville handed her the cocktail. 'And a Gimlet for you, darling.' He set Lady Fetherstone's drink on a side table and pulled up a chair.

'Now, Matty, I can't restrain myself a moment longer.' He had the look of a mischievous boy, confident that when his crime was discovered he wouldn't be punished.

'Tom, do come and sit with us. I want to tell Matty all about my plan.'

Tom had been chatting to Will and Feathers and now the three joined them. Matty held Tom's gaze. 'A plan? Why is it you always know the plans before I do?'

'Don't blame the poor chap. I swore him to silence. He's not the person to persuade you about anything at the moment. He's far too soft on you to make you do anything you don't want to!'

Matty was getting uncomfortable. 'I think I'll say "no",' she said, pleased to see that she'd wiped the smile off Neville's face.

'Before you've heard my suggestion? You can't!'

She saw Tom give a secret smile.

'Classic mistake, Neville,' Will said, laughing. 'Try to tell Matty what she should do and you've already lost. Her other nickname was Matty the Mule, you know.'

Neville looked uncertainly towards her, opened his mouth and then shut it again. 'All right, Tom, you tell her,' he said, crossing his legs and sitting back.

Matty laughed. 'No! You tell me. I'm pulling your leg, Neville. I'm listening.'

'All right then. How would you like to make a film?'

'I make films all the time, or I did before...'

'No, not those, a *real* film!'

Matty could see that Tom was about to take issue with Neville's dismissal of their carefully crafted Bermondsey films, but she launched in first. 'Our films *are* real, Neville. They've helped cut fever and TB rates – Bermondsey used to have the highest rate in London! And infant mortality has dropped by what?' she appealed to Tom.

'By half,' he said.

'Half! How many mothers are not mourning their dead babies because of our films!' She felt the eyes of everyone on her and she lowered her voice. 'Sorry, Neville, but they are real.'

Lady Fetherstone laid a hand on Matty's. 'I'm sure Neville had no wish to denigrate Bermondsey Borough Council's sterling efforts, Matty dear.'

'I beg your pardon, Matty,' Neville continued. 'What I should have said is a film with a wider distribution... a film for general release.' He let that sink in and took Matty's silence as his cue to continue.

'Last week I was asked to attend a meeting with a rather boring civil servant by the name of Herbert Minor, most off-putting nasal voice I've ever heard, but I digress. He has been tasked with improving the national morale, and has a very modest budget to achieve it. The government's feeling is that with factories closing and unemployment pushing three million, we all need a bit of cheering up and jollying along. So Herbert Minor has been appointed as a sort of unofficial morale monitor. And the rather plain little man had the good sense to call upon me for help! Of course I suggested we make some films with the express purpose of showing how much this country depends upon the labour of ordinary men and women, and how we can pull ourselves out of this malaise if we work together!'

Neville had stood up and with a messianic glint in his eye asked her, 'You've been making films for the good of Bermondsey. Now I'm asking if you'll make them for the good of your country?'

She could see he was thoroughly enjoying the role he'd cast for himself as some British Eisenstein.

'I don't know about all working together, Neville. Some work and some don't...' This was as near as she could get to pointing out the vast difference in wealth represented in the room, without being rude to her hostess, and she left the point hanging in the air.

'But what if the film I'm talking about could cast ordinary working people as the heroes – show their value and worth? Would you be interested in that?'

'But why me?'

'Why you? Well, because – and I don't say this to bend you to my will – you're beloved! Everybody loves you, Matty. Doesn't matter a jot who they are: working classes, aristocracy...' Here he tipped his head to Lady Fetherstone. 'Even mobster monsters are apt to fall under your spell – we all love you, Matty darling, and when you perform you make us smile, you cheer us up. And did I mention the film will have *singing*?'

Matty didn't answer him directly. It had been a day of declarations and her heart was too full. 'I like the bit about cheering you all up. There's some miserable sods about these days.'

Neville trilled his high, brittle laugh and slapped the arm of his chair. 'I knew you'd agree! Didn't I tell you, Tom? Now let's see if she likes your storyline...'

'Yours?'

'Don't look so surprised. I've helped out D.M. with his scripts before now,' Tom said.

'And I had to occupy the poor chap somehow. He's been pining like a lovesick puppy since he got here.'

Tom coughed, his colour heightening. 'Well, the story is about a factory girl – played by Matty, of course – who's laid off when the biscuit factory she works at is forced to close down. She and all her friends have to go on relief, but then she has an idea for making the biscuit-baking process more efficient, and she goes to the boss, who dismisses her idea. But the boss's son, a handsome young charmer with no interest in the business, happens to overhear her and persuades him to give it a go. Of course we'll need a bit of romance with the young charmer before the end...' And the corners of his eyes crinkled with amusement.

'But the point is to show that both sides have to listen and pull together if we're to get out of this mess. Bosses can't afford to dismiss workers as wage slaves and workers can't tar all bosses with the same brush,' Neville declared.

Will snorted. 'Forgive me for saying it all sounds a bit naive. Workers need representation – they only get listened to when they stick together.'

'Yes, yes, but we aren't making a film in Russia, dear chap. We're in good old Blighty and we had our revolution a long time ago. But there's another consideration that was brought to my attention by Herbert Minor – if his fears about Herr Hitler are well-founded, a time might come when rich and poor will be fighting a common enemy. When that day comes we'll need to have put aside all this class warfare nonsense you young fellows are so intent on stirring up.'

There was silence in the room for a minute and Will leaped to tear down Neville's assessment of his views. Interrupting his friend, Feathers chipped in. 'But don't you see, Neville, true communism is the only thing that can save us from those fascist bully boys!'

The chorus of male voices grew louder and their faces grew redder as neither side would give way. On the pretext of getting another drink, Matty stood up and walked out on to the terrace. It was a cool night and she needed to think, somewhere away from the men's fighting. She wanted to leave the terrace doors open, let in the cold air to bring them to their senses. Neville's prophecy of another war had sent a chill through her. Matty could feel even now the agony of waiting for news of Sam at the front. What if she had to face that again with Tom one day? Back then she'd sung those rousing songs on stage at the Star, to keep their spirits up while they waited for news of sons, husbands, lovers, and part of her dreaded having to do that again. But if a war did come, then a divided country would have no chance against the ridiculous little man with the moustache. Neville was right about that. The country of haves and have-nots would need to find some common ground, and if she could help by singing in a film, then she would do it.

*

The last of the summer evening sun glanced through their bedroom window, falling across Matty's hands as she sat at the dressing table. The burn scars were still visible, but less livid now.

'Fancy coming to the pictures, Mrs Roberts?' Tom asked.

'Depends what's on up the Star,' she said, putting the finishing touches to her lipstick.

'I was thinking of the Empire, Leicester Square, actually, but if you prefer the fleapit... sorry, Star...'

She laughed. 'It's a good job Bernie can't hear you.'

She stood up and smoothed the front of her dress, her hand lingering on her swollen stomach. Tom came up behind her, laying his hand over hers and kissing the nape of her neck. 'Is the baby moving?'

She smiled and pressed his hand to the spot where she had felt the fluttering. 'There, feel?' And she turned into his arms, meeting his smile with her own.

Just then there came a knocking on the door. 'That'll be the car. Are you ready? You look beautiful.'

'I'm ready.'

He draped the gold velvet stole over her shoulders, and offered his arm. 'No first-night nerves?'

'Oh no. It's done now – for better or worse. I just hope it achieves what we set out to do.'

'Pull people together?'

'Lift them up.'

Tom nodded. 'It will.'

Neville had arranged for a chauffeur-driven limousine to collect them and when Matty slipped into its leather interior she was greeted by the excited chatter of Billy, Sammy and Albie. Nellie was vainly trying to calm them.

'If you lot don't settle down you'll end up being carsick.'

The boys ignored her, but Nellie seemed to have shed her motherly self. With her thick chestnut hair beautifully waved and a touch of make-up to bring out her still perfect complexion, Matty had a vision of the pretty young woman she'd been when they'd first met.

'You look lovely, Nellie.' Matty kissed her and Sam nodded in agreement. 'Doesn't she?' He smiled, and added hastily, 'You too, duck.'

The boys managed to avoid carsickness and were stunned into silence by the time they entered the palace of dreams, the Empire, Leicester Square. They skipped the long queue and were ushered into reserved seats. She'd insisted there must be tickets for all her friends and family. Winnie and Wally were there, with Nellie's brothers Freddie and Bobby and their wives, Kitty and her greatest fan Elsie. As she took her seat, Queenie stood up at the far end of the row and pointed to her own hat. 'Oi, Mat, where's yer titfer? What did I tell you, always come prepared, gel!' Sugar, who looked as sharp as the leading man, though not as handsome, pulled her down into her seat. Behind Matty were the Peek's Tiller Girls, who'd all acted in the film as the unemployed biscuit girls. Even Edna was there, as a thank you for allowing them another close-up of her biscuit-leg veins. Peek Frean's had been only too happy to offer the factory as a location. Matty looked round as the lights dimmed, craning her neck to find Will, and was relieved to spot him at the other end of their row. She blew him a kiss and one for Feathers too. Will had been reluctant to attend the premiere, which he'd dismissed as government propaganda. But eventually she'd worn him down. 'I'm only coming so I can hear you sing, not because I agree with Neville,' he'd insisted.

She looked behind her, anxious that everyone should be here. Then with relief she saw Bernie and Esme hurrying towards her. Esme reached a hand to Matty. 'I knew this day would come, darling,' she said and Bernie beamed at her. 'Never lost faith in my Cockney Canary!' As her two mentors took their seats beside Neville and Lady Fetherstone, the Wurlitzer organ rose from the pit. The thrill-inducing chords trumpeted forth and even had she not been the star of the film, that sound alone was enough to stir up an almost painful anticipation in Matty's heart.

When the last strains of the organ overture finally faded, the lights dimmed to leave the auditorium in darkness. The screen flickered into life and she heard her own voice, singing the familiar theme music.

Midnight, you heavy laden, it's midnight.
Come on and trade in your old dreams for new,
Your new dreams for old.
I know where they're bought, I know where they're sold...

An aerial shot of the sprawling Peek Frean's buildings appeared against a backdrop of smoke-spewing factory chimneys and terraced streets. On the railway viaduct hard by the factory, a train sped past, trailing a plume of steam. The engine's haunting whistle was echoed by the factory hooter, and the camera zoomed in to a group of factory girls streaming through the entrance gates. As the film's title unfurled above the factory: *NEW DREAMS FOR OLD. Starring Matty Gilbie – The Cockney Canary,* she heard herself singing again.

> *Dreams broken in two can be made like new,*
> *On the street of dreams...*

She had tried to fill her voice with all the yearning and all the hope she'd felt in her own long struggle to rebuild her dreams. It wasn't hard to do. It was the song Neville had played on the night she'd risen phoenix-like from the ashes of his burning house. She reached for Tom's hand and drew him in closer. His eyes shone bright in the darkness as he turned to kiss her, his face lit by the flickering screen.

> *Gold, silver and gold, all you can hold, is in a moonbeam.*
> *Poor, no one is poor, long as love is sure*
> *On the street of dreams...*

And though the tune she sang might be a melancholy one, to Matty it had become a hymn of hope, reminding her that however many wrong turns and dead ends she had encountered along the way, love had always been leading her back here, to the place where her dreams were made new.

Author's Note

Between 1923 and 1948 Bermondsey Borough Council's Public Health Department made thirty-four public health education films. For the purposes of my story I have taken some liberties with the filmography and production dates. Matty Gilbie's 'Modern Woman' films were made only in my imagination – though I like to think they might still be lying somewhere in a council archive waiting to be discovered!

I've also imagined the characters of the actual film producers: the photographer, C.F. Lumley; writers and directors Dr Connan, (MoH) and Mr H.W. Bush. I hope I've managed to evoke their visionary resourcefulness, good humour and pioneering spirit.

Many of the films can still be viewed at the Southwark Local Studies Library, the BFI, Imperial War Museum, also online at the Wellcome Foundation website and on Youtube. A fascinating account of the making of Bermondsey Borough Council's education films, and a full filmography, can be found in *Forgotten Futures* by Elizabeth Lebas.

Acknowledgements

Once again I am indebted to my agent, Anne Williams, and my editor, Rosie de Courcy, for sharing their expertise and wealth of editorial knowledge with me; thank you for always guiding me in the direction of a better story! A huge thanks, also, to the dedicated team at Head of Zeus for all their hard work in bringing this book to publication.

Thanks are due to Maria Pia Brusadelli for help with Italian and also to Kim Neumann. Any mistakes are entirely my own.

I would like to acknowledge the many people who have generously shared their family stories of old Bermondsey and the Peek Freans biscuit factory, especially Violet Henderson; Bette Crickmar; Ann Eldridge; Irene Lock; Ivy Carpenter; Sally Innes and her father; Amanda Ward and her mother Valerie Gates; Rosie Peake and her mother; Pat Jarman and her mother Mary Teather; Jane Gaskell; Catherine Archer and her father. My apologies if I have forgotten anyone – without your stories my books would be the poorer.

Thanks to my friends at Bexley Scribblers and to my lovely family for their continuing support. Finally, special thanks to Jo, without whom this book could not have been written.

A letter from the publisher

We hope you enjoyed this book. We are an independent publisher dedicated to discovering brilliant books, new authors and great storytelling. Please join us at www.headofzeus.com and become part of our community of book-lovers.

We will keep you up to date with our latest books, author blogs, special previews, tempting offers, chances to win signed editions and much more.

If you have any questions, feedback or just want to say hi, please drop us a line on hello@headofzeus.com

 @HoZ_Books

 HeadofZeusBooks

www.headofzeus.com

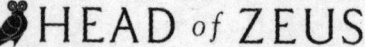 HEAD of ZEUS

The story starts here